D0463726

ARNPRIOR PUBLIC LIBRARY

THE RESTLESS SEA

THE RESTLESS SEA

E.V. Thompson

MACMILLAN LONDON

ISBN 0 333 35796 5

First published 1983 by
MACMILLAN LONDON LIMITED
London and Basingstoke
Associated companies in Auckland Dallas Delhi
Dublin Johannesburg Lagos Manzini Melbourne Nairobi
New York Singapore Tokyo Washington and Zaria

Photoset by Wyvern Typesetting Ltd, Bristol.

Printed in Hong Kong

Man is born with ambition, it is the power source that spurs him on, subjugating adversity and opposition and raising a man above the circumstances to which he was born. Yet neither ambition, determination nor the application of man's labours can avail against the might of the restless sea, that while possessing none of these attributes can put an end to the vain dreams of all men.

BOOK ONE

Chapter One

'KILL him, Ned.'

'Take him now. . . .'

'Your right, Ned lad. Use your bleedin' right. . .!'

Ignoring the shouts of encouragement hurled at his opponent, Nathan Jago kept his left fist extended well in front of him, not taking his eyes from his adversary's face for even a moment. A quick flick of his right wrist was sufficient to wipe away the perspiration that filtered through his thick, black eyebrows, threatening to blind him with its saltiness.

This was London Fields. Once the waste land beyond the walls of London Town, the fields were now at the heart of London's crowded 'East End' and home ground for Nathan's opponent, Ned Belcher, champion prize-fighter of all England. A Hoxton man, Belcher's home was hardly more than a gargle and a spit away.

Suddenly, Ned Belcher tucked his chin down tight on his chest. Crouching low, he moved in to the attack, swinging heavy fists that were stained dark brown from hours of soaking in a hardening mixture of vinegar and walnut juice.

One of the champion's punches caught Nathan a glancing blow on the side of his face. Ducking low, Nathan slipped beneath the next punch and brought his own fist across in a short, jarring blow that caught Belcher just below the right ear. Belcher grunted with pain and dropped to one knee on the flattened grass. He kneeled there, shaking his head in the manner of a puzzled dog that had just snapped at a wasp, and the referee declared it to be the end of a round.

Nathan walked gratefully to his corner and slumped down on the stool quickly provided by his seconds. Across the ring, Belcher's seconds ran to help their man back to his own corner before the precious thirty-second interval was over.

Spitting a mixture of wine and water on the muddy turf just outside the ring, Nathan asked, 'How many rounds is that?'

'Twenty-nine.' A man of few words, Sammy Mizler had himself been no mean light-weight fighter, before a broken knuckle put an end to his career. 'The rest of the rounds are yours. Belcher's kissed the gin bottle too often to take a long fight.'

Nathan looked across the ring to where Ned Belcher sat sprawled back in his corner, legs stretched out before him, the loose flesh of his stomach spilling over the leather belt that held up his trousers.

Nathan thought that Sammy Mizler was probably right. Belcher was not the man he had been ten years before, when he fought Hen Pearce to a standstill and took the title from him. Something had gone wrong along the way. Nevertheless, although Nathan was not a small man, Belcher weighed at least three stone more – and he boasted a punch that could stun a bullock. He was an opponent not to be underestimated.

A murmur of concern rose from the vast crowd that stretched back as far as the dingy, grey, gardenless houses fringing the northern edge of London Fields. Looking up, Nathan saw long, sulphurous fingers of mist beginning to reach out into the crowd. The fog had been lurking among the close-packed houses of London's crowded suburbs all day, held at bay only by the weak rays of the autumn sun. Now it was evening, and as the last rays of sunlight left the stinking squalor that was Hoxton the fog emerged to take over England's ancient capital.

Nathan shivered. He knew he would have to chance the power of Ned Belcher's fists in order to bring the fight to a rapid close. As the fog moved closer to the ring, so would the crowd. When the fog became thicker, and the crowd was able to advance no farther for the press of those in front, they would become first restless, then angry, and finally violent. This was a London crowd. An 'East End' London crowd, ever ready to riot.

A disturbance of such a nature would bring the fight to a premature conclusion, the three-hundred-guinea purse being taken home by neither man. And Nathan had plans for the money.

'Time!'

From the side of the ring, the referee called on both men to advance to the centre and assume their stances to his satisfaction.

Ned Belcher's seconds heaved their charge to his feet, and he lurched forward to the centre of the ring, raising his fists when he was two paces away from his opponent.

Nathan's unexpected assault took Belcher by surprise. Until now the challenger had been content to box a mainly defensive fight, allowing the London champion to use up his strength. The two-fisted onslaught brought the crowd to their toes. Partisanship was momentarily forgotten as they revelled in the sight of a skilled and superbly fit prize-fighter moving in for the kill.

As Nathan's punches drove home, Ned Belcher retreated rapidly, his arms raised in ineffectual defence. At one stage his knees buckled beneath him and he almost went down, but Belcher was an experienced and tough fighter. Lungeing forward, he wrapped his arms about Nathan and held on grimly as Nathan pummelled him about the kidneys.

When Nathan attempted to throw Belcher from him, the heavier fighter whispered hoarsely: 'Go easy on me, son. You'll be an old fighter yourself one day.'

So unexpected was the older fighter's plea that Nathan stopped his punishing pummelling. Immediately, Belcher stepped a short pace backward – then brought his balding head forward sharply. The unorthodox blow struck Nathan on the forehead, and a carnival of coloured lights exploded inside his head.

It was only an instinctive sense of self-preservation that kept Nathan's guard up as he was battered backwards across the ring by Ned Belcher. Caught in his own corner, Nathan slipped on the turf, which had become saturated by liberal use of sponge and water-bottle. As he fell, Sammy Mizler protected his boxer from the continuing assault, calling upon the referee to intervene.

The referee had to pull Belcher away from Nathan, so desperate was the ageing champion to ensure that Nathan would not make the mark at the end of the half-minute rest brought about by the fall.

Nathan shook his head in protest as water poured over his head, and Sammy Mizler slapped his cheeks frantically in a bid to bring him back to his senses.

'What d'you think you're doing out there? One minute I'm cheering myself hoarse because you've got him going. A moment later you're standing doing nothing, with Belcher's arms about you. Did you think he was going to kiss you, maybe?'

Nathan grimaced. His head felt as though it had been resting against an exploding cannon. 'He appealed to my better nature. It won't happen again.'

'Better nature, you say? Is it an alms-giver you are now? Or are you fighting for the title of Champion of all England, and a three-hundred-guinea purse? Oi! But the ref's calling "time" now. You'd better make up your mind what it is you want.'

Nathan jumped to his feet and was waiting in the centre of the ring when Ned Belcher came to the mark. Hardly giving him time to raise his guard, Nathan launched an attack that drove the champion before him. It was too much for Belcher. He walked heavily, heels to the turf, the elasticity gone from his legs. Forced to a neutral corner, Ned Belcher lay back against the taut rope, and his hands dropped helplessly to his sides. Blood dribbling from a cut lip, he stood slack-jawed, staring blankly at Nathan.

For one brief moment, Nathan hesitated. Then he remembered Belcher's whispered appeal – and the head butt that had followed. He brought across a straight left that caught Belcher on the side of his jaw. The champion sagged at the knees; but, before he struck the ground, Nathan landed a hard right between Belcher's eyes, and every man in the hushed crowd heard the crack of knuckle upon bone.

Belcher's seconds darted forward to drag their man to his corner as Nathan made his way back to Sammy Mizler.

'You've got him, Nathan. You're the new champion, already.' The phlegmatic Jewish second was more excited than Nathan had ever seen him.

Declining to take the stool for the mandatory thirty-second break, Nathan stood nursing the aching knuckles of his right hand, looking to where Ned Belcher's seconds worked frenziedly on their champion. He, too, doubted whether Belcher would come to the mark for the next round. The punch that had put him down was one of the hardest Nathan had ever thrown.

At a nod from the timekeeper, the referee called upon both fighters to take up their stances in the centre of the ring. Confidently, Nathan made his way to the mark, helped on his

12

way by a resounding slap of encouragement from Sammy Mizler.

Ned Belcher's corner was the scene of utter confusion. The seconds had their champion on his feet, but he seemed not to know what was happening and was shouting in near-hysteria. Nathan could not hear his words because they were drowned by the noise of the crowd, many of whom had bet large sums of money on the locally born champion.

To make matters worse, thick fog was now rolling across the fields. Unable to see what was happening, the spectators at the rear of the huge crowd were pressing forward, clamouring noisily to be told what was going on inside the thirty-foot-square ring.

Ned Belcher was dragged to the centre of the ring by his seconds just in time to beat the referee's deadline. As the seconds scuttled back to their corner, Nathan took his stance. Ned Belcher advanced for only two shuffling paces and then he dropped to his knees, his hands going up to cover his face.

Nathan hesitated, in a quandary. A fighter was not allowed to go down without a punch being thrown but, equally, a man on his knees was deemed to be 'down' and should not be struck.

The crowd entertained no such doubts. Angered at Ned Belcher's unprecedented behaviour, they called to Nathan to 'finish him off'. Their howls of rage mingled with the cries of those frustrated specators prevented by fog from seeing what was happening inside the ring.

As the fog began swirling across the ring, the noise reached an ugly crescendo. It was now that Nathan saw tears begin to seep between Ned Belcher's fingers.

Convinced at last that this was no trick on the part of the champion, Nathan advanced cautiously towards him and laid a hand upon his head.

Ned Belcher reached up and grasped Nathan's hand in his own. In a hoarse, terror-filled voice, he whispered desperately: 'I can't see! I'm blind, boy. So help me, I'm blind!'

Nathan was still wary of the man kneeling before him. Ned Belcher was an ageing and weary champion, desperate to keep his title.

'It's the fog, Ned. A few more minutes and it will have closed in altogether. . . .'

The battle-scarred fingers closed tightly on Nathan's hand. 'It's not fog, boy. I've lost my sight. I'm as blind as a maggot. God help me. . . .'

The referee was as uncertain as Nathan.

'Get up and fight, Ned. Get to your feet now, or I'll have no option but to give the title and purse to Jago.'

It was doubtful if Ned Belcher heard the words, so loud was the din from the disgruntled spectators. He turned his head this way and that, in total confusion.

Nathan was no longer in doubt. The last blow he had landed had robbed the champion of his sight.

'He says he's blind. I believe him.'

Clods of earth and stones began landing in the ring, hurled by the howling spectators. The situation was rendered more malignant by the foul-smelling fog that now reduced visibility to no more than a few yards. The referee waited no longer.

Raising Nathan's free arm, he declared him the winner of the contest, and the Champion of all England. Thrusting a bag containing the three-hundred-guinea purse at the new champion, the referee scurried away. Ducking beneath the rope, he was quickly swallowed up by the fog and the angry, gesticulating crowd.

Sammy Mizler appeared at Nathan's side, an arm crooked above his head to shield himself from the volley of missiles bombarding the ring from every direction.

'Let's go before half that crowd gets in the ring with us. They're out for blood – yours mainly. But I've no doubt the colour of mine will serve them as well.'

Fighting had already broken out among the crowd at the ringside, and now one of the ropes sagged inwards beneath the weight of struggling bodies.

Snatching his shirt from the worried Sammy Mizler, Nathan turned to where Ned Belcher was being helped to his feet by equally anxious seconds. Thrusting the purse into Belcher's groping hands, Nathan shouted: 'Here. . . . It's the purse. Put it to good use. Buy an inn. . . .'

The side of the ring collapsed. As the crowd spilled through, Ned Belcher was hustled off; and Nathan Jago, undisputed Champion of all England in the illegal sport of prize-fighting, followed after.

The date was 10 August 1810. At the age of twenty-seven, Nathan had achieved the ambition that had been his since he had left the Navy to become a prize-fighter five years before.

Chapter Two

THE day had not started well for Elinor Hearle, and it became progressively worse as it wore on. It began when her maid failed to awaken her and Elinor overslept. When the maid finally put in an appearance she had such a dreadful chill that Elinor sent her straight back to her bed.

Then, when Elinor reached the stables to take her stallion Napoleon for a morning gallop, the horse had gone. The animal had been taken out by the groom in the belief that Elinor was foregoing her usual morning ride.

The decision to exercise the stallion, although taken in the best interests of the horse, cost the groom his post at Polrudden Manor.

The nagging realisation that the groom had been dismissed unjustly did nothing to improve Elinor's humour as the day wore on. By noon a foul temper possessed her. The few servants in the big house did their best to keep out of her way, but it was not easy. Sir Lewis Hearle, Elinor's father, was returning from London today, and there was much to be done about the house.

Elinor's mother had died when she was a child, and Sir Lewis, Member of Parliament for the nearby port of Fowey, was away in London for most of the year, engaged in parliamentary affairs. He hoped one day to gain high office, and so recoup the dwindling family fortunes. Consequently, the task of running the household staff fell to Elinor.

Elinor was a very capable housekeeper, but the responsibilities thrust upon her so early in life combined with an unusually strong character to produce a wilfulness that had frightened away even the most ardent suitor. Elinor was twenty-five years old now and one of the most attractive girls in the district, but there was no hint of romance in her life. Women in the nearby village of Pentuan shook their heads in disapproval as she galloped through the village on her high-spirited stallion, sitting the horse like a man. They swore that Elinor, heiress to the decrepit manor house and scant fortunes of Polrudden, would end her days an impoverished and eccentric spinster.

If Elinor knew of their disapprobation, she did not allow the knowledge to alter her way of life – and there was not a villager who dared express such views to her face.

Sir Lewis Hearle had written to tell Elinor that he would be travelling from London on the Royal Mail coach, due to reach the Queen's Head inn in St Austell at three o'clock that afternoon. Elinor was to meet him there.

Usually, she would have travelled in a chaise driven by the groom but, smarting under her injustice, the groom had already left Polrudden. Elinor had gone to his house, intending to give the conscientious man another chance. She had been met by his red-eyed wife and three wailing children, and had learned that he had gone to seek the recruiting sergeant in Bodmin Town to take the King's shilling. He had told his wife that he preferred the bayonets of Bonaparte's army to the tongue of the mistress of Polrudden.

Because of this, Elinor was obliged to take the smaller gig and drive the horse herself.

It was a distance of five miles to St Austell, and Elinor set off rather later than she had intended. She drove briskly from the house, situated high on the hill above the busy little fishing village of Pentuan, urging the horse on through the narrow, high-banked lanes.

It was a hot day and, unlike her own riding-horse, the pony pulling the gig had not been exercised daily. Lazy days and lush summer grass had made it fat and out of condition. By the time they had covered less than half the distance to St Austell, the steep hill and Elinor's urging had brought the horse out in an unhealthy sweat.

There was a well-used watering-place nearby and, cursing the delay, Elinor turned aside to give the pony a brief rest and the opportunity to drink.

The watering-place was no more than a shallow pond, fed by a spring and the ground about it muddy and uneven. Climbing down from the seat of the gig, Elinor led the animal to the water's edge. Suddenly, her foot slipped and she tugged hard at the bridle. Startled, the horse threw back its head and pranced nervously in the shafts of the gig. Elinor's feet went from beneath her, and she fell heavily in the pond, catching her dress on a piece of broken fencing as she went down.

Scrambling out as quickly as she could, Elinor grabbed the

horse's trailing reins before the animal could bolt. Backing horse and gig away from the slippery bank of the pond, she secured the reins and then examined the state of her dress.

She was soaked through, and muddied from shoulder to toe.

The ill-humour that had been simmering inside her since early morning flared up once again. She cursed the horse, the pond, and the groom she had dismissed that morning. Not until it was out of her system did Elinor pause to think of what to do next. She could not continue her journey to St Austell in her present state, and to return to Polrudden Manor to change her clothes was out of the question. She was late already.

About a quarter of a mile away was the cliff-edge farmhouse of Venn. Leading the horse and gig, Elinor made her way there.

A small farm of some fifty acres, Venn had a steep, difficult-to-work patchwork of fields. It belonged to Elinor's father, but was currently rented out to a young yeoman farmer named Tom Quicke. Elinor knew he had married no more than six months before and hoped she might borrow a dress from his young wife.

The first sight of the farmhouse immediately raised her hopes. For many years it had been occupied by a retired sea-captain who had merely played at being a farmer. Widowed for more than thirty years, the sea-captain had allowed the farm and himself to run down towards the end of his ninety-four years. Tom Quicke had changed all that. Gates had been repaired and rehung, and the small farmhouse was bright with new paintwork.

The door of the house stood open and, looping the reins of her horse over a fence-post, Elinor walked inside. She found herself in a low-beamed room with large blue-slate flagstones on the floor and only one small, open window to allow light inside. Full of cool shadow, the room was as clean as the outside of the farmhouse had promised.

Elinor could hear sounds coming from the back of the house and, ducking through a low doorway, entered the farmhouse dairy. A young woman with dark hair tied neatly behind her neck stood at a stone sink. She was busily scrubbing the dismantled workings of a butter-churning machine.

As Elinor entered, the girl looked up, startled at the sudden appearance of this dishevelled, uninvited visitor.

Elinor wasted no time on irrelevant greeting. 'I'm Elinor Hearle and I have had an accident at the watering-place. I need to borrow a dress – and be quick about it. I'm to meet my father in St Austell at three.'

Flustered, the girl stepped back from the sink with soap suds clinging to her bare arms. Dropping Elinor a hurried curtsy, she said: 'I'm Nell, ma'am. Wife of Tom Quicke.'

Elinor thought the girl looked hardly old enough to be a farmer's wife, but she had neither the time nor the inclination to exchange chitchat with the young wife of one of her father's tenants.

'Well, don't stand there gawping. Help me off with these clothes, then run upstairs and bring me some of your dresses to choose from.'

'I . . . I haven't got many, ma'am.' The girl moved towards the door as Elinor began impatiently unfastening those hooks she was able to reach on the back of her dress. 'You'd best come upstairs to the bedroom. Tom will be in from the fields in a minute or two. . . .'

'Then Tom will just have to go out again. I'm not staying in this dress for one moment longer. Help me undo these wretched hooks.'

Hastily drying her hands on her apron, Nell Quicke moved behind Elinor and unfastened the metal hooks securing the dress. As she worked she made low sounds of distress.

'You've made a terrible mess of this, ma'am. 'Tis not only muddy, it's torn, too.'

Elinor wriggled the dress down over her hips and it dropped to the floor at her feet. Picking it up, she examined it quickly, then threw it down again petulantly.

'Damn!'

'I can wash and mend it for you, but it won't be ready for you to wear again today.'

'Then take me upstairs and show me what you have. You must have *something*.'

Without waiting for the girl's reply, Elinor strode from the dairy and headed for the staircase in the corner of the living-room. On the way she swept past Tom Quicke, who had just entered the house from the yard. His mouth dropped open at the sight of his titled landlord's daughter advancing upon him dressed only in a wet and bedraggled petticoat. But he hardly had time to snatch the hat from his head before Elinor passed by without a word, Nell in close pursuit.

There were two doors opening off the head of the stairs. One door stood open, displaying a bed, a handmade rag carpet, and marble-topped washstand. This was quite obviously the bedroom in use by the Quicke family, and Elinor swept inside. She looked in vain for a wardrobe.

With a murmured apology, Nell Quicke slipped past her and dropped to her knees beside a leather chest, hidden on the far side of the bed. Of a type used by sea-captains, it had been left behind by the previous occupant of Venn. Raising the lid, Nell Quicke reached inside and carefully lifted out three neatly folded dresses.

Two Elinor rejected immediately. Of gaudy silk, they had evidently been bought for Nell Quicke when she was a much younger girl. The third, made from coarsely woven woollen cloth, was more suitable than either of the others, but it was well worn.

Elinor looked questioningly at the farmer's young wife, and Nell Quicke met her glance with an expression that was a mixture of embarrassment and defiant pride.

'That's all I've got, ma'am. My father's a poor man. I came to Tom with no dowry.'

For a fleeting moment, Elinor felt an unexpected surge of sympathy for this wife who had so little – and was unlikely to gain more while her husband worked Venn Farm as a tenant. But Elinor had a coach to meet. Taking up the woollen dress, she held it against her body. 'Then this will have to do. But first I'll need a wash. I'm covered in mud.'

Nell Quicke hurried from the room. Moments later Elinor heard the sound of urgent whispering from downstairs as pans and kettles clanged upon the kitchen fire.

Elinor's expression softened. There was an intangible, calming quality about Nell Quicke. It was not difficult to understand why Tom Quicke had been ready to take his young wife without a dowry.

Nell Quicke returned with a jug of hot water and convinced Elinor that her petticoat would have to be left behind, too. Not only was it too elaborate to be worn beneath Nell's simple

20

woollen garment, but it was also as wet and mud-stained as Elinor's dress.

After a hurried wash, Elinor put on Nell Quicke's dress. She was not able to confirm Nell Quicke's statement that the dress fitted well. When she asked for a mirror, Nell Quicke produced a small and cheap hand-mirror, proudly declaring it to be a wedding gift. It was the only mirror in the house.

When Elinor went outside, she found Tom Quicke brushing down her pony.

'I gave him a drop of water, Miss Hearle,' he said as he handed her up into the gig. 'He seemed to be thirsty.'

Guiltily, Elinor recalled that she had been so concerned with her own plight that she had not given the horse a drink at the watering-place.

'I'm obliged to you, Quicke.'

To his wife she said: 'Bring my clothes to Polrudden when they're washed and mended. I'll see you're paid for your trouble.'

Flicking the reins over the horse's back, Elinor set the animal off at a smart trot, heading back along the farm track that led to the St Austell road.

When she was out of sight, Tom Quicke scratched his head ruefully and replaced the battered hat upon his head. 'That's the first time I've spoken to Sir Lewis's daughter. I can't say I've been missing much. Attractive she may be, but she's no more grateful for anything that's done for her than her father.'

'Oh, she's grateful enough, Tom. I could see that.' Nell Quicke took her husband's hand as they walked inside the house together. 'She's just not used to thanking folks, that's all. Life can't be easy for her up at that big house – alone for most of the time, I shouldn't wonder. I feel sorry for her.'

They had reached the kitchen now, and Tom Quicke looked at the dirty but expensive dress and petticoat lying on the table. Elinor Hearle probably had two or three wardrobes crammed with such clothes. All of Nell's treasured possessions were packed inside a single sea-chest – and yet *she* felt sorry for Elinor Hearle!

Tom Quicke squeezed Nell's hand affectionately. He knew he had married a very special girl and was very much in love with his young wife.

Elinor Hearle arrived at the Queen's Head inn a few minutes after three o'clock. There was no sign of the Royal Mail coach. In answer to her question, a serving-girl informed her that it had not yet arrived.

There was a great deal of noise coming from the Queen's Head and the other inns of the town. Elinor remembered that this was the last Friday of the month, the day when both the weekly paid labourers and the more highly skilled miners received their pay.

St Austell was surrounded by tin and copper mines. In recent years the opening of the china-clay quarries to the north of the town had begun to change the age-old landscape of the Cornish countryside, throwing up tall mounds of china-clay waste, and attracting a great deal of labour to the area. The quarry-owners, members of the local trading fraternity, had learned from their mining associates that a great deal of trading profit could be gained by paying their workers in the St Austell inns. Much of the hard-earned money would return to the businessmen over the tavern bars. More would be spent later in the nearby shops, on gifts for irate wives whose meagre housekeeping money had been further depleted in the convivial atmosphere of a smoke-filled ale-house.

For almost an hour Elinor sat in the gig, growing ever more impatient and annoyed by the remarks and hopeful attentions of passing miners in varying stages of insobriety.

When half-past four came and the mail coach had still not arrived, Elinor tied the pony to a hitching-post outside the Queen's Head and sought the shadows of the archway that led to the yard beside the inn.

Inside the yard was a brewer's wagon. It had arrived earlier in the afternoon, heavily laden with barrels of locally brewed ale. Unloading the barrels and trundling them to the cellars of the Queen's Head inn was hard and thirsty work, calling for constant refreshment for the drayman and his mate. By the time the last full barrel had been replaced on the wagon by an empty one, both brewery employees were red-faced and loud-voiced, their talk liberally laced with oaths.

When the last empty barrels were tied down, the drayman began to turn the wagon around in the narrow yard. It was not an easy manoeuvre. The yard was cluttered with the gigs and light carriages of the inn's wealthier customers.

The brewery horses did not make the drayman's task any easier. They were an ill-matched pair. One horse was aged and experienced, and stood quietly in the shafts, head hanging low. But the other was young and nervous. Ears twitching at every sound, it rolled its eyes fearfully whenever anyone passed by. Had the drayman showed more patience, he might have *coaxed* this horse to do his bidding, but many pints of best brewery ale had drowned all reasonableness.Careless handling soon caused the heavy wagon to jam against the inn wall. In his efforts to work it free, the drayman had the horses moving backwards and forwards time and time again. Thoroughly confused, the inexperienced animal became even more nervous than before and continually tried to back away from the shouting drayman. The wagon jammed tighter against the wall and there came the noise of splintering wood.

Bellowing at the young horse, the drayman picked up a heavy stave that had been used to lever the big barrels from the wagon. Swinging it high in the air, he brought it down upon the horse's flank with a sickening thud. The horse snorted in fear and tried to bolt. The other horse did not budge. With the dray stuck fast, the frightened horse slipped on the cobbles of the yard and crashed heavily to the ground.

The horse's predicament enraged the drayman. He began raining heavy blows on the animal's side and stomach as it struggled in a vain attempt to rise.

Watching the incident from the very beginning, Elinor had first been faintly amused at the drunken drayman's antics, but when he began beating the horse with the heavy stave she had seen enough. Rushing across the innyard, she pushed herself between the drayman and his horse and called upon him to leave the horse alone.

Elinor was behaving as she would at Polrudden, where she was used to being obeyed. The drayman, who did not know her, saw only a young woman in a cheap and ill-fitting, homespun woollen dress.

He gave her a half-blow, half-push that sent her sprawling to the cobblestones six feet away.

'Mind your own business, girl, or it'll be your arse I'm

23

paddling, not this bloody useless horse.'

There were a few muffled guffaws from behind Elinor, and she realised for the first time that the happenings in the innyard had attracted an audience.

The drayman turned his back on Elinor and resumed his belabouring of the horse as Elinor scrambled to her feet. Glaring angrily at the amused men standing about in the yard, she cried: 'Will you stand here and do nothing while he beats the poor animal to death?'

'I wouldn't take on Bill Coffin for you, my beauty, let alone for some stupid carthorse,' replied one of the bystanders. 'If you've got any sense, you'll be on your way. Bill Coffin's a man of his word.'

'Aw, leave 'er alone, won't 'ee? Let Bill get to work wi' 'is paddling-stick. I'd give a half-pint of brandy for a flash of what she's got under that there dress.'

Incensed by the coarse laughter of the amused bystanders, Elinor pushed her way through them. Running to her waiting gig, she snatched up the short whip from its holder and ran back to the innyard.

Bill Coffin never saw her return. He had dropped the stave and was now standing over the fallen horse, kicking it heavily in the ribs with hard-toed boots while his mate was trying more conventional methods of raising the horse.

Elinor's first blow cut across the side of Bill Coffin's neck and he bellowed in surprised pain. Her second blow caught him across the cheek as he turned. The third never landed. The drayman snatched the whip from her hand and broke it into four leather-linked pieces. Throwing the whip to the ground, he touched a fingertip to his cheek. It came away tinged with blood, and Bill Coffin howled with rage.

'You vicious little cow! I'll give you some of your own medicine. . . .'

Before the angry drayman was able to carry out his threat, a young man stepped from the crowd. Almost casually, he pushed Elinor out of Bill Coffin's reach. When the drayman moved after her, the young man stepped into his path.

'Leave her. I didn't agree with what you were doing to that horse, but that's between you and the brewery. This isn't. I won't stand by and watch you beat a woman.'

There was a quiet confidence in the young man that caused Bill Coffin to hesitate – but only for a moment. The drayman stood a head taller than the newcomer, and he knew his mate was behind him.

'Did you hear that, Seth?' Bill Coffin called the words over his shoulder as he eyed the newcomer's stylish, if somewhat dusty, clothes. 'We've got a young dandy here. Reckons he can tell Bill Coffin what he should or shouldn't be doing.'

'Then ye'd best put him right, Bill. Unless thee'd like me to do it for 'ee?'

'No, I'll do it – and gladly. You see that the maid doesn't run away. I've a score to settle with her.'

Without warning, Bill Coffin rushed at his opponent, arms held wide to secure him in a hug that would squeeze the breath from his body. The sudden move was wasted. With a quick movement, the stranger sidestepped out of reach.

Someone in the crowd let out a muffled titter, and Bill Coffin flushed angrily. He bored in once more, this time with fists flailing. What occurred next happened so quickly that it was the subject of heated argument in the St Austell hostelries for many months to come. A few onlookers would hotly declare that Bill Coffin was hit by a number of blows. Others, also present, swore it was no more than one.

No one cared to ask Bill Coffin. Had they done so, he could have told them he took three of the mightiest punches he had ever experienced in his rough-and-tumble life. The first sank wrist-deep into his ale-inflated stomach. The second took him on the forehead even as his body doubled up in pain. He straightened involuntarily, positioning his chin perfectly for an impeccable straight right.

Arms akimbo, Bill Coffin was knocked back into the crowd, his momentum and unconscious weight carrying upwards of half a dozen men to the ground with him.

The drayman's mate watched the destruction of his colleague in wide-mouthed amazement. A man of great strength but limited discernment, he never paused to ponder upon the character and skills of the man who had so effectively demolished his companion. Placing a heavy hand on the victor's shoulder, he said: 'I'll show 'ee. . . .'

The next moment the hand on the stranger's shoulder was

25

clutching air. What happened next, though often talked about in St Austell and the surrounding district, was never a subject of argument. Every man there agreed that the single uppercut travelled no more than six inches to the chin of the drayman's burly mate. Nevertheless, it had sufficient explosive power to stretch the man until his toes barely touched the uneven cobbles. A moment later he crumpled to the ground, no more aware of his surroundings than his horse-beating workmate.

There was a momentary awe-filled hush before the watching crowd roared their loud appreciation of the stranger's skill.

Ignoring their noisy approval, the victorious young man went to where Elinor stood, slightly bemused by the turn events had taken.

'Are you all right, miss?' He nodded towards the inn. 'Would you like to go inside and sit down for a while?'

Elinor shook her head. 'No. No, I'm quite all right.'

The young man grinned suddenly. 'Only a very brave girl, or a stupid one, would take on a drayman for the sake of a horse. You don't look particularly stupid to me, so I compliment you on your courage.'

Elinor was torn between gratitude for this man's intervention on her behalf and indignation at his words. Then she remembered she was not dressed as the daughter of Sir Lewis Hearle, but was wearing an old woollen dress belonging to Nell Quicke. Realisation came that for possibly the first time in her life someone had helped her simply because she was a woman, and not because she was Elinor Hearle, daughter of Sir Lewis Hearle, local landowner and Member of Parliament for the borough of Fowey. It was an unusual and strangely uncomfortable discovery.

In a bid to cover her confusion, Elinor unfastened the small leather bag she wore dangling from a long thong about her neck. Taking out a sovereign, she proffered it to her rescuer.

'I am grateful for the assistance you rendered me. Please take this.'

It was customary for gentry to reward those who performed outstanding services for them; but the expression on the young man's face told Elinor she had blundered.

Taking her hand in his, he folded her fingers back upon the gold coin.

26

'Keep your money, young lady.' He fingered the sleeve of her dress where there was a neat but noticeable darn. 'Put it towards the cost of a new dress.'

As he turned away, her rescuer was joined by a thin-faced companion who looked down upon the fallen drayman approvingly before the crowd parted respectfully to allow both men through.

Elinor suddenly realised she had not asked the name of the man who had come to her aid in such a ready and positive manner. Then she became aware of the excited talk about her.

'Did you ever see such a punch?'

'Who was he? Does anyone know him?'

'I do.' The speaker was a ferret-faced little miner. 'Recognised him as soon as I set eyes on him. It were Nathan Jago. Son of the preacher down to Pentuan.'

Chapter Three

THE Royal Mail coach from London rattled into the yard of the Queen's Head inn only minutes after the landlord and his potman had raised the fallen brewery horse. The wagon was sent back to the brewery with two semi-conscious draymen lying between the empty barrels.

Climbing stiffly from the coach, Sir Lewis Hearle gave his daughter a gruff greeting. Then, eyebrows drawn together in a disapproving frown, he demanded to know what she was doing 'dressed like some kitchen drab'.

Elinor offered him no explanation until his luggage had been stowed in the small two-wheeled gig and they were on the road to Polrudden. Only then did she detail the many happenings of the eventful day.

Sir Lewis's reaction was one of amusement when she described her soaking at the watering-place, but his mood changed abruptly when she told him of the incident in the yard of the Queen's Head.

Erupting in a sudden bout of irascibility that did much to explain Elinor's own explosive nature, he shouted: 'Dammit, Elinor! Isn't it enough that you come to meet me dressed like a servant girl? Do you also have to brawl with draymen as though you were some Mevagissey fisherwoman? Such behaviour would be bad enough in a son. In a daughter it's . . . it's *intolerable*. I won't have it, do you hear me?'

Elinor was unperturbed. She knew that the story of how she had horsewhipped a brewer's man for beating a horse would be proudly related in a dozen London gatherings within a week of her father's return to Parliament.

'Who is this fellow who stopped the drayman from giving you the hiding you deserve? Is he a local man?'

'I've never seen him before, but some of the crowd seemed to know him. Nathan Jago was the name I heard mentioned.'

'Nathan Jago? The prize-fighter? What the devil is he doing back in these parts?'

Elinor looked at her father in surprise. 'You know him?'

'I've heard of him. I'm surprised you haven't. He was fishing

28

from Pentuan as a boy, but was too wild to stay in one place. He ran off to join the Navy when he was no more than fourteen or fifteen. He was Admiral Nelson's helmsman, first in *Elephant* at the battle of Copenhagen, and again in *Victory* at Trafalgar. They say Nelson would have no other man at the helm of his ship in battle. Jago was wounded at Trafalgar and discharged from the service. But it couldn't have been a bad wound. Only a year later he fought Ted Laxton, the London prize-fighter, to a standstill over forty rounds.'

Elinor remembered the unmarked features of her rescuer. He certainly did not have the appearance of a prize-fighter. No doubt this was testimony to his skill.

'It seems I could not have chosen a better champion.'

Sir Lewis Hearle snorted. 'He might have saved you a paddled backside, but I'm damned if I'm happy about the Hearle family owing a debt of gratitude to a Jago.'

Before Sir Lewis Hearle could say more, the gig rounded a sharp bend and they found the narrow lane blocked by a pair of yoked oxen. The smocked countryman driving the two beasts gave no indication that he knew the gig was behind him and continued on his way, oblivious of the baronet's mounting anger.

'You there! Get those oxen out of the way. Move them off the road. Damn you, man! Do you hear me?'

The countryman never even turned his head, and Sir Lewis Hearle made a strangled noise in his throat.

Elinor flicked the reins and the pony edged forward uncertainly until it nudged the countryman, causing him to stumble and look behind him.

Muttering beneath his breath, he turned back to his slow beasts and drew them to the side of the road, where they immediately began cropping the grass.

As Elinor and her father drove past, the countryman raised his soft hat of stitched line, and gave the occupants of the gig an enigmatic smile.

'There! That's the reason I want nothing to do with the Jagos. You saw that man's insolence? A peasant thinking he's being clever by holding up his betters.'

Elinor smiled tolerantly at her father. 'I don't think he was being insolent. It is far more likely that he is deaf. He never realised we were behind him until the pony nudged him.'

'Nonsense! The man's been listening to the teachings of your young hero's father. He's a dangerous bigot. He and his kind are stirring up the scum of the earth, seeking to destroy all that's good in this land of ours. Unless he and those like him are checked, England will go the same way as France. Preacher Jago is a rabble-rouser. A sower of sedition. A Wesleyan Methodist.'

At dusk that day, Nathan Jago and Sammy Mizler paused at the top of Pentuan Hill. A few hundred yards to their left, hidden behind a copse of tall trees, was Polrudden Manor. Below them, a quarter-mile break in the cliffs was filled by a wide scimitar of smooth, golden sand, unevenly bisected by a narrow, fast-flowing river. Huddled on the near bank of the river was the small fishing village of Pentuan.

Nathan filled his lungs with air, expelling it again noisily.

'Breathe in that air, Sammy. Go on, you can *taste* it. You won't find air like it within a hundred miles of London Town.'

Sammy Mizler sniffed more cautiously. 'It smells like Billingsgate to me.'

Nathan grinned. 'The wind must be blowing from Mevagissey. All the offal from the fish-cellars goes into the harbour there. It's a smell you'll need to get used to, Sammy. This is Cornwall, and we're here to go into the fishing business.'

Sammy Mizler grimaced. 'So you've been telling me for more than two hundred and fifty miles. The idea would have more appeal had we come by mail coach and not walked every step of the way.'

'You'll feel different about it when we come to buy a boat and nets. We'll need every penny we've saved. Had we come by coach and then found we were a few guineas short, you'd have begrudged every bone-jarring mile we'd travelled.'

Sammy Mizler shrugged. 'You're the fisherman, not me. I just want to be around when you come to your senses and return to your prize-fighting – and to London. Why, you could be undisputed *world* champion within twelve months! Just think of it, Nathan. The world would be yours! To give all that up for' – he sniffed disdainfully – '*this*. It's madness!'

Sammy Mizler spread his hands in a gesture of helpless

frustration. 'It's not too late. Go and visit your ma. Stay for a week – a month. You've earned yourself a rest. But don't throw away the very real gift that God has given to you. There's magic in your fists. It showed itself back there, in St Austell, when you downed the two draymen. It was beautiful to watch. Beautiful. . . .'

Sammy Mizler stopped talking and hurried to catch up with Nathan, who, his face devoid of expression, had begun to walk down the steep hill to Pentuan village.

'All right, so Ned Belcher was blinded. It was unfortunate – a tragedy, even – but nobody blames you. His own seconds told me his sight had been going for years. He'd been in the prize-fighting game for too long and was never very clever at dodging a punch. Nathan boy! To give up now is nothing short of . . . felonious! If you take the world title, you'll be able to come home in a year or two and buy a whole armada of fishing-boats. Yes, and a house like that, too.'

Sammy Mizler pointed to where the roof and high chimneys of Polrudden Manor rose through the trees far to the left of them.

Nathan checked his stride and looked towards the great house. 'When I was a boy I used to hide on the hill behind Polrudden for hours, wondering what it would be like to live there. But it was just a boy's dream. Save your tongue for tasting my ma's cooking. You'll find it a sight more satisfying, I promise you.'

Sammy Mizler shook his head in despair. But he found consolation in remembering the manner in which Nathan had disposed of the two draymen. Nathan might *think* he was through with prize-fighting, but a man who possessed such devastating power in his two fists would be a fool not to put them to good use. And Nathan Jago was no fool.

Annie Jago bustled about her kitchen-cum-living-room. As she lifted a heavy iron skillet from the fire and raked hot ashes from the cloam oven, she could scarcely contain her happiness. It was a rare occasion for her to have her only son in the house. Indeed, this was only the third time he had been home since coming ashore after Nelson's great, yet tragic, victory at Trafalgar. Over the mantelshelf were proudly displayed the medals presented to Nathan for his part in this battle and in the earlier victory at Copenhagen.

'Why didn't you let me know you were coming?' asked the hot and beaming Annie Jago. 'I'd have got in something special for you. I might even have persuaded your father to stay home to greet you – though I doubt if I'd have succeeded in that, even for you. The Lord's been calling loudly of late, and your father has never been a man to allow His voice to go unheeded. No, not even if his only son were to be here for no more than five minutes.'

Nathan grinned. 'It's good to know some things in life never change. But where's our Nell? Working in the fish-cellars?'

'Working in the cellars? Lord bless you, no. I'm forgetting how long it's been since you were last home. Your sister's been married for six months. She's not Nell Jago any longer, but Nell Quicke. The wife of young Tom Quicke from over by St Ewe. You'll remember him when you meet him. He's a fine man. It was a good marriage for her, Nathan.' Annie Jago could not keep the pride from her voice as she added: 'Tom's a farmer – a *yeoman* farmer. He rents Venn Farm from Sir Lewis Hearle.'

It mattered not to Annie Jago that her daughter probably had less money to spend on herself than a miner's wife, or the lowest-paid worker in a fish-cellar. She was married to a *farmer*, a man making his own way in life. Nell had married well.

She turned to Nathan, holding a kettle of boiling water, her apron wrapped about its handle. 'You haven't said how long you'll be staying?'

Nathan hesitated. He had told Sammy Mizler that his prize-fighting days were over. He had told himself the same thing. Yet now he was at home in the house he had known from childhood, the house in which he had been born, he was suddenly unsure. Everything was somehow smaller than he remembered: the house, the village, the fields – even his mother. He had grown both mentally and physically since leaving Pentuan. He wondered whether he might have grown too big to be part of this tiny community ever again. Aware of Sammy Mizler's quizzical gaze, Nathan did his best to ignore the unwanted doubts.

'I'll likely be around for a long time, Ma. I've come back to buy a boat – perhaps my own cellar, too. I'm going to do a spot of fishing once more.'

An expression of incredulous joy spread over Annie Jago's face, and Nathan leaped to his feet to relieve her of the kettle of steaming water which, unnoticed, had begun to tilt alarmingly in his mother's hands. Placing the kettle on the granite stone of the hearth, he shook his hands in pain. The kettle was very, very hot.

'Do you mean that, Nathan? But what about the money? Boats are not cheap, you know. Colin Arthur's been saving for years to buy his own boat. Even with a couple of good fishing seasons behind him he still hasn't got enough. And to be talking about a fish-cellar, too. . . .'

'I've got the money, Ma. At least, me and Sammy together have. Not only that; Sammy has the keenest business brain outside of Threadneedle Street. We'll stay here and grow rich. All of us.'

Annie Jago's pleasure at Nathan's announcement that he was home to stay was diluted by doubts. The Jagos were a poor family, and Josiah Jago's dedication to evangelism would ensure that he and his wife remained poor to the end of their days. It did not matter overmuch. Their friends were poor, too, and the county in which they lived was a poor one. Even Nell, who had made such a good marriage, had gained nothing but pride in her change of status. Now here was her son talking of *owning* a fishing-boat.

Annie Jago knew nothing of the rewards to be gained in the prize-fighting ring and she was concerned that Nathan might have come by his money dishonestly.

'You'll need more than a business brain to grow rich from pilchards,' she said eventually. 'Last year there were no more than two shoals came close enough to shore to be taken – and there's been but one this year so far. We have four fish-cellars in Pentuan, yet not enough fish is being caught to keep one of them going. If you've got money to spare, you'd do better looking for something else on which to spend it.'

Sammy Mizler looked at Nathan triumphantly. 'Isn't this what I've been telling you every step of the way from London Town? Come back there, Nathan. If you've a mind to put your money into a business, let me find something that will make money for you while you carry on with the thing you do best –

prize-fighting.'

Ignoring his friend's plea, Nathan leaned forward in his chair, addressing his mother: 'You're talking of *seine*-fishing, Ma. I'm not. Any fisherman who sits around on the shore waiting for the fish to come to him deserves to go hungry. The boat I'm going to buy will be a deep-water drifter. I intend going out *looking* for the fish.'

Once again Annie Jago came close to dropping a kettle, but this time there was no joy in her expression. She was genuinely horrified. 'Drift-fishing? You can't do that. We have no drift-fishermen in Pentuan. Never have had. We've always been seiners here.'

'Not any more.' Nathan stood up and walked to the window of the small, warm, comfortable kitchen. 'Look out there. What do you see? A fishing village that's dying through poverty, ignorance and an unwillingness to change. If they'll listen to me and follow my example, the village will come to life again. Children won't need to move away to make a living; they'll have a future here.'

Such talk was beyond Annie Jago's understanding. She shook her head unhappily. 'It will take more than fine words to persuade Pentuan fishermen to take up drifting.'

Sammy Mizler had been looking from Nathan to Annie Jago as the two talked, his dark eyebrows drawn together in a puzzled frown. Now he spoke to Nathan.

'You didn't tell me you were setting out on a fishing crusade when you persuaded me to come to Cornwall as your partner. What's all this talk of drift-fishing and seine-fishing? I've always thought one fisherman was the same as another.'

'So he is – but Cornish fishermen are too stubborn to admit it. Drifting and seining are two different ways to catch fish, that's all. About this time of year the pilchards suddenly appear close inshore in their millions. Every available boat puts to sea, and the pilchards are encircled in long nets – seine-nets – and hauled as close inshore as possible. Then the fish are "tucked in" and taken ashore to the salting-cellars. Tucking might last a week. Salting, bulking, pressing and packing might provide work for the village for another two months. If it's a good season, there might be another run of pilchards before the season's out. On the other hand, if luck's running against the seiners, a storm

34

might blow up while the fish are held in the nets. Then they'll lose fish and nets as well. When this happens the whole community comes close to starving for the remainder of the year. *That's* seine-fishing.'

'What's so different about drift-fishing?'

'Drifting's the only sensible way to fish. You go out to where the fish are and put out a net that stretches like a barrier for perhaps half a mile. When you hoist the net back on board you empty out your fish and bring them ashore. It's a year-round business – and the only way to fish, to my mind.'

'There are many men in these parts who'd argue against you – and that includes the whole of Pentuan. They say it's a selfish way to fish. By laying those nets across the bay you stop the pilchards from coming close inshore and deprive everyone else of a living.'

'That's a load of nonsense, Ma, as every thinking fisherman knows very well. Over the years all sorts of laws have been passed in a bid to control drifters and make fishing more difficult for them. It's made no difference at all. The pilchards still come inshore some years and stay away for others.'

'I'd rather you kept such views to yourself, especially when your father's around. He's as strong against drifting as anyone else when he thinks of *anything* other than doing the Lord's bidding.'

'When do you think Pa will be home?'

Nathan deliberately changed the subject. There had always been a deep and unreasonable division between deep-sea drift-fishermen and those who pursued the more traditional fishing methods. Cornish fishermen had always resisted change, whatever form it took, and Annie Jago came from a long line of seine-fishers. Nathan would keep his thoughts to himself until he had both a boat and a cellar. There would be time enough then to tackle opposition.

'Your father won't be home until he's saved enough new souls to satisfy him, or until he falls off his donkey with sheer exhaustion because he's forgotten to eat or sleep.'

Chapter Four

PREACHER JOSIAH JAGO had still not returned home two days later, when Nathan set out early to visit his sister and her husband at Venn Farm.

Sammy Mizler remained behind at Pentuan. Later in the day he would hobble to the nearby harbour wall, there to bask in the warm autumn sunshine, but he had done enough walking in recent weeks.

Instead of taking the road direct to Venn Farm, Nathan set off along the cliff path that passed behind Polrudden Manor. He paused along the way to gaze down into the deep, overgrown cleft in the cliff face from which great blocks of Pentuan stone had once been quarried. He remembered, as a boy, watching the huge blocks of stone being winched into the dark holds of blunt-bowed, dust-coated merchantmen. Pentuan stone was a distinctive buff colour, and Nathan had recognised it in many of the fine London buildings.

Not far from the disused sea-edge quarry, Nathan passed within a few hundred yards of Polrudden. He was close enough to view with sadness the air of neglect that the old house wore like a shabby cloak.

Nathan had business to discuss with Sir Lewis Hearle, but it would have to wait for another day.

Nell Quicke was sweeping the flagstones immediately in front of the small farmhouse door when Nathan came into view. She saw him when he was still some distance from the house. With a hand shielding her eyes from the slanting sun, she squinted uncertainly until he came closer. Then, dropping the broom, she ran to greet him.

'Nathan! It *is* you, isn't it? How wonderful.'

Nell Quicke flung herself at her brother, and Nathan hugged her to him, swinging her clear of the ground as her arms tightened about his neck.

'How long have you been home? Why didn't you let us know you were coming?'

'I'm no letter-writer, Nell, as well you know. But you're a fine one to talk. I come home expecting to be cared for by my loving young sister, only to find she's up and married some rich young farmer!'

Nell laughed happily. Releasing her grip on Nathan, she took him by the hand and led him towards the house. 'Hardly rich, Nathan. There are so many things we need. A good milking-cow, for one thing. But we'll get one sometime. Tom says so.'

'Where is this husband of yours?' Nathan looked about the empty yard. He had seen no one working in the fields on his way to the farm.

'Tom's taken a litter of pigs to St Austell market. It's the first litter we've raised at Venn,' Nell added proudly.

Nathan ducked his head to enter the house through the low doorway. It was warm in here and smelled of wood smoke.

'I'll get you a drink. One of Tom's friends gave us a barrel of cider as a wedding present.'

Nathan nodded. Glancing around the room while Nell was fetching the drink, he observed the lack of luxury. Yet there was an air of serenity, almost well-being, that put him immediately at ease.

Nell returned to the room and placed a cider-filled jug on the white-scrubbed table in the centre of the room before reaching down a mug from a shelf.

'Are you enjoying married life, Nell? You're happy with your Tom Quicke?'

The answer was in Nell's eyes when she looked up at her brother. 'I'm *very* happy, Nathan. Tom's a wonderful man. He's good to me.'

'I'm glad. I've often worried about the sort of man Pa might have found for you. I felt sure he would be some ageing, lonely circuit preacher.'

Nell and Nathan were very close to each other, even though they had seen little of one another in recent years and there was ten years between the two. Nell idolised Nathan. He, in his turn, felt very protective towards her.

'You can stop worrying about me now. You'll like Tom. He's. . . . Oh, he's just a *wonderful* man. He makes me feel really good.'

Sheer happiness threatened to choke Nell, and Nathan held out his arms and hugged her to him.

37

At that moment a long shadow reached into the room. Still holding Nell, Nathan turned and saw Elinor Hearle.

The mistress of Polrudden had Nell's woollen dress in her hands, and her eyes opened wide in astonishment as she recognised Nathan. Recovering her composure, her manner became icily cold. Ignoring Nathan, she threw the woollen dress on the table and spoke to Nell Quicke.

'I came to return this. I had expected you to bring my clothes to Polrudden before this.'

Flustered, Nell Quicke said: 'I . . . I had to borrow some cotton of the right colour. I had none at the farm. I was going to bring them to Polrudden this afternoon. I'll fetch them; they're upstairs.'

Nell Quicke hurried from the room. She had made no introductions, but they were not necessary as far as Nathan was concerned. Polrudden Manor had been mentioned. There would not be two girls like this one at the old manor-house.

'Well. . . . So you are Elinor Hearle. I had no idea I was rescuing the squire's daughter from a beating.' He lifted the woollen dress from the table, then allowed it to fall back again. 'This fooled me. Do you often visit the town in borrowed clothes?'

Elinor's head went up haughtily. 'I had an accident and fell in the watering-place pond. I borrowed this dress because I had no time to go home and change.' Elinor owed this man no explanations and she could not understand why she was giving him one. 'If it makes a difference to you that I have no need to buy more clothes, I still have the sovereign I offered to you. I believe you *usually* fight for money?'

There was an edge to her voice that caused Nathan to respond in a similar vein.

'My fights are arranged in advance – and for considerably more than a guinea.'

'Oh? And are your assignations arranged for you, too? Or do all young married women fall into your arms when they learn they are in the presence of Nathan Jago, champion prize-fighter of all England?'

The scorn in her voice came as more of a surprise to Elinor Hearle than to Nathan. She had no reason to be concerned with the liaisons of a *prize-fighter* – and she certainly cared nothing for the young wife of a farmer, even if he *were* one of her father's tenants.

To add to her chagrin, Elinor saw that Nathan was grinning broadly. 'I don't confine my embraces to married women. Single girls are high on my list, too.'

At that moment Nell Quicke returned to the room, unaware of the strained atmosphere. Over her arm lay Elinor's dress and petticoat, both neatly pressed and folded. Placing them on the table, she carefully opened out the dress to show the neatly repaired tear. 'I mended this. It hardly shows at all. You'll be able to wear it again'.

'I have no doubt you have repaired it adequately.' Throwing a coin on the table, Elinor snapped: 'Here's a shilling for your work.'

Keenly aware of the amused expression upon Nathan's face, Elinor refused to meet his eyes. 'I'm sorry if I've interrupted anything.' With this remark, she turned about abruptly and strode from the house.

Behind her, Elinor's barbed words were lost on the young wife. Nell Quicke's mind was filled with thoughts of how she would spend the welcome shilling.

Elinor's horse was grazing on the lush grass just beyond the farmyard. Placing her left foot in the stirrup, she grasped the pommel of the saddle and was about to swing herself on to the horse when she heard a step behind her.

It was Nathan. Still grinning, he said: 'I'd better set matters straight before you go – about Nell and me.'

'Why?' Elinor shrugged. 'The morals of our tenants, or of their wives, are no concern of mine.'

'All the same, I think you should know that Nell is my sister.'

Elinor felt the colour rise to her face. She had made a fool of herself in front of this exasperatingly self-assured man. It was not a comfortable feeling. She swung her leg across the saddle in a masculine fashion and found the second stirrup.

Nathan felt he had goaded Sir Lewis Hearle's very attractive daughter enough for one day. Resting a hand upon the horse's neck, he looked up at her and smiled. 'I would like to discuss a business matter with your father sometime. When would be a good time to call at Polrudden?'

Elinor wondered what business Nathan Jago could possibly

have with her father. She did not ask. Instead, she said: 'He's a busy man. Is it urgent?'

Nathan wanted to speak to Sir Lewis Hearle about the fishing tithes payable to the manor of Polrudden by all boats fishing out of Pentuan. He said: 'It will keep for a day or two. It's a matter that I'd like to discuss with my father first.'

Nathan's reply touched a sudden chord in Elinor's memory. Her father had told her that Nathan was the son of a Methodist preacher, and now she remembered the St Austell court messenger who had come to Polrudden seeking her father late the previous evening.

'Your father . . . where is he now?'

The question took Nathan by surprise. 'Out riding his circuit. He's a Methodist preacher.'

'Does he ride the Mevagissey and Tregony circuits?'

'Yes. Why?'

Elinor remembered the exact words of the messenger to her father: 'The Methodist minister who rides the Mevagissey and Tregony circuits has been arrested. The other magistrates feel the case is important enough for a full bench to meet to hear his case.' She told Nathan.

Absent from home not on the Lord's business, but held in St Austell lock-up in the name of His insane Majesty, King George III, Preacher Josiah Jago was a bewildered and unhappy man. He had been arrested, quietly and discreetly, whilst homeward bound from Fowey. The constables making the arrest told him only that he was being arrested as a result of a complaint lodged by the Reverend Nicholas Kent, rector of the busy south Cornish port of Fowey.

Taken in custody to St Austell, Josiah Jago was charged with being an itinerant preacher, contrary to the Toleration Act of 1689. This ancient Act of Parliament, enacted in the year that William of Orange and Mary took the throne vacated by the Catholic King James II, decreed that a dissenting preacher had to be settled in the parish in which he preached. The Act had been intended to give dissenters a greater degree of freedom than they had hitherto enjoyed. Now, more than a century later, it was being resurrected as a weapon to curtail the activities of the most popular religious movement England had known since Christianity ousted paganism.

Such popularity was spreading alarm and hypocrisy among the leadership of the Established Church and its political counterparts.

For very many years the Church had neglected the people it claimed to serve. Parish clergymen who should have been protecting the interests of miner, fisherman and farmworker had long ceased to see the Church as a heavenly-inspired vocation. It had become a business – a very lucrative business for many – and an ambitious curate had more prospect of furthering his career by riding with the local hunt and dining frequently at the manor. Ambition apart, it was a far more *comfortable* way of life than sharing the many insurmountable problems of the poor.

But the Church was not yet ready to relinquish its age-old hold on the poor and allow them to seek their God outside the high grey-stone walls of the churches of the established faith. Nonconformists had always aroused the fury of the church of the land. *Successful* nonconformists, especially those with the fervour of the Methodist movement, did far more. They posed a long-term threat to the wealthy and powerful bishops who ruled profitable sees from feudal palaces.

Acting as the spokesman for the bishops, the Archbishop of Canterbury drew the attention of Spencer Perceval's government to the dangers that were posed by the followers of Wesley. The Wesleyan Methodist movement was a church of the common people. Most of their preachers were themselves *of* the people. Yet the disciplines they imposed upon themselves and their followers would have done credit to the army of Viscount Wellington, Britain's popular new hero.

The Archbishop reminded Prime Minister Perceval that the flood of war currently engulfing Europe had sprung from just such a deep well in eighteenth century France. He convinced Britain's traditionalist Prime Minister that untutored preachers with the ability to rouse the masses to such heights of fervour were dangerous men.

To add weight to his arguments, the Archbishop was able to point to the industrial discontent that had recently erupted in the Midlands and the North of England. Much of the discontent was mistakenly – or perhaps maliciously – blamed upon the Methodists.

Spencer Perceval, himself destined to die a violent death only two years later, needed no further persuasion. Word went out from London that the preaching of Methodism was to be 'discouraged'.

This was all that was needed by the Cornish gentry – as represented by the county's magistrates. Seriously alarmed already by rioting miners protesting against the high price of corn, they were eager to deflect blame from the landowners. Methodist preachers would make excellent scapegoats.

Josiah Jago spent most of his day and night in St Austell lock-up asking the Lord for strength to face whatever might be in store for him. The Wesleyan preacher knew the Reverend Nicholas Kent. The Anglican rector was an unremitting opponent of Methodism. Nevertheless, he would not have laid his complaint without the full backing of his own Church Authority.

It was this that worried Josiah Jago more than anything else. In common with most Methodists, he felt an affection, a family bond, with the mother church. Wesley himself had been ordained in the Church of England and had urged his followers to pursue his particular brand of evangelism within the established faith. It was impossible, of course. Such a vital and energetic movement soon left the conservative Established Church far, far behind. Yet the older members of the Methodist Church were still keenly aware that they had sprung from the church founded by Henry VIII. An organised campaign against them by the mother church would cause such men great distress.

The magistrates' court was due to sit at eleven in the morning. Long before this time, Josiah Jago became aware of a gradually swelling hubbub beyond the walls of the lock-up. At first, he dismissed the sound as being that of the Cornish market-town awakening and gathering pace as the morning wore on; but there was no levelling-off in the unseen noise, and it puzzled the imprisoned preacher. Josiah Jago wished he could see outside, but there was only a tiny, barred aperture, far up in one corner of his cell, higher than he could reach.

Then, when the blue-faced clock in St Austell church tower

chimed the hour for ten o'clock, a single voice beyond the barred window began to sing one of John Wesley's hymns. As Josiah Jago thrilled to the sound, the words were taken up by more voices, until all the noises of the busy market-town were lost in the defiant words pouring from the throats of a thousand men and women.

Joyful though the sound was, Josiah Jago found himself at a loss to think of the reason for such a religious gathering. It was not a feast day. Even if it had been, he had never known a holy day to be celebrated with such a rousing display of religious fervour.

When the hymn ended it was followed by another. Then, in a brief pause before another hymn was called for, the powerful voice of a speaker rang out, drawing prolonged cheering from the unseen crowd. Josiah Jago could not hear what was being said, but he caught three words. Those words were 'Preacher Josiah Jago'!

Enlightenment filled him with a sense of emotional awe. The crowd gathered outside the lock-up were there to show support for him – Josiah Jago.

The preacher was a simple man, a truly humble servant of the Lord. Men listened to him, but only because he was guiding them to God. As a man he had never claimed to amount to much. The thought of all those people gathered outside to protest at his arrest and to offer him encouragement in his time of need overwhelmed him. Sinking to his knees, his voice choked with emotion, Josiah Jago begged the Lord not to make a martyr of him. He asked only that he be released and allowed to serve Him in a comfortable, familiar way.

At ten-thirty, the church bells began to ring, the bell-ringers hurriedly summoned by the vicar of St Austell in an angry bid to drown the voices of the Methodist hymn-singers. The battle between bells and hymn-singers was still going on when a nervous Town Constable arrived at the lock-up to take Josiah Jago up the stone stairs to the magistrates' court.

Sir Lewis Hearle, MP and Justice of the Peace, entered St Austell while the Methodists and the church bells were vying with each other for supremacy. He frowned angrily at the size of the crowd in front of the court-room. It extended the whole length of the road, making entry to the magistrates' court impossible.

But Sir Lewis Hearle was not going to the court-room immediately. A second messenger had intercepted him while he was on the road to St Austell.

The Sheriff of Cornwall, Richard Oxnam, had also been told of Josiah Jago's arrest and had immediately hurried to St Austell. He sent a message to Sir Lewis, suggesting that the baronet meet him before taking his place on the bench at the magistrates' court.

Sir Lewis Hearle found Richard Oxnam lounging in the best room of the White Hart inn. The Sheriff had a scowl on his face, and a jug of best claret on the table at his elbow. Waving Sir Lewis Hearle to a seat, he poured him a glass from the jug.

Richard Oxnam took the opportunity to top up his own glass, and promptly poured half the contents down his throat.

'Those blasted bells! At least the singing was *half*-musical. I trust it will remain so. I would hate to see such a crowd turn ugly. How many would you say were there, Sir Lewis? A thousand? Two?'

Sir Lewis Hearle merely nodded. He would have placed the total closer to two thousand than to one.

The Sheriff of Cornwall pursed his lips, and Sir Lewis Hearle was undecided whether the Sheriff was savouring his drink or was lost in thought. His next words proved that Richard Oxnam was deeply concerned about the situation that had brought about the scene in the streets outside.

'You've been called in to hear the case against the Wesley preacher, Jago, I believe?'

'That's right. It's high time action was taken against these Methodist rabble-rousers. They are driving the country to the brink of revolution. You have only to look at the mob outside. If the Constable hasn't dispersed them by the time the court sits, I'll have the Riot Act read out to them.'

Richard Oxnam's eyebrows had risen just sufficiently to cause Sir Lewis Hearle to pause in his tirade.

'Because they are singing hymns? I trust you'll take the same line with those wretched bell-ringers. They're causing a breach of the peace, if ever I heard one.'

The baronet could not disguise his surprise.

44

'You're not telling me you approve of the Wesleyans? Why, the Prime Minister himself is anxious to curb their activities.'

Richard Oxnam snorted derisively. 'Spencer Perceval was incapable of forming an opinion of his own during the years we spent at school together. I doubt he's changed. Perceval's views on the Methodist Church are those of my Lord Archbishop of Canterbury – and he can hardly be said to be impartial! The Wesleyan movement has gained more converts in the last thirty years than the Church of England during the whole of its existence. Whether or not I approve of Methodism doesn't matter. I'm a realist.'

The Sheriff of Cornwall topped up his glass again before fixing a shrewd look upon Sir Lewis Hearle. 'I'm going to do you a favour, Sir Lewis. Don't sit on the bench for this case against the preacher. Not only that; do your best to see he's given a sentence that will enable him to walk free from the court-room, in full view of his fellow-Methodists.'

Sir Lewis Hearle opened his mouth to register a protest, but Richard Oxnam raised a hand to silence him.

'Hear me out before you say anything. That crowd is going to double, perhaps even treble, by midday. Send Jago to prison and you'll have a riot on your hands, whether you've read the Act to them or not. What's more, you'll have given them a leader – a martyr to the Methodist cause. He will become an inspiration to every malcontent Methodist in the county – and, just in case you don't already know, *one in three of Cornwall's population is a Methodist.* It means that the county you represent in Parliament is a *Methodist* county. I know . . . I know, you're about to tell me that these people are miners, fishermen and farm labourers – non-voting peasants, whose views don't matter a damn.'

Richard Oxnam leaned forward in his chair and emphasised his next words with an admonishing finger. 'You're wrong, Sir Lewis. Dangerously wrong. Oh, I don't doubt that in London and these new industrial towns of the north, the Wesleyans are attracting riff-raff. The Methodists are organised. They have discipline and communications, and are reaching the people. No agitator worthy of the name will miss the opportunity to join such an organisation and use it for his own ends. But things are different here in Cornwall. Our people don't follow like sheep just because someone happens to bleat louder than his fellows.

45

Methodism is becoming respectable here. One day it will be the same elsewhere. It's showing men the way to God. Before you know it, Methodism will be attracting respectable men of substance to its ranks – your artisan, yeoman farmer and merchant. Householders, Sir Lewis. *Voters.* Men who put you into Parliament at the last election – and who'll damn soon vote you out again if they don't like what they see.'

Richard Oxnam sank back in his chair once more. 'Be very careful, Sir Lewis, very careful indeed – whatever your personal feelings about Methodism. No doubt you'll have many opportunities to make life difficult for them but, for now, be circumspect, I beg you.'

Satisfied that he had put his message across to the baronet, Richard Oxnam picked up his glass and sat looking at his visitor across the rim of the glass.

Sir Lewis Hearle viewed Cornwall's sheriff with suspicion. 'If I were the Prime Minister, I would go much farther than Perceval in putting down dissident religious groups, such as the Wesleyans. They are spawning-beds for disaffection and revolution. However, I am grateful to you for expressing concern about my future. Perhaps you will tell me why you have this sudden interest? As far as I am aware, we have never met socially. Are you one of Wesley's converts?'

'I find you offensive, Sir Lewis, and I don't give a damn about your future. But, if the Methodists are pushed too hard, they – and other dissenters – are likely to follow the example of the Luddite reformers and other malcontents. Such unrest will bring about the downfall of your party. This would not please me at all just now; the Whig opposition is far too committed to reform. It might also light the fires of a popular revolution, enthusiastically aided by France, of course. If you and your government wish to curb the power of the Methodists, I suggest you resort to more subtle means than you appear to favour at the moment. Make the practice of their religion difficult for them. They have few enough places of worship at the moment – be sure you keep it that way. God's bounty is less apparent when a man's family stands in the open for two hours every Sunday, with rain trickling down their necks. Make them discontented with their church, and with one another. It should not be impossible for a determined man. Without Wesley, Methodism is a church without a leader. The movement is already falling apart in other parts of the country. There is a breakaway group calling itself "The New Connection", or some such. Before long there will be another, the "Primitive" Methodists. Your Preacher Jago will become one of these. As the groups become smaller and more introspective, their following will fall away and members will return to the Established Church. But use a sledgehammer to crack them and they will band together so tightly they will break the Government.'

The Sheriff gave Sir Lewis Hearle a disarming smile. 'Even if the consequences for the remainder of the country are far less serious than I have painted them, there will be a major disturbance here if Jago is convicted. Couple this with the demonstrations staged by the miners against rising food-prices and it might be sufficient to deny my son the baronetcy I am determined he will one day inherit from me. Do you understand my concern now, Sir Lewis?'

Sir Lewis Hearle rose to his feet and extended his hand. 'I owe you an apology, Mr Oxnam. I assure you I will do nothing to put your baronetcy in jeopardy.'

Nothing Richard Oxnam had said had changed Sir Lewis Hearle's opinion of Methodism. He detested their pious dedication and narrow-minded views on religion. He saw them as a threat to the rural way of life he and his ancestors had enjoyed for centuries and which was beginning to crumble away throughout the land. But Sir Lewis Hearle was no fool. Richard Oxnam had offered him sound advice. He would act upon that part of it which affected him.

Josiah Jago might be convicted in the St Austell magistrates' court, but Sir Lewis Hearle would not be sitting on the bench.

Chapter Five

AS PREACHER JOSIAH JAGO emerged from the St Austell court-room, the cheers of the huge crowd greeted a thoroughly bewildered man.

Even as he waited on the stairs that led from the dark and dank cells to the magistrates' court above, a gloating gaoler had informed him that he was likely to meet many of his fellow-preachers in prison. The gaoler had added darkly that in other parts of the country Methodist preachers were being referred to higher courts, with recommendations for transportation to the Australian penal colonies.

Josiah Jago knew he had done nothing to bring such a dreadful sentence upon himself, but, then, he *had* been arrested without reason. Anything was likely.

Then Josiah Jago's name was called, and suddenly everything became confused. Following a heated exchange between magistrate, constables and the rector who had laid the charges, it appeared there had been an error in the wording of the charge for which he had been arrested.

The matter was discussed in a three-cornered, shouted argument that was more often than not drowned in the din made by the church bells. A constable had been despatched to order the bell-ringers to cease their vigorous enterprise for the duration of the court hearing, but he returned to shout an explanation for his lack of success. The bell-ringers had locked themselves inside the tower and would not open the door to anyone.

Upon receipt of this information, the magistrate made a ruling that left the rector of Fowey angry and red-faced. The charge against Josiah Jago was reduced to that of causing an unlawful obstruction in the streets of Fowey whilst holding a prayer-meeting.

The case was swiftly proved and he was fined ten shillings, or fourteen days in prison in default. Josiah Jago declared himself unable to pay the fine when, much to his surprise, the voice of his son called from the back of the crowded court-room, offering to pay the fine into court immediately.

Passing the money to a court official, Nathan grasped his father's arm and bustled him from the court, half-afraid that the determined preacher would take a stubborn stand on the sheer injustice of his arrest and conviction.

Fortunately, Josiah Jago was much too confused to invoke his principles. The events of the morning had proved too much. The unexpected appearance of his son came as a great relief.

Josiah Jago's confused state of mind was not helped when he saw the huge crowd waiting beyond the doors of the magistrates' court. As their cheers momentarily rose above the bell-ringers' determined cacophony, Nathan felt his father's fingers tighten their grip upon his arm.

There followed a wild scene on the steps of the magistrates' court, as joyful Methodist well-wishers surged forward to shake the hand of the circuit preacher and slap him on the back in boisterous greeting.

A cry went up calling for a prayer of thanksgiving to the Lord for His servant's release, and Josiah Jago sank to his knees, grateful for the opportunity to perform such a familiar act.

Preacher Josiah Jago had been found guilty of obstructing a little-used footpath on the outskirts of Fowey village. Here, in busy St Austell Town, with more and more Methodists pouring in from the surrounding countryside, three thousand men, women and children sank to their knees in prayer in the main thoroughfares, bringing the whole town to a standstill. It made a mockery of the preacher's conviction. None was more aware of the irony of the situation than the Reverend Nicholas Kent. Unable to pick his way through the kneeling throng, he was forced to stand in silent fury and observe the paean of an alien congregation, one larger than any he had ever seen before.

The prayers over, father and son made slow progress through the ecstatic crowd until they arrived at the stable where the St Austell Constable had boarded the preacher's donkey.

The preacher led the animal through the waiting masses until Nathan insisted that he ride the beast, and eventually they left the people and the deafening noise of the bells behind them.

For the first mile, Josiah Jago rode in a deeply troubled silence, reliving the events of the last couple of days, his mind trying to grasp the implications of his arrest.

Glancing frequently at his father, Nathan saw a thin, ageing man, dressed soberly in a black serge suit, his low-crowned hat pulled down over his forehead, the wide brim misshapen by many inclement seasons. Josiah rode the donkey with only a threadbare blanket for a saddle, and rope harness with which to guide the beast. It was a small donkey, and more than once the preacher's feet touched the ground as he swayed on his thoughtful way.

In a bid to break into his father's morose mood, Nathan said: 'I would have thought a pony better for your work. You'd find it quicker, surely?'

With a visible effort, Josiah Jago brought his thoughts back to the present. 'Speed isn't essential to an itinerant preacher. I've composed many a fine sermon sitting on the back of old Barnabas here. Besides, he's not such a fussy feeder as a horse.'

Suddenly, Josiah Jago smiled wanly. 'I'm sorry, son. I haven't yet told you how pleased I am to see you. But, then, I doubt if you expected to arrive home to find your pa in prison! It's a strange homecoming. How did your mother take the news?'

'I don't know. I was at Venn Farm when I learned of your arrest. I sent Nell to Pentuan and arrived at St Austell just in time to pay your fine. What's it all about? You must have upset someone very important to have them turn the full force of the law upon you. If the magistrate hadn't reduced the charges, you'd be on your way to Bodmin Gaol to await sentencing at the Quarter Sessions, with the certainty of transportation ahead of you.'

'I know . . . I know,' Josiah Jago nodded grimly. 'But I am guilty only of bringing the message of the Lord to His people, and of leading them to Him. I've caused hurt to no man, though I may have pricked the pride of a few Church of England clergy.'

There was a pained expression upon Josiah Jago's face. 'That's the truth, Nathan. It was the Church who brought the prosecution. It was aimed, not at me, but at the Methodist movement as a whole. The gaoler told me preachers are being arrested throughout the land.'

'Something must have happened to upset the government,' mused Nathan. 'They'll be behind the Church, you can be certain. You'd best remain at home in Pentuan for a week or two. The situation will be clearer by then. We'll know what's happening.'

As Nathan had expected, his father shook his head vigorously. 'I won't be turned from my duty. I'll go about the Lord's business as usual – and so will every Methodist preacher in the land. This is a time for determination. We need to show both the Government and our friends that the Methodist Society is here to stay. Perhaps I'll be arrested again, but there will be another preacher eager to take my place. You saw that gathering in St Austell today. They came to show the world we are no "hole-in-a-corner" society. We are a church, Nathan. One day the Government will have to recognise us. When that glorious day arrives I want to be able to thank the Lord for allowing me to be a party to His will. But enough of my chatter. There will be much thinking and even more praying before such hopes are realised. Tell me about yourself. How are you keeping? Are you home for long? And this . . . this "prize-fighting" – are you still earning your living in a manner that's shameful to the Lord?'

Nathan knew the futility of attempting to persuade his father to change his mind. Josiah Jago was a stubborn man. Once he made up his mind about something, he closed his mind to all argument. It had happened many years before in respect of Nathan's prize-fighting. John Wesley was known to have been opposed to wrestling, Cornish hurling, and all other aggressive forms of sport and recreation. Therefore, Josiah Jago had never approved of his son's career as a prize-fighter, even when success and fame came Nathan's way.

Nathan told his father he had retired from the ring. He had, he said, returned home to Cornwall to resume fishing for a living.

Josiah Jago was overjoyed to know his son had forsaken the temptations of the great cities to take up the way of life followed by generations of Cornish Jagos. Then Nathan informed his father that he intended to break from Jago tradition in favour of drift-fishing.

Josiah Jago's dismay caused him temporarily to forget his own problems. As Annie Jago had predicted, her husband echoed the argument of the majority of Cornish fishermen, declaring that drift-fishing deprived inshore seine-fishermen of

51

a living and ought to be banned.

Nathan could be almost as stubborn as his father when he chose to be, and he had been prepared for such opposition. He pointed out that the laws of the land provided more than ample protection to the seiner, and were as outdated as the law that had resulted in Josiah Jago's arrest. In support of drift-fishing, Nathan repeated the argument he had given to his mother and to Sammy Mizler. A drift-fisherman could operate all year round. He used a large boat that would give work to a fair-sized crew and employment for many women in the fish-cellars.

Josiah Jago would not allow himself to be convinced, and Nathan thought the argument was closed when he remarked that, as everyone felt the same about drifting, it was doubtful if he would ever be able to purchase a cellar.

For some minutes the preacher struggled with his conscience as he weighed the evils of drift-fishing against those of prize-fighting. Eventually, he said quietly: 'I don't agree with drift-fishing. I never will. But John Wesley pointed out the evil in prize-fighting. He said nothing against drift-fishing. I know of a fish-cellar for sale. It's in Pentuan – or as near as makes no difference.'

Reaching out excitedly, Nathan brought his father's donkey to a not altogether unwilling halt in order to hear more.

'You know of a *Pentuan* fish-cellar for sale? Who's selling?'

There were only four fish-cellars in Pentuan, each owned by a number of shareholders. Shares were occasionally offered for sale, but unless a concern had suffered a particularly disastrous season it was rare for a whole cellar – which included boats, nets and equipment – to come on to the market.

'Two weeks ago I buried Ned Hoblyn. You've heard of him?'

Nathan nodded silently.

'He moved to Portgiskey Cove a few years back and went into business with a few partners – most of them as dubious a set of characters as Hoblyn was himself. Over the years he bought them all out. Now there's just a widow and a daughter left behind. No doubt they'll be pleased to sell to the first customer who comes along. Try them. Perhaps when you start thinking like a fisherman again you'll come back to seining.'

Nathan's interest had been whetted far more than his father knew. Ned Hoblyn had once been the south coast's most notorious smuggler. That was when he lived farther west, in Prussia Cove. Nathan had once known him *very* well, but he could not tell his father that *he* had once worked for the well-known smuggler.

Nathan also knew Portgiskey Cove. Situated just off the end of Pentuan's half-mile strip of sandy beach, it would have suited Hoblyn's clandestine purposes admirably. Hidden from the view of the fishing village by a protruding fold of the cliff, Hoblyn could have carried out his chosen trade in absolute secrecy. Access to Portgiskey was easy enough from the beach at low tide, but when the water rose it could only be reached via a tortuous path from the adjoining cliffs, or by a long and steep-sided, wooded valley that stretched inland from the late smuggler's cottage.

In addition to the house and fish-cellar, Portgiskey also boasted a tiny deep-water berth. It was an ideal spot for a smuggler – or a fisherman who intended earning his living with an unpopular drifter.

Once he had obtained a cellar, Nathan knew his biggest problem would be over. He had already placed a provisional order for a boat. It was a Brixham-built lugger, one of the best small sea-boats in the world, built in the large Devon fishing village sixty miles away along the English Channel.

Nathan was impatient to hurry to Portgiskey and make an offer to the widow of Ned Hoblyn, but there was no hurrying either Josiah Jago or his donkey.

When father and son reached Pentuan they found that news of the popular preacher's release had gone ahead of them. The whole village, together with Methodists from surrounding communities, waited to give Josiah Jago a triumphant homecoming.

Not until dusk did Nathan manage to slip away from the celebrations, taking Sammy Mizler with him. The tide was on its way in, but they were able to walk to Portgiskey along the firm sand of Pentuan Beach and into the shadow of the cliff separating the beach from Portgiskey Cove.

When they came within sight of the cottage and fish-cellar, Nathan stopped and looked at them with a professional eye. They were in shadow, but he could see enough to fuel his enthusiasm. The incoming tide lapped against black, barnacled rocks lining both sides of the cove and pressed close to the tiny quay wall that rose to twice a man's height. The boat Nathan had ordered would berth here comfortably.

Behind the quay was a tiny cottage. It was surrounded by a low wall that served little purpose, but would prove useful as a seat for men repairing nets. The 'cellar' was attached to the side of the cottage. With an adjacent store and a loft for fishing-tackle, it was larger than the cottage itself.

There was a low, uncertain light burning inside the cottage, but Nathan knocked for many minutes before there was any movement within.

Through the lightly curtained window he saw a shadow cross the room, then the flickering lamp was turned down so low that everything inside became indistinct. A few minutes later there was a sound from behind the door and a woman's voice called in a hoarse whisper.

'Who's there? What do you want at this time of night?'

Nathan and Sammy Mizler looked at each other quizzically. Although it was quite dark in the shadowed cove, it was hardly more than six o'clock.

'It's Nathan Jago. Preacher Jago's son. I'd like to talk to you – about the fish-cellar.'

'I've not met any son of Preacher Jago. Away with you and come back at a decent hour, when I can see your face in the light of day.'

A quickly stifled giggle escaped from Sammy Mizler. In London the working day would just be drawing to a close. Men and women would be looking forward to the delights of the evening. Yet here was a woman complaining that it was too late to receive callers.

Nathan frowned in annoyance. His was the impatience of a man anxious to secure his chosen future.

'I'd like to talk to you about your fish-cellar, Mrs Hoblyn. I'm prepared to make an offer to buy it from you.'

After a long pause, the unseen woman replied: 'You'll need to talk about that to my daughter, Amy. I don't have nothing to do with the business.'

'Fine. Ask Amy to come to the door. I'll talk to *her*.'

'You can't. She's not at home.'

Exasperated by the futile conversation, Nathan asked:

'Where is she? I'll go and find her.'

'Amy's out. . . . She's fishing,' came the reply.

'Fishing? At this time of night?' Nathan was momentarily puzzled. She would not be seine-fishing in the darkness, and Nathan knew his father would have told him had the Hoblyns been engaged in drifting. Then a thought occurred to him. After all, Amy *was* a Hoblyn.

'Who's with your daughter? Can I wait to meet her when she comes back?'

'She's on her own – line-fishing. Now, go away – right away. Don't think that because I'm a widow-woman you can do as you like. I've got a blunderbuss here. It's loaded and it's pointing straight at the door.'

Sammy Mizler scrambled away from the thin wooden door, and Nathan hastily moved to one side of the doorway.

'All right, Mrs Hoblyn. I'm going. I'll be back to see you and your daughter tomorrow.'

Calling an unanswered 'Good night', Nathan walked away. He headed to where the low waves broke against the shore, the sea-water swirling across the gently sloping beach until, all momentum spent, it percolated through the sand.

'The sooner we're away from here the better,' said Sammy Mizler, looking anxiously over his shoulder at the shadowy outline of the dimly lit cottage. 'Guns make me nervous at the best of times. Put one in the hands of a woman who thinks we're going to break into her home and attack her and I become terrified!'

'We're not leaving,' said Nathan unexpectedly. 'We'll go as far as the rocks and wait there for Amy Hoblyn.'

'I don't understand. The woman in the house said her daughter was off somewhere, fishing. Our business will wait until morning.'

'I don't believe she *is* fishing,' explained Nathan. 'Ned Hoblyn was once the most notorious smuggler along this coast. I doubt if he gave it up when he moved here. It's my belief that his daughter is carrying on the family business. It's something I'll need to know about before I make an offer for the fish-cellar. If the Hoblyn women are out to make as much money as possible before selling up, they'll take chances. If word gets about that Portgiskey is being used for smuggling, we'll never be free of the Revenue men. They'll stop and search our boats most nights, raid the fish-cellar and generally do their best to ruin us.'

'But what if this girl and her friends find us here and mistakes *us* for Revenue men?'

Nathan smiled in the darkness at Sammy Mizler's fears. 'Then we'll have a fight on our hands. It will be just like old times. Remember the prize-fight you arranged for me in Whitechapel – when the referee gave me the verdict and the crowd disagreed? Now, that was a fight to remember.'

'I didn't have a blunderbuss pointing in my direction then.'

'Don't worry, Sammy. She'll probably miss,' said Nathan unsympathetically. 'We'll settle down on these rocks. But keep quiet. Sound travels for miles across the water on a still night like this.'

Sammy Mizler pulled his coat collar high about his ears and wedged himself between two damp rocks. He thought longingly of the familiar narrow streets of London. There would be a hint of fog there on such a night as this, and the sounds and smells of a busy city all about: the clip-clop of horses' hooves on cobbled streets; the rattle of carriage wheels; hoarse voices of hawkers advertising their wares; and the all-pervading smell of pitch hanging on the air from the flaming torches borne by carriage-boys. But, most of all, Sammy missed the people who filled the litter-strewn streets – busy, lounging, chattering, drunken, happy, belligerent people.

An hour after the two men had settled themselves among the rocks, the lamp in the little Hoblyn cottage was turned up and placed in a window, its arc of light falling just short of the spot where they sat. It was quite obviously a signal to a boat, but nothing occurred immediately. After remaining in their positions for another half-hour, Nathan and Sammy Mizler were obliged to move to higher ground as the tide came in farther.

Another hour went by before Nathan suddenly reached across and touched Sammy Mizler's arm.

'Listen,' he whispered. 'Can you hear anything?'

Sammy Mizler had heard the sound at the same moment as Nathan. It was the squeak of a small pulley, as a boat's sail was lowered. It was some little distance out, probably at the entrance to the small cove. Moments later there came the sound of muffled oars, straining against cloth-bound rowlocks.

Easing himself from his uncomfortable position, Nathan moved stiffly and cautiously in the direction of the cottage. Sammy Mizler, heart beating rapidly in nervous anticipation, followed. The two men skirted the cottage and moved into the shadow of the fish-cellar. A few minutes later a boat bumped against the quay steps. A small figure jumped from the boat into the dim light, rope in hand, and secured the vessel.

Nathan waited to see how many others had taken part in Amy Hoblyn's nocturnal 'fishing' trip. To his surprise, Peggy Hoblyn had been telling the truth. The girl had been out alone.

As he watched, Amy Hoblyn went to the door of the cottage and knocked softly, calling: 'It's me, Ma. Let me in.'

There was the loud sound of bolts being drawn, the door opened and the girl slipped inside, the door being quickly closed and bolted after her.

'Now's our chance. I want to look at that boat.'

Crouching low, Nathan ran across the space between fish-cellar and quay, scrambling down the steps to the boat riding easily below. Sammy Mizler followed, but hesitated at the bottom of the steps.

'What are we looking for?' Sammy Mizler could just make out Nathan's shadowy figure at the stern of the small boat.

Nathan's reply took the form of a grunt of satisfaction as he located a thin rope leading out over the stern of the fishing-vessel. He began to haul on the rope. It was hard work, and he knew that the other end had been weighted with a heavy rock. It took fully five minutes of determined heaving and straining before something hard bumped against the wooden stern of the boat.

Reaching over the side with both hands, Nathan lifted a small barrel into the boat. He did not need to trace the chiselled words on the side of the barrel to know it contained French cognac. The taut rope extending from the barrel out towards the bay was a clear indication that there were more out there.

Suddenly there came the rasp of flint upon steel above them, and a crude pitch-coated brand spluttered into life on the quay. In the inconstant light, Nathan and Sammy Mizler saw two women looking down at them. The one who held the torch was a scrawny, wild-eyed woman of middle-age. The other was young, with short, dark hair. In her hands she held a brass-barrelled blunderbuss, its bell-shaped mouth yawning in their direction.

'That's them,' screeched the older woman. 'That's them, I tell you. I'd know Revenue men anywhere. Knew it as soon as I saw them from the window. Preacher's son, indeed! Shoot them now, Amy.'

Sammy Mizler moaned in fear and crouched at the bottom of the steps as the young woman raised the gun menacingly.

'I *am* Preacher Jago's son,' declared Nathan firmly. He was as aware as Sammy Mizler of the danger they were in.

'Oh? Then what are you doing in my boat, preacher's son?'

Amy Hoblyn's voice was steady, but the tone was no more friendly than her mother's had been.

'I was wondering what fishing you'd been doing in the darkness. Before making an offer for your fish-cellar I wanted to satisfy myself that I'm not likely to have Revenue men tramping through the place at all hours of the day and night.'

'Don't listen to his crafty talk, Amy. If we don't kill them, we'll end our days rotting in the straw of a gaol cell.'

'Hush Ma.' To the relief of both men, Amy Hoblyn lowered the barrel of the blunderbuss slightly. To Nathan she said: 'The cellar's not for sale. Who told you it was?'

'My father. He told me he'd buried Ned Hoblyn two weeks ago. I was sorry to hear the news. Your pa was a good fisherman, as well as being one of the best sailors I've ever met.'

'You knew Pa? How? When? I've never seen you before.' Amy made her mother hold the spluttering torch out over the edge of the quay in a bid to see Nathan more clearly.

All the time they had been talking, Nathan had been holding the keg of brandy in front of him. Now he lowered it slowly to the bottom of the boat. Straightening up, he said: 'When I was fifteen. I was finding it difficult to live up to my father's standards. I ran away to sea, and made my way to Falmouth. Getting a berth in a ship wasn't as easy as I thought it would be. Then I met up with your pa. He gave me work. You and I *have* met, but you were hardly more than a babe then – and Ned Hoblyn liked to keep his family and his work separate.'

Amy Hoblyn was still undecided whether or not to believe

58

Nathan, although she knew that what Nathan had said was true. When they were living farther west, her father *had* tried to keep work and home life apart.

Her mother was less easily won over. 'Take no notice of him, girl. He's said no more than any Revenue officer would know about your pa. It's a trick.'

'No, Mrs Hoblyn,' Nathan said evenly. Ned Hoblyn's widow was evidently not in her right mind. He did his best to humour her. 'I knew your husband. I knew Beville, too. He and I were impressed into service with the Royal Navy together.'

The effect of Nathan's words upon Peggy Hoblyn was astounding. Her attitude changed immediately. After twice trying unsuccessfully to mouth the words, she whispered: 'You knew Beville? You knew my boy?'

'I was with him when he died in *Victory*. Some of the grapeshot that killed him is still lodged in my leg.'

Sammy Mizler breathed a sigh of relief at the sudden easing of tension. He was interested, too. He knew little of Nathan's life before he had taken up prize-fighting.

The brand in Peggy Hoblyn's hand was spluttering in its death throes, and Amy said: 'You'd better both come inside the house where we can see you better – but don't come empty-handed. Bring two of those kegs with you and haul the others close to the boat. There are eight altogether. Ma and I will bring them in later.'

She paused, then added: 'Just in case you aren't all you claim to be, remember I'll have this blunderbuss with me.'

Sammy Mizler helped Nathan to haul in the remainder of the brandy-kegs, then they each brought one up the steps and carried them to the empty fish-cellar. Here they were hidden in a tomb-like hole beneath one of the flagstones.

There were already more than a dozen kegs inside the stone-lined hole. It was clear that this was not the first occasion on which Amy had been 'night fishing'.

Peggy Hoblyn led the way inside the house, with Amy bringing up the rear. The lamp was turned up and, in its steadier light, Nathan saw that Amy was no more than seventeen years of age – the same age as Nell, Nathan's sister. Her next words confirmed that Amy, in fact, knew her.

'If you're telling me the truth about being Preacher Jago's

son, you'll have no difficulty in naming your sister.'

'Nell? She's married to Tom Quicke now, living up at Venn Farm. You know her?'

'Yes. Pa might have been a smuggler, but he came from a Methodist family. He wanted me to learn to read and write a little. He sent me to classes in Pentuan chapel. Nell was there, too.'

The conversation was interrupted by a pitiful plea from Amy's mother: 'Tell me about Beville. I never saw him from the time he was taken. He was my only son. . . .'

Peggy Hoblyn screwed up her eyes in an unsuccessful bid to dam the tears that trembled there.

Nathan looked questioningly at Amy, and she nodded her head. Then, in the little room, lit by a single pilchard-oil lamp, Nathan told his story, the noise of the sea lapping against the quay outside providing a background to his words.

He told how he and Beville, with two other men, kept a rendezvous with a French merchantman on behalf of Ned Hoblyn. They were transferring an undutied cargo to their boat when they were surprised by a frigate of the Royal Navy, on her way to join Nelson's fleet in Mediterranean waters. The frigate captain put a prize-crew on the French ship, hanged the two experienced smugglers for trading with the enemy, and pressed the two fifteen-year-old boys into service with the Navy.

Once in the Mediterranean, Nathan and Beville were transferred to *Vanguard*, Admiral Nelson's flagship. They were just in time to take part in the battle of the Nile.

For two years the boys gained experience of shipboard warfare in the service of King George III's most famous admiral. Then, in 1800, Nelson resigned his command to travel overland to England from Naples with Lady Hamilton and her ageing ambassador husband.

Soon afterwards, Nathan and Beville were chosen to help sail a captured French man-of-war to England, where they transferred to *Elephant*, another English man-of-war.

In 1801, called back to the service he loved, Vice-Admiral Lord Nelson hoisted his flag in *Elephant*. On two foggy March nights, Nathan and Beville crewed an open boat from which Nelson himself took vital soundings in the treacherous waters of Copenhagen. They were to enable him to take his ships within cannon range of the Danish capital.

Nathan was at the helm of *Elephant* when the three ships in line ahead of the flagship ran aground on their way to do battle with the enemy. With the assistance of Beville, Nathan put the helm over and led the remainder of the fleet past the stranded men-of-war. The result was another glorious victory for the brilliant British admiral.

In 1803, when Nelson raised his flag in HMS *Victory*, he scoured the fleet to locate his Cornish helmsman and transferred him to the flagship. Yet again, Beville Hoblyn went with Nathan. Together they pursued the fleet of the French Admiral Pierre de Villeneuve from the Mediterranean to the West Indies, and back again to the waters of Europe.

On Monday, 21 October 1805, within sight of Cape Trafalgar, Nelson's fleet and the combined fleets of the French and Spanish navies met in battle. At one o'clock in the afternoon a shot shattered the wheel of HMS *Victory*, fatally wounding Beville and driving splinters of wood and metal deep into Nathan's legs. Beville died that same evening, within minutes of England's adored admiral. Nathan was with him.

When Nathan ended his narrative, husky-voiced with emotion, Peggy Hoblyn, eyes red from prolonged weeping, clasped his hands in hers and drew them to her face.

'God bless you, boy. When my time comes I'll rest easier for knowing what happened to my Beville.'

Dropping his hands, the weeping woman drew her apron to her face and scuttled from the room, and Amy hurried after her.

'Was that really how it happened?' Sammy Mizler put the question.

Nathan nodded, not trusting himself to speak again just yet. He felt emotionally drained after reliving the dramatic events of five years before. It was the first time he had related the story of Trafalgar to anyone.

When Amy returned to the room, she looked at Nathan with new respect. 'Thank you for telling Ma about Beville. The news of my brother's death affected her very deeply at the time. Not long after that the Revenue men raided our house down the coast, while Pa was away. Ma fought them off as best she could, but one of them hit her on the head with his musket. She was unconscious for days and was never the same again. Since then, the only things in life that have had any meaning for her have been the memories of Beville – and a deep hatred of Revenue men.'

Nathan nodded sympathetically. 'She'll have had as much excitement as she can take for one night. We'll leave you now. Before we go, Sammy and me will bring the rest of the brandy to the cellar. Your ma will be in no state to help you tonight, and by dawn they'll be high and dry. A Revenue man will be able to see them from a mile away.'

Nathan turned to leave the cottage, but Amy Hoblyn put out a hand to stop him. 'I thought you came here because you wanted a fish-cellar?'

Nathan looked puzzled. 'But you said your cellar isn't for sale.'

'It isn't. But I can't run a fishing business by myself. If I could, I wouldn't need to spend the night hours in an open boat, waiting for a French night-runner who might keep the rendezvous or might not. If he does come, I'll have to spend at least half an hour convincing the captain and his crew that my body isn't part payment for their brandy. I may even have to draw the pistol I carry before they believe me. One day I'll need to use it. I don't want that.'

For a moment, Amy Hoblyn looked very young and vulnerable. 'I'm not going to part with the cellar, but I *could* do with a partner. I'll put up the cellar and pay a fair amount towards nets and any other equipment we'll need. The profits can be shared equally.'

Nathan's interest quickened. It was a generous offer. In the few minutes they had spent in the cellar he had seen that it was fully fitted out for fish-curing. But there was another matter to be settled.

'I've already got a partner – Sammy. I also have firm ideas about the kind of fishing enterprise I want to run. Sammy is the man who'll organise the sale of all the fish I catch, and he's ready to risk his own money on his ability to sell.'

Amy looked from Nathan to Sammy, and back again. After some hesitation, she said: 'I'll not allow others to have a bigger share of the business, but I'm willing to make it a four-way partnership. You and Sammy . . . me and Ma. You'd run the fishing side of the business and I'd organise the cellar with Ma.

She may not be able to think as straight as she once did, but she knows as much about curing, packing and salting as anyone in Cornwall.'

'Right! We'll need to employ two crews and keep them busy night and day if we're to fish my way – and they won't have to mind being unpopular. I'll be bringing a deep-water boat here, for year-round fishing. For drifting.'

Amy's expressive eyes widened. Drift-fishermen were as welcome as lepers in this part of Cornwall. She lapsed into deep thought. When the seconds had become minutes, Nathan said: 'You've had a busy evening, and I've given you much to think about. Discuss what I've said with someone whose opinion you value. Let me know your decision when you make up your mind. I'm staying with my family in Pentuan village. You know the house.'

Amy looked directly at Nathan for the first time in many minutes and met his gaze. To Sammy Mizler it seemed they had forgotten that he was in the room with them.

'I've thought about it as much as I'll ever need to. What name are we going to give our boat?'

Chapter Six

NATHAN realised that in the small, gossip-hungry community of Pentuan his new fishing venture would not remain a secret for very long. Before it became general knowledge, he wanted to have a word with Sir Lewis Hearle. As squire of the manor of Polrudden, he claimed the tithe rights of the fishing village.

Every fisherman in the village paid tithe money to Sir Lewis Hearle on the amount of fish he landed. The origins of such payments had been lost along the tortuous path of history. It was believed tithes at one time provided an income for the Church. In return, the Church fulfilled the spiritual needs of the community. The money would also have subsidised the lord of the manor, who was responsible for the defence of surrounding villages and contributed heavily towards poor relief, asylums and law and order.

Many of the responsibilities of both Church and landowner had fallen away over the centuries, but the tithe payments remained, a source of irritation to those forced to pay them.

Nathan had only ever seen Polrudden Manor from a distance. As a village lad he had fallen in love with the beautiful old house, but had never dared to come close. To have approached the manor-house along the curving tree-fringed driveway as he was doing now would have been quite unthinkable. The driveway had been reserved for the gentry of the county and their families. In all probability it still was, but Nathan was no longer a young village boy wearing a threadbare jersey and clumsy boots roughly put together from leather remnants. He had travelled the world, earning the respect of great men such as Admiral Lord Nelson. He was also a prize-fighting champion, and had been entertained in fashionable London clubs by aristocratic supporters of the prize-ring.

As he approached the manor-house that had overawed him only a few years before, Nathan observed that the magnificently proportioned house had an unmistakable air of genteel neglect. Nathan was reminded of an aged member of the Naples royal family he had seen in a welcoming party assembled to greet

Nelson after his great victory of the Nile. She had been an elegant but infirm old lady, her clothes faded tokens of an earlier, splendid age.

The first person Nathan saw in the grounds of the house was Elinor Hearle. Bloodied from fingertips to elbow, she had just acted as midwife to one of her father's prized mares. Coming round the side of the house from the stables, she was on her way to tell Sir Lewis that the mare had produced a splendid black filly, sired by her own stallion, Napoleon.

Recovering from her surprise at seeing Nathan, she exclaimed: 'Are you looking for me?' She was in a rare good mood. Holding both hands out in front of her, she added: 'I've just delivered a foal. It was a messy business.'

Seeing Elinor Hearle like this, her hair hanging untidily about her face, he was reminded of the first occasion on which they had met, when he had mistaken her for a town girl. He preferred this image to the haughty, autocratic girl who had come to Venn Farm.

'I'm here to see Sir Lewis, but I *have* been hoping I would see you again. I want to thank you for telling me of the arrest of my father. I was able to get to St Austell in time to pay his fine and save him from prison.'

Elinor shrugged. 'It cost me nothing – but don't mention the matter to my father. He'd not thank me for keeping a dissenter from prison – especially a Methodist preacher. I hope you're not here because of that incident?'

'No, I'm here to discuss business with Sir Lewis.'

Elinor's face suggested disbelief, but they had arrived at the front door now and she said: 'Wait here. I'll find him and see if he wants to speak to you.'

Elinor Hearle was gone for twenty minutes. When she returned she had washed her arms and brushed and drawn back her long, dark hair.

'My father is in his study. I'll take you to him.'

She did not mention that Sir Lewis Hearle had watched Nathan's arrival from the window of his study and angrily declared that he should have come to the back door of Polrudden. The very fact that she kept his words to herself surprised Elinor. She attributed her unaccustomed tact to the manner in which she and Nathan Jago had first met.

65

Sir Lewis Hearle was seated at a large rosewood desk, close to the study window. Panelled from floor to ceiling in the same wood, the room contained an impressive carved marble fireplace. Around the walls, the portraits of successive Hearles cast stern-faced disapproval upon the visitor. It had once been a truly magnificent room but, in keeping with the remainder of the house, the wooden panels were dulled by years of neglect and the room smelled damp and musty.

On the desk were a number of letters to which Sir Lewis Hearle appeared to be writing replies. The baronet did not look up immediately, neither did he acknowledge Nathan's presence. For some minutes his quill pen continued to scratch across the page, occasionally replenished from a squat, silver-capped inkpot.

Elinor stood silently beside Nathan for a couple of long minutes. Then she strode to the door, opened it and slammed it noisily before returning to the centre of the room.

Sir Lewis Hearle looked up and frowned at his daughter.

'I thought you probably had not heard us arrive,' she said defiantly.

Ignoring her outburst, the baronet MP turned his unsmiling attention to Nathan.

'So you're Nathan Jago, the prize-fighter. Champion of all England, I believe? Well, what business do you have with me? If you're looking for a sponsor for one of your prize-fights, you can forget it. Prize-fighting is outside the law. As far as I'm concerned, that is where it will stay.'

'It's a matter on which you and my father seem to be in full agreement,' said Nathan easily. He did not miss the sudden tightening of the baronet's expression at mention of Josiah Jago. It came as no surprise; Sir Lewis Hearle's opposition to Methodism was no secret. 'But I'm not here to discuss prize-fighting. I'm setting up a fishing venture, buying into the Hoblyn cellar and drift-fishing the year round.'

'Hoblyn a fisherman? Why, the man's a scoundrel. A notorious smuggler. Are you telling me he's had a change of heart and intends earning an honest living? If drift-fishing can be called "honest".'

'Ned Hoblyn is dead and buried, but many so-called "honest" men acquired a rich source of income because of him,' retorted Nathan, stung by Sir Lewis Hearle's attitude. He brought himself under control quickly. He would gain nothing by antagonising the bigotted landowner. 'I'm going into partnership with Ned Hoblyn's widow and daughter. As for drift-fishing, it will bring more work and prosperity to Pentuan than seine-fishing ever has.'

Sir Lewis Hearle glared at Nathan. In truth, he knew little about either drifting or seining, and he cared less. He kept the tithes as high as he dared. Just so long as they were paid on time, he was happy for the fishermen to stay with the smells of their work at the bottom of Pentuan Hill.

'You know the arrangement I have with the seine-fishers, Jago? I take eight pence for each hogshead of fish that leaves the cellar. If sold fresh, it's a twelfth of the value. In addition, owners of boats pay me six guineas a year for each seaworthy boat they own.'

Nathan hid the anger he felt at the sums mentioned by Sir Lewis Hearle. They were exceedingly high. The huge shoals of pilchards might come close inshore once or twice a year – three times in an exceptional year, none at all during a bad one. In these brief and uncertain periods, the fisherman had to catch enough fish to support his family and the families of the cellar workers for a whole year. In an age when a man considered himself fortunate if he averaged a weekly wage of ten shillings throughout the year, Sir Lewis was taking most of the profit and ensuring that the fishermen of Pentuan remained poor. He possessed this right because of an ancient custom that had little or no relevance in early nineteenth-century life.

Sir Lewis Hearle leaned back in his chair and looked up at Nathan arrogantly. 'Of course, if you intend fishing the whole year round, you'll be using your boat more than a seiner, so you'll pay me more boat money. Shall we say twenty guineas a year?'

It was a disgracefully high sum, and Nathan heard Elinor suck in her breath in a gasp of surprise.

Nathan struggled to keep his temper, but only partially succeeded. 'You could as easily say *two hundred* guineas, Sir Lewis, but I'll pay none of the sums you've mentioned. I'll not run the risk of bankruptcy for you. I intend eventually owning a whole fleet of drifters, and there are many tithe-owners along the coast who'll be glad to welcome my business in their ports. I apologise for taking up your time and bid you "Good day".'

'Not so fast.'

Now it was Sir Lewis Hearle's turn to hide both pride and anger. Nathan Jago's name was mentioned with a proprietary approbation by both squire and hired man throughout Cornwall. There was no doubt that he would be welcomed in any fishing community – Fowey, for instance, the town represented by Sir Lewis in Parliament. Sir Lewis's re-election was by no means assured. He needed to woo every voter. If Nathan Jago set up business there, his assets would be sufficient to make *him* a voter. Such a man would also make many friends among the voting community.

'If it's your intention to work a number of boats, you'll naturally employ many local men. I have no wish to do anything that might take work away from them. I'll make it twelve guineas a boat.'

'You'll make it six guineas, the same as a seiner – and *five* pence per hogshead, or a twentieth for fresh fish,' declared Nathan defiantly. He was not certain why Sir Lewis Hearle had not allowed him to walk from the room and seek a cellar outside Pentuan, although he knew it had nothing to do with the well-being of Pentuan fishermen. He thought the answer might lie in the neglected state of Polrudden Manor. Sir Lewis Hearle was in sore need of money.

Sir Lewis Hearle shifted his gaze to the desk in front of him, not trusting himself to look at the man who stood before him. It was bad enough that he should have a Methodist preacher's son here in his own house. To listen to him dictating his own terms on a business matter was more than any man of his breeding should have to bear.

However, Sir Lewis Hearle realised that more than money and political security might be gained by having Nathan drift-fishing from Pentuan. He had no doubt that the prize-fighting champion of all England would be able to ride the anger of the Pentuan fishermen, but some of their anger might be directed against Nathan's father. The fact that Nathan was going into business with the family of Ned Hoblyn would also excite comment. Smugglers were known to have been anathema to John Wesley. If it were hinted that Nathan Jago had taken on the mantle of the late Ned Hoblyn under the cover of his drift-fishing business. . . .

The Member of Parliament for Fowey looked up from his desk and smiled at Nathan. 'I admire enterprise, Jago – especially when it's likely to improve the lot of Cornishmen. All right, I'll have an agreement drawn up along the lines you suggest. It will be ready for your signature before I return to London.'

Turning to his astonished daughter, Sir Lewis Hearle said, 'Perhaps you will be kind enough to show Mr Jago out, my dear.'

Without another glance at his visitor, Sir Lewis Hearle picked up his quill and the sharpened point of the long goose feather began once more to hurry across the surface of the paper on the desk before him.

Outside the house, Elinor looked at Nathan with new, if slightly bemused, respect. 'I never thought I would ever hear anyone dictate to Father as you did without provoking a reply that would have been clearly heard in Pentuan village.'

'It couldn't have been my tactful manner,' Nathan admitted truthfully. 'When I *demanded* tithe reductions I thought I'd gone much too far.'

'So did I!' Elinor laughed and, in a warm, impulsive gesture, laid a hand upon Nathan's arm. 'I held my breath then, hoping you wouldn't mention your father again. That would have been more than he could have accepted – even from *me*.'

'You *hoped* I wouldn't mention my father?' asked Nathan softly. 'Are you telling me you were on my side in there?'

Colour rushed to Elinor's cheeks, and she took her hand from Nathan's arm. 'My father is not the only one who admires enterprise.'

She gave Nathan a look that, had it come from anyone else, he would have regarded as coy. But coyness had no place in Elinor Hearle's character. 'You are a rather remarkable man, Nathan Jago. War hero, champion prize-fighter. . . . And now you are turning your talents to fishing. Drift-fishing at that. Had my father been more business-minded, he would have offered to finance your new venture. I am quite certain it will prove highly successful.'

'I'll do my best to justify your faith in me,' mocked Nathan.

'But thank you for your help – and for your support.'

He had taken no more than a dozen paces when Elinor called to him.

'Nathan Jago . . . do you ride?'

'No, I've had very little opportunity to learn.'

Elinor was disappointed, but she did her best to give her shrug the appearance of nonchalance. 'I thought you might be interested in the new filly, but it doesn't matter.'

Turning away, she hurried off round the side of the house. After a moment's hesitation, Nathan walked from Polrudden Manor, heading for Pentuan village.

In his study, Sir Lewis Hearle was watching Nathan's departure. The baronet's expression combined anger and parental concern. He had witnessed Elinor's spontaneous gesture when she rested her hand on Nathan's arm. He had also been watching her face when she called to Jago to ask if he rode. Sir Lewis Hearle knew his daughter well enough to recognise that Nathan Jago's reply *had* mattered to her.

With an oath, the baronet brought his clenched fist down hard upon the wooden windowsill. It was the first time, to his knowledge, that Elinor had shown any interest in a man – and it had to be a man with Nathan Jago's background.

Sir Lewis, in common with his daughter, recognised the exceptional qualities possessed by the prize-fighting champion; but Jago was a villager, a man from common fishing stock. It was unthinkable that Elinor should ever cast more than a glance in his direction. He, Sir Lewis Hearle, third baronet, Member of Parliament for Fowey, and Senior Magistrate of the St Austell Bench, would have to ensure there never was more than a *look* between them.

Chapter Seven

Now the matter of tithe money had been settled, Nathan was ready to collect his new fishing-boat from the Brixham boatyard. At a meeting held that evening at the Hoblyn cottage, Nathan told Sammy Mizler and Amy of his intention.

'How will you travel?' asked Sammy Mizler.

'By carriage from St Austell to Plymouth, then either by carriage or on foot from there. It's little more than thirty miles to Brixham from Plymouth. It would be quicker by fishing-boat from Mevagissey, but I want to put off any questions from the Mevagissey men until we have the boat here.'

'I'll travel with you as far as Plymouth,' declared Sammy Mizler. 'I have a feeling we'll be able to market most of our fish there. I would like to go and have a look around.'

'I was hoping you'd come on to Brixham with me. It will need two of us to sail the boat back to Portgiskey.'

'You thought *I* would help you to sail a *boat?*' Sammy Mizler looked at Nathan incredulously. 'Oh, no! I've put money into this dream of yours, I'll direct all my efforts into ensuring its success – but I stay on dry land. Why, I feel ill if an innkeeper rocks my soup when he puts it on the table before me.'

'I'll come with you.' The offer came from Amy, and both men looked at her in surprise.

'Can you think of anyone better to crew the boat? I'm a partner in the business, and I can handle a boat as well as any man.'

Nathan thought of Amy's activities the night before. Few men would have relished the thought of bringing a small boat into Portgiskey Cove on a dark night, as she had done. He shrugged. 'I agree. But who'll look after your ma?'

'She'll be all right for a few days. She can cook and do things that are familiar to her.'

Suddenly the air of mature capability dropped away from Amy as she allowed the eager excitement of a seventeen-year-old girl to come to the fore.

'I've never travelled by coach. How long will it take to get to Plymouth? Will we travel inside or outside?'

Sammy Mizler watched Amy's enthusiasm directed towards Nathan and there was an aching emptiness within him. He looked at Nathan questioningly, wondering if he knew how Amy felt about him. Sammy doubted whether he did. Nathan accepted the admiration of others as a matter of course. Very often he did not even notice. It was most unfair on those like Sammy Mizler who could only stand back and watch the world fall at Nathan's feet.

Nathan thought about Amy's question. The fare to Plymouth was a guinea for an inside passenger, but only half this amount for a seat outside. He was about to declare that they would travel outside, when he looked up and saw her eager anticipation.

'We'll travel inside, in a style befitting partners in a great new fishing venture.'

Amy squealed with delight. Stretching up on her toes, she reached up and kissed Nathan quickly on the cheek. 'Thank you, Nathan. When do we go?'

'Tomorrow morning. There's no sense wasting time. With any luck there will still be some pilchards about when we get back to Portgiskey. I'd like to have a share in them. Does this suit you, Sammy?'

Sammy Mizler shrugged. 'Who wants my advice? I'll be with you in the morning.'

With this enigmatic remark, Sammy walked out of the cottage, leaving Nathan and Amy gazing after him, wondering what had happened to upset him.

Sammy was not certain himself. Less than a year older than Nathan, Sammy Mizler's acquaintance with women had been confined to those he had met in London's inns. Many of these had possessed Amy's self-assurance and determination, but not one of them had ever known her natural innocence. Amy was unique in Sammy Mizler's limited experience. He was jealous of Nathan's easy relationship with her – and of the affectionate kiss she had just given him.

In truth, Sammy Mizler was himself something of an innocent, certainly as far as women were concerned. Brought up in London's 'East End', one of a Jewish tailor's over-large family, Sammy Mizler had quite literally to fight for recognition, if not his very existence, from an early age. From fighting

72

his brothers and the brutal Jew-baiting youths of Shoreditch, it was a small step to the prize-ring. Here Sammy Mizler fought brilliantly and with great success for many years. Unfortunately, Sammy was not a big man. In an age when prize-fighting had no weight division he was frequently matched with larger opponents and forced to absorb an increasing amount of punishment. When Sammy met Nathan he left the ring and became advisor and matchmaker to the man who, even then, was tipped as a future champion of all England.

In this world of men, Sammy Mizler felt at home, confident of his own ability. With women he was shy and reserved, unable to express his thoughts. This was how he felt with Amy Hoblyn. After only two meetings with her, Sammy Mizler found himself floundering well out of his emotional depth.

The journey to Plymouth took eight hours and the trio shared the coach with two clergymen from Truro and a very large farmer from Falmouth, who sat in a corner sneezing and snuffling the whole way. The presence of the farmer caused Sammy Mizler great concern. Sammy had an unreasonable fear of colds and illness. It was as much as Nathan could do to prevent his friend from leaving the carriage and travelling outside.

The last part of the journey involved a crossing of the River Tamar at Saltash Passage. At the water's edge the horses were unhitched and the carriage manhandled on to the flat-bottomed ferry boat. A fresh south-easterly wind was blowing and Sammy Mizler spent the journey huddled dejectedly in a corner of the carriage as the ferry bobbed on the water.

Sammy found some consolation in Amy's very real concern for his well-being, but he breathed a sigh of relief when the ungainly craft was driven ashore on the soft mud of the Devon river bank. The passengers climbed inside the carriage beside Sammy Mizler, four reluctant horses were backed into their traces and, with a jolt, the coach was driven off the ferry, lurching dangerously as it dropped into the mud at an acute angle.

The road from the ferry was both narrow and steep and the coach passengers were tumbled against each other frequently as the coachman whipped up his horses around every sharp bend.

73

It was not long before the brow of the hill was reached and the coach began the long, gradual descent into Plymouth Town. Soon the high-hedged country road gave the passengers glimpses of muddy creeks and tide-grounded cargo-ships, their masts leaning at a hundred different angles. Around the merchantmen were clustered groups of sailors. Knee-deep, occasionally waist-deep, in black, foul-smelling mud, they scraped and painted, caulked and tarred keels that had gathered barnacles from every ocean of the world.

Then all talking ceased inside the coach as it rattled over the cobbles of Devon's great port. The cobbles soon gave way to stone blocks, and now there were houses on either hand, crowding in upon the coach as it travelled the narrow streets of Plymouth Town. Here Sammy Mizler suddenly blossomed into life, his temporary indisposition cured by the street cries and the bustle of a busy seaport town.

Watching his friend's rapid recovery, Nathan grinned wryly. Sammy Mizler was an irredeemable city-dweller. A man of his word, Sammy would remain with Nathan and find markets for all the fish that were caught, but his heart would always be in the city. Nathan knew that one day he would return to London.

There was an unmistakable smell of fish in the air as the coach rolled to a halt at the heart of the Barbican. This was the harbourside area of Plymouth, a tangle of inns, narrow streets and alleyways.

This was where Sammy Mizler would find the fish-dock, the market and the merchants. He was to make his own way back to Pentuan – and he had already determined he would find an alternative route to the Saltash passenger-ferry.

Nathan and Amy were fortunate enough to catch a coach from the Barbican inn within minutes of their arrival. It would take them to Dartmouth, from where they would catch a ferry across the river that gave its name to the town, and walk the final two or three miles to Brixham.

There was hardly time for last-minute instructions from Nathan to Sammy Mizler and a breathless 'Goodbye' from Amy as they clambered inside the waiting coach. Then, with horn sounding stridently to clear their path, the coachman slapped the reins over the backs of his horses and the coach moved off on slim, well-greased wheels.

The roads were much better on this side of the River Tamar. As a result, the coaches in use were built for speed, and not for rugged endurance. The coach and horses clattered through tiny villages of thatched houses, covering the miles to Dartmouth in under three hours, Amy enjoying every moment of the speedy journey.

In Dartmouth there was an hour of daylight remaining, and Nathan booked rooms for them in the coaching inn, close to Dartmouth's busy harbour. He told Amy they had travelled far enough for one day. They would make an early start the next morning.

That evening, Nathan and Amy sat down to a meal in the dining-room of the inn, grateful for the fire which crackled cheerfully in the great stone hearth, keeping the chills of the autumn night from the room. The inn was busy, and the talk and laughter from the tap-room beyond the dining-room provided a comforting background for an excellent meal.

Nathan was beginning to feel at peace with the world, warmed by the fire, good ale and Amy's happy chatter, when the sounds coming from the tap-room under went a dramatic change. Men's voices rose in shouted warning, and the sudden uproar was accompanied by the noise of crashing glasses and splintering wood.

As diners ceased their conversations and serving-girls stopped their work in consternation, the door from the tap-room crashed open and three men hurtled into the dining-room. The door swung shut behind them, and two of the men ran between the tables, fleeing through the door that led to the kitchen. The third man, in search of a way out of the inn, chose the door to the cellar. He disappeared down the steep stone steps with a shout that ceased abruptly as he cannoned off the wall somewhere in the region of the tenth step and fell into the darkness below.

Moments later four blue-jacketed sailors, armed with cudgels, crowded inside the dining-room. Behind them Nathan could see two more sailors carrying a wildly struggling form between them from the now deserted tap-room. It was a naval press-gang.

A scowling man wearing the uniform and insignia of a boatswain entered the dining-room and glared about him, apparently looking for the three men who had made their escape.

'I'm looking for deserters from one of His Majesty's ships. Where did they go?'

Not a person in the room said a word, and the boatswain's scowl deepened. To his men he said: 'Question every man in the room. If they don't satisfy you as to their identities, take 'em aboard. The Cap'n says he wants ten men. These will do as well as any – and they'll be better fed than most we're likely to gather.'

When the three fugitives had fled from the tap-room, Amy had started up in alarm. Now Nathan stood up slowly, putting himself between her and the men of the press-gang.

'You won't find your deserters in here, bos'n. They'll be long gone by now. I suggest you and your men go off and search elsewhere, leaving us to finish our dinner in peace.'

'You suggest . . .?' The boatswain glared across the room, head thrust forward aggressively. 'I've seen you somewhere before, mister. Why, you might be a deserter yourself. What's your name?'

'Nathan Jago – and my discharge papers are in order, but they're staying where they belong, in my pocket.'

It was by no means unusual for an able-bodied sailor's discharge papers to be 'lost' by a press-gang desperate to gather crewmen for one of His Majesty's men-of-war.

'Call off your men, or your captain will find himself short of another five members of his crew.'

Nathan's warning was unnecessary. At the mention of his name, the closest member of the press-gang took a hasty step backwards and the boatswain's expression underwent a sudden change.

'Nathan Jago of *Elephant* and *Victory*? The prize-fighting champion of all England?'

Nathan ignored the question, wary of those members of the press-gang close enough to jump him if the boatswain gave them the order. But the leader of the press-gang had lost all interest in securing Nathan for the Royal Navy.

'That's where I've seen you before – in *Elephant*. I was a gun-layer then.'

Nathan nodded his head in acknowledgement. There was a

proud sense of comradeship between men who had served in any ship which Admiral Lord Nelson had commanded, but he had a message for the press-gang boatswain.

'I was in *Elephant* because *I'd* been pressed into service. These days I get nervous when a press-gang begins to crowd me.'

The boatswain signalled for his men to fall back. At that moment the cellar door crashed open. The man who had fallen down the cellar steps staggered into the dining-room, blood pouring from his nose.

'That's one of them.' A member of the press-gang pointed to the unfortunate and confused deserter. Nathan was temporarily forgotten as the sailors of the press-gang pounced upon their colleague, a dining-table crashing over in their eagerness.

'Take him outside.' The boatswain saw his order carried out, then returned his attention to Nathan. 'I'm proud to renew your acquaintance, Mr Jago. You and your good lady enjoy your dinner, sir. We won't be bothering you again.'

As Nathan pulled out the chair for Amy, the boatswain backed to the door. Pausing there, he called: 'Are you here for a prize-fight, sir? If you are, I'd like to see it.' Giving Nathan a jovial wink, he added: 'I've got a few guineas put aside that I'll wager on your winning.'

'I'm here to buy a fishing-boat and sail it home to Pentuan.'

'Oh!' The boatswain sounded disappointed. He was about to leave when the full significance of what Nathan had said sank into his none-too-agile brain.

'Taking a boat to Pentuan, you say. Then I'll give you a word of caution, Mr Jago. The French are busy about that way. That's why we're here trying to pick up men. We fought a French privateer off Mevagissey only yesterday morning. *Montendre* was her name. She put up a stiff fight. Before we sent her to the bottom with all hands more than ten of our own men were wounded. The Cap'n sent them ashore today. That's when the three men deserted. We're only a frigate, and with ten crew short we need to impress more.' He looked apologetically at Nathan. '*You* know how it is, sir.'

Nathan said nothing and, looking about the dining-room for a last time, the boatswain left, closing the door behind him. Immediately, a buzz of excited conversation rose from the diners and more than one grateful look was cast in Nathan's direction. Had it not been for him, there would have been a number of empty seats in the dining-room by now. A press-gang was supposed to impress only seamen, but when desperately short of sailors they would carry off any able-bodied man, enquiring as to his calling afterwards.

At a nearby table were a number of men dressed in the style popularised by the future King George IV, and later to be termed the 'Regency' style. Their noisy hilarity was proof that they had not feared the press-gang. Now one of their number stood up and came to Nathan's table.

Bowing first to Amy, and then to Nathan, the stranger asked: 'Were you telling the truth about not being here for a prize-fight?'

'I was.'

The stranger's shrug expressed disappointment. 'A pity. I've seen you in action twice, Nathan Jago. I'd put up an uncommon purse to watch you fight again.'

He dropped a card casually on the table beside Nathan's plate. 'When you decide to fight again, make no arrangements before you've spoken to me. I'll put up a stake that will make you the envy of every prize-fighter in England. I won't discuss it now. I can see the events of the evening have distressed your lady. Sir . . . Miss. . . .'

Inclining his head at Nathan and Amy in turn, the man returned to his own table.

Turning to Amy, Nathan saw tears in her eyes.

'Nathan, take me out of here, please.' Her voice was a distressed whisper.

Hurriedly, Nathan pushed back his chair and helped Amy to her feet. Aware of the stares of their fellow-diners, he led her from the room. He would have taken her upstairs, but at the doorway she said: 'I . . . I would like to walk for a while.'

'Of course.'

Nathan led her outside, and she clung to his arm as they walked along the uneven pavement, sheltered beneath the upper storeys of houses propped up by granite pillars. Whenever they passed by a lighted window he could see she was still distressed.

'You mustn't upset yourself because of what happened at the

inn. The press-gang isn't something of which I approve, but the Navy isn't a bad life for a man.'

Amy shook her head vigorously. 'It's not that. It's what he said about *Montendre*.'

For a moment Nathan was baffled, then he remembered the boatswain's story of the sea-battle.

'*Montendre*? You mean the French ship sunk off Mevagissey? Why should that upset you? We're at war with the French.'

'The crew of *Montendre* weren't at war with anyone. Only the other night you hid the brandy they'd carried to England.'

Now Nathan understood. *Montendre* had been a smuggler's vessel.

'But you said you'd be happy if you never had to deal with them again. That they'd made . . . "suggestions" to you.'

'Did they deserve to die because of that?' Amy rounded on Nathan. 'They were . . . they were just *men*. Like you and Sammy. Oh, this war!' she wailed. 'It's so senseless.'

They walked on in silence for a while. Then, as they turned a corner, they came within sight of the river and could see the lights of the British frigate anchored offshore.

'Yes,' Nathan said unexpectedly. 'It *is* a senseless war. It would have ended years ago had it not been for one man's selfish ambition. Because of it the country has lost some of its greatest men. Lord Nelson . . . Sir John Moore. . . . Aye, and a good, honest man like your brother – and a dozen more I was proud to call my friends.'

Immediately, Amy's own sorrow was forgotten in her concern for Nathan. Gripping his arm in her two small hands, she pulled him to a halt. 'Nathan, I'm so sorry. I must have stirred up so many unhappy memories for you – memories you would rather forget.'

'Some I wish I *could* forget. Others I am proud to remember.'

Amy looked up at Nathan's face as they stood at the water's edge. 'Are all your unhappy memories to do with war, Nathan?' she asked quietly.

'No. But the things that have happened during this war are the only ones that ever bother me now.'

Back in his room later that evening, something dropped to the floor from Nathan's pocket when he hung his clothes over the back of a chair. It was the card given to him by the man in the dining-room.

Picking up the card, Nathan carried it to the light. With considerable astonishment, Nathan learned that the man who had offered to finance his next fight was none other than William, Duke of Clarence. Third son of the reigning monarch, George III, the Duke was a renowned patron of the prize-ring. The area about his estate at Bushy Park had been the venue for more than one great championship bout.

Nathan was glad that Sammy Mizler had not witnessed the offer made by the sporting royal duke. He would never have been satisfied until he had persuaded Nathan to take part in the richest fight ever staged in Great Britain.

Chapter Eight

THE next morning Nathan and Amy crossed the River Dart estuary in a small, one-oarsman ferry and walked the remaining three miles to Brixham.

Nathan had recognised the qualities of the Brixham-designed boats many years before and, once he had made up his mind to use his prize-ring winnings to become a fisherman on his own account, he had ordered a lugger from a small Brixham yard. It was an astute move. Many other fishermen were learning to appreciate the exceptional qualities of Brixham-built fishing-craft. Demand for them now far outstripped production.

Amy and Nathan arrived at the fishing village at low tide and found the lugger they were to purchase standing proudly on the mud beside the quay. It was a much larger craft than Amy had been expecting. With its deep-water keel, half-deck and tadpole-shaped belly, it should prove to be a good sea-boat and one with an incredible carrying capacity.

The boat-builder was proud of his vessel and explained its construction, inside and out, in great detail. For full-time fishing the boat would require a crew of at least five men. The boat-builder looked horrified when told that Nathan and Amy alone would be crewing the boat on its maiden voyage to Mevagissey. When he was able, he took Nathan to one side and suggested that one man and a young girl could not hope to handle a forty-two-foot fishing-boat without help. Nathan merely smiled, saved from making a reply by the return of Amy.

That afternoon, when the tide had risen sufficiently to float the fishing-boat, Nathan, Amy and the boat-builder took the new craft to sea. The vessel handled beautifully, delighting its new owners. By the time the trip ended, the boat-builder no longer entertained doubts about Amy's ability to crew a fishing-boat. He confessed that she could handle a boat more skilfully than he could himself.

Nathan and Amy remained at Brixham for three days, staying with the boat-builder and his family. During this time Nathan purchased the drift-nets and other fishing equipment he would need at Portgiskey. He knew that none would be made available to him in Pentuan, Mevagissey or any of the other fishing villages on Cornwall's south coast.

Nathan also had the opportunity during these few days to observe Amy in the kind of family surroundings to which he had been accustomed as a young boy. The boat-builder had a young wife and three active young children. The children took to Amy immediately, and it was evident to everyone that she thoroughly enjoyed their attentions. The three days spent in Brixham re-awoke in Nathan some almost-forgotten memories of the more pleasant days he had spent in Pentuan before constant arguments with his father had driven him from home.

The youngest of the boat-builder's children, taking Nathan's hand when they went walking, reminded him of how his young sister Nell's hand would seek his on the frequent occasions when their preacher father thundered his wrath at Nathan's 'evil ways', swearing that his only son was destined for damnation.

It was the first time Nathan had experienced any form of family life since then, and he was glad that Amy was part of this experience. It showed her in an entirely new light and gave an added depth to their unusual partnership.

Nathan and Amy set off on the sixty-mile sea-voyage to Portgiskey on an overcast morning. There was a fresh south-easterly wind that hinted at an autumn storm to come. However, Nathan thought that if the wind held from the south-east they would be safely moored in Portgiskey Cove long before the storm broke.

It was not to be. By the time they stood off Plymouth the wind had veered to the south-west and was already blowing a gale. It was now that the Brixham-built boat proved her seaworthiness. Tacking into the wind involved a number of changes to the sail arrangement, and Nathan found it comparatively easy to slacken off a halyard here and tighten somewhere else, while the wind whistled exhilaratingly through the rigging.

The strength of the wind and the acute angle of their tacking meant that they alternated between steering dangerously close to the rocky shore and heading far out into the grey rain-mist of the English Channel, with the land out of sight, far astern.

On one of these outward tacks, when the boat rose from a deep trough and lurched drunkenly up the uneven slope of a high-sided wave, Nathan spotted the outline of another vessel, indistinct in the damp, grey mist.

Fighting the heavy wheel as wind and tide vied with each other for control of the boat, Nathan shouted to Amy as she crouched close to his feet, sheltering from the wind and spray behind heaped nets and baskets.

'There's a ship out there.'

Amy rose unsteadily to her feet and ducked hurriedly again as the lively craft shipped a wave. Rising for a second time, she peered into the grey gloom.

'There it is.' Nathan pointed as the lugger rose on a wave and the ship came into view once more. Broadside on, it was about half a mile away.

'What is it?' Looking up at him, Amy retied her short hair behind her neck. 'Do you think it's French?'

Nathan shook his head. He did not want to alarm her unnecessarily, but the unusual lines of the ship, coupled with an absence of any form of national flag, told their own story. The ship was undoubtedly a corsair from the Barbary Coast of north Africa. Corsairs were the scourge of the high seas, ranging far and wide in search of slaves and booty to carry back to their Mediterranean kingdom. Knowing full well that the British navy was engaged elsewhere with the French, the corsairs had recently become very active around the coasts of Ireland and south-western England, claiming more victims than the rich annual harvest reaped by the sea.

Nathan hoped the corsair would pass down-Channel without seeing them. His hopes were dashed when the lugger rode the next wave. The masts of the corsair tilted towards the sea as the foreign craft executed a tight turn. When the ship righted itself, more sails snaked up the masts as the Mediterranean pirates prepared for a chase.

Amy had witnessed the other vessel's change of direction and she, too, now realised what type of vessel they had encountered.

'Quick, turn about and make for Plymouth.'

'No.' Nathan put the wheel over and called for Amy to hoist more sail. 'Give me as much sail as she'll take,' he called as Amy made her way forward. 'If we try to run before them, they'll overhaul us in no time. Our only chance is to outmanoeuvre them.'

Guessing his intention, the master of the corsair sailed across their stern in an attempt to bring his guns to bear on the fishing-vessel.

Nathan saw small clouds of black smoke erupt from two cannons on the corsair's deck, but wind blew the sound away, while the condition of the sea made accurate shooting an impossibility. Bringing the lugger over to the opposite tack, Nathan waited only until the corsair followed suit before swinging back to resume his original course, heading for the grey and indistinct shoreline.

Nathan had made up his mind to wreck the new vessel rather than allow Amy and himself to fall into the hands of the corsairs. After the battle of the Nile, *Elephant* had rescued some American seamen taken prisoner by a corsair ship. Every one of them had been crudely emasculated in readiness for their duties as harem guards. Nathan did not dwell on the thought of what such men would do to Amy.

Through the mist he could now see the outline of Cornish cliffs, and he strained his eyes for a break in the cliffs that would indicate a beach or cove. Meanwhile, the corsair ship gained rapidly on the lugger.

Suddenly, Amy climbed up beside him. 'Quick, give me the wheel.' Seeing his uncertainty, Amy added: 'I know this part of the coast well. Go forward and be ready to do as I say.'

There was little alternative. The sound of the corsair's bow gun was close enough to carry to them now, and a plume of water rose in the air not twelve feet from the lugger.

Amy took the wheel and pursued a zig-zag course towards the shore. They gained no advantage on the other craft, but the irregular course spoiled the aim of the north African gunners.

When the shore was no more than a couple of hundred yards away, Amy suddenly spun the wheel desperately. As the lugger leaned away from the wind Nathan gasped with alarm. The boat was sliding past a cluster of foam-encircled rocks protruding from the sea only yards away.

Amy spun the wheel back again, and Nathan was given a similar view on the other side of the boat.

'Drop the sail – quickly!'

Spurred on by the urgency in Amy's voice, Nathan untied the halyards holding up the sails and allowed them to drop in a most unseamanlike manner. Moments later the fishing-boat slid into smooth, deep water, the wind cut off by a wall of glistening black rock.

Leaving the wheel, Amy scrambled over the tangle of sail and rigging to heave the anchor over the side. The lugger was left riding comfortably, a hundred yards of rock-encrusted water between boat and shore.

Looking out to sea, Nathan was in time to witness the confusion on board the corsair ship. Already aware of the proximity of the shore, they had been waiting confidently for the lugger to come about and fall into their hands. Expecting this to happen, they had taken in much of their sail – and it was this that saved them from total destruction.

The corsair's master saw the partially submerged rocks only seconds before Nathan. He screamed out his orders, and the highly manoeuvrable pirate-ship slewed around in little more than its own length. Frenzied activity was needed to raise every square inch of sail, and when it seemed that disaster was imminent the Mediterranean craft began slowly to edge its way to safety, grazing the farthermost rocks on the way. It was enough to deter the corsair master from pursuing the English fishing-lugger any further. One small boat was not worth the risk posed to his own vessel.

As the corsair sailed away into the mist, Nathan hugged Amy to him, filled with exhilarated relief. 'Amy, you were wonderful. I know of no man or woman who could have done better. The way you put the boat between those rocks was nothing short of brilliant. . . . Amy, what's the matter? It's all over now.'

Amy had begun to shake in his arms. Now she turned a white face up to him. 'I didn't even see the rocks until we were almost on them. . . .'

As the full implication of Amy's words sank in, Nathan went cold with horror. They had been within seconds of wrecking the lugger – and of almost certain death. Then he remembered how quickly she had changed the boat's direction in order to avoid the second group of rocks, and how she had dashed forward to drop the anchor. Amy might have been taken by surprise, but her actions proved she lacked neither courage nor resourcefulness.

'Amy, you saved both our lives – and almost wrecked a Barbary pirate. You're the finest sailor I've ever put to sea with – and I've sailed with the very best.'

Giving her a hard but brief kiss on the lips, Nathan released Amy with an affectionate hug, then began gathering in the sail that hung flapping over the side of the boat.

Had Nathan turned round, he would have seen Amy standing watching him, a strange expression on her pale face, her fingers touching the lips he had just bruised.

The blustery, grey October day had brought more than Barbary pirates to the coast of Cornwall. Three hours after the encounter with the corsairs, Nathan and Amy sailed the lugger into Portgiskey Cove and saw that Pentuan beach was the scene of fevered activity. Boats were offshore shooting nets, encircling shoals containing millions of pilchards. So vast were the shoals, it seemed the whole sea was a heaving silver mass. It was the harvest for which Cornish fishermen had been waiting and praying for almost a year.

Proud as he was of his new vessel, this was not the moment for Nathan to show it off to the seine-fishermen of Pentuan. Leaving Amy to take her mother on board, Nathan hurried along the beach and here met up with Sammy Mizler. The one-time London prize-fighter had good news. The fish-markets in Plymouth would take all the fish Nathan could land – fresh or salted. There were also rumours that buyers in Bristol were outbidding all their competitors and buying all the heavily salted fish they could lay hands on. From Bristol it was being shipped to West Indies sugar plantations to feed the many thousands of negro slaves employed there.

It was the news for which Nathan had been hoping. Not only did they now have a well-proven boat, but the partners also had assured markets should the hostility of local men towards the drift-fishermen prove too great for them to make local sales.

Yet, even while Sammy Mizler was giving him the good news, Nathan found himself caught up in the age-old excitement that swept over a fishing community when the pilchards were 'running'.

This was a huge shoal, the largest seen in the vicinity for very many years. Every boat and every net was being pressed into service as still more fish came shorewards. Those villagers who were not at sea crowded the sands of the beach, screeching encouragement and advice to those who were. Others – men, women and children – heaved on long, stout ropes, to which were attached great nets drawn about a writhing mass of fish.

The aim was to draw the net to shallower water. Once here, the ropes were secured on land and the fish left trapped inside a circular mesh wall until the hard-pressed fishermen could scoop them out and carry them away to the fish-cellars.

A boat scraped ashore on the sand not ten feet from Nathan and Sammy Mizler. Yelling almost unintelligibly for assistance, a fisherman leaped ashore, one end of a long rope held in his hand. Instantly, Nathan sprang to his aid. Not certain what it was all about, Sammy Mizler followed his example and they were joined by some girls and a few old men. Most were related to the man in the boat and they had deserted other seine-nets to secure their own harvest from the sea.

Those holding the rope heaved with every ounce of muscle they possessed, yet it was thirty minutes before the fish were close enough inshore to be secured. Immediately, the happy Pentuan villagers hurried away to join another tug-of-war.

Offering a reluctant 'Thank you' to Nathan, the fisherman who had brought the rope ashore said: 'I'm obliged to you, Nathan, but I saw your new boat come in. We'll be working against each other from now on.'

'Nonsense, Dan. We've known each other since we could first walk. I'll not work against you – or any other Pentuan man. We're all fishermen here.'

'You'll find few to agree with you hereabouts, not if you intend shooting a mile or two of net every night to keep the fish away from us. No, Nathan,' – the fisherman waved away Nathan's protest – 'don't try me with any of your arguments. I've heard them all before, I dare say. You're Pentuan-born. Because of that you'll have no trouble here – just as long as we continue to make a living. But you'll not find the Mevagissey men of the same mind. They boast of having forced two drifters out of business in their own village. A third disappeared at sea with all hands on a flat-calm night. No, you'll not find them as kind to you as we. They'll give you plenty of trouble, you mind my words.'

'Thanks for the warning, Dan. But there's fish enough for all of us out there. You'll learn that soon enough.' Nathan hesitated. 'I don't suppose you know any good fishermen who are looking for work?'

While Nathan and the Pentuan fisherman had been talking, a thin-faced man had been loitering close enough to overhear their conversation, although he seemed to be interested in nothing more than the sand he was aimlessly kicking at his feet. Now he straightened up and spoke eagerly.

'I'll crew for you, Mr Jago. I can fish and handle a boat as well as anyone.'

Nathan could scarcely hide his delight. Then the fisherman to whom he had been talking let out a snort of derisive laughter. 'Before you take him on you'd better ask him to shake hands on the agreement.'

The man who had offered his services to Nathan had been standing sideways-on to him. Now, with a despairing look at the fisherman who had spoken, he turned to face Nathan.

His right arm was missing, cut off at the shoulder.

'Having only one arm has never stopped me from doing things that other men do, Mr Jago – except find work. You come to my house and you'll find it as clean and up together as any other, and my garden grows more than Dan Clymo's. *Please*, Mr Jago. I've got five little 'uns to feed.'

'How did you lose your arm? In the King's service?'

'Calvin Dickin in the King's service?' Dan Clymo's derisive laughter contained no humour. 'Not unless King George is in the habit of drinking smuggled brandy. You don't like folk talking about such things, do you, Calvin? But I reckon Nathan has a right to know, seeing as how you've asked him for work. Shall *I* tell him how you came to lose your arm, Calvin?'

'I doubt if I'll be able to stop you, Dan Clymo.'

The one-armed Calvin Dickin spoke with an air of defeat that was ignored by the seine-fisherman.

'Where shall I begin? With the years you worked for Ned Hoblyn – when ships were lured on to rocks with no survivors around to say why? Somehow you were always there on such occasions, Calvin, I remember. Or shall I simply tell him about the night the Revenue men were waiting above Portgiskey and surprised some night-runners? They weren't part-time smugglers like the rest of us, content with a keg or two of Spanish brandy. Oh, no, they were Ned Hoblyn's men, carrying guns and only too ready to use 'em.'

Dan Clymo glared malevolently at Calvin Dickin. 'Two Revenue men died that night – but that wasn't all. Ezra Partridge and his Revenue men caught a fifteen-year-old Pentuan lad. They wouldn't believe him when he said he'd been excited by the noise of the fighting and had just gone out to see what was happening. The Revenue men had him transported – for life. There wasn't one 'of Ned Hoblyn's men with the courage to step forward and say the boy had nothing to do with night-running. Not one. Yet they were quick enough to help one of their own who'd been sabre-slashed to the bone. Took you to an inland doctor, didn't they, Calvin? Kept you out of the way until you were fit to return to the village – leaving your arm behind you.'

'Who was the boy, Dan?' Nathan asked the question, aware that the fisherman's bitterness went far deeper than a sense of community injustice. 'Couldn't Ned Hoblyn have been asked to sign a sworn statement before he died?'

'He might, but it would have come two years too late. The fifteen-year-old was my brother. You'll remember him as a lively two-year-old. You and I took him to chapel with us more than once when we were boys.'

The fisherman paused to gain control of his emotions. 'He died on the transport, before it reached Australia.'

Dan Clymo turned away abruptly and walked off, up the gently sloping beach.

'Is his story true, Calvin? You worked for Ned Hoblyn?'

Calvin Dickin nodded defiantly. 'Yes. But I knew nothing about Dan Clymo's brother being caught. After the loss of my arm I fought for my life for weeks. By the time I was well enough to return to Pentuan he'd been sentenced and transported.'

Nathan inclined his head. 'It's a sad tale, but it was the Revenue men who were responsible for his sentence, not you. Can you really do a man's job with only the one arm?'

Calvin Dickin's face lost its expression of despair. 'Try me,

Mr Jago! Try me.'

'All right. My boat is at Portgiskey. Go there and help get it ready for fishing. We put to sea on tomorrow night's tide.'

Chapter Nine

WHEN Nathan's 'crew' gathered at Portgiskey to prepare both boat and equipment for their first fishing trip, the men wanted to give the boat a name, as tradition demanded. Nathan refused to be drawn on the subject. He would name the vessel, he said, when circumstances suggested a suitable name.

Looking at the men about him as he helped to secure corks to almost a mile of nets, Sammy Mizler wondered, as he had many times before, why he had risked so much of his hard-earned capital on such a venture. Only Nathan would have satisfied the minimum requirements of an underwriter from Lloyd's, London's shipping insurers. His crew would have brought on hysterics.

In truth, there were only three. First was the one-armed ex-smuggler, Calvin Dickin. Next, Nathan had found Ahab Arthur, an aged fisherman who had been the owner of the two drifters put out of action by Mevagissey seiners. The last member of the crew was Amy Hoblyn.

Because of Nathan's difficulty in obtaining more men, Amy had insisted upon becoming a crew member. Nathan had refused at first, but he had experienced the standard of her seamanship and the situation *was* desperate. Even with four of them it would be a herculean task to haul in almost four hundred fathoms of net at the end of a night's drift-fishing – especially if they had a good catch.

Sammy Mizler had listened to the argument between Amy and Nathan, and at first it had amused him to hear the young girl argue with the prize-fighting champion of all England to such effect. Then Sammy Mizler saw her expression when Nathan turned away after a curt refusal, early in the argument. Sammy saw that Nathan had the power to hurt Amy deeply. It was a responsibility of which Nathan was unaware, and one he certainly did not want, yet it *was* there. In that moment of realisation, Sammy Mizler's heart went out to Amy. Sammy too knew what it meant to have one's future hinge upon Nathan's arbitrary decisions.

At mid-morning, a horse and rider came round the headland

into Portgiskey Cove from Pentuan beach, splashing through the shallow waters of a receding tide. It was Elinor Hearle. Casting a quick glance at the busy group, her eyes lingered on Amy for a few moments. Then she gave her full attention to Nathan.

'My father returned to London yesterday. Before he left he had an agreement drawn up, setting out the tithes you are to pay him. I have it at Polrudden. It requires your signature.'

Nathan wanted to have the matter of tithe payments settled beyond all dispute before he began fishing. Strong hostility to him from local fishermen might induce Sir Lewis Hearle to change his mind.

'When can I come to Polrudden?'

Elinor shrugged in exaggerated indifference, 'Whenever you please.'

'Today?'

Elinor nodded. 'I'll be riding for another hour, but I'll be home for the remainder of the day.'

'I'll come to Polrudden early this afternoon.'

With no acknowledgment that she had heard him, Elinor Hearle pulled on the rein and turned the horse, cantering away in the direction from which she had come.

Watching Elinor Hearle leave, Amy felt all the pleasure she had derived from becoming a member of Nathan's crew drain away.

Nathan said: 'With luck we should have these corks tied on and the nets stowed on board before I go to Polrudden.'

'Don't let us hold you up,' snapped Amy irritably. 'Her ladyship might get the impression she's less important than your livelihood. *That* wouldn't suit her at all. If the agreement is so important, why didn't she bring it *here* for you to sign?'

Nathan grinned at her indignation. 'Perhaps I should have told her that. It's of importance to us at Portgiskey, not to Elinor Hearle.'

Amy snorted, only slightly mollified. 'Nobody *tells* Elinor Hearle to do anything – not even her father. She does only what *she* wants to do, and no more. I can't understand why she bothered to come here to pass on her father's message.'

'She owes me a favour. Sammx will tell you all about it sometime.'

'Elinor Hearle accepts favours as her due. I saw Nell just before we set off for Brixham. She told me how Elinor Hearle came to the farm *demanding* Nell's best dress.'

Fiercely, Amy jerked the thin rope she was holding and pulled it into an unwanted knot. 'I don't *like* Elinor Hearle.'

She said it emphatically and with such determined unreasonableness that Nathan smiled to himself.

By the time Nathan set out for Polrudden the sky had become dark and overcast. A storm was building up over the sea. If it was accompanied by a fierce wind, it would delay the maiden fishing voyage of the Brixham-built boat. However, the storm was still holding off when Nathan arrived at Polrudden.

Elinor Hearle met him before he reached the house. She had been occupying herself within sight of the entrance to the driveway for some time. The excuse she gave to herself was that she was inspecting the newly cut and layered blackthorn hedge. The work had been carried out by a team of out-of-work labourers from the inland farms who were now begging for more work. Desperate for any form of employment, the whole team had contracted to work for less money than one man would have received in better times.

When Elinor saw Nathan, she told the delighted men to trim all the remaining hedges on the Polrudden estate, then hurried away to meet him.

By the time Nathan saw Elinor coming towards him she was no longer hurrying, although inside she had the same eager feeling she had experienced only once before. When visiting friends on Exmoor she had been taken stag hunting. The same tight thrill of anticipation had come to her when she sighted a superb stag bounding up a steep hill, closely pursued by a pack of excited, baying hounds.

'You are prompt, Nathan Jago. I thought you might have been so busy you would put off coming to Polrudden until another day.'

'I'll be even busier soon. Tonight, weather permitting, we begin fishing.'

'I'm impressed. I admire a man who knows what he wants and who wastes no time in going out after it. I'm surprised you have been able to find a crew so quickly. Are they local men?'

Nathan gave an amused chuckle. 'You saw my crew when you came to Portgiskey – and you can leave out Sammy Mizler. He wouldn't make a fishing trip if it meant the difference between life and death to him.'

Elinor Hearle knew immediately which man was Sammy Mizler; his clothes had set him apart as a city man. Her mind ranged over the others who had been at Portgiskey Cove that morning and she looked at Nathan in disbelief. 'You're going deep-sea fishing with a one-armed smuggler and an old man who should be at home in a rocking-chair?'

'There's a girl, too. Amy came with me to pick up the boat. She's probably a better sailor than any of us.'

Elinor Hearle frowned. 'You're talking of Amy Hoblyn, the smuggler's daughter?'

'Yes. You know her?'

Elinor Hearle sniffed disparagingly. 'There can be few people in Cornwall who don't know *of* Amy Hoblyn. I have heard it rumoured she has taken over her father's activities. Why should she work for you?'

'We're partners. I've provided the boat, she's put up the fish-cellar.'

'Oh, yes, I forgot. You told my father.' Elinor Hearle was silent for some moments. Sme looked at Nathan's face as though expecting to learn more there. Then she shrugged. 'Who you work with is your business. The agreement is in my father's study. I'll take you there and you can sign it.'

It was dark and gloomy in the house, the windows reflecting the overcast sky outside.

Halfway up the stairs Elinor placed a warning hand upon Nathan's arm. 'Be careful. There's a broken stair here. I must get someone in to fix it soon.'

Nathan negotiated the broken stair with no trouble, but Elinor Hearle kept her hand on his arm and Nathan was acutely aware of her closeness, experiencing a sense of disappointment when she released his arm to open the door of the study.

Inside the study Elinor moved to her father's desk, beside an open window. 'Here is the agreement. You'd better read it through. You *can* read?'

Nathan nodded and bent over the document. It was written in bold, lawyer's writing on a large sheet of stiff paper. Beside him, Elinor leaned close, reading over his shoulder. He found his concentration wandering, distracted by the headiness of the perfume she wore. It was a perfume that was out of place here in Cornwall. It belonged beneath the chandeliers of the fine salons of London. No doubt her father had bought it for her – or was it a present from someone else?

There had been few girls in Nathan's life. He had been brought up by his father to believe that involvement with a nice girl led inexorably to marriage – and marriage for a prize-fighter was the first step to disaster. Consequently, Nathan had kept well clear of marriageable girls. There had been others, of course, girls of whom his father had said nothing – probably because Josiah Jago *knew* nothing of them. Then there were the girls who could be found in the hostelries frequented by prize-fighters. Girls eager to please, who asked for little but who, more often than not, passed on a debilitating disease to ruin the career of more than one promising champion.

Nathan brought his straying thoughts back to the present. He was no longer a champion prize-fighter, idol of the London 'Fancy'. He was a Cornish fisherman – and Elinor Hearle was the haughty daughter of a man who was a landowner, Member of Parliament and baronet. Nevertheless, try as he might to be rational, the stirrings within his body mocked at common sense.

In order to put an end to such disturbing fantasies, Nathan took up the goose-quill pen, dipped it in the ink and scratched his signature at the foot of the page. Suddenly he stopped, quill in hand. He could smell something more than Elinor Hearle's perfume. It was smoke. It appeared to be drifting in through the open window.

'Do you have a garden fire going?'

The question startled Elinor, but she shook her head. 'No, the gardener is cleaning out the well.'

Nathan flung the window open wider, and immediately they both heard an ominous crackling sound.

'It sounds like thatch. . . .'

Elinor paled. 'The stables!' Turning, she ran from the room and down the stairs. Nathan followed her.

In the darkness of the downstairs hall, Nathan almost bowled over a startled maidservant. Steadying her, Nathan said urgently: 'Fetch all the servants you can find – and the men cutting the hedge by the lane. There's a fire in the stables. Quickly now!'

Running from the house after Elinor, he rounded the corner just as a section of the stable roof ignited with a frightening roar.

'There are horses inside,' Elinor cried above the din of flames devouring the dry straw roof.

'Get some water organised. I'll release as many as I can.'

Without waiting for a reply, Nathan ran to the stable-door. The door was closed, but not secured. Flinging it open, Nathan put up an arm in an instinctive, if useless, gesture, warding off the thick black smoke that billowed out, engulfing him.

As the smoke thinned temporarily, Nathan moved cautiously inside the stables. He could hear horses snorting in terror as they crashed about inside their loose-boxes. Reaching the first of them, he slipped the bolt and threw back the gate, jumping clear as the horse inside bolted for the exit.

He started coughing as he reached the second loose-box, and for a moment he thought he might have to abandon his rescue attempt. Then he remembered how, in the thick of battle on the gun-deck of a man-of-war, the gunners would crouch low beside the guns to escape the acrid smoke that collected in dense clouds about the low deckheads.

Dropping to all fours, Nathan found he could breathe a little easier. Occasionally, he could even see a few feet ahead as a breeze from outside cut a thin path through the smoke. One by one he slipped the bolts, flinging himself to one side as the panic-stricken horses slipped and slid on the cobbled floor in their haste to reach safety.

The smoke was thickening now, catching at his throat as the dirty straw in the boxes, and the boxes themselves, began to burn. In the last loose-box he found a terrified mare and a near-helpless foal. The mare bolted the moment Nathan opened the gate of the loose-box, but the foal was confused and had to be manhandled to the stable-door.

Outside, Nathan sat on the ground, sucking in clean air, ignoring the sparks that showered about him. Wiping his streaming eyes on the back of a sleeve, he saw Elinor and Will Hodge, her new groom, catching the horses and turning them out in a nearby paddock.

At that moment a young woman came running up, looking about her in wide-eyed horror. To the groom she screamed: 'Sarah? Where's Sarah?'

Will Hodge stared at her, not understanding. 'Why, when last I saw her she was at home with you.'

'No!' The young woman's fingers clutched at her face. 'She came to the stables to find you!'

Will Hodge stared stupidly from his wife to the burning stables. 'Then it must have been her. She must have knocked the lamp over. I set it on a box, up by the tackle-room. It was dark, you see. . . .' The groom was too stunned to think rationally.

'Perhaps she ran out again, frightened at what she'd done.' Nathan spoke to the groom's distraught wife.

Ann Hodge shook her head, her face twisting and distorting in anguish. 'She'd have come home if she were frightened. She's only four. She must be in there.'

She started towards the stables just as a section of the roof collapsed with a snapping of blazing beams and a roar that blew sparks and fragments of burning straw as high as the roof of the manor-house.

Grabbing the wife of the groom as she began screaming, Nathan thrust her at Elinor. 'Hold her here – and get some water on the fire. *Now!*'

He dived towards the open stable-door. Pausing to take a deep breath before plunging inside, he thought he heard Elinor shout, telling him not to be a fool, but the sound was quickly lost in the noise of the conflagration about him.

Nathan knew exactly where he was going. Alongside the loose-box which had housed the foal he had seen a closed door. It had to be the tackle-room. If young Sarah had fled inside and closed the door when the lamp fell to the floor and started the blaze, she might still be alive.

The woodwork inside the stables was well ablaze now. As Nathan sidestepped a burning loose-box, the heat reached out and struck him in the face with the strength of a prize-fighter. Putting both arms over his head, Nathan stumbled on to the far end of the building.

He cannoned into the closed door of the tackle-room and

blindly fumbled for the latch. When he found it he realised it was too high for a child to reach. Either the door had been open when Sarah reached here, or she was not inside.

As he pushed open the door, smoke billowed out to meet him and a bundle of burning thatch dropped to the floor at his feet. Kicking it to one side, Nathan tripped over another obstacle and fell to his knees. He was choking for breath now. Above him there was an angry hiss of steam. Someone outside, with a knowledge of the building, was trying to damp down the roof of the tackle-room. It was too late to have any lasting effect. The fire had far too strong a hold on the whole building.

Nathan crawled across the floor, his arms moving ahead of him with the action of a breast-stroke swimmer in his search for the missing girl. Twice he was fooled by tumbled horse-blankets. Then, when he knew his lungs could take no more of the heat and smoke, he touched something soft. It was a small arm. He had found the missing child.

Sarah was lying in a tangle of harness, and Nathan hurriedly extricated her. She was a small four-year-old and weighed very little. Nathan held her close to him with one arm as he crawled from the tackle-room. The fire in the main stable was fearsome now. For a moment Nathan hesitated, but he could afford to waste no more time. He was having great difficulty in breathing, and his senses were beginning to fail him.

Rising to his feet, Nathan put his head down and ran, a large hand protecting Sarah's head. As he plunged through the flames he heard a deafening roar in his ears, but he felt no pain. Once he stumbled and almost fell. Then, staggering helplessly, his shoulder bouncing off the cob wall at every other step, his shoulder suddenly missed the wall and he fell sideways – out through the open doorway.

A moment later the child was snatched from him and Nathan was dragged away from the almost-gutted stables.

As Nathan lay coughing up smoke, tears streaming from his eyes, he heard the crying of the child's mother and thought his rescue bid must have been in vain. But when he was able to sit up and wipe his eyes sufficiently to see what was going on about him, he saw the daughter of the groom in her mother's arms, retching as healthily as Nathan himself. Her mother was crying from sheer relief.

The employees of the estate had now been joined by fishermen from Pentuan who had seen the plume of black smoke rising high in the sky above their village. Although they would be unable to save the stables, there was now little danger that the fire might spread to the house.

'And how is the hero of the day?'

The mocking words were belied by the expression of concern on Elinor Hearle's face as she looked down at him. Putting out a hand, she touched his shoulder where a piece of burning thatch had landed on him. It hurt.

'You've burned yourself. You had better come inside to clean up and have something put on that shoulder.' She smiled at him. 'I'm afraid you've lost most of your eyebrows, too.'

There were no servants inside the house. The few who remained in the service of Sir Lewis Hearle were outside, helping to fight the blaze. Elinor took Nathan upstairs to a bedroom heavy with the perfume she herself wore. Off the bedroom was another, smaller room. Here Elinor poured water from a jug into a bowl and put soap and a large towel on the marble-topped table beside it.

'That shirt is ruined. Take if off and wash yourself. I'll go and find some balm and an old shirt of my father's. It will be too small for you, I've no doubt, but it will serve.'

When Elinor had gone, Nathan stripped off his shirt. It had been badly holed by flying sparks and was so charred in parts that if fell to pieces beneath his touch.

Elinor returned to the room carrying a small earthenware jar in her hands. Nathan was drying himself and Elinor made disapproving noises. 'There's a whole area of your back that hasn't been touched. It looks as though you have another burn there, too.'

Taking the sponge from the bowl, she rubbed it gently over his back, dabbing the area dry with the towel afterwards. When she had finished, she began applying the ointment to his burns. She rubbed it over most of his back before turning her attention to his shoulders, and finally smearing it carefully over his chest, on which numerous red scorch-marks showed now the grime of the fire had been removed.

As she worked, Elinor murmured reassuringly that,

although Nathan was burned here and there, he was not seriously hurt.

Elinor Hearle was a tall girl, but the top of her head came no higher than Nathan's chin and she was standing so close to him that he could smell the fire smoke, lingering in her hair.

Suddenly, with both hands resting on his chest, her voice took on a new, strangely fierce note. 'God! Nathan Jago, you have a magnificent body. . . . A Greek god. . . .'

When Nathan looked down at her face he saw the same hunger he had witnessed on the faces of men when they first saw a woman after spending months at sea. He had never before known such a need in a woman.

She was looking up at him. Waiting. . . . Willing him to make the first move. He told himself it would be madness. It *was* madness, but he reached for her and she came to him, mouth on his, with a ferocity that was unlike anything he had ever experienced. His whole body became aware of her as she strained to him, hands at first kneading his scorched back before her nails dug into his flesh.

Her mouth moved fiercely beneath his, and suddenly her teeth sank into his lower lip and he tasted his own blood.

With a stifled oath, Nathan jerked his head back. Elinor was looking up at him, and in her eyes was an animal hunger that called up an equally primitive need deep within him. Picking her up, Nathan carried Elinor to the bed.

Nathan awoke, aware that he had been disturbed by an alien sound. Raising his head from the soft pillow, he was momentarily confused by his surroundings. There was a drowsy protest from the pillow beside him – and he remembered.

Elinor's leg was trapped beneath his. As she pulled it free, a rumble of thunder rolled across the sea beyond the window. A gust of wind brought a rattle of heavy raindrops against the diamond-paned windows.

'What are you doing?'

Elinor spoke without moving her head from the pillow as she freed an arm from a tangle of bedclothes and slipped it about Nathan's neck.

'I must go. We both should. You to see what's happening at

the stables, me to my boat. I have to get it ready for a night's fishing.'

'Damn the fire. If the servants haven't put it out yet, the rain will do the job for them. As for your boat, it will wait. I won't.'

Propping himself up on one elbow, Nathan looked down at Elinor, and she squirmed the smooth roundness of her body beneath his before pulling him down to her.

'Love me again, Nathan. Love me again. . . .'

Her voice was hoarse with desire. Moments later the storm, the fire and Nathan's boat were all forgotten as he was swallowed up by the passion of the woman whose bed he shared.

Chapter Ten

BY THE TIME Nathan returned to Portgiskey the storm had blown inland, washing the pale sky clean and leaving the world to await the arrival of night.

As he approached it was apparent from the manner of the men that there had been much speculation about the reason for his long absence. Nathan tried to put some spring into his step. It was not easy. His feet felt as though they were encased in lead.

When he reached the small group waiting on the quayside, the men would not meet his eyes. It was left to Amy to voice their thoughts.

'No doubt Elinor Hearle had more to offer you than a wet afternoon spent preparing a fishing-boat for sea?'

Nathan was too honest not to feel a sense of guilt at the sarcastic question. But on the walk from Polrudden he had anticipated the resentment of Amy and the others. He had convinced himself that whatever he did was none of their business. Nevertheless, he felt the need to defend himself to Amy.

'I would have been here sooner had I not needed to go home first to change my clothes.'

Amy gave a derisive snort. 'If you intend taking up fishing seriously, you'll need to get used to getting wet. You can't run home to change every time it rains.'

'I said nothing about rain. There was a fire at Polrudden. My shirt was scorched. I left the manor wearing one of Sir Lewis Hearle's shirts. I didn't think he would approve if I wore it for fishing.'

'A fire? Was it a bad one?'

The question came from Ahab Arthur, the oldest man there. He hurried to explain his concern. 'My daughter's living up by the house. She's married to Will Hodge, Sir Lewis Hearle's groom. He's been there only a week.'

'The stables caught fire. They were gutted. Will Hodge left a lamp alight inside while he went off and did something else. Your grand-daughter came in looking for her father and knocked the lamp to the ground, starting the fire.'

Ahab Arthur's face paled. 'Was young Sarah harmed?'

'No, but she had a very narrow escape. The blaze terrified her and she ran into the tackle-room. Fortunately the door slammed shut behind her and held the flames back. When I found her she'd been overcome by smoke, but hadn't a burn on her.'

'You brought her out? But there's no way into the tackle-room except through the stables. If they were burning . . .?'

Nathan shrugged, wishing he had not gone into such detail. 'As I said, she had a very lucky escape.'

'And all the time I thought. . . .' Amy choked on her words. 'Was that how your shirt was burned? Bringing out Ahab's grand-daughter?'

'Yes.'

Nathan was embarrassed by the hero-worship he saw in Amy's eyes. His bid to keep the real reason for his absence from her and the others had worked too well. Gruffly, he said: 'We've wasted enough time in talk. Come on, into the boat. Pilchards will be at a premium. The seiners at Pentuan lost all their fish and most of their nets in this afternoon's storm.'

The Portgiskey drifter arrived at Nathan's chosen fishing-ground a few minutes after nightfall. Some four miles from the coast, it was close enough to the land to enjoy shelter from a westerly swell, yet far enough out to avoid any risk of drifting ashore during the night.

Amy took the helm while the three men shot half a mile of nets in a line across the wide mouth of St Austell Bay. Once this task had been completed and a sail set to hold the boat steady, Calvin Dickin and Ahab Arthur enjoyed a late-night smoke before settling down on hard canvas-sail beds to await Nathan's call to stand watch in his stead.

In a talkative mood, Amy stayed up for a while, declaring she was not tired. Nathan would have welcomed an opportunity to think about what had happened between Elinor Hearle and himself at Polrudden Manor. Instead, he was obliged both to listen and to reply to an inexplicably happy Amy.

'I love being out here at night. Don't you, Nathan? You and I could be the only people in the whole world. Even the lights of Pentuan and Mevagissey could be so many fallen stars scattered on the ground.'

The residents of the two fishing villages did not keep late hours, and there were no more than two dozen lighted windows to be seen.

'I feel so contented. More than I have for years. Pa was ill for a very long time and I've missed the nights he and I would spend out here together, waiting for a French smuggler. We'd just sit here like this, talking together for hours.'

Nathan struck a light for his pipe and saw her sitting hugging her knees, one cheek resting lightly against one arm.

'We talked lots, Pa and me. He missed Beville. I suppose that's why I always tried to do everything Beville would have done with him. I was very young when he was taken off to sea. I hardly remember him, really. What kind of man was he?'

'He was a good man, Amy. A great sailor and a wonderful friend. I miss him, too.'

Nathan could not see Amy's face, but he sensed that he had made the reply she wanted to hear.

'That's what I've always believed, but I've never before met anyone who *really* knew him – not in the way you did. It's strange really, the way things have worked out. You and Beville being such good friends, and now the Jagos and Hoblyns being partners. It's unexpected, too, I suppose, after what happened between your pa and mine.'

Nathan's brow creased in a puzzled frown, and he took the pipe from his mouth. 'What *did* happen between them?'

'You don't know? But of course you wouldn't. They had an awful row. When we lived farther west Pa always went to church every Sunday, without fail. He was a Methodist for years, ever since he met John Wesley himself. Pa went to the Sunday meetings here, too, until your father criticised him in front of the whole congregation for night-running. Preacher Jago said John Wesley had called smuggling "the work of the Devil". Pa stood up and told your father he reckoned he'd known Wesley a sight better than anyone in Pentuan. Everyone took sides, the meeting became a bit heated – and then fighting started. It almost wrecked the inside of the chapel, and Pa was thrown out of the Methodist Society. We had nothing more to do with Methodism until Preacher Jago came along and offered to say the prayers when we buried Pa. It made Ma very happy.'

Nathan shook his head. 'That was my father's way of saying he was sorry. He's never found it easy to forgive anyone who disagrees with him – and I should know. I wondered why he told me about your fish-cellar when he is so opposed to drift-fishing. It was his way of making amends for the way he'd behaved towards your pa. He thought you and your mother might need money.'

'I'm glad he did tell you. I . . . I like working with you, Nathan.'

Nathan broke the embarrassed silence that followed Amy's simple admission. 'I hope it will prove to be a profitable partnership for all of us. But having you crew the boat with us is only a temporary arrangement. When we can find enough men you'll remain ashore, supervising the cellar.'

Amy opened her mouth to argue, then snapped it shut again. She had plans of her own, but it would not do to bring them all into the open just yet. Rising to her feet, she hesitated for a moment, then she leaned forward and kissed Nathan on the cheek.

'Good night, Nathan. Thank you for listening to me.'

As she went forward to find a place to sleep, Nathan compared Amy's kiss with the kisses of Elinor Hearle. Remembering the hours he had spent in the bedroom at Polrudden Manor, all thoughts of Amy Hoblyn slipped away.

Nathan and his crew began hauling in their nets before dawn. They soon learned they had spent a very successful night at sea. It had been light for two hours before all the nets were inboard. By then the boat was heavily laden and everyone was in a jubilant mood.

Ahab Arthur was standing in the bow of the boat as they sailed into Portgiskey Cove on a light breeze and he called back: 'It looks as though Sammy has gathered a welcoming party to cheer us in.'

Nathan leaned over the side of the boat. There was a large black-and-white-painted cutter drawn up on the tiny beach beside the waterside cottage and a dozen or more men stood flanking Sammy Mizler on the small quay.

105

Nathan frowned. 'That's no welcoming party. Unless I'm very much mistaken, the Revenue men are waiting for us.'

Amy appeared at his side. 'You're right. The fat one in the middle is Ezra Partridge, Chief Revenue Officer of the Mevagissey preventive men. He's the most hated man in Cornwall. He was responsible for having a Polperro man hanged for smuggling last year. I wonder what he's doing at Portgiskey.'

'We'll soon find out,' replied Nathan grimly. He had remembered the casks of brandy he and Sammy Mizler had carried ashore for Amy's boat and hidden beneath the fish-cellar. If Chief Revenue Officer Partridge had found them, they would all be in serious trouble.

The next few moments were too busy to speculate on the presence of the Revenue men at Portgiskey, as sails were lowered and the boat brought alongside the quay. When the boat was secured, Chief Revenue Officer Partridge stepped aboard with two armed Revenue men in close attendance. The remainder formed an armed line on the quayside.

Without offering to identify himself, Ezra Partridge asked: 'Your name is Jago?'

Nathan nodded.

'I have reason to believe you have contraband spirits on board this boat. My men are here to carry out a search.'

'You'll find no spirits on this boat, Chief Officer Partridge – and I'll have no clumsy-footed Revenue men trampling on good fish. Your men can search my boat when the catch has been landed. That's unless you want to be taken to court for the value of the catch?'

Chief Revenue Officer Ezra Partridge hesitated, speculating whether Nathan was trying to bluff him. Finally deciding that Nathan meant every word, Partridge scowled angrily. He knew that a Cornish magistrate would delight in convicting him and awarding Nathan whatever damages he claimed. Speaking to the Revenue men who had boarded the boat with him, he ordered: 'You men remain here. Check everything that's taken ashore. The others on the quay can come with me and search the house and fish-cellar.'

Nathan's heart sank. He had been hoping to take the pilchards ashore and begin stacking them over the flagstone that concealed the smuggler's hiding-place. He tried to catch Amy's eye, but she would not look at him.

Nathan hurriedly filled a large basket with pilchards and carried it himself to the fish-cellar. He was too late. Ezra Partridge had already located the underfloor hiding-place. As Nathan dumped his fish on the stone floor, the Revenue men were prising up the huge flagstone, using iron bars they had brought with them in their boat.

The Chief Revenue Officer turned to Nathan triumphantly. 'Is this why you were so confident I'd find no contraband on your boat, Jago? Because you'd brought it ashore earlier?'

Nathan shrugged; it would be no use denying all knowledge of the brandy. It was his cellar. His and Amy Hoblyn's. She was standing impassively nearby and still would not look at him.

Nathan wondered what would happen to her. He had never heard of a woman being convicted of involvement in smuggling, but there was always a first time.

With cries of triumph, the Revenue men raised the flagstone – and the shouts died on their lips. Ezra Partridge looked from the hiding-place to Nathan. 'What's this?'

Nathan crossed the floor of the fish-cellar as casually as he could. Looking down into the hole he saw it was filled with a white substance that resembled hard-packed snow.

'It's salt.' The unexpected explanation came from Amy.

'Salt? Salt? What's it doing here?'

'Keeping dry.' Amy looked at Ezra Partridge scornfully. 'How long have you been stationed in fishing villages? You should know that damp salt loses its strength, and there's no way salt can be kept dry at Portgiskey if it's exposed to the air. It needs to be kept in a dry, sealed place. That's a specially made salt-store.'

Ezra Partridge looked from Amy to Nathan suspiciously. 'I don't believe you.'

Amy shrugged. 'Please yourself. You asked why there's salt here. I've told you.' With that she turned her back on the Chief Revenue Officer and walked from the fish-cellar.

'You men. Find something to probe into this . . . salt. I want to know if there's anything hidden beneath it.'

There was nothing. But not until the Revenue men could see the bare boards of the fishing-boat beneath the small amount of fish remaining in the hold did they accept that their early-morning raid had been a waste of time.

Standing beside Amy on the small quay as the Revenue men rowed Chief Revenue Officer Ezra Partridge away from Portgiskey Cove, Nathan said quietly: 'You had me scared for a while, Amy. When did the brandy go?'

'It was collected the very next night after you and Sammy brought it ashore for me.'

'And the salt?'

'Delivered while we were in Brixham picking up the boat.'

'Amy, you're a truly remarkable girl. I'll never doubt you again, I promise.'

Amy grinned delightedly. 'Good. But I must admit I was worried for a while. I thought Ezra Partridge was going to ask me some awkward questions about the salt. It's best Brittany salt, delivered from France – duty unpaid.'

In London, Sir Lewis Hearle was both surprised and excited to receive an invitation to have lunch with Spencer Perceval, the Tory Prime Minister, at 10 Downing Street. Such invitations were issued to backbenchers when they were being considered for promotion to Cabinet rank.

The Cornish baronet was not disappointed. After an exchange of pleasantries, and some meaningless chitchat about the progress of the war, the state of the rural economy, and the disarray of the Whig opposition, the two men sat down to eat and to discuss the purpose behind the invitation.

'I thank you for your report on the growing strength of Methodist dissidents, Sir Lewis. A very well-written and detailed communication. Indeed, I confess to finding much of your information quite startling. It has given my colleagues and myself much food for thought. To have such a popular dissident movement in the land in time of war is causing us all much concern. We have little control over their actions, and there's not a damned fellow of note among the lot of them! You've produced a first-class report, Sir Lewis; but can you put forward any ideas on how we might bring these Wesleyans to heel?'

Sir Lewis Hearle took a swig of burgundy, still readily available in London, even after many weary years of war with

France. Leaning back in his chair he gazed speculatively at his Prime Minister. He had submitted the report on the dangers of Methodism, uncertain of its reception. Perceval had made public utterances against 'Methodist rabble', but such words may have been intended merely to appease the Archbishop of Canterbury, who had powerful support in the House of Lords. Now Sir Lewis felt that perhaps the Prime Minister's stated dislike of Methodism was genuine. He determined to speak his mind.

'I have given this matter a great deal of thought, Prime Minister. As you know, these Wesleyans have taken a firm hold in my own county. Nevertheless, serious cracks are developing in their organisation, and I feel we should take full advantage of such a situation. Divide and rule would appear to be the order of the day. Part of the Wesleyan movement is calling for more militant evangelism. They point to the example set by their founder, who took the Methodist message to the masses. Others favour consolidation, and wish to gather the trappings of respectability about themselves. Yet another group resents the central ruling body of the Wesleyan movement and is calling for more power to be given to local Methodist societies. Such dissension comes as no surprise to me – certainly not where Cornish Methodists are concerned. Rebellion against all forms of authority is part of the Cornishman's nature. Yet my information is that this state of affairs exists throughout the whole Methodist movement. It had to happen, of course. Since John Wesley died his followers have had no leader. They are reliant upon a "Council". I suggest, Prime Minister, that the time is ripe to remove the threat posed to this country by these dissidents – once and for all.'

'And how do you suggest we pursue such a policy?' Spencer Perceval leaned forward eagerly to hear what Sir Lewis Hearle had to say. The Cornish baronet had been recommended to him as a capable man whose hatred of Methodism matched the Prime Minister's own mistrust of their aims.

'There are a number of courses open to us. At a local level we must prevent Methodists from building new churches and, wherever possible, close down those already in existence. Force the Wesleyans to hold their meetings in the open air. Not only shall we be able to see and hear what is happening, but it will be a simple matter to introduce agitators, should we find it necessary. The expectation of violence will deter decent, law-abiding people from attending such meetings and attract riff-raff. Consequently, it will come as no surprise to anyone when magistrates appear among them to read the Riot Act and arrest their ringleaders – the so-called "preachers". Indeed, before long the whole country will no doubt be clamouring for legislation to put an end to such disturbances.'

Spencer Perceval looked at Sir Lewis Hearle speculatively. 'You have some interesting ideas, Sir Lewis, but to implement them on a national scale would involve my government. The risk is considerable.'

'Not necessarily, Prime Minister. Any government in time of war would be lacking in its duty if it did not examine very closely the activities of a dissident group established in its midst, even though such a group were operating under the cloak of religion. But I realise that it would be necessary to proceed with a great deal of discretion.'

'Of course, and it would be embarrassing if no substantial evidence of subversion were to be proven against these Methodists. Very well, Sir Lewis. I intend giving you the opportunity to put your beliefs to the test. I am offering you the post of Under-Secretary at the Home Office. You will have special responsibility for investigating the affairs of dissident groups in His Majesty's Kingdom.'

Sir Lewis Hearle rode home from Downing Street in a mood of great self-satisfaction. He had worked tirelessly for years to achieve Cabinet rank. Now at last he had a foot on the ladder to his goal, together with a mandate to destroy a dissident organisation he loathed with an intensity that had become obsessional over the years.

There was only one matter that cast a shadow over Sir Lewis Hearle's happiness. Money. If he were going to attain and hold Cabinet rank, the Tory baronet knew he would need to win over a great many influential men. His bills for entertaining would soar to frightening heights. Somehow he had to raise more money. Lack of money was an embarrassment that had been with him for many years. But now there was an end in sight. A Cabinet Minister could amass a fortune securing posts for the sons of grateful acquaintances, accepting directorships on the

110

boards of suitable companies, and generally performing favours for men of means.

In the meantime, Sir Lewis Hearle decided he must sell off a number of his less profitable Cornish farms for which the rents were negligible – Venn, for instance.

Thinking of Cornwall set Sir Lewis Hearle to think of Elinor. She would be pleased at the news of his appointment. He would write and tell her when time permitted. She might be more inclined to come to London when he began entertaining. She might even find herself a husband here. Yes, he would have to persuade her to join him in the capital. Elinor had spent far too long going her own way in a remote corner of Cornwall. He sometimes thought she had forgotten her station in life. He had observed the casual and informal manner in which she had touched the arm of the Jago upstart. A prize-fighting fisherman was no fit company for the daughter of a baronet.

Sir Lewis Hearle would have run Nathan Jago out of Cornwall at the time had he not believed that the new fishing venture would add a considerable sum to the income of Polrudden Manor. Once Sir Lewis was established in the Government the need would not be so pressing. Then Nathan Jago would go the way of his Wesley-preaching father.

Chapter Eleven

FISHING from Portgiskey continued to prove highly profitable for Nathan and his partners, but it was not without incident. One morning, as Nathan and his crew were hauling in their nets, they were surprised by a daring French man-of-war. Cutting free the two nets still in the water, Nathan put on every inch of sail the lugger possessed and made the safety of Mevagissey harbour just ahead of the French warship.

The incident was watched by dozens of astonished fishermen and a few early-rising villagers who quickly roused the Revenue men from their beds. Led by Chief Officer Partridge, the Revenue men turned the small coastguard signalling-cannon on the daring raider from across the English Channel.

The shots from the ineffectual weapon drew a broadside from the French vessel, and the cannon-balls fell close enough to Ezra Partridge's men to send them scurrying for cover. After firing another scornful broadside, the man-of-war put about and headed out to sea.

It was a lucky escape for the crew of the Portgiskey drifter. Only a few miles along the coast the crews of two Looe drifters were less fortunate. Scooped up by the same man-of-war, they were taken captive to Verdun. Here they joined Captain Nicholas Lelean and the crew of *The Seven Brothers*, a Mevagissey vessel taken outside its home port seven years before.

Serious though this incident might have been, it caused Nathan less concern than an occurrence a few nights later. Under cover of darkness, a number of fishermen in small seine-boats slipped out of Mevagissey harbour and cut away Nathan's nets as his craft drifted across the entrance of St Austell Bay.

Nathan feared it might herald the beginning of a war between the Portgiskey boat and the seine-fishermen of Mevagissey. To his great relief, it proved to be an isolated incident – little more than a savage expression of disapproval.

Paradoxically, the night attack actually worked to Nathan's advantage. Because the action had been taken by Mevagissey

112

men, it angered some of the Pentuan fishermen. The result was that Nathan was able to make up a full crew of Pentuan men who would otherwise have remained unemployed until the next pilchard season came around.

It was now November, and winter was close. Sometimes the weather proved too rough for the Portgiskey boat to put to sea. Nathan spent these nights at Polrudden Manor, with Elinor Hearle.

Nathan thought his bedroom romance with Sir Lewis Hearle's daughter was a well-kept secret, until one stormy evening his mother tackled him as he prepared to leave the house.

'Where are you off to tonight?'

Nathan did his best to appear nonchalant. 'I'm a fisherman, Ma. A drift-fisherman. Where do I usually go when I leave home at this time of night?'

'Is that supposed to be an answer? You're squirming like a Mevagissey eel, my son. No, don't say any more. I'd rather you didn't tell me a lie. Rumour has it that you've taken up with Sir Lewis Hearle's daughter. I've scoffed at such silly talk. Elinor Hearle is far too high and mighty for the likes of us. Am I right or wrong?'

'I see her sometimes. We enjoy each other's company. Is there anything wrong with that?'

Nathan's very defensiveness told Annie Jago that the incredible half-rumours were true. She was aghast. Annie Jago had not always been married to a preacher. She knew what went on in the soft thyme of the Winnick, the rough pastureland behind Pentuan Beach. But that was between the girls and boys of the village, sons and daughters of fishermen.

There were also a number of bastards dwelling in the surrounding countryside who bore a remarkable resemblance to generations of Hearles. Indeed, bastards sired by men of good family were in great demand as husbands and wives. The paternal consciences of those who dwelled at Polrudden meant that *their* families would never go hungry in hard times.

All such relationships were accepted as part of the pattern of rural life. But for a village *man* to form such a relationship with the daughter of a great house was unheard of!

'There's everything wrong with it, as well you know. The

113

Lord only knows what Sir Lewis Hearle will say when he hears what's going on behind his back – and he *will* find out, you can be sure of that. Oh, heaven help us! This could kill your father.'

Nathan was white-faced but unrepentant. 'Would you rather I moved out of the house, and found somewhere else to live?'

'And cause tongues to wag all the more? No, you're a grown man now, but you're still my son. Your road may not be my road – and it's certainly not your father's – but you'll never be turned out of this house while I'm alive.'

Annie Jago's words troubled Nathan greatly, but they did not prevent him from making the walk to Polrudden Manor that same night.

Between dusk and dawn, in Elinor Hearle's bed, Nathan entered a world far removed from the lot of a Pentuan fisherman. Not for him the cold comfort of a dingy, rough-blanketed room and a wife smelling of sweat and fish, her hands calloused and red-raw from constant immersion in rough preserving salt. Nathan lay with Elinor in a spacious bed, with clean linen covering their newly bathed bodies, and the fresh woman-smell of her in his nostrils as they made love in the darkness.

Nevertheless, after his mother's talk of rumour, Nathan was even more cautious than before. Labouring up the hill on his way to Polrudden Manor, he kept to the shadows, moving back out of sight if he heard anyone approaching along the pathway. In the mornings he always left the house before dawn, making his way direct to Portgiskey, where he would be hard at work on the boat by the time the others arrived.

One rough night the wind was gusting a gale from the south, driving heavy belts of rain inland off the sea. In the small cottage at Portgiskey, Amy lay awake listening to the thunder of the sea on the nearby rocks. Above her the beams creaked and groaned as the wind roared from clifftop to clifftop on either side of the house. Occasionally, lightning illuminated the room, but none of these noises was responsible for her wakefulness. They had all been part of life at Portgiskey Cove for as long as she had lived there. The cause of her sleeplessness was far more difficult to define.

Since Sammy Mizler and Nathan had gone into partnership

with Amy and her mother, the days had been more fully occupied than any since the death of her father. Sammy had found a ready market for all the fish they could catch. All day long Portgiskey Cove rang to the voices of the fishermen and their wives, elbow-deep in fish and brine in the busy cellar. Yet deep inside Amy there was a dull emptiness that had not been there in the long, lonely days following her father's death. The pleasure and anticipation of working with Nathan had ebbed away. Nathan no longer talked of the plans he had for the future of the drift-fishing partnership. There were no longer exciting days when he carried everyone along with his enthusiasm. True, Nathan still worked harder than anyone when the weather permitted fishing, but his mind was elsewhere. His heart and soul had gone from his work.

Amy was certain she knew where the responsibility for the change lay, but she did not know what *she* could do to make everything right once more.

As Amy lay in her bed, she thought she heard a stone turn on the path outside. It was followed by what might have been a man's voice, uttering a muffled curse. Throwing back the blankets, Amy took two swift paces to the rattling window overlooking the path outside. As she opened the window the wind rushed in, billowing out the curtains. Carried on the wind was the sound of running footsteps, receding along the path that led inland from the cove.

Pulling a coat over her nightdress, Amy made her way to the living-room. Here she took down a pistol from a peg on the wall. Checking its loading and priming, she slipped the gun inside her coat and let herself out through the cottage door.

The wind out here was so strong that there was no way she could have kept a lamp alight; but she had sensibly placed a lamp in the window before leaving the house, and the light reached far enough to show Amy that the door of the fish-cellar was closed and did not appear to have been tampered with. Puzzled, Amy turned back to the darkened quay.

The boat was gone! Horrified, Amy ran to the edge of the quay. Kneeling in the rain and spray, she saw that the ropes used to secure the boat had been cut through.

The loss of their boat would be disastrous for the enterprise. Looking out into the darkness, Amy called upon all her years of experience of Portgiskey tides and topography in an effort to guess where the boat might now be.

It was three hours after high tide. Amy estimated that, if the boat had been cut adrift shortly before she had heard the footsteps, it would now be somewhere close to the rocks dividing the cove from Pentuan Beach. Once past the rocks the boat would be fully exposed to the wind and running sea. As the tide came in it would be swept on to the shore and quickly battered to pieces by the ferocious waves.

Without pausing to think of the dangers involved, Amy ran from the jetty to the pebble beach where her own small boat was drawn up beyond the reach of the swirling waters. There were several inches of rainwater in the bottom of the boat, making it heavier than usual; but, exerting all her strength, Amy heaved and slid the small boat down the beach until an incoming wave lifted the bow. It took only a moment for Amy to scramble on board and, unshipping the oars, she rowed the boat into the darkness of the cove.

Amy's one chance of saving the fishing-boat lay in locating it before it drifted clear of the cove. The bay beyond the cove was much too rough for her small craft, and it would be suicidal for her to attempt to go any farther.

Amy searched close to the rocks, gauging her distance from them by the white froth bubbling about their dark outlines. She found no trace of the large fishing-boat. Soaked by heavy rain and spray she twice searched the perimeter of the cove before accepting that the fishing-boat must already have been swept out into the heaving waters of St Austell Bay.

She had begun the hard pull back towards the light in the cottage window, when a dark shape suddenly loomed up ahead of her. Although Amy desperately tried to hold off the small rowing-boat, the two vessels collided with a thump that brought a screech of protest from the smaller vessel's timbers, and pitched Amy from the thwart. She had located the missing drifter.

Amy regained her feet as the two craft collided for a second time. For the next fifteen minutes, unable to climb on board the fishing-boat, she worked hard to secure a line from the rowing-boat to the larger fishing-craft. By the time she succeeded, the movement of the two vessels told her that she

116

was passing from the comparative shelter of the cove into the bay.

Then began the most exhausting half-hour of Amy's young life. With her sodden clothes clinging to her body, and battered by wind and sea, she struggled to tow the fishing-boat to safety. Inch by hard-fought inch she pulled the dinghy towards the light, but it never seemed to get any closer. Finally, Amy knew she could go on no longer. She was weakening so much that, before long, the sea must win and carry both boats out to sea.

But she had gained the few yards that might make all the difference between saving or losing the drifter. It would have to suffice; she had no more strength in her.

There was an anchor in the rowing-boat. Too small to hold the drifter for long, it would have to do. Untying the rope that joined the two craft, Amy secured the anchor to the free end, trusting the other end would not break free from the drifter. It was a dreadful moment when she tossed the anchor out into the water. She felt as though she had deserted the fishing-boat, but she could do no more out here, alone.

At Polrudden, the ferocity of the storm had penetrated the self-induced exhaustion cocooning the two lovers. Nathan lay awake listening to the wind howling about the tall chimneys of the manor-house as lightning cast dancing shadows about the bedroom. He fancied the wind was shifting round to the east. An easterly gale brought the worst possible weather conditions to this part of the coast. It was the only gale that could seriously threaten the otherwise sheltered cove at Portgiskey.

He shifted an arm that was trapped beneath the naked body of Elinor. She lay with her back towards him, curled into the contours of his body. Untroubled by anything that might be happening beyond the bedroom walls, she slept easily, her breath a feline purr in her throat.

Nathan had been lying awake listening to the storm for about half an hour, when he heard another sound. It brought him to a sitting position in the bed, and Elinor stirred sleepily, protesting at the sudden movement.

'Sh! Can't you hear? There's someone at the door, downstairs.'

'In this weather? You're imagining things, Nathan. Something's broken loose in the wind, that's all.'

'There it is again! You must be able to hear it. . . .'

The sound was unmistakable now. The heavy iron knocker on the front door of the house was being wielded determinedly by the late-night caller.

'Who on earth . . .? Where are the servants? They can't *all* be deaf. . . .'

'Hadn't you better go down and see who it is? What if it's someone with an urgent message and the servant brings him up here? It might even be your father!'

'He has more sense than to be out on a night like this. But you are right.' Elinor swung herself reluctantly out of bed. 'I had better go downstairs. Where's that blasted tinder-box . . .?'

A moment later there was the repeated sound of steel on flintstone, and a flicker of flame as Elinor lit a candle.

A white silk dressing-gown lay on the floor at the foot of the bed. Picking it up, Elinor slipped it on to cover her nakedness. Then, with candle held aloft, she opened the door and went out, leaving the bedroom in darkness.

A few minutes later Nathan heard voices in the passageway outside the room and he had a brief moment of panic. What if it were Sir Lewis Hearle and he was insisting upon coming upstairs to his daughter's room? Then Nathan heard Elinor speak – and the answering voice was that of another woman. It was probably one of the servants. Nathan relaxed. They must have got rid of the visitor and were both returning to their beds.

But when the door opened Nathan could see in the candlelight that the other woman was still with Elinor, although only her dripping cloak was visible as she stood behind the baronet's daughter.

With malicious amusement, Elinor said: 'You have a visitor, Nathan. I told her you weren't dressed for company, but she insists that she must speak to you.'

Moving to one side, Elinor allowed the light from the candle to fall upon the wet and dishevelled figure of Amy.

Nathan would have given much to have been able to pass responsibility for Amy's expression of deep hurt to someone else; but, even as he cringed in self-remorse, Amy's chin came up defiantly.

'Someone's been to Portgiskey and cut the boat adrift. I

managed to get out to her and put an anchor down, but it's too small. It won't hold in this wind. I've sent Mother to rouse the others, but they'll not risk their lives for someone else's boat.'

There had been no hint of a tremor in Amy's voice while she passed on the dramatic information. Now her resolution faltered and she looked away from Nathan unhappily. 'I . . . I thought you ought to know.'

Nathan's embarrassment vanished. Much to Elinor's chagrin, his immediate concern was for his fishing-boat – and for Amy.

'You put to sea in this storm? To save the boat . . .?'

'You weren't there to do it. What else could I do . . .?' The words died in Amy's throat.

'Would you two mind if I return to my bed while you continue this conversation? Your little friend has brought the cold in with her, Nathan.'

Quite unashamedly, fully aware of the effect it had, Elinor Hearle undid the cord at the neck of her dressing-gown and allowed it to slide to the floor at her feet. Quite naked, she stepped clear of the tumbled heap of silk and climbed into bed beside Nathan.

Unable to control the tears that had threatened to shatter her outward composure from the moment of her arrival, Amy turned and fled from the room.

Nathan caught up with her halfway down the muddy track that led down the hill to Pentuan.

'Amy. . . . I'm sorry that happened. Very sorry.'

'Sorry? Why, because I disturbed your love-making? Shouldn't *I* be the one apologising for that?'

Amy spoke fiercely, grateful that Nathan could not see her eyes in the storm-black night.

'That isn't what I meant. I'm sorry I caused you the humiliation of having to come and find me at Polrudden.'

Nathan reached out for her arm as she slipped on the mud of the track and fell against him. She shook his hand away angrily.

'Why should *I* feel humiliated? I wasn't the one in someone else's bed – and *she* certainly didn't feel humiliated. I got the impression she was actually enjoying it. Besides, how you live your life doesn't matter to me. We're partners, not husband and wife. Ma and me have put up the fish-cellar and you've provided the boat. The arrangement works very well – although I'll no doubt be looking for another partner when Sir Lewis Hearle learns what's going on. Now, save your breath – and mine. We'll both need it if we're to save the boat.'

With this final remark, Amy surged ahead at a furious pace that did not slacken until they were at Portgiskey.

Amy's mother had roused Calvin Dickin, Ahab Arthur and one of the new young members of the fishing crew. When Nathan and Amy arrived they were all standing in the shelter of the fish-cellar doorway. Peering out into the darkness, they were nervously debating their first move. If they wondered why it had taken Amy so long to find Nathan, no one voiced his thoughts aloud.

'It doesn't seem right that someone should cut another man's boat adrift in this weather,' said Ahab Arthur. 'Not that it surprises me. They did some terrible things before they managed to put me out of business. D'you have any idea who did it, Nathan?'

'Never mind that now. We need to get out to the boat. Amy's been out to her and put an anchor down, but it's too small. It won't hold in an easterly gale. We'll need to get on board, take her out to sea and ride out this storm well clear of land.'

Three faces turned to him, yellow-white in the lamplight. 'Put to sea – in this? 'Tis madness, Nathan, and no mistake.'

The young fisherman spoke for them all.

'Damn you! While we're here saying what we *can't* do, my boat is probably dragging anchor and heading for the rocks. I'll not ask any one of you to go farther than the mouth of the cove. Take me there and I'll go on board and take the boat to sea myself.'

Nathan ran from the cellar doorway to Amy's boat, riding in the shallow surf at the edge of the beach. With considerable trepidation, the three men followed. Amy went with them.

Nathan stood in the bows, scanning the darkness to catch a first glimpse of the drifter as the men pulled away from the shore. Amy called directions from the stern. She guided them to where she thought the fishing-boat should be, but it was not there. When Amy's small boat nosed from the cove into the agitated waters of the bay, it began pitching alarmingly. Without waiting for an order, the three crewmen hastily back-oared the boat to the shelter of the cove once more.

They made another search, this time closer to the rocks – and here they found the drifter. It had dragged its ineffectual anchor, and was pitching and bucking close to the black, sea-washed rocks, only a matter of yards from the cove entrance.

With the changing direction of the wind, it could only be a matter of minutes before the drifter dragged anchor once more and was dashed to pieces on the rocks.

'Go alongside – on the lee side,' Nathan called. 'I'm going on board.'

'It's madness,' Calvin Dickin shouted as he leaned on his oar, holding it firm between his body and his one good arm. 'Leave her be. Better to lose a boat than your life.'

'We've lost neither yet – and we're not going to. Get me to the other side of her. *Pull!*'

The fishermen brought the small boat to the far side of the wildly bucking drifter. In the scant shelter offered by the larger craft, they eased Amy's boat in towards it, stern first.

'Take it steady now.' Nathan had made his way to the stern and now he crouched beside Amy, his face protected from the driving rain by an upflung arm.

The dark bulk of the drifter loomed above the small boat now, but neither vessel was still. At one moment the two boats were almost touching, the next they were many feet apart.

'Hold it now. . . . *Hold it!*' Nathan was reaching out but could not quite touch the other vessel. The men behind him heard his cry and strained on their oars to hold the small boat in position. The drifter rose above Nathan; then, as it dropped away, Nathan leaped into the darkness.

For one frightening moment Nathan thought he had misjudged the distance. Then the drifter rose hard to meet him and he tumbled on the half-deck.

'Nathan, *help me! help* . . .!' Amy's cry came from nearby as Nathan scrambled to his knees.

'Where are you? Keep shouting!'

'Here, close to the backstay. Help me – quickly!'

Nathan scrambled across the boat to where the taut rope-stay securing the mast was attached to the side of the boat. He found Amy hanging over the side, her arm hooked about the water-tautened rope. Her body, from the waist downwards, being dipped in the sea every few moments as the drifter rocked violently from side to side.

Putting an arm down, Nathan secured a grip on the sodden dress Amy wore beneath her waterproof coat. Waiting until the roll of the drifter was to his advantage, Nathan heaved Amy inboard and dropped her ignominiously to the bottom of the boat.

'That was a damned foolish trick! What were you doing?'

'C-coming on board w-with you. You can't manage the sails and steer the boat in this w-weather.'

Amy's teeth were chattering as much from fright as from the repeated ducking she had received in the cold water. She had leaped from the smaller boat only seconds after Nathan, but the leap had been badly mistimed. While she was in mid-air the drifter had reared from the water and passed her by. She only just managed to grip the gunwale and hook an arm about the backstay. There she clung like a limpet while the movements of boat and sea combined in a wild attempt to fling her off.

Nathan realised how close Amy had come to death, and the knowledge frightened him as much as it did her. But Amy was right. It would take two of them if they were to have a real chance of saving the drifter. The weather was far more severe than he had realised.

'Help me to shorten the anchor rope.' He shouted the words, his lips close to her ear. 'We've got to get away from the rocks before we risk raising any sail.'

They both made it safely to the bow of the drifter, and then began the gruelling task of hauling the rope in, and so pulling the boat away from the rocks. They had to be very careful. If they brought the boat too close to the anchor, the force of the swell would combine with the movement of the drifter to dislodge the anchor from the bed of the cove.

They worked for twenty minutes before Nathan called a halt.

'That's it. You take the wheel while I hoist a sail. Steer across the cove. When I feel the wind begin to take us I'll cut through the anchor rope.'

Amy crawled away towards the wheel. Giving her time to unlash the rope that held the wheel, Nathan close-hoisted the foresail. He dared not hoist the larger lugsail in this wind; it was

122

strong enough to overturn a larger boat than the drifter. As it was, the wind threatened to sweep them inside the cove, complete with dragging anchor.

When the boat started straining into the wind, Nathan cut through the anchor rope with a couple of slashes from the sharp knife he wore at his belt – and the drifter was free.

Amy held her course for no more than a minute before bringing the boat about and sailing on the opposite tack. Meanwhile, Nathan worked frantically to adjust the sail and so gain maximum controlled propulsion from the wind.

They tacked twice more before Nathan estimated they must now be well clear of the tiny cove. The violent movement of the boat tended to confirm his view. On the last occasion Amy brought the boat about it seemed they would capsize, and Nathan had to scramble aft to help Amy hold the wheel as the rudder was caught between the will of man and the incredible power of the sea.

'We're clear of the point now.' Amy echoed Nathan's thoughts.

He nodded. 'We'll make for clear water, then put out a sea-anchor and ride this out.'

With the initial excitement over, Amy once more had great difficulty in stopping her teeth from chattering noisily. She had been thoroughly soaked by sea and rain, and the chill of the November night was biting deep into her bones.

By the time Nathan felt they were far enough out from shore to put out a sea-anchor, Amy could no longer hide the effect the cold was having on her. Teeth chattering, she shook uncontrollably. When Nathan came to lash the wheel he was thoroughly alarmed. Then he remembered the dripping figure standing outside the bedroom at Polrudden, and later clinging to the side of the boat. It had been a long, cold and exhausting night for Amy.

'Come on, you need to get out of those clothes and into something dry.'

As he put an arm about her shoulders to help her inside the shelter of the small and shallow hold, Amy tried to protest that she could manage by herself, but she was unable to stop her teeth from chattering for long enough to put the words together.

Sheltered from the wind, Nathan rummaged through a locker and found the spare shirt and trousers he always kept there.

'Get your things off and put these on.' Nathan thrust the dry clothing into her hands, and she promptly dropped them again.

Picking them up, Nathan said: 'You'd best let me do it for you.'

Amy jerkily voiced her protest, but by the time it was out Nathan had unfastened her soaking 'waterproof' coat and eased it over her shoulders. He unfastened the buttons on the top of her dress, too, but as he tried to slip it down over her shoulders she stopped him. 'I c-c-can do it.'

She was wrong. Amy was so cold that her hands would no longer function. After she had fumbled at the dress for more than five minutes, Nathan completed the task for her.

'Come on now. Everything off – and no arguments.'

In the darkness, Nathan stripped the clothes from Amy's shivering body, pausing only when lightning beyond the open hatchway bared her body to him and Amy vainly attempted to shield her nakedness with her arms.

He slipped the rough flannel shirt over her head and then gave her the trousers to pull on, tying the waist with a piece of cord and rolling up the bottoms of the oversized trousers. Finally he took off his waterproof coat and, pulling off his heavy, fisherman's jersey, handed it to her.

Forestalling her objections, he said: 'Keep it on until you're warmer. There isn't another waterproof, so you'd best stay down here for a while.'

He helped to pull the neck of the jersey over her head and could not prevent a grin as another flash of lightning showed him the small, tired and cold figure in the oversized clothes.

'That was a foolish thing you did back there in the cove. You could have got yourself killed. But it's something I'll never forget. Without you we'd have lost the boat.'

He put an arm about her shoulders in an affectionate gesture, but she shrugged it away, determined not to let him know how much pleasure his words gave her. 'Save your embraces for Mistress Hearle. You and I are business partners, that's all. Without the boat we'd both have suffered. I did what needed to be done. I went to Polrudden for the same reason.'

124

Nathan suddenly realised that he had not thought of Elinor Hearle once since setting out from Polrudden, and he doubted whether he had occupied her thoughts for a moment more. She would be lying in her bed, safe and warm, the storm no more than a rattle of wind against the window.

Nathan wondered how Elinor would have behaved in circumstances such as those he and Amy had encountered tonight. Elinor was a strong-minded girl – a *wilful* girl – but would she have risked her life to save his boat?

Nathan checked his thoughts. He was making unfair comparisons. Elinor was risking much – not least, her reputation – because of their relationship. She, too, was a remarkable girl – and he had fallen in love for the first time in his life.

The dawn brought a welcome improvement in the weather. Thunder still occasionally grumbled far out in the English Channel, but the rain had stopped, and the wind was now no more than a stiff breeze.

Nathan and Amy sailed the drifter to Portgiskey Cove and a welcome from the whole of the crew, Peggy Hoblyn and Sammy Mizler. The relief of everyone was evident, although it was noticeable to Nathan that most of Sammy Mizler's concern was for Amy. She, in her turn, was embarrassed as much by the fishermen's expressed admiration for her heroism as by her unusual garb.

When the boat was safely moored alongside the quay, the events of the night caught up with Nathan and he suddenly felt very, very tired. Picking up his waterproof coat, he announced brusquely that he was going home to Pentuan to sleep, and told Sammy Mizler to ensure that Amy did the same.

'When you've done that I've another job for you. You can paint a name on the boat.'

The fishermen beamed their delight. Putting to sea in an unnamed vessel had troubled them. It was a break with tradition. Such things were likely to bring ill-luck. They would have pointed to the events of the previous night as an example, had not the cut mooring-ropes pointed to the more positive influence of a Mevagissey or Pentuan seiner.

'What's the name to be?'

125

The question came from Calvin Dickin. 'After last night it should be something like *Storm Queen*, I'm thinking.'

'I've a better name than that, Calvin. She'll be called *The Brave Amy H*, and there'll be no fishing-boat with a prouder name.'

Chapter Twelve

IT SEEMED that the wild weather of 1810 had spent itself in the storm which almost wrecked the newly named fishing-boat. From that night the weather steadily improved, and December brought crisp, clear days and skies unscarred by a single cloud.

The first week of December also saw the return of Sir Lewis Hearle to Polrudden. With him came some of the glory the ancient Cornish manor had enjoyed in former days. It seemed that the whole of the country's gentry wished to call upon Sir Lewis in order to offer him their congratulations on his Home Office appointment. There were so many visitors that Sir Lewis was obliged to take on more staff to work in the house, and Elinor assumed the unaccustomed role of hostess to her father's guests.

Suddenly, Polrudden was no place for a lovelorn fisherman.

But not all of Sir Lewis Hearle's visitors came to Polrudden to murmur insincere good wishes and drink his rather less than excellent sherry. There were those who came on more serious business. Among these was the Reverend Nicholas Kent, the Methodist-hating rector of Fowey.

The Reverend Kent was closeted with Sir Lewis Hearle for two hours and left the house a happy man. He believed that at last there was a man in government office who *really* understood the threat posed to the country by the followers of Wesley.

Others spent less time in Sir Lewis Hearle's study – and left Polrudden deeply unhappy. Some even had tears streaming down their sunburned cheeks. These were the tenant farmers who rented their farms from the baronet MP. Many had worked their rented lands for a lifetime, as had their fathers and grandfathers before them. Now Sir Lewis had told them they must prepare to leave. The farms were being sold to raise badly needed money for the newly promoted Member of Parliament.

One of the farmers so affected was Tom Quicke, husband of Nathan's sister. The young farming couple came to Pentuan to break the news to the Jago family when Nathan, Amy, and Sammy Mizler were there. Nell was in a particularly distressed state. She sat in a high-backed chair in the kitchen of the tiny cottage, wringing her hands, the tears that filled her eyes threatening to overflow at any moment.

Nell's undisguised misery surprised Nathan. He was aware that she loved the farm where she and Tom lived, but Nell had always been such a selfless girl. It would have been more in keeping with her nature had she tried to shrug off the grim news in a bid to lessen the blow for her husband.

It was not long before the reason for her deep distress became known, eased on its way by a sudden flood of tears. Nell imparted the news that she was expecting a baby. It would arrive in May 1811. She and Tom had delayed telling anyone until they were absolutely certain.

The news brought delighted congratulations from both Annie and Josiah Jago.

'It's wonderful news . . . just wonderful.' Annie Jago hugged her daughter, then looked pointedly at Nathan. 'I was beginning to wonder whether your father and I would live long enough to see grandchildren in our home.'

'But it's *not* wonderful.' The flow of Nell's tears increased. 'That's what makes Sir Lewis Hearle's decision so heartbreaking. We've nowhere to live, and Tom will have no work. You know what things are like for men who work on the land. More than half are in the county's poor-houses. . . .'

Tom Quicke put an arm about his young wife's shoulders, murmuring that they would manage somehow.

Josiah Jago was embarrassed by his daughter's anguish. An unemotional man himself, he found his aloofness an asset when dealing with those who looked to him for comfort in times of grief, even though it set him apart from the members of his own family. But he cared for his children in his own way and he agonised because he expressed less feeling for them than he had for others.

'Did you tell Sir Lewis Hearle about the baby?'

Tom Quicke nodded ruefully. 'I did. He was quick to tell me that the decision to have a child was mine and not his. He said its future was my concern.'

Josiah Jago shook his head sadly. 'Sir Lewis Hearle is an uncharitable man for one in his position. Now, if he only came to listen to my preaching, I would give him a sermon taken straight from the New Testament. Jesus himself once said—'

128

'What price does Sir Lewis Hearle put on your farm?' Nathan interrupted his father's homily brusquely. The sermon had always been Josiah Jago's answer to the many problems of life. It was one of the reasons why Nathan had run away from home at the age of fifteen.

Tom Quicke was less accustomed to the ways of father and son. He felt uncomfortable at Nathan's abrupt interruption.

'What difference does it make? Be it a thousand guineas, or a hundred, I can raise neither. We've been scratching a living at Venn, no more. The land's improving, but it will – it would have been a while before we made any money. Now, if only I'd had a milking-cow, we'd have brought money in, make no mistake. . . .'

He caught Nathan's eye and blushed.

'I'm sorry; I'm day-dreaming. Even with the best milking-cow in the land I'd never be able to raise enough money to buy Venn. It's beyond the likes of me, as Sir Lewis Hearle knows full well.' For the first time since coming to the cottage, Tom Quicke allowed some of the bitterness he felt to show. 'He's asking a thousand guineas.'

Nathan looked across the room at Sammy Mizler. Correctly interpreting the unasked question, Sammy shook his head. There was not nearly enough money in the partnership to buy a farm, even had the other two partners agreed to the suggestion. There had been a lot of nets to replace, in addition to the everyday expenses associated with fishing.

'Don't give up all hope yet, Tom. Or you Nell. I'll see if I can think of something.'

'Do you think because there's something between you and Elinor Hearle her father will change his mind? Huh! You don't know Sir Lewis – or his daughter.'

In her anger, Amy had spoken without thinking of who was in the room. Now she caught her breath in dismay when Preacher Josiah Jago pounced on her words.

'What kind of talk is this? What can there possibly be between Nathan and the Hearle girl?'

Annie Jago provided the answer that neither Nathan nor Amy could find: 'Amy means that Nathan earned the gratitude of Sir Lewis Hearle by saving his daughter from a beating at the hands of a drunken drayman when she tried to prevent a horse from being mistreated.'

Josiah Jago looked from mother to son suspiciously. 'Why haven't I heard anything about this before?'

'It happened in St Austell when Nathan was on his way home from London. You were too busy getting yourself arrested to know about anything else that was going on. Now, you can all sit down at the table while I serve something up for you. Then we'll talk of babies and the like – not of Sir Lewis Hearle and his doings.'

It was an order that Annie Jago would allow no one to disobey for the remainder of the evening.

Later, Nathan and Sammy Mizler walked Amy to the small cottage at Portgiskey. Since the night the mooring-ropes on *The Brave Amy H* had been cut, one of the men always slept at Portgiskey Cove, in the fishing-store beside the cellar.

Tonight was Sammy Mizler's turn. Sammy would have preferred to walk with Amy without any other company, but Nathan had something to say to his friend.

The opportunity to speak to Sammy alone did not come until the night was well advanced. The three partners sat on the quayside talking until then and, for the first time, Nathan became aware of the easy relationship that now existed between Sammy Mizler and Amy. Indeed, Amy seemed intent upon provoking Nathan into commenting upon their close friendship, but Nathan refused to be drawn and eventually Amy announced that she was going to bed.

When the two men reached the fishing-store, Sammy Mizler said: 'All right, what's on your mind? You've been simmering like a tripe stew all evening. What is it?'

Instead of replying, Nathan took a card from his pocket and handed it to his companion.

Sammy Mizler read the name printed upon the card and looked at Nathan in bewilderment. 'The Duke of Clarence? Where did you get this?'

Nathan told Sammy Mizler of the evening he and Amy had spent at the Dartmouth inn.

Weighing the card in his hand as though it were a nugget of pure gold, Sammy Mizler whistled softly. 'Oi! What an opportunity! What a wonderful opportunity. When I was finding fights for you I'd have given my right arm for such a chance. . . . But why are you showing this to me now?'

The look he saw on Nathan's face caused Sammy to leap to his feet in excitement. 'You've come to your senses at last? Nathan, tell me you're giving up this idea of chasing small fishes for a living. You're going back to the prize-ring?'

'Not quite. But I'll fight again if the purse is right.'

'With the Duke of Clarence as your backer? You'll be able to name your own purse. Five hundred. Six . . . *seven* hundred guineas, even.'

To Sammy's astonishment, Nathan shook his head. 'It needs to be more than that, Sammy. I want you to take that card to the Duke of Clarence in London. Tell him I'm ready to defend my championship against any fighter of his choice – but only if he's prepared to put up a thousand guineas.'

'A thousand!' Sammy Mizler gasped. 'You'll never get it, Nathan. Who has ever heard of a thousand-guinea purse for a prize-fight?'

'Hen Pearce. He defended the title I hold for a thousand guineas in 1805. And who do you think put up the money?'

Sammy Mizler nodded his head vigorously, acknowledging Nathan's prize-fighting knowledge. 'It was the Duke of Clarence. So what do you want me to do?'

'I want you to take a fast coach to London. See the Duke, and tell him my terms. If he agrees, have him use the thousand guineas to buy Venn Farm and make it over to Tom and Nell. Sir Lewis will sell Venn to the Duke of Clarence without asking questions. If *I* try to buy the farm, he'll probably refuse to sell it to me.'

Sammy Mizler had already guessed the reason behind Nathan's return to the ring, but he could not hide his astonishment that Nathan should fight for such a colossal sum – and then give it all away.

'If the Duke of Clarence agrees to put up the purse, I'll leave it to you to arrange everything. Try to get the fight staged close to Cornwall, if you can. I can't spare too much time away from my boat.'

'*Our* boat,' corrected Sammy Mizler softly. 'And what about my share of the purse? Or are you going to give all this money away without consulting me, just as you did with the purse you won from Ned Belcher?'

131

Nathan was unsure whether Sammy Mizler was joking or serious. They *did* have a longstanding arrangement that Sammy should take a percentage of the purse, and he was quite within his rights to demand that Nathan should honour the agreement.

'You'll get your share, but it will have to come from the profits I get from fishing. Nell and Tom need that money desperately.'

'All right! All right!' Sammy Mizler threw up his hands. 'Forget my share. With you in this mood I can guarantee to win twice as much on bets. I just wanted to remind you that I'm doing you a favour, that's all. Besides, what do I want with money – unless I need to get married, maybe?'

Nathan frowned, remembering how Amy and Sammy had behaved together that evening. He wondered if Sammy was trying to tell him something, but the Jewish ex-fighter was already talking about something else.

'When do you want me to leave? I haven't a lot on just now.'

'Good, then go tomorrow. Return to the house and pack your things now. There's a coach from St Austell in the morning that will have you in London in forty hours. I'll stay here tonight.'

Sammy Mizler was taken aback by such haste, but he knew Nathan too well to argue. Besides, this was an opportunity that was too good to pass up. For a while Sammy would be back enjoying the camaraderie of the prize-ring, the fluctuating fortunes of the fighters, and the hurly-burly and feverish excitement of a championship fight.

After Sammy Mizler had gone, Nathan extinguished the fish-oil lamp and lay on the makeshift bed in the fishing-store. No more than a couple of blankets laid upon a pile of new fishing-nets, it was more comfortable than many beds he had known, but sleep was slow in coming. He was not surprised. The prospect of fighting again was both exciting and daunting. In common with Sammy Mizler, Nathan shared a love of the atmosphere of a prize-fight: the noisy crowd; the well-dressed men of the 'Fancy' – the gentlemen who followed the sport; and the awareness that prize-fighting was still illegal. At any moment the local magistrate might appear on the scene with his constables or the militia, bringing a fight to an end amid scenes of wild pandemonium.

Yet, in spite of the thrill of ducking beneath the rope of a ring to the accompaniment of a mighty roar from the crowd, every champion prize-fighter always knew that the man standing in the far corner of the ring at the start of a fight might be the one to beat him and take away his title.

No champion had yet come back from defeat to regain a title. For this reason many tried to enjoy the glory of their titles for as long as possible without fighting in its defence. Others – and Nathan had hoped to be one of them – simply faded from the prize-fighting scene. Investing his hard-earned purses in a small business, more often than not an inn, the ex-champion would content himself with rapidly fading local fame, enjoying a way of life he might otherwise never have known.

All these thoughts came to Nathan as he lay on his fishing-net mattress. He had many other thoughts, too, not all connected with the prize-ring.

There was a strong wind outside, and breakers crashed heavily against the rocks beneath the cliff-base. But it was not raining, and after lying awake for more than an hour Nathan decided to take a walk.

The lights were off in the Hoblyn cottage; Amy and her mother had gone to bed. In the sky above, scattered cloud fled before the wind, intermittently covering the moon.

Turning his jacket collar high about his neck, Nathan walked along the sand before turning inland, returning to Portgiskey after about an hour, approaching the cove along the narrow valley from the Mevagissey road.

He was close to the house, all sound of his approach muffled by the booming surf, when he saw a flicker of light in the vicinity of the quayside, where *The Brave Amy H* was moored. Seconds later the light became a flame that leaped into the air, fanned by the wind.

Nathan began to run. The moon was temporarily hidden behind a cloud, but he was guided by the flickering yellow flames that grew with every second. Nathan's running footsteps on the soft grass of the little-used pathway made no sound – and suddenly the figure of a man loomed up before him.

The other man uttered an exclamation of surprise, but even as the sound left his lips Nathan's fist moved to shut it off.

Nathan knew his blow was a good one, but he did not stop to make certain. He could see now that the fire was inside *The Brave Amy H*. It needed to be extinguished quickly.

There was a second man running along the path from the quay, but he saw Nathan and turned to flee back the way he had come. Nathan was close on his heels by the time he reached the cottage. Unable to escape any other way, the unknown arsonist jumped from the quay. Unfortunately for him, he chose the end of the quay where a huge flat rock was embedded in the sand. Landing awkwardly, he gave a scream of pain that quickly gave way to agonised howling.

Nathan ignored the man's cries. The fire was burning in the nets stowed on board *The Brave Amy H*. Someone had emptied a couple of bags of wood shavings inside the boat and struck a flint to them. Loaded ready to put to sea the moment the wind dropped, there was almost a mile of nets on board. They were valuable – and highly inflammable.

Nathan began pulling the nets from the boat, concentrating on those that were already well alight. He had not been working long when he heard a shout from the quay above him. Looking up, he saw Amy and her mother holding a large wooden tub between them. He just had time to leap out of the way before they tipped the contents of the tub over the edge of the quay.

A cascade of water descended upon the blaze inside the boat. It hissed loudly and raised a cloud of steam, but seconds later the flames were regaining lost ground.

However, with Nathan pulling nets from the boat as fast as the flames would allow, and Amy and her mother attacking the blaze from above, it was possible to prevent any permanent damage being caused to the boat. By the time the last net was pulled clear, the fire had been extinguished, charring no more than a thwart and scorching the boat's paintwork.

As the remains of the nets smouldered on the quay steps, or trailed on the damp sand beside the boat, Nathan strode to where the unknown arsonist had dragged himself to a sitting position, his back propped against a rock. He was groaning less noisily now, but both his hands clutched his right leg, just beneath the knee. The moonlight showed the lower section of the leg extending sideways at an unnatural angle, indicating a serious fracture.

134

'It's broken. . . . My leg's broken.' The man gasped the words painfully.

'You'll wish it was your neck by the time I'm finished with you,' growled Nathan angrily. 'Likely it will be. Setting fire to a man's property is a hanging offence. Why did you do it? I've never seen you before.'

It was the truth, although there was something about the man that was vaguely familiar.

Nathan received no reply and he called for Amy to bring a lantern. In the meantime, he ran back along the path to where he had knocked the second arsonist to the ground. The man had gone.

Returning to the quayside, Nathan found Amy bending over the injured man. She had slit his trousers to the knee and was examining the area about the break. Looking up at Nathan, she said: 'This leg will need to be set. Mother can do it, but she'll need your help.'

'There will be no help from me. He'll hang as well with one leg as with two. What I want to know is, why did he set fire to our boat?'

'He's a seiner. I suppose that was reason enough for him.'

'Perhaps, but it's not for me. You know him?'

'Yes, it's Dick Coffin, from Mevagissey.'

'Coffin?' Nathan looked at the man more closely. Now he thought he knew why he looked so familiar. 'Is he a brother to the Coffin who's a drayman in St Austell?'

'He was a drayman until you cost him his job.' The man on the ground spoke through his pain.

'Is that the man you knocked unconscious in St Austell?' Amy asked the question.

'And again tonight, unless I'm mistaken. You pick up the lantern. I'll drag this one to the storeroom. He can wait for the constable in there.'

'Nathan. . . .' Amy touched his arm as he leaned over the injured man. Leading him some paces away, she said softly: 'Don't inform the constable . . . please. I know Dick Coffin's family. His wife and children – all six of them. The youngest is blind, and Dick is her whole life. He's wonderful with her, he really is.'

'He should have thought of her before coming here and

trying to destroy our boat. It isn't the first time, you know that?'

Amy nodded. 'You have every right to have him arrested. But please don't, I beg you.'

Nathan thought he knew why Amy and his sister Nell were such good friends. They both cared too much about other people.

'Dick Coffin and his brother have cost us a lot of money tonight, Amy – and they damn near cost you your life, too, the last time they came calling. I can't think of one good reason why he shouldn't hang.'

'I can. A little blind girl named Sophie Coffin.'

Nathan looked seriously at Amy for a long while, and she thought he was going to insist on informing the magistrate. Instead, he shrugged. 'Very well. But we're not standing the loss we've suffered tonight. Dick Coffin and his brother will pay for those nets. I don't care how they raise the money, but they *will* pay.'

Amy's whole body sagged in sudden relief. Few people would have criticised Nathan had he insisted upon handing Dick Coffin over to the constable. Not even the Mevagissey fishermen themselves.

'Thank you, Nathan.'

'Go and fetch your mother,' said Nathan gruffly. 'I'll carry Coffin to the store. She can set his leg there. I'll find his brother tomorrow.'

Nathan did not find Bill Coffin the next day, or any other day. Returning home during the night, Bill Coffin made up a bundle of his clothing and left hurriedly, never to be seen in his native Cornwall again.

Chapter Thirteen

UP AT THE first hint of dawn, Sammy Mizler walked to St Austell, arriving in good time for the mail coach. As on the much shorter journey to Plymouth a few weeks before, Sammy travelled inside the coach. He was on his way to call on the Duke of Clarence, son of the reigning monarch. He could not arrive in clothes that had been subjected to rain and spattered by mud thrown up from country roads.

It was the boast of the coach operators that their forty-hour service to London was the fastest the West Country had ever known. It undoubtedly was, but in order to achieve such a time all else had been sacrificed to speed. The journey was a nightmare of jolting and jarring on indifferent roads, and was accompanied by constant noise. There were squealing coach springs, complaining passengers, drumming hooves, the shouts of the driver, and the long, drawn-out note of the coach horn warning tollmen of their rapid approach.

For Sammy Mizler, all discomfort became worthwhile when potholed, rutted roads gave way to the cobbled streets of London. Life inside the coach became more bearable as the volume of traffic and the hazards of London at dusk forced the coach driver to slacken his pace.

That night, with the sounds of London in his ears, and its sulphurous night odour in his nostrils, Sammy Mizler slept more soundly than he had for many months.

The next morning he rose late and dressed slowly and carefully. At noon he summoned a hackney carriage, taking snobbish delight in instructing the cabbie to take him to Almack's Club, the most fashionable establishment in London's St James's. Sammy had been told by reliable friends that it was here he was most likely to find the sporting Duke of Clarence.

Sammy Mizler's pride suffered a blow at Almack's, when an immaculately liveried doorman blocked his path and directed him to the back door before Sammy had uttered a single word. His reply was to grasp the haughty doorman about the waist, lift him with deceptive ease to one side, and stride in through the open doorway. Immediately, he was surrounded by a whole host of club employees and bustled hurriedly to a large office. Sammy could have taken them all on and beaten them without too much difficulty, but he had come here to arrange a fight, not to become involved in one himself.

In the office a man jumped to his feet and one of the men surrounding Sammy explained quickly what had happened.

'This man was stopped at the entrance, Mr McAlmack, but he forced his way in.'

'I was told to go to the back door before I had time to state my business,' Sammy Mizler interrupted the speaker. 'I objected – peaceably.'

The club employee began speaking again, but McAlmack cut him short with an impatient wave of his hand. Speaking in a clipped Scots accent, he asked Sammy Mizler: 'And just what *is* your business?'

'I'm here to see the Duke of Clarence.'

McAlmack's eyebrows rose so high they merged with the grey hair that hung down over his forehead. 'Indeed? And who shall I tell his Grace is here to speak to him?'

'My name is Sammy Mizler, but I'm here on behalf of Nathan Jago.' Sammy reached inside his pocket and drew out the card the Duke had presented to Nathan. 'The Duke gave him this, some time ago.'

McAlmack glanced at the card and waved his staff from the room, brushing them before him with his hands. When they had all gone, he said to Sammy: 'You'll stay here while I speak to his Grace. But I give you due warning, Mizler. If he doesn't wish to talk to you, I'll call the constables and have you charged with forcing your way in here.'

'He'll see me,' replied Sammy Mizler, with more confidence than he felt. Without even putting his mind to the matter, he could think of many reasons why the Duke of Clarence might not wish to speak to him. Prize-fighting *was* an illegal sport, and even dukes of royal blood were not above the law.

Sammy Mizler need not have worried. A few minutes later McAlmack hurried to the office and held the door open for him.

'If you'll come this way, Mr Mizler, his Grace will be pleased to receive you.'

Sammy Mizler's relief was tinged with nervousness. He was

138

over the first hurdle, but now he had to persuade the Duke of Clarence to back Nathan on terms that Sammy himself believed to be unrealistic.

McAlmack knocked at a door and waited with his ear pressed against it until he heard a muffled 'Come in!' Opening the door, he pushed Sammy inside and bowed low.

'Your Grace, my Lords. Mr Mizler.'

There were four men seated about a table on which were strewn cards, money, and a number of glasses and bottles. At the far end of the room a fire burned cheerfully. The heat inside the room was such that Sammy wished he had removed his heavy worsted overcoat before stepping inside.

As McAlmack backed from the room, Sammy Mizler bowed to each of the men about the table in turn. He had seen them all before – at prize-fights. In addition to the Duke of Clarence, there was the Marquess of Queensberry, Lord Pomfret and Sir Francis Boynton. Each was an enthusiastic follower of prize-fighting.

'I believe you've come here on behalf of Nathan Jago? What does he want, sponsorship for a fight, I suppose, eh?' The Duke of Clarence's manner was as bluff as his appearance, but he was smiling and Sammy Mizler was given new hope.

'Yes, your Grace. He says he'll fight anyone of your choosing – but he wants a purse of a thousand guineas.'

'A thousand guineas?' The Duke of Clarence's astonishment was echoed in the gasps of his companions. 'I could be tempted to step inside a ring myself for a thousand guineas. What does Jago want with such a sum? Is he in trouble?'

Sammy Mizler realised that his only hope of persuading William, Duke of Clarence to put up a purse for Nathan's fight lay in telling him the truth.

The four men listened in silence until Sammy Mizler had finished talking, then they exchanged glances among themselves.

'So this is to be Jago's last fight,' mused the Duke of Clarence.

'Jago's always drawn a good crowd,' declared the Marquess of Queensberry. 'I'm willing to put up two hundred and fifty guineas of the purse.' He looked at his companions. Both Lord Pomfret and Sir Francis Boynton nodded.

'Then I'll gladly put up the other two hundred and fifty.' The Duke of Clarence looked thoughtfully at Sammy Mizler. 'Jago has his thousand guineas. But I'm damned if I'll get involved in any village politics – and I'll act as no estate agent for a prize-fighter. I'll arrange for the purchase of this farm to be made through my brother's Duchy of Cornwall office. They are buying and selling land all the time, as far as I can make out. What they do will excite no curiosity. Now, about the fight itself. I'm not going to be made to look a fool by having Jago fall to the ground at the first punch and walk off with a thousand guineas in his pocket. Jago gets his money, but only if he wins, or is still on his feet after, say, *twenty* rounds? Is this understood?'

Sammy Mizler nodded. He was confident that Nathan could beat any fighter in the British Isles.

'I've not finished yet. There is one more condition. If Jago wins this fight, he'll defend his title again – at Bushy Park. But this time for a nominal purse.'

Bushy Park was where the Duke of Clarence lived. It had been the venue for many famous prize-fights in recent years.

Sammy Mizler hesitated, reluctant to commit Nathan to two fights.

'Those are my conditions, Mizler. You can accept them or refuse. Just as you wish.'

'I accept them, your Grace.' Sammy Mizler fervently hoped that Nathan thought his sister Nell's future was worth *two* fights.

'Good. Pull up a chair and have a drink while we discuss a suitable opponent for Jago. It will need to be someone very good if we're to draw a crowd large enough to cover a thousand-guinea purse.'

Sammy Mizler did not return to Pentuan until seventeen days after his departure, with Christmas only a week away. His return journey had not been without incident. First, the coach had been held up by a highwayman when no more than ten miles out of London. The would-be thief had been shot dead by one of the passengers, a wounded artillery officer returning from the Peninsular Wars. Then, crossing the high expanse of Dartmoor, the coach was caught in a blizzard. For a whole night passengers and coachman huddled together inside the coach to keep warm while the driver floundered through deep snow with the unhitched horses, in a desperate bid to find help. The shivering passengers were dug out the following day by French prisoners-of-war from Dartmoor prison. Afterwards, the same prisoners dragged the carriage through the snow until they reached a more sheltered spot, where fresh horses were hitched up to take the coach on its way.

But the story of Sammy Mizler's adventures would have to await a quiet evening beside the fire in Amy Hoblyn's Portgiskey home. Nathan was eager to know the result of Sammy's mission to the Duke of Clarence.

As Sammy had anticipated, Nathan was not pleased with the condition that meant he would have to fight again at Bushy Park. It would mean a long spell away from fishing. However, that was in the future. The main consideration was that he had saved Venn Farm for Nell and Tom – providing, of course, he did not lose the first fight. But Nathan entertained no thought of losing. Sammy Mizler had done well. Nathan told him so and asked who he would be fighting.

Some of Sammy Mizler's pleasure at Nathan's praise faded a little.

'You're to fight Abraham Dellow, an American sailor. His ship is expected in Bristol from Africa, bound for America, some time in January. A horseman will be sent to tell us of its arrival. He'll also carry a letter with full details of where the fight is to be held, but I've been assured it will be in the Bristol area. I spoke to the London agents of the ship and I've been able to make a good deal for our fish with them. They'll take all the pilchards we can let them have in Bristol. But they want them double-cured. They'll be going to the West Indies. They also insist on thirty-two-gallon hogsheads, but they're willing to pay fifty shillings per hogshead.'

Nathan made some rapid mental calculations. 'That's half as much again as normal rates!'

Sammy Mizler nodded. But Nathan was already thinking of something else.

'What ships would ask for double-salted pilchards on the West Indies run . . .?' Sudden enlightenment came to Nathan. 'Slavers! We'll be selling to slave-ships.'

141

'So? We'll be doing the slaves a service. From us they'll **get** good fish. Many others aren't so fussy about what they sell.'

'I thought the slave trade had been abolished. I seem to remember Methodists throughout the world holding a day of prayer and thanksgiving.'

Sammy snorted. 'Slavery has been abandoned *here*, and British ships aren't supposed to carry slaves anywhere in the world, but hang an American flag on the yardarm and the business becomes legal. Anyway, such matters are best left to the reformers. We're running a business – and we give good value for money. Leave me to attend to the sales. You catch the fish – and train for your fight.'

Chapter Fourteen

THE messenger from Bristol reached Pentuan at the end of January 1811, on a day when breath hung on the air like a formless spectre. Arriving at the house when Preacher Josiah Jago was at home putting the finishing touches to a new series of sermons for the coming year, the startled messenger scarcely had time to catch his breath before he was hustled from the house. Nathan sent him on his way with half a guinea for board and lodging in St Austell.

Nathan had managed to keep the forthcoming fight a secret from his family. Indeed, Sammy was the only other man in Cornwall who knew that the prize-fighting champion of all England would soon be defending his title.

Prior to the arrival of the messenger, Nathan and Sammy Mizler spent at least an hour each day in sparring practice on the lonely cliff-edge above Portgiskey Cove. But Nathan continued to fish, taking *The Brave Amy H* out on the unseasonably calm waters of St Austell Bay, adding to the large amount of fish being double-salted in the Portgiskey fish-cellar.

Nathan had tried on more than one occasion in recent weeks to speak to Elinor Hearle, but Polrudden remained a very busy manor-house. Coaches and riders arrived and left at all hours of the day and night, and Nathan could never get close to her. He did see Elinor once from a distance as she rode in the company of a man of considerable elegance. Nathan thought she looked in his direction, but she showed no recognition and he consoled himself with the belief that she probably had not recognised him.

The journey to Bristol was to be made in *The Brave Amy H*, and the boat would be heavily laden with salted pilchards for the West Indian trade. Sammy was unhappy about making a sea-voyage around the toe of England, but he would not allow Nathan out of his sight with such a short time to go before the fight.

Calvin Dickin and Ahab Arthur were to crew the heavily laden fishing-boat to Bristol. Neither had been told of the forthcoming fight. Such secrecy was necessary in order to keep

Preacher Josiah Jago from learning the truth. Nathan knew his father would not hesitate to send word to his fellow-Methodists in Bristol. They would inform the authorities and have the fight stopped.

Because of the need for secrecy, it came as a shock to Nathan when he arrived at Portgiskey on the day of departure to find Amy waiting in the boat with Calvin Dickin and Ahab Arthur.

Bubbling with excitement, she answered Nathan's sharp question happily. 'I'm coming with you to Bristol. I'm looking forward to it very much. My pa used to tell me that Bristol is the finest sea-port in the land. He went there many times. Now I'll be able to see it for myself.'

'This isn't a holiday trip. Who said you could come?'

Nathan's tone of voice was sharply disapproving. Amy's elation vanished with the realisation that Nathan did not want her on board *The Brave Amy H* for the voyage to Bristol.

'Sammy told me I could come – and you don't have to worry yourself about carrying a passenger. I'll do my share of the work, and I won't get in your way.'

With this remark, Amy turned away from Nathan and went forward, out of sight behind the hogsheads of pilchards piled dangerously high in the boat. Nathan realised that he had robbed Amy of much of the thrill she had felt at going to Bristol. The knowledge did nothing to improve his temper when he tackled Sammy Mizler a few minutes later.

'Why did you tell Amy she could come to Bristol with us? It's a damned foolish idea.'

Sammy Mizler's eyebrows rose only very slightly. 'I thought we were all partners? I mean, if she wants to come to Bristol in *our* boat, who has the right to say "No"? Not me. Not even you.'

'That has nothing to do with anything, and you know it.'

'I know only that you're angry with Amy for no good reason. I was speaking to her about Bristol, telling her what a wonderful city it is. She hung on every word, as though I were talking of Paradise, maybe. When she says how much she would like to go there, I ask: "Then why not come with us?" You don't have to worry about her, Nathan. You should know that already. She's a sensible girl – and I'll look after her.'

'Your job is to look after *me*,' Nathan snapped, but at that

144

moment the two members of the crew who were to remain behind put in an appearance and he did not pursue the matter further. During the absence of *The Brave Amy H* the crew would be kept busy repairing nets and overhauling fishing-tackle.

Sammy Mizler knew from past experience that much of the all-England champion's edginess was due to thought of the forthcoming fight. Nathan was always this way for days before a contest. It was as though he needed to build up a deep reserve of aggression that would spill out when he entered the ring with his opponent.

But Amy knew nothing of this. She believed Nathan was in a bad mood simply because he did not want her to go to Bristol with him.

The voyage turned out to be far smoother than Nathan and Sammy had dared hope. Rounding Land's End on the afternoon of the first day, they picked up a useful westerly breeze. Anxious to make the most of such favourable conditions, Nathan decided they would sail all night instead of putting into shelter. Taking the boat out a couple of miles from shore, a course was set for Bristol.

In spite of such good weather conditions, Sammy Mizler was extremely sea-sick, but he received no sympathy from anyone but Amy. Ignoring the grins and jibes of Calvin Dickin and Ahab Arthur, she crouched on the deck beside Sammy and held his head in her lap, talking to him as though he were an invalid child.

During the night Sammy Mizler's stomach seemed to accept the unaccustomed, gently rocking environment in which it found itself, and by morning he was able to make his groggy way aft to where Nathan stood at the wheel. Well wrapped up against the cold, Sammy settled himself in the stern – upwind of Nathan's pipe.

'Feeling better now, Sammy?'

Sammy Mizler nodded unhappily. 'This morning I'm satisfied I'll live. Last night I didn't *want* to. You don't understand such a feeling, Nathan?'

Nathan took the pipe from his mouth. 'If you're asking if I've ever been sea-sick, the answer is "No". But I can think of at least two great sailors who were always sick for the first day or two of every voyage. One was an admiral, the other a commodore.' Nathan gave Sammy Mizler the first grin he had seen from him in thirty-six hours. 'But neither of them ever had such a comfortable pillow as you.'

'Amy's a good girl, Nathan. A very special girl. I . . . I'm very fond of her.'

Something in Sammy Mizler's voice stopped Nathan from making a flippant reply.

'You're not thinking of taking things any farther, Sammy?'

'Why not? Because I'm Jewish?'

It was the first time Sammy Mizler had ever mentioned his Jewish origins to Nathan, and it came as a shock to realise that Sammy thought of himself as 'different' from his fellow-men. It had never mattered to Nathan. Yet this was an age when Jews were still barred from governmental posts, foreign-born Jews were not allowed to take out British citizenship, and there was much prejudice levelled against them. It would be another fifty years before Great Britain afforded them the full benefit of its laws.

'You know better than that, Sammy. I'm concerned only because you're city born and bred. Amy is part of Cornwall. She would never settle to city life – any more than you'll ever be able to make the country your permanent home.'

'I'll stay in Cornwall, if that's what Amy wants,' retorted Sammy Mizler. 'If she would agree to marry me, I'd even become a fisherman. . . .'

Nathan turned away from Sammy Mizler and studied the sea ahead of the drifter. He knew he should be wishing Sammy well, telling him he hoped he would win the girl he loved, but the words would not come. He told himself it was because he cared for both Amy and Sammy Mizler; because they were totally unsuited for each other. A marriage between them would prove disastrous.

At that moment a heavily laden merchantman, outward bound from Bristol, and only a few hundred yards from *The Brave Amy H*, changed course. Tacking close to the wind, the vessel bore down upon the Cornish drifter. Nathan had to put the wheel hard over very quickly to avoid being run down. The movement brought Calvin Dickin hurrying to the stern of the boat.

146

After cursing the helmsman on the merchantman for a fool, Calvin Dickin settled down to tell his companions of his escapades when he had last visited the port of Bristol.

Nathan found he was not in the mood to listen to sailors' tales. Handing over the helm to Calvin Dickin, he found a space between the barrels shielded from the wind. Wrapping a couple of blankets about him, he went to sleep.

When Nathan awoke, *The Brave Amy H* was in the Bristol Channel. The rugged cliffs of Devon, backed by the green heights of Exmoor, were to the south. Farther away, on the port side, were the dark hills of Wales, with the tall, foul-smoking chimneys of the Swansea smelting-houses in the foreground.

There was much more shipping about now, boats of every description: wide, flat-bottomed estuary barges; fishing-boats; merchantmen from all the continents of the world. Among them was a sleek, Baltimore-built schooner. With its raked masts and combined fore-and-aft and square rig, such a vessel could outsail any ship afloat. The Baltimore schooner overtook *The Brave Amy H* rapidly, its sharp bow slicing through the water like a knife, leaving a single, narrow wake to mark its passing.

The Brave Amy H reached the entrance to the Avon river soon after noon, then waited for two hours until the tide was sufficiently high for the waiting vessels to enter the river safely. The port of Bristol was some six miles up-river. Ships making their way there had to negotiate a series of narrow bends and high-walled gorges along the way.

A pilot vessel was the first to enter the river, followed closely by the first of the merchantmen. A small vessel, her captain took advantage of his ship's shallow draught to gain an early berth. *The Brave Amy H* entered the river sixth in line, passing many larger vessels still awaiting deeper water.

Reaching the Bristol Docks, Nathan haggled with the Bristol Docks boatmen before *The Brave Amy H* was taken in tow by an eight-oared longboat and taken to a pre-arranged berth at Welsh Back, close to the Llandoger Trow, an old and noisy tavern.

Darkness was falling, but in spite of the late hour a lighter was brought alongside *The Brave Amy H* and the unloading of the hogsheads of salted pilchards went on until the drifter had been emptied of its cargo. But the day's work was not over yet. The boat reeked of fish and fish-oil that had leaked from the hogsheads. The small crew set to, cleaning the boat from stem to stern, until Amy declared she was satisfied.

By now it was almost midnight, but the noise from the Llandoger Trow had not diminished and Nathan suggested they should take advantage of the tavern's facilities. Not wishing Amy to be subjected to the attentions of the tavern's noisy customers, Calvin Dickin and Ahab Arthur were sent to fetch brandy with which to celebrate the sale of their cargo.

Although she was tired, Amy was too full of excitement to contemplate sleep. She chattered about the places she intended visiting while she was in the great port. However, when she found her companions would not tell her of their own plans, she lapsed into a hurt silence.

Neither Sammy Mizler nor Nathan could say anything about their plans until they had visited Clifton Down, the venue for the prize-fight, on the following day. Whilst there Sammy Mizler would satisfy himself about the arrangements for seconds, timekeeper, referee and all the other officials, in discussion with the men responsible for staging the championship fight.

The two men left *The Brave Amy H* together the next morning. After inspecting the natural amphitheatre where the fight was to be staged, they walked back to the heart of Bristol for an early lunch with the Duke of Clarence's men. Afterwards, Nathan left Sammy to complete the final arrangements for the fight and returned to *The Brave Amy H*.

He found Calvin Dickin and Ahab Arthur splicing new stays on the drifter's mainmast. They were in good humour, having spent an hour at the Llandoger Trow enjoying good Bristol ale.

In sharp contrast to the two fishermen, Amy sat on the jetty dejectedly lobbing pebbles at the still waters of the harbour. Her expression lightened momentarily when she saw Nathan, but then she resumed her desultory pastime with increased vigour.

Nathan hesitated for only a moment. He knew she was unhappy because he and Sammy had not taken her with them when they set off that morning, and had not told her where they were going. It had been Nathan's hope to keep the fight forever a secret from his father, but he had already accepted that it was a forlorn hope. When Nathan secured Venn Farm for Nell and her husband, Josiah Jago would have to know from whence the money had come. He spared little thought for anything other than his religion, but he would know that such money could not be earned from a few months' fishing. But Josiah Jago would not learn of the fight in time to have it stopped now, so there was no reason why Amy and the two crewmen should not know the real reason for the voyage to Bristol.

Nathan sat down beside Amy, but she chose to pay no attention to him and viciously aimed pebbles at a worm-eaten piece of wood floating six feet from the side of the quay.

'I'm sorry Sammy and I couldn't take you with us this morning. There was something we had to do.'

'I'm *sure* there was!' Amy's stone splashed a full ten feet away from the inoffensive target.

The two fishermen had stopped their work to listen, and Nathan addressed his next words to them.

'Sammy and I couldn't tell you before we left Pentuan why we were coming to Bristol. Had word got back to my father, he would have found a way to stop us.'

Nathan had Amy's full attention now. 'The *real* reason . . .? We came to sell fish.'

'No – although bringing the hogsheads here provided us with a very profitable excuse. I'm here for a prize-fight. The Championship of all England will be at stake tomorrow afternoon on Clifton Down, above the gorge. There's room for the whole of Bristol there, should they choose to come along. Sammy and I have been to inspect the place this morning.'

Calvin Dickin gave an evil chuckle. When Nathan looked at him quizzically, the fisherman glanced mischievously at Amy.

'That isn't where Amy thought you were. She was certain you was spending your time with some of they women Ahab and I saw cavorting in the Llandoger Trow last night.'

Looking at Amy, Nathan saw her cheeks had turned a fiery scarlet. But her eyes met his boldly, and he knew she was thinking of the stormy night when she had called him from the bed of Elinor Hearle.

Her expression dared him to comment on Calvin Dickin's observation as she said briefly: 'We all make mistakes.'

Nathan felt happier now there were no secrets between them. When the many questions about the fight had been answered, he said to Amy: 'Put your things in a bag. We have rooms at an inn for a couple of nights. We'll go there now and you can change into that pretty dress I'm sure you've packed. You and I are going to see something of Bristol. You haven't come all this way to spend your days throwing stones in the dock.'

Some of the excitement that Amy had shown before leaving Pentuan returned to her. She leaped from the edge of the quay to the drifter and disappeared inside the hold.

Ahab Arthur watched her go and shook his head wistfully. Turning to Nathan, he said quietly: 'It doesn't take more than a kind word from you to make that maid happy, Nathan. Take care; it's a heavy responsibility. You can break her heart just as easily.'

Thinking of what Sammy Mizler had said to him on the voyage, Nathan made no reply. Instead, he flipped two golden guineas to the two fishermen. 'Here, finish your work, then go off and enjoy yourselves. We have rooms at the Golden Fleece, hard by the bridge. We'll all meet up there later.'

Amy came from the hold carrying a bulging leathern bag over her shoulder. She reached a hand up to Nathan and, taking it, he lifted her easily to the jetty and relieved her of the bag.

Walking beside Nathan, Amy took three happy steps to two of his, occasionally skipping to keep up when she fell half a pace behind.

'Am I going too fast for you?' Nathan had been walking along lost in his own thoughts about the fight that was to take place the next day.

Amy shook her head and took his arm happily. 'No. If I had to walk any slower, I'd bust.' She gave him a coy, sidelong glance. 'I thought this was going to be the most miserable birthday I'd ever spent.'

'Your birthday? Amy, why didn't you tell me before?'

He gave her a hug. 'Does Sammy know?'

When Amy shook her head, Nathan said: 'He should be at the inn by now. We'll meet him there and go out for a special celebration.'

Sammy Mizler was not at the Golden Fleece inn. After waiting for half an hour, Nathan declared they could waste no more of the day, or Bristol would be in darkness before they had seen any of its sights.

The innkeeper provided them with a small open carriage and a driver. Leaving a message for Sammy Mizler, Nathan and Amy set off from the inn.

Bristol was a large and ancient city, but for Amy much of the thrill came from riding in the open carriage, a warm blanket over her knees, tucked about her by the carriage driver.

After they had marvelled at the lofty magnificence of St Mary Redcliffe Church, once described by Queen Elizabeth as 'the fairest, the goodliest, and the most famous church in England,' the driver took them to Clifton Downs. Here they stood on the very edge of the deep, tree-lined gorge of the River Avon. The knowledge that they stood just a single pace from eternity was an exciting, yet frightening, experience.

Next, Amy asked Nathan to show her the spot where the prize-fight was to take place.

Viewing the site from the carriage, Amy asked Nathan a number of questions about prize-fighting, then she fell silent for some minutes. Nathan was about to order the driver to move on, when Amy suddenly looked up at him.

'Why have you decided to fight again, Nathan? I thought you had given up the prize-ring.'

'So did I.'

'Then . . . *why?*'

Nathan found himself tongue-tied, and Amy took his silence as an indication that he did not want to tell her.

'Do you look upon fishing as something you can give up when the prize-ring calls to you, Nathan? Is it just something to keep you amused? It's more than that to me. I look upon fishing as a way of life – a *respectable* way of life. Can you understand what that means to the daughter of a smuggler? Do you know what it's like to spend the whole of your life frightened of everything and everyone? At sea you're suspicious of every boat that draws near. On land you hide whenever a stranger approaches the cottage. I don't want that sort of life any more.'

'I understand, Amy. Fishing isn't just a game for me. It means more to me than any other way of life – more than prize-fighting.'

'Then this will be your last prize-fight?'

151

Nathan thought of the conditions the Duke of Clarence had attached to his thousand-guinea purse. 'No . . . I'll be fighting again.'

Amy bit off the angry retort that came to her lips and turned her head away. 'Then there's no more to be said.'

'Not at the moment,' Nathan agreed. 'But there *is* a reason for what I'm doing. Trust me, Amy.'

She turned to look at him, and for the second time that day he had an uncomfortable feeling that she was thinking of Elinor Hearle. Unconvinced, she said stiffly: 'I'll try.'

Back at the Golden Fleece they found Sammy Mizler waiting for them. He looked hurt that they had been out without him until Nathan explained.

Sammy Mizler was as indignant as Nathan had been that Amy had not mentioned her birthday earlier. Kissing Amy warmly, he hooked his arm through hers. 'Well, now it's my turn to give you a treat. Tonight you'll enjoy the best meal that Bristol can provide.'

Sammy was as good as his word. The landlord of the Golden Fleece provided his guests with a meal that had Amy gasping with delight.

During the meal Sammy Mizler was at his amusing best, and Amy's happy laughter brought smiles to the faces of even the most dour diners at the inn. So happy was she with Sammy that Nathan, by nature more serious than his light-hearted partners, felt himself an interloper. But when he found an excuse to go to his room and leave them together Amy protested that there were still a couple of hours of her birthday remaining. She demanded that her two escorts take her for a walk through the streets of the great sea-port. She would probably never visit Bristol again, she said, and wanted to take away enough memories to last her a lifetime.

Outside the inn they were pounced upon by torch boys carrying pitch torches. For a sum that began at a shilling, and eventually dropped to tuppence, they were offered a light to guide them about the city. Amy refused all their offers. It was a bright, moonlit night and she wanted to savour the atmosphere of the city without the distraction of a flickering, spitting torch held in the hands of a mercenary and garrulous torch boy.

'Where shall we go?' Nathan asked, as they walked three

abreast along the rough cobbled road.

'Let's just go where the whim takes us,' Amy replied. 'But first let's make certain all is well with our boat.'

The boat was as securely moored as when they had left her, and they resumed their walk past the Llandoger Trow. The lights of the waterside tavern shone out like a beacon, attracting many sailors. Ahab Arthur and Calvin Dickin were probably among their number; they had not yet found their way to the Golden Fleece. The din from inside was considerable. Fiddlers were ensconced in every bar room, each playing a different tune, accompanied by an enthusiastic but less-than-tuneful choir. Outside the inn were a number of drabs, either too drunk or too well known to be welcome inside the seamen's tavern.

As the trio passed by the door it opened and two women fell shrieking and clawing into the street. An excited crowd of onlookers swiftly gathered about them, shouting words of encouragement to the combatants.

Soon Amy, Nathan and Sammy Mizler left the sounds of the Llandoger Trow behind and walked beside the docks, the moon reflected dully in the dark, dirty water.

'I have an idea,' said Sammy Mizler suddenly. 'Let's go and have a look at the ship in which Nathan's challenger arrived. She's the *Seneca*, lying at Redcliffe Wharf. We might even see Abraham Dellow training on the deck.'

'At this time of night?' snorted Nathan. 'If he's got any sense at all, he'll be below decks, sleeping in a warm bunk.'

'Is he a good prize-fighter?' Amy asked anxiously. 'I mean, do you think you'll beat him, Nathan?'

'He's good enough to claim he's the "world" champion,' Sammy Mizler replied seriously. 'But Nathan's better. Of that I'm certain. Abraham Dellow has fought no one I've met – and I know all the best prize-fighters.'

Amy shuddered. 'I think it's dreadful that two men should fight each other for money. It's even worse that other men pay money to watch them.'

'If it weren't for prize-fighting, we wouldn't all be partners, with a fine boat and a thriving business,' Nathan pointed out.

'No, and if it hadn't been for prize-fighting I'd as likely as not be skulking in a dark London alley, waiting to relieve some unsuspecting gent of his watch and purse. There were a dozen

153

boys of my age in the street where I was brought up. So far, two have been hanged as footpads and five transported for petty thieving. Thank God for prize-fighting, I say.'

Sammy spoke with great feeling, and Amy hugged his arm sympathetically. 'I'm sorry, Sammy. I was talking without thinking.'

'You were merely expressing your opinion – and why shouldn't you?' Sammy Mizler patted her hand affectionately. 'Would you rather return to the inn?'

'No, let's go and see this ship.'

There were surprisingly few vessels moored in this part of the port. Judging from the accumulation of rubbish, and the derelict warehouses visible in the moonlight, it seemed that this corner of Bristol's sprawling docks was little used. Nathan wondered why *Seneca* was moored here. The answer was soon provided for him.

They saw the ill-lit ship at the far end of a long quay. As they drew closer, Amy wrinkled her nose. 'Ugh! What's that smell? It's foul.'

Sammy Mizler shook his head, but Nathan knew. He had experienced such a smell before. When he was in the Navy his ship had come downwind of a slaver that was sailing with its hatches open. It was the smell from hundreds of captive bodies, shackled together and imprisoned in cramped quarters, with insufficient air and no sanitation.

'*Seneca*'s a slave-ship,' he said. Pulling Amy and Sammy to a halt, he added: 'I don't think we should go any closer. Do you hear that?'

From somewhere ahead of them they could hear the sound of clanking chains. There were other sounds, too. The regular 'crack' of what might have been musket shots – and a low, continuous moaning that set the hairs on the back of Amy's neck tingling. The sound was an expression of human helplessness and despair.

'This is no place for a young girl on her birthday. We'll get you back to the inn.'

'No!' Amy hissed her refusal. 'I want to get closer, to see what's going on.' Snatching her arm from Nathan's grip, she ran towards the sounds.

Taken by surprise, Nathan and Sammy Mizler ran after her.

154

They caught up with Amy as she rounded the hulk of a rotting brigantine, drawn up on the quayside. The sight that met their eyes brought all three to a sudden halt and Amy gasped incredulously.

In the light of no more than three torches held by seamen, a long line of wretched humanity – men, women and small children – stretched from the ship to a man-made cave set high in the cliff beyond the quay. Shackled at wrist and ankle, they were linked to each other by heavy chains that passed through iron belts fastened about their waists. The African slaves moved slowly and painfully, driven on by two men wielding whips.

One of these men, a heavily built white man, wielded his whip enthusiastically, and the bodies of those selected as his targets jerked in pain as the leather lash curled about them. They were unable to escape. All movement was restricted by the slaves in front and behind. It was the sound of this whip that Nathan had mistaken for musket shots.

The second man wielded his whip with rather less enthusiasm. A giant African, his whip cracked for much of the time on empty air, but he shouted all the while, calling to the slow-moving slaves in a language that was unintelligible to Nathan and his two companions.

'Get moving! Jesus, I've never carried a lazier cargo of niggers. You'll need to move faster when you reach America. If you don't, you'll taste more whip than water.'

The whip-wielding white man had the accent of America's deep south.

'Johanson . . .' he called to one of the torch-bearing sailors. 'Get on board and make sure they've made a start washing out the holds. I want this lot back on board before morning.'

One of the female slaves tripped and fell. As she struggled to rise, the movement of the long line of slaves dragged her along with them across the cobbled quayside. The white man used his whip on her brutally, until she finally ceased her efforts to rise and was bumped, a limp, unconscious figure, across the rough stone quayside.

'Check this one when you've got them inside,' the man called to another torch-bearer. 'If she's dead, throw her down with the others. If not, give her a beating she'll remember.'

For the first time, Nathan noticed a heap of some twelve or

fourteen bodies lying on the quayside beside the ship. No doubt they would be carried on board before morning, to lie in a corner of the hold with their live fellows. Once at sea they would be thrown overboard and lost for ever, or perhaps washed up on the shore somewhere, to be buried without ceremony below the high-tide line.

Amy watched the whip-wielding seamen in horror. As the woman, inexorably linked to the other slaves, bumped away like a rag puppet, she cried: 'Nathan . . . *do* something. Stop them . . .!'

'Sh! There's nothing that can be done. Let's get out of here. Now!'

During his naval days, Nathan had experienced more than one encounter with slavers. They were a thoroughly ruthless lot, the very nature of their chosen trade rendering human life cheap. The British government had made slaving in British ships illegal, but slaves were still employed on British plantations in the West Indies and they still occasionally entered British ports when carried in foreign ships. However, William Wilberforce was pursuing a vigorous anti-slavery campaign in Parliament and his cause had many supporters throughout the land, notably among the country's Methodists. This was why *Seneca* had been given a berth as far from inquisitive eyes as possible. It was also the reason why the ship's slave-holds were being cleaned during the hours of darkness.

Nathan had called for the horrified Amy to be quiet, but it was already too late. Her cry had been heard. Peering into the darkness, the big, whip-wielding white man called for a torch. As one of the seamen ran after him, he advanced towards Nathan, Amy and Sammy Mizler.

'What are you doing here? Who are you?'

'We're three people who were enjoying a pleasant moonlit walk until we came across you.'

'Ah! So you've got delicate innards, have you? I don't suppose it'll put you off enjoying a spoonful or two of sugar in your toddy when you get home. And you' – the slaver reached across and fingered the cloth of Amy's coat – 'who do you think picked the cotton for this? I'll tell you. It was slaves.'

He jerked his head derisively in the direction of the slaves who were now disappearing into the cavern opening. 'They're

156

like animals. Show 'em who's boss and you'll have no trouble. Treat 'em like humans and they'll turn on you. This is what they understand.' He cracked the whip in his hand expertly.

Unexpectedly, Sammy Mizler reached out and casually took the whip from the seaman's hand. Before anyone could make a move to stop him, he snapped it in two across his knee and tossed it far out into the waters of the harbour.

'What the hell?'

The American took an angry step forward. Sammy Mizler held his ground and, putting his face close to the seaman's, said: 'I once heard a man say similar words about my people. I'm a Jew.'

Sammy Mizler made the flat statement softly and proudly, but it brought a sneer to the slaver's face. 'I don't know who that man was, but I reckon I wouldn't argue with him. There ain't much to choose between niggers, Indians and Jews when you get right down to it. They all need to be taught their place.'

The seaman made a grab at Sammy Mizler – but he grabbed air. Sammy Mizler ducked quickly and poked out two swift left jabs. As the American seaman staggered back, Sammy went after him. Seizing the dazed man by the shoulder, he turned him around. With his other hand gripping the back of the seaman's belt, Sammy propelled him to the edge of the quay and hurled him into the dock.

The American's cry of protest ended abruptly as the water closed over his head. Behind him on the quayside the seaman holding the blazing torch shouted. Answering cries came from the ship, demanding to know what was happening.

'Good work, Sammy,' Nathan took Amy's hand. 'Now it's time we got far away from this place – and I'll have no arguing from you, young lady.'

With Sammy holding Amy's other hand, they ran back the way they had come, until the cries behind them were lost in the familiar sounds coming from the waterside taverns.

When they eventually stopped running, Amy was so breathless it was difficult to know whether she was laughing or crying.

'Sammy, you were wonderful! But those people. That poor woman . . .'

Used to standing in the shadow of Nathan's prize-fighting

achievements, Sammy Mizler was unaccustomed to taking on the role of a hero. He held Amy self-consciously as she clung to him. 'There's nothing we can do tonight, but I don't doubt we've saved more than one slave from a whipping.'

'We might have done much more than that,' said Nathan thoughtfully. 'The man you threw into the dock had the build of a prize-fighter. You might have just thrashed the so-called "world champion".'

Chapter Fifteen

NATHAN was wrong. Emile Levinsky, boatswain of the Baltimore-built clipper *Seneca*, was in the ring opposite Nathan the following day, but he was acting as a second. The man Nathan would fight was the huge African who had been wielding the second whip on Redcliffe Wharf.

Levinsky recognised his assailant and glared angrily across the ring at Sammy from his one good eye. The other was tightly closed and impressively discoloured. Sammy did his best to ignore the American seaman, but as he went about his business in the corner he gave Nathan a whispered warning.

'Watch Dellow for dirty tricks, Nathan. His corner will desperately want to win the fight now, and we already know what manner of men they are.'

Nathan nodded, eyeing his opponent across the ring. The African was huge, being at least four inches taller than Nathan, and more than forty pounds heavier. But it was also apparent that the cold weather was not to his liking. He had a heavy blanket thrown about his shoulders, yet still shivered uncontrollably.

Sammy had also seen the challenger's discomfort. 'Make the fight last, Nathan. The longer it goes, the better it will be. And make the rounds short. The more time Dellow spends sitting in his corner, the colder he's going to be. If a round looks as though it's lasting too long, take a drop. None of the spectators will complain about a long fight. The only one who won't enjoy it is Abraham Dellow.'

Nathan nodded once more, only half-listening. He was busy watching the other corner. *Seneca*'s boatswain was instructing his fighter in very much the same way as Sammy Mizler – but Abraham Dellow was listening as though his very life depended upon remembering every word.

With Nathan and Sammy Mizler in the ring was Calvin Dickin. He was to act as Nathan's 'knee man'. His job was to provide Nathan with a knee to sit on in the intervals between rounds. In London, the knee had been replaced by a stool for a while, but there had recently been an unfortunate incident when an irate second, incensed at a referee's decision, had cracked the misguided adjudicator's skull with the stool. Referees were now insisting that fighters should revert to the more traditional knee man.

Calvin Dickin's secondary role would be to help Sammy Mizler get Nathan to the mark in the centre of the ring at the end of each thirty-second break. This was a most important task. If a boxer failed to come up to the mark and stand there unaided, the fight was given to his opponent.

Amy was also watching the fight, but from the outer ring. The only woman to been seen anywhere near the prize-ring, she had been taken into the Duke of Clarence's party and they had taken up a position close to Nathan's corner.

The Duke of Clarence was accompanied by two other dukes, three marquesses, and a large number of earls and barons. Looking at them, Sammy Mizler commented drily that one could be forgiven for thinking it was Agincourt, and not Clifton Down.

The Duke of Clarence brought Amy to Nathan's corner shortly before the fight began, to wish him well. After a lengthy conversation with Sammy Mizler, carried on in low tones that did not carry to Nathan, the Duke made Amy take his arm. He then escorted her back to his party with great dignity.

'The Duke wanted to know what I thought of your chances,' said Sammy casually, when the Duke of Clarence had gone. 'I told him you were a sure winner, so he's gone to lay a few wagers. He'll cover your purse *and* make himself a handsome profit, too, I don't wonder.'

'I hope you're right,' grunted Nathan. Abraham Dellow was a big man. No doubt he also possessed a big punch. Nathan would need all his skills to avoid walking into one of them.

The referee for the fight was a serving cavalry officer, approved by both sides. Now he stepped inside the single-rope ring, inspected the mark, then called both fighters to the centre of the ring to ask if they both understood the rules of prize-fighting. Still wrapped in his blanket, Abraham Dellow stared at Nathan and appeared to be paying scant attention to what the referee was saying, but he nodded vigorously enough when pressed for an answer.

Both fighters returned to their corners for last-minute

instructions while the referee spoke to the two timekeepers. Suddenly, Amy was at Nathan's corner, just outside the ropes. Unfastening a blue silk scarf, a very recent purchase, from about her neck, she tied it to the rope beside Nathan. The act brought a chorus of howls and catcalls from the huge crowd that had gathered to view the prize-fight.

Her face scarlet, Amy said breathlessly: 'The other man has a scarf in his corner. The Duke of Clarence says most prize-fighters show them, but you never have. I thought it was time you did.'

She hesitated, very much aware that the eyes of every man in the vast crowd were upon her. 'The Duke also told me why you're fighting – for Nell and Tom. I'm proud of you, Nathan. Very proud. I wanted you to know that before you started fighting.'

Leaning over the rope, she kissed Nathan quickly, then fled back to the Duke of Clarence as the whole crowd erupted in a tumult of cheers and whistles.

Displaying no outward signs of jealousy, Sammy Mizler said dourly: 'Well, Amy might have swung the crowd over to your side, but don't expect Abraham Dellow to kiss your cheek. His corner is warming him up for action.'

In the far corner, Boatswain Levinsky had his man running hard on the spot in an effort to warm up his muscles. Moments later the referee ducked out of the ring and called on the fighters to take up their stances at the mark.

Nathan was wearing a heavy jersey and he slipped it over his head. Stripped to the waist, he took up a position in the centre of the ring. At the same time, Abraham Dellow let the blanket fall from his shoulders. A gasp went up from the crowd. Dellow was magnificently muscled, but his back was criss-crossed with the scars of a lashing such as few men might have been expected to survive.

Abraham Dellow took up a stance facing Nathan. At another signal from the referee, both men began to circle cautiously about each other. Their seconds shouted encouragement from inside the ring, where they would remain for the whole of the fight.

Nathan struck the first blow after half a minute of wary circling. It was a good punch, landing high on Dellow's cheek, and brought a faint show of blood from the broken skin. Dellow brushed at it as he might a fly that had settled on him and immediately countered with a right that sang past Nathan's ear. There followed a flurry of blows before Nathan was tripped and knocked to the ground. It was a perfectly legitimate move, and the end of the first round was called.

In his corner, the fighter from the slave-ship was fed brandy and water in an attempt to put more warmth in his body. Boatswain Levinsky was also drinking heavily from the same flagon, possibly for the same reason.

The second round got off to a brisker start than the first, Dellow coming off the mark full of aggression. As Nathan had already realised, the huge African had little prize-fighting skill, but he carried a devastating punch in each of his fists. This round lasted for eight minutes before one of Dellow's mighty blows exploded against the side of Nathan's head and he fell to the ground, stunned.

Dragged to his corner by Sammy Mizler and Calvin Dickin, Nathan received their anxious attentions for the full thirty seconds in a desperate and successful bid to get him to the mark. He then avoided Dellow's punches as best he could for another minute before allowing his opponent to hurl him to the ground with a cross-buttock throw, rolling away quickly as the heavy African attempted to drop on him.

'You're doing all right,' said Sammy Mizler encouragingly. 'Dellow isn't enjoying these breaks. It's giving him time to remember just how cold it is. Keep away from him and take a drop whenever you get the opportunity.'

Nathan looked to where a jubilant Boatswain Levinsky towelled his man down enthusiastically, convinced it was only a matter of time before he scored a knockout punch. If the fight continued as it was going, Levinsky might well prove to be right. Nathan came to a sudden decision.

'I'm changing my tactics, Sammy. By letting him set the pace I'm laying myself open to a lucky punch – and he's a might hard hitter. I'm going to take charge now. Abraham Dellow will know he's in a fight.'

Sammy Mizler began to argue, but moments later the referee called for the two men to recommence fighting. As Nathan and Abraham Dellow came from their respective corners the

162

spectators were strangely hushed. Nathan realised they were expecting to see him lose his title to the African. Dellow was equally confident that the undisputed championship of the world would be his before the afternoon was over. He was taken completely by surprise when Nathan switched from dogged defence and launched a two-fisted attack that drove Dellow all the way back to his corner.

The negro fighter recovered quickly, however, and for the remainder of the twelve-minute round the two prize-fighters had the great crowd roaring approval. The round ended when Nathan caught Dellow off guard. A punch to the stomach sent Dellow to his knees on the turf, gasping for air.

This round set the pattern for a fierce fight that kept the huge crowd on its toes, and men shouted themselves hoarse at the skill of Nathan and the courage of his opponent. Twelve gruelling rounds lasted an exhausting hour and forty minutes, and for nine of them Abraham Dellow was on the ground when the referee called a break.

In Dellow's corner, Boatswain Levinsky leaned over his battered fighter, gesticulating angrily. The African's eyes rolled in fright as he listened to a tight-lipped summary of his fate, should he lose the fight. Sammy Mizler did not miss the drama being enacted across the ring and he was quick to warn Nathan.

'Be on your guard now, Nathan. Dellow knows he's a loser and he's been ordered to win *at all costs*. It looks to me as though his life may depend upon winning.'

Nathan nodded. He had kept his eyes on his opponent during every break. He, too, realised that *Seneca*'s boatswain was putting Dellow under tremendous pressure.

Called to the centre of the ring for the thirteenth round, Nathan looked at his opponent's bloody face with some pity. It was short-lived. Lowering his head, Abraham Dellow charged at Nathan as though he were an angry bull. The unorthodox attack ended in disaster for the challenger. Sidestepping, Nathan brought his fist down hard behind the negro's ear. Dellow crashed to the ground and lay still on his face.

Boatswain Emile Levinsky and his fellow-second worked hard on their prize-fighter, pouring a bucket of water over his head, and spilling a generous measure of brandy down his throat. When the end of the break was called, the two men

163

dragged Abraham Dellow to the mark in the centre of the ring, supporting him for as long as they dared. When Sammy Mizler protested in a loud voice, the referee ordered Levinsky and his companion to their corner. They went reluctantly, and behind them Abraham Dellow sank heavily to his knees, supporting himself shakily with both knuckles resting on the turf.

Crossing the ring to the challenger, the referee bent low to look into his eyes. Straightening up, he declared Dellow unable to defend himself.

Nathan had won!

As the crowd erupted in roars of jubilation, Nathan stood looking down at Abraham Dellow's brutally scarred back. While members of the Duke of Clarence's party, and others, crowded inside the ring to offer him their congratulations, Nathan squatted beside the African as he attempted to rise upon legs that refused to support him.

'It's all right; the fight's over. Just stay down for a while.'

Abraham Dellow looked up at him, and Nathan had never seen such fear on a man's face.

'He'll kill me for this, boss. That Bos'n Levinsky's going to kill me for sure.'

Across the ring, Boatswain Levinsky was watching his defeated fighter, his face distorted with rage. Nathan did not doubt Abraham Dellow's words.

'You don't have to go back to *Seneca*. Come with me. I'll see that you're looked after.'

Instead of providing the defeated boxer with hope, Nathan's words seemed to add to his terror. 'You don't understand. I can't do that. I'm not a free man. I *belong* to Bos'n Levinsky.'

Now Nathan understood Abraham Dellow's fears. As a slave on an American slave-ship he had no rights at all. He belonged to Emile Levinsky. The boatswain could do with him whatever he wished. Having seen Levinsky's love of the whip, and Abraham Dellow's scarred back, Nathan had no doubts about the fate in store for the negro prize-fighter.

'Forget Levinsky. You're not in *Seneca* now. This is England. We no longer recognise slavery. Come with me.'

Helping Dellow to his feet, Nathan forced a way through the throng to the corner where Sammy Mizler was surrounded by many of his prize-fighting friends and a few members of the

Duke of Clarence's party.

Brushing aside their jubilant congratulations, Nathan said: 'Sammy, we need to get Dellow back to the inn. Don't let him out of your sight for one minute.'

Startled, Sammy Mizler began to protest that Nathan had just won a fight. The Duke of Clarence wanted to speak to him to offer his own congratulations.

'The Duke of Clarence knows where we're staying – and it will be better if he leaves here right now. Abraham Dellow's a slave. He's owned by Boatswain Levinsky – the man who's so handy with a whip. I've told Dellow he's not going back to the ship. There are a number of *Seneca*'s crew here. That means there's going to be trouble. Get Dellow away – and make certain Amy goes with you, too.'

A North Country peer who had been listening to Nathan's story immediately set off to warn William, Duke of Clarence. The Duke would not wish to become involved in a brawl at an illegal prize-fight where one of the participants was a slave!

On his way, the peer intercepted Amy as she tried to reach Nathan's side. Ignoring her protests, he forced her to return with him to the Duke of Clarence.

He was none too soon. As Nathan had feared, crewmen from *Seneca* were gathering about their boatswain – but formidable support was also rallying to Nathan's side.

Before and during a long prize-fight, the outer ring – the area immediately adjacent to the prize-ring itself – was reserved for those gentlemen of the 'Fancy', who paid considerable sums of money in order to watch the fight with a degree of comfort, without being jostled by the noisy, unwashed and frequently unruly crowd. In order to keep the mob beyond the limits of this outer ring, a number of 'would-be' and 'has-been' pugilists were employed. Now, with the fight over, the pugilists' task was to fall back upon the prize-fighting ring to escort Nathan away.

They reached him in ones and twos, until there were a dozen of them, keeping a breathing-space for the man who was being hailed as the champion of the world. Among the prize-fighters was Jem Belcher, cousin of Nathan's unfortunate last opponent and himself once Champion of all England. Among the others were men with whom Nathan had sparred on more than one occasion.

Above the din of the excited crowd, Nathan managed to convey to his prize-fighting bodyguard what was happening. Some of the spectators also heard Nathan's words and they began howling for the blood of Boatswain Emile Levinsky and his slaver colleagues. Minutes later, Levinsky abandoned all thought of repossessing his frightened slave as he and his fellow-Americans were set upon by the crowd.

Abraham Dellow had won the respect of the Bristol men for the courageous fight he had put up against Nathan. Many of those close to the ring had seen the ugly scarring on his back and rightly attributed it to the big American boatswain.

'You'll have little trouble with the American now, I'm thinking,' said Jem Belcher. 'You put up a good fight, Nathan Jago. I couldn't have done much better myself.'

Nathan grinned. Jem Belcher had been a good champion, but had never been strong on modesty. 'Thanks. How's that cousin of yours?'

'Ned? He's dead. Died three months since. Drank himself to death, didn't you know?'

Much of Nathan's exhilaration left him, and Jem Belcher said hurriedly: 'It was none of your fault, Nathan. Don't you think it was. He'd been slowly killing himself with drink for years, ever since he reached the top in the prize-ring. Blind or sighted, he wouldn't have lasted no longer than he did. It was a happy release really, you might say.' Jem Belcher handed Nathan a blue silk scarf. 'Here, don't leave your lady's favour tied to the rope. She'd never forgive you – and pretty young things like her are hard to come by for scarred old veterans like you and me.'

Nathan was about to protest that there was a tremendous age difference between himself and the former champion, but he stopped himself quickly. Jem Belcher, himself blind in one eye, had fought his last two prize-fights with a broken hand. Consequently, his battered features had taken far more punches than was good for them. Belcher also had the sickly pallor of ill-health, and would be dead within six months. Yet Bristol-born Belcher was only twenty-nine years of age – barely two years older than Nathan.

.   .   .

That night the private room of the Golden Fleece witnessed a party such as the inn had not known in all the years of its existence.

The Duke of Clarence was in a jovial mood and provided the highlight of the evening with his rendering of between-deck naval songs. He had good reason to be well pleased. The prize-fight on Clifton Down had netted him a great deal of money – though he admitted to suffering 'palpitations' during the early rounds of the fight.

The Duke and his companions also had lengthy discussions during the course of the evening with Abraham Dellow – the name had been given to him by Emile Levinsky, when Dellow had been purchased as an oversized boy of fourteen.

Subjected to all forms of humiliation on board *Seneca*, Dellow had been thrashed many times by his owner, the worst beating being the one that had left him scarred for life.

The cause had been a young slave girl. Selected by Emile Levinsky to provide the boatswain with some of the pleasures of life during the long voyage from Africa to America, she had preferred the charms of Abraham Dellow. The two Africans were surprised by the boatswain when they were making love in Levinsky's own cabin.

The boatswain had gone berserk. The screaming girl was taken to the side of the ship in mid-Atlantic and thrown overboard. Abraham Dellow, pinned to the deck by a dozen seamen, had been given a choice. Castration, or a beating that would last until Emile Levinsky was too exhausted to wield a whip.

Abraham Dellow chose the beating. It lasted for two hours, by which time even the crew of *Seneca*, hardened by years of slave-trading, were sickened.

All night long Abraham Dellow lay twitching and groaning on the deck of the ship in a pool of his own blood, the flesh on his back in ribbons. The boatswain had forbidden anyone to go to his aid.

Dellow lived, but the boatswain boasted that he had broken his slave as he might have broken a horse and would have no more trouble from him. To prove his words, Emile Levinsky took every opportunity to demonstrate Dellow's incredible servility, degrading the slave in every possible way before the

European crew and the African slave cargo. With the memory of his cruel beating in his mind, Abraham Dellow was careful to ensure that only the slaves ever saw the looks of hate he occasionally cast in the direction of his brutal owner.

To the Europeans, Abraham Dellow became all that a 'good' negro should be: trustworthy and servile, a model for his fellows. Because of this he was given the post of slavemaster on board *Seneca*.

When Nathan asked him why he had never tried to escape, Abraham Dellow shrugged his shoulders. 'Where would I have gone?' He went on to explain that he came from a tribe of Africa's interior. Had he tried to escape when *Seneca* called at an African port, the tribesmen of the coast would have taken great delight in handing him back to Boatswain Levinsky. After explaining all this, Dellow added: 'Before this trip the only ports we called at were either in Africa, the West Indies or America. They are not healthy places for a runaway slave.'

Abraham Dellow had drunk heavily at the Golden Fleece and he now added something that made Nathan wonder whether they had heard the whole truth of Dellow's experiences on board *Seneca*.

'Besides, it wasn't such a bad life when Bos'n Levinsky was in a good mood. I could have as many of the slave women as I wanted – except those chosen by white men. I took them whether they wanted me or not. When they were put up for auction, Boatswain Levinsky would have me stand on the platform with them, then he'd tell the buyers that most of the women were probably in child by me.'

The huge African smiled proudly. 'It sure did put up the price of them slave girls.'

'Ahem!' William, Duke of Clarence looked at Dellow with faintly raised eyebrows. 'I doubt if we can provide you with pleasures on the same scale as those you enjoyed on board *Seneca*, but if you wish to stay in England as a free man I can place you with someone who'll improve your prize-fighting technique. I, and the gentlemen with me today, will sponsor you. I think we can promise you a satisfactory life.'

There were murmurs of agreement from the men of the 'Fancy' gathered about the Duke. Abraham Dellow had the strength and courage required of a prize-fighter. Once he had acquired some of the art of a boxer he would be a tremendous crowd-pleaser.

'Now that's settled, I propose a toast to Nathan Jago, prize-fighting champion of the world. He gave us all a wonderful display of skill today.'

While the party in the private room of the Golden Fleece was at its height, the slave-ship *Seneca* was passing from the River Avon into the wider waters of the Bristol Channel. It marked the premature end of the vessel's first and last visit to an English port.

The reason for *Seneca*'s deviation from her usual run between Africa and America had been twofold: she had come to load preserved fish, provided by Nathan and his fellow-fishermen – and also so that her master and crew might make a fortune in wagers when Abraham Dellow beat the all-England prize-fighting champion.

Instead, *Seneca* left Bristol with a furious boatswain and a disgruntled crew. Their champion had been beaten and was now lost to them. In addition, the ship had been driven from the port of Bristol by angry anti-slave demonstrators before it had taken on a full load of provisions.

Much worse was to come. Caught in a howling snowstorm when no more than twenty-four hours outward bound from Bristol, *Seneca* blundered blindly on her way for the whole of one terrifying night. Then, on Sunday, 17 February 1811, hopelessly off course, *Seneca* drove on to the infamous Gilstone Reef, on the fringe of the Scilly Isles. While the snow held back the dawn, two hundred and seventy slaves entered eternity chained together. With them went the captain of *Seneca* and all forty men of his crew, swallowed up by the cold, grey, undiscriminating sea.

Chapter Sixteen

THE February blizzard raged for four days and nights, before ceasing as suddenly as it had begun, leaving the land hushed and white. For these four days, Nathan, Amy, Sammy Mizler and the two fishermen shared the warm intimacy of the Bristol inn. The Duke of Clarence and his entourage had left for Gloucestershire in the early hours of the morning after the fight, taking Abraham Dellow with them.

Amy was pleased to see the former-slave go. She, too, felt they had not heard the truth of Abraham Dellow's role in the slave-ship *Seneca* and she hoped Nathan would never regret his part in rescuing the slave.

Nathan welcomed the delay caused by the snow. He had absorbed a certain amount of punishment from the prize-fighting slave, and his face was bruised and grazed. The few days spent in Bristol would allow the wounds to heal and perhaps excite less anger from Josiah Jago.

But Preacher Jago was concerned with far more serious problems than his son's prize-fighting activities.

South Cornwall had escaped the blizzards that swept the remainder of the country. A little snow fell during the course of a single night, but by noon it had melted, leaving only tiny pockets of snow in creases of the hills and beneath sheltered hedgerows. It meant that Preacher Jago, well wrapped up against the wind, was able to go about the Lord's business as usual.

On the Sunday following the fight, Josiah Jago preached in four of the tiny fishing hamlets to the west of Mevagissey. Each of the congregations was given the benefit of one of his newest sermons, entitled 'I look upon all the world as my parish', based on the stirring evangelical words of John Wesley.

Warmed by the belief that his message had entered the hearts and minds of his flock, Preacher Jago continued on his circuit on Monday morning, well pleased with life. At noon he stopped to share a meal with two elderly spinsters who worked a corn-grinding mill in a lonely valley, two miles inland from the coast. It was here that he was finally traced by the young son of one of his Pentuan lay preachers. Chosen for his fitness, the youth had run nine miles to find the Methodist preacher.

The news he carried hit Josiah Jago with more force than any blow landed on his son by Abraham Dellow.

Sir Lewis Hearle had sent men to Pentuan to demolish the Methodist chapel. The young runner reported that by the time he had left the village the roof had already been stripped of slates, and the men were putting axes to the rafters.

Filled with shock and disbelief, Josiah Jago tried to conjure up coherent speech. 'But . . . but Sir Lewis Hearle has no right . . .! The land on which the chapel is built was given to us by old Captain Dunne before he died.'

'Ah, so 'twas,' agreed the exhausted youngster. 'But it seems it weren't his to give away. That piece of land and a whole lot more was sold to Polrudden by Captain Dunne's father, many years ago. The Dunnes were allowed to carry on using it, but 'tis part of Lower Polrudden Farm. Sir Lewis only found out about it when he put the farm up for sale. He says the chapel's got to come down.'

Still trying to grasp the situation, Preacher Jago could only keep repeating: 'I can't believe it . . . I just can't believe it.'

'It's right enough, Preacher Jago. Sir Lewis has brought in St Austell men to do the job – and you know what they're like. They'll hang their grandmothers for the price of a pint of ale – ay, and draw and quarter 'em afterwards for an extra shilling. Folks in Pentuan have begged 'em to stop knocking the chapel down, but they won't listen. *You'll* need to persuade Sir Lewis to leave chapel be, I reckon. . . . But you'd best hurry, or there won't be much of 'en left standing.'

Josiah Jago had his thoughts under control now, disbelief giving way to anger. Leaving the two agitated spinsters to tend to the blistered feet of the young Pentuan youth, Josiah Jago mounted his old donkey and set off homeward, urging the startled animal to a faster gait than it had ever before achieved.

News of the destruction of the Pentuan chapel had spread to the surrounding countryside by the time Josiah Jago rode into Pentuan that afternoon. The tiny village was thronged with angry Methodists.

His arrival prompted an outbreak of cheering, and cries of 'Here comes the preacher,' and 'Make way for Preacher Jago.

He'll soon put a stop to it.'

Preacher Josiah Jago was aware of the hopes of his Methodist parishioners, but he looked in horror at the destruction already achieved by the St Austell men. The roof of the chapel had been totally demolished, and an end wall was reduced to little more than a heap of rubble. Inside the half-destroyed chapel, the pulpit rose above the rows of wooden benches, the whole being covered in dust and debris.

The sight of such desecration brought Preacher Josiah Jago close to tears. He had collected the money for this building himself, much of it in pennies and twopences, the most the donors could afford. He had gone without many meals during his circuit-riding in order to put a few extra pence in the chapel fund. Much of the actual building work had also been carried out by his own hands, and all had been done for love of the Lord.

In this emotional mood, he appealed to the St Austell men to cease work. He *begged* them to destroy no more of the Lord's house.

The St Austell men's refusal brought an angry swelling of sound from the listening crowd. Finally, Josiah Jago pleaded with the demolishers to cease their work at least until he had spoken with Sir Lewis Hearle, and they grudgingly agreed, moved more by the ugly mood of the Wesleyan crowd than by the preacher's arguments.

Still stiff from his long ride, Preacher Josiah Jago remounted his donkey and kicked his heels into the animal's flanks. Old Barnabas had just carried his agitated rider for nine miles at an unaccustomed speed. The ageing donkey was tired, thirsty – and exceedingly stubborn. It refused to move. Bystanders came to the aid of their preacher, and the donkey was poked and prodded, his tail twisted, and his ears tugged until he threw back his woolly head and kicked out at his tormentors in protest. But he took not a single pace forward. When some of the younger members of the crowd began to laugh, Preacher Jago dismounted. He would need to walk to see Sir Lewis Hearle.

This was to be the only moment of humour in a day of disaster for the Methodist community.

Preacher Josiah Jago toiled up the hill to Polrudden Manor,

accompanied by a number of his friends. Along the way all offered their breathless, disjointed advice. At the entrance to the manor driveway, Josiah Jago asked his companions to wait and leave him to carry out his mission alone.

Not knowing that the preacher was absent from Pentuan, Sir Lewis Hearle had been expecting Josiah Jago much earlier in the day. In fact, he had become more and more anxious as the hours passed and he did not arrive. Watching the ageing figure in a shabby serge suit making his way wearily along the driveway to Polrudden Manor, Sir Lewis Hearle was filled with a sense of relief. It was late, but there was still time to effect the main object of his carefully prepared plan.

Preacher Josiah Jago received short thrift at the hands of Spencer Perceval's Under-Secretary for Home Affairs. Tongue in cheek, Sir Lewis Hearle expressed sympathy with the preacher at the loss of his chapel, but Josiah Jago had to understand the baronet's own position. He had put Lower Polrudden Farm on the market. Indeed, he felt the Duchy of Cornwall was prepared to purchase if from him, just as they had bought another of his farms. But the Duchy was the property of the future King of England. It could not be expected to buy land upon which there was a dissenting place of worship.

Sir Lewis Hearle reminded Josiah Jago that the chapel had been illegally built on Polrudden land and he would be within his rights to sue the Methodists for the costs incurred in having the chapel knocked down. He would not do this, of course, but he wanted the preacher to understand the legalities of the situation.

Preacher Jago was a simple man. He had been brought up to believe that the lord of the manor – any manor – was a man of honour. It was certainly not for men like himself to question either his rights or the manner in which he exercised them. He accepted the cruel setback to his life's work.

Murmuring incoherently that Sir Lewis could have given him due warning of his intentions, in order that the chapel records and some of the fittings might have been carried to safety, he bowed to the baronet's authority.

'Oh! Weren't you given notice? I feel certain I asked one of my servants to tell you – last week some time, I believe,' Sir Lewis lied jubilantly as he rang for a servant to show the preacher out of the study.

The friends waiting outside the manor gates listened to the story of their preacher's failure in dismayed silence. Each knew how much the loss of the chapel meant to him personally. They took little notice of the groom who kneed his horse between them, a sealed note from Sir Lewis Hearle tucked inside a pouch at his waist.

The crowds at Pentuan were less restrained. They maintained their silence only long enough to catch the gist of what Josiah Jago had to say and then they let out loud howls of anger.

The St Austell men had been listening, too, and now they resumed knocking down the Wesleyan place of worship. Immediately, the workmen became the focus for the crowd's frustration and anger. At first it involved no more than shouted abuse. It might have become nothing more, had one of the workmen not made a ribald comment about the barrackers. It was made in a moment of bravado, but when the other workmen laughed at his words the mood of the Methodist crowd became ugly.

A clod of grass and earth hurtled through the air, landing close to one of the workmen. There was a brief hesitation before another missile, this time a stone, was hurled with more accuracy. It struck one of the workmen on the leg.

Even now all might not have been lost had the workman chosen to ignore the provocation. Instead, he picked up a piece of masonry and hurled it back into the crowd. It was not large, but it struck a young girl on the face. Her cry was more of fright than of pain, but it became a scream when she put a hand to her face and it came away streaked with her blood.

Given an example of how best to vent their feelings, the crowd erupted in violent anger. Stones, earth and even wooden fence-staves flew through the air towards the St Austell workmen. One was struck on the head by a stone and fell off the half-demolished wall, to lie sprawled in a grotesque heap on the rubble below.

Greatly alarmed at the sudden turn events had taken, Preacher Josiah Jago climbed on a mounting-block outside the Jolly Sailor tavern and called upon the crowd to show restraint. His words were lost in the uproar, as missiles continued to fly through the air in the direction of the St Austell workmen.

174

This was the moment chosen by a magistrate from St Austell to arrive upon the scene accompanied by forty mounted men of the North Cornwall Yeomanry, mustered at Bodmin.

The fact that the yeomanry arrived so swiftly was certain evidence that the authorities had anticipated trouble. In fact, they had been waiting since dawn at Nansladron, no more than a mile along the valley. The messenger sent to summon them urgently to Pentuan had left Polrudden Manor while Preacher Jago was admitting the failure of his mission to his friends, outside the manor.

The magistrate's words, calling on the angry mob to disperse, were lost in the general din. Only one or two people standing nearby guessed that the Riot Act had been read.

One of these few was Preacher Jago. He shouted himself hoarse in a bid to bring the people in the packed village square to their senses, but missiles continued to rain down on the workmen, who now cowered in the ruins of the Methodist chapel.

The magistrate gave the crowd no further warning. At a word of command, the yeomanry drove their horses into the surprised and angry crowd, using the butt ends of their muskets to clear a path. The bulk of the crowd scattered before the determined drive of the part-time soldiers, but not before seven of their number had been arrested, on orders from the magistrate. One of the seven was Preacher Josiah Jago.

Across the square, Annie Jago had been watching events from her kitchen window, determined not to leave the house while the noisy, unruly crowd remained. Then she saw her husband summarily and roughly arrested. Running from the house, she tried to force a way through the fleeing crowds to reach him. As frightened Methodists fled past her, Annie Jago inched her way forward until she reached those who were hardest pressed by the horses and flailing muskets of the mounted yeomanry.

Unable to make further headway, Annie Jago found herself being carried backwards by the terrified crowd. Caught up in their mood, she began pummelling those about her in a bid to break through to reach her husband. Suddenly her ankle turned on a rock dropped to the ground by one of the protesters and she stumbled to her knees. As she tried to rise someone fell

175

over her and bore her to the ground. Within moments there were a dozen men and women lying in a heap, among them a member of the yeomanry whose horse had been downed.

When the last of the fleeing Methodists finally cleared the square, four men and a woman still lay on the ground. The four men moaned in agony, but Annie Jago lay quite still.

Josiah Jago recognised the still figure of his wife as one of the part-time soldiers was in the process of shackling his wrists with heavy iron bands joined together by a chain.

Pushing the surprised man to one side, Josiah Jago ran towards his wife, forgetting the chains that already secured his ankles.

The soldier of the yeomanry called that the preacher was trying to escape. One of his companions, crossing the square on his horse, ran the preacher down. As Josiah Jago shouted and tried to explain his actions, he was beaten into insensibility by the butt end of a musket wielded by another soldier.

Two of the arrested men helped to lift the unconscious form of the preacher inside an enclosed prison-wagon, thoughtfully provided by the magistrate for the occasion. The injured St Austell workman, nursing a broken arm, rode with the driver of the wagon, escorted by the magistrate and thirty members of the yeomanry.

Not until the wagon and horses had clattered from Pentuan Square did the stunned residents of the fishing village leave their houses to tend to those who still lay where they had fallen, watched by ten men of the yeomanry. Left behind to protect the workmen who were completing their task in silent haste, the part-time soldiers fingered their muskets nervously.

They had nothing to fear. The violent scenes had shocked the Methodist villagers and they went about their administrations in silent grief.

Two of the injured villagers had broken limbs. A third suffered internal injuries.

Annie Jago was dead.

Chapter Seventeen

NATHAN was told of the death of his mother and the arrest of his father when *The Brave Amy H* tied up alongside the quay at Portgiskey.

Amy watched helplessly as he struggled to control his anguish and bewilderment, and she was filled with an urge to hold him to her. She knew he needed someone to comfort him. Nathan Jago, prize-fighting champion of the world, needed someone to help him bridge this terrible chasm that had suddenly appeared before him.

Amy could have provided the bridge. She desperately wanted to help – but she hesitated too long. The moment came – and as quickly went.

Drawing a deep breath, as though sucking new life into his body, Nathan questioned his fisherman informant. 'Does my father know that Ma is dead?'

'Yes. Your sister Nell went to see him in Bodmin Gaol. Word is that he's taken the news badly. He feels that he's responsible.'

It was on Nathan's tongue to retort that his father's narrow interpretation of his religion could be blamed for most of the misfortunes that had befallen the Jago family, but he bit back the words. This was not the time to air such thoughts, and they were probably not true. He realised his father must have been desperately unhappy to have made such an admission.

Then Nathan seized upon something else the fisherman had said.

'Why is he in Bodmin Gaol, and not in St Austell lock-up?'

'He's been charged with inciting the riot in Pentuan. It's an offence that needs to be tried at Bodmin Assize. He's also been charged with repeatedly preaching in the open air. But, whatever the charges, we all know he's been arrested simply because he preaches Methodism.'

'I'll go and see him straightaway.'

To Amy and Sammy, Nathan said: 'I might be away for a day or two. There's Pa to see . . . and a funeral to arrange. Can you keep things going here?'

'Of course,' Amy and Sammy spoke in unison, and Amy

added: 'We'll keep things going. But hurry back. We need you here with us.'

The fisherman who had given Nathan news of the happenings at Pentuan said quickly: 'About the funeral. . . . It might not be so easy to arrange. You see . . . she's been refused burial by the Church.'

It was a strange anomaly of the country's religious laws that the Methodists, young and dynamic as they were, and so often in conflict with the Church of England, were reliant upon the Established Church for the sacraments. Indeed, John Wesley, founder of the Methodist Church, was himself ordained in the Church of England and had never originally intended that his great revivalist movement should advance outside the Church of England.

'I don't believe it!' Nathan stared at the fisherman in disbelief. He had heard of dissenters being refused burial elsewhere in the country, but never here in Cornwall. The vicar of St Austell was responsible for the spiritual needs of Pentuan. He disapproved of the Methodist separation, but had never before refused them any of the benefits of his church.

'The vicar of St Austell's been taken ill. He'll likely not live long. Until a new vicar is appointed, the Reverend Kent, rector of Fowey, has taken over from him.'

Now Nathan understood. The Reverend Nicholas Kent was as notoriously opposed to Methodism as Sir Lewis Hearle – and he had a particular dislike for Josiah Jago.

Turning away, Nathan strode off without another word. Behind him, Sammy Mizler was watching the expression upon Amy's face and he reached for her hand. When Nathan rounded the rocks separating Portgiskey Cove from Pentuan Beach, he looked back briefly and saw his two partners standing hand in hand. He felt very much alone. He did not see Amy dissolve in tears as he passed out of sight.

Nathan called first at Venn Farm. He found Nell and Tom Quicke deeply unhappy. Married life had begun for them with such high hopes for the future. Now, it seemed, their whole world was crumbling about them. Tearfully Nell began to tell Nathan about the death of their mother. He told her he already knew and led her to a seat close to the wood fire that defied the despondent gloom in the room with its crackling cheerfulness.

'It's a sad business, right enough,' echoed Tom Quicke, Nell's serious and steady husband. 'First the farm's taken away, then your father's arrested and your poor ma killed in Pentuan square. They called an inquest on her, but they held it in St Austell. "Fear of inflaming local opinion" was the reason they gave for not having it here. We knew better. They knew full well that if they held it far enough away from Pentuan no one from here would go and tell the truth of what happened. "Misadventure" was the verdict they recorded. "Murder" would have been a more honest finding. I've spoken to some who said one of the soldiers rode his horse right over your poor mother while she lay helpless on the ground.'

'Then it's a pity they didn't have the courage to go to St Austell and say so,' said Nathan bitterly. 'Tell me about Kent's refusal to bury Ma.'

'What is there to say?' asked Nell. 'Tom and I went to see the Reverend Kent, on our way back from Bodmin, after visiting Pa. He said that by supporting Pa in his ways she'd forfeited the right to a decent Christian burial. He swore she'd not have a single inch of Church ground.'

Tom Quicke put an arm about his wife. 'Kent said a whole lot more, but what Nell's told you is about the strength of it.'

'Where is Ma now?'

'Upstairs. We didn't like to leave her down at the village – alone. But she'll need to be buried soon, Nathan. We've got to get out of the farm, Nell and me. We had official notice yesterday from Sir Lewis Hearle. Venn's been sold already.'

'Did Sir Lewis mention the name of the buyer?'

'He didn't, but his solicitor did. I've been to see him this morning. It's been bought through the Duchy of Cornwall Land Agent – for the Duke of Clarence. Why he should want a farm like Venn beats me. . . .'

Nathan's shoulders sagged with relief. There and then, he told Nell and Tom Quicke about the arrangement he had made with the Duke of Clarence.

If Nathan had ever entertained any doubts about his decision to fight again in order to give Nell and her husband Venn Farm, one look at their faces now would have dispelled them for ever.

Tom Quicke was utterly dazed at the sudden change in his fortunes.

'You . . . you fought to give us the farm? Why, Nathan? Why should you do so much . . .?'

'I can give you two reasons,' replied Nathan slowly. 'I've gained a lot from prize-fighting. I have a good boat, and a fishing business. It's always been my wish to help Ma and Pa, but Pa has strong feelings about prize-fighting. He'd never accept anything from me. If he ever did, he'd give it away again – to his church.'

Nathan managed a wan smile. 'That left you, Nell. You and Tom wanted Venn Farm. Well, thanks to prize-fighting, you've got it.'

Tom Quicke, still in a daze, gripped Nathan's hand in a fierce grip. 'I just don't know what to say, Nathan. "Thank you" don't hardly seem enough. I'm sorry. . . . I'm lost for words. Me and Nell want to keep Venn Farm, more than anything in the world. I . . . I wish your ma could have known about this. . . .'

Tom Quicke choked on his words as Nell rose and flung her arms about her brother's neck. Her own emotions were such a tangled mixture of grief, relief and happiness that she dared say nothing at all.

Nathan remained at the farm that night, going on to Bodmin at dawn the following day. He travelled on foot. Tom and Nell Quicke had Josiah Jago's donkey at the farm, but the animal was a one-man mount. He allowed Nathan to sit upon his back, but when Nathan tried to persuade him to move forward he was unceremoniously dumped to the ground.

Nathan knew there was little he would be able to do to help his father. Before leaving Bristol he had heard disquieting rumours that Methodist preachers were being arrested throughout the land. There seemed to be a determined plan afoot to destroy Methodism, once and for all.

Before Nathan left Venn Farm, Tom Quicke said something to him that appeared to indicate that the plan was succeeding.

'Your father's arrest has taken the heart from Methodism in this area,' said the slow-thinking farmer. 'We've suffered a blow that has put Methodism back fifty years. With your pa's support we might have survived the loss of the chapel. Without him . . .?' Tom Quicke shrugged. 'Do what you can for him – and for *us*, Nathan.'

When the heavy cell door swung open with a loud squeal of protest, Josiah Jago did not even look up to see who was there. He sat hunched on the straw-strewn floor. It was a very small cell, the focal point and only form of furnishing being an iron-bound wooden slop-bucket.

'Pa? It's me, Nathan.'

Josiah Jago turned pain-filled eyes up to his son, and Nathan was deeply shocked at what he saw. One of the preacher's eyes was blackened and the side of his stubble-cheeked face discoloured by an ugly dark bruise.

Nothing Nell or Tom had told him had prepared Nathan for this.

Rounding on the gaoler angrily, he demanded: 'Who did this? Who gave my father a beating.'

The gaoler was an aged, limping ex-soldier and he cowered before Nathan's anger.

'No one in here's touched him, Mr Jago. I'll swear to that. I've never struck a prisoner in my life – though I've had many as I'd like to have looked at along the barrel of a Baker rifle, I don't mind telling thee. No, sir. Your father was struck by a musket at the time of his arrest. He was out for nigh on three hours, so the St Austell turnkey told me.'

'All right. Leave us for a while.'

It had cost Nathan a golden half-guinea to grease the gaoler's key in the rusty locks of Bodmin's decaying and stinking old gaol. Nathan had not paid the money to have a gossiping old turnkey listen to all that was said.

The gaoler touched a finger to his hat respectfully. 'That's all right, Mr Jago, sir. If there's anything you want afore you go, just you let me know. I'll be pleased to oblige.'

The gaoler went out, shutting the rusty-hinged door behind him.

'He's right,' mumbled Josiah Jago suddenly, painfully fingering the bruised side of his face. His bottom lip trembled in the manner of a hurt child. 'I was only trying to reach your mother. She was running to me – concerned for me, as she always was. She didn't deserve to die, Nathan. She'd done nothing wrong. I don't think she ever did a wrong thing in the whole of her life. She was a good woman, such a good woman.'

Preacher Josiah Jago's chin sank to his chest, his eyes closed. His whole body shook in spasm after spasm, as the painful memory of that dreadful afternoon returned to him.

Nathan dropped to his knees beside his father and put an arm about his shoulders. It was the first physical demonstration of affection he could ever remember between them.

Josiah Jago leaned against his son for about two minutes. Then he pulled away and struggled stiffly to his feet. Putting a hand against the crumbling stone wall, he stood looking up at the small, barred window, his back to Nathan.

'I'm finished, son. My life's work is in ruins, the Methodist cause in disarray. I've failed myself, I've failed your mother – God rest her soul – and I've failed the Lord.'

Nathan had never heard his father accept defeat before. He said so.

'Perhaps I've never been honest with myself before. I am now – and I'm deeply troubled. I'm beginning to question all that I've ever done in my lifetime. Was I right to sacrifice the affection of you and Nell – yes, and of your mother, too – for my own beliefs?'

Preacher Josiah Jago turned an agonised glance upon his startled son. 'Did you think I didn't know what was happening? I knew, Nathan. I took *pride* in the sacrifices I made for Him. *Pride* in building His Church. *Pride* in being looked up to by other men and called "Preacher". *Pride*. That's what's brought me down. I, who dedicated my life to spreading the Lord's Word, forgot what it says in Proverbs 16, verse 18: "Pride goeth before destruction, and an haughty spirit before a fall." Well, now the Lord and the whole world bear witness to my downfall. I spend my days sitting in the corner of a cell measuring three paces by two. Surrounded by my own filth. A pig in his pen.'

Josiah Jago's bitter laugh became a cough that hunched his body and alarmed Nathan. The robust preacher who would ride miles in all weathers, defying rain and storm with a hymn on his lips, had become a frail old man.

Nathan looked about the gloomy cell. The walls were scratched with names, dates and primitive calendars.

'I'll speak to the gaoler on my way out. I'll have you moved to a better cell. That will be a start. Then we'll see about having these ridiculous charges dropped, and get you out of here.'

'Don't waste your time, Nathan. The authorities are out to destroy Methodism. I don't really matter to them – or to anyone else, for that matter. But they'll convict me. It's all part of their scheming. Go back to your fishing, my son. Live your own life. I've given you little enough happiness in the past. Don't allow an old fool to ruin your *future*, too.'

'Pa. . . .' Nathan took hold of his father's stooped shoulders and turned him round to face him. 'You just quoted the Bible at me. Now I'm doing the same to you. It's something you made me learn when I was a small boy. I've never forgotten it and I refuse to believe you have. It's from the New Testament. St Matthew, chapter 17, verse 20.'

Josiah Jago's face became animated for the first time since Nathan had entered the gloomy, depressing cell. 'You remember it? After all this time?'

'Every word. But I want *you* to quote it to me.'

Josiah Jago licked his dry lips. Looking up at his son, he said in a hoarse, emotional whisper: ' "If ye have faith as a grain of mustard seed, ye shall say unto this mountain, Remove hence to yonder place; and it shall remove; and nothing shall be impossible unto you".'

Nathan nodded. 'You've lived your life by those words, Pa – and you've proved them true. I've always admired you for that. Are you going to cast them aside now?'

For a few moments the old religious fervour shone from Josiah Jago's eyes. Then the fire died and his shoulders shrugged helplessly beneath Nathan's hands. 'Will faith bring your ma back to life? Or raise my chapel again?'

'You and I will always look at our Nell and see Ma in the way she walks, and talks, and smiles. Ma will never be dead for us. And, yes, faith *will* raise your chapel. What's more, it will have its own burial-ground – and Ma is going to be the first Methodist buried there.'

Nathan was trying desperately hard to rekindle the fires of faith burning so low in the heart of his father. He was also expressing the ideas that had occupied his thoughts on the long walk from Pentuan. The things he had promised Josiah Jago would not be easy, but the promises *would* be fulfilled.

Josiah Jago shook his head. 'There will never be another chapel in Pentuan. Sir Lewis Hearle will see to that. He and his

183

friends own every inch of land about Pentuan.'

'Not any more. Listen to me, Pa. Tom and Nell own Venn Farm now. True, it's not right in Pentuan, but it's close enough to serve well enough. They'll give you a plot of land for a chapel and burial-ground. There's an ideal piece of rough ground close to the road that will suit you perfectly.'

'They *own* Venn Farm? What nonsense is this? They can't afford to buy a cow, let alone a farm. . . .'

'I've bought it for them.'

'You? Where did you get the money?'

'I had another prize-fight. It was a big purse. Big enough to buy Venn Farm.'

Nathan expected his father to be angry. He *hoped* he would be angry. Any positive state of mind would be better than the present mood of depression. But Josiah Jago was in no mood to quarrel with his son.

'I don't hold with prize-fighting, Nathan. You know that. I've told you so many times. But if you've used money from it to buy Nell and Tom their farm, then I'm proud of you. It's more than I've been able to do.'

'And the chapel?' Nathan prompted his father.

Josiah Jago shook his head. 'Where would the money come from? It took me almost three years to raise enough for the chapel Sir Lewis Hearle destroyed. Now there isn't even a preacher for my circuit. People are frightened to stand up and address an open-air congregation for fear of being arrested. Three of my lay preachers are in St Austell lock-up now, awaiting trial before a magistrate on charges of preaching in the open air.'

'That's one of the charges levelled against *you*. How long has it been an offence to preach to people in places where there is no church – of any denomination?'

'Since the St Austell magistrate decided it should be. We won't be the first Methodists to be convicted for nothing more than preaching the Word of the Lord – and convicted we shall be. I'm convinced Sir Lewis Hearle planned my arrest, and I believe the Prime Minister is behind him.'

Nathan was sceptical, but he said nothing. Josiah Jago was talking rationally now.

'I've had time to think since I've been in here. Sir Lewis

Hearle is now an under-secretary at the Home Office, appointed by the Prime Minister. He is responsible for various aspects of law and order. I believe he must have sent out orders telling magistrates to make things harder for us Methodists. One thing is certain: since he took office there have been more preachers arrested than ever before. It's happening all over the country. When I was arrested, the magistrate and the yeomanry couldn't have been more than a few minutes away. Sir Lewis Hearle knew I would be in Pentuan when they arrived because I had only just left him at Polrudden. I seem to remember, too, that a rider came from the house while I was outside talking. He went as though the Devil were after him. I suspect he'd been sent to inform the magistrate and his men that I was on my way to Pentuan.'

Nathan was still sceptical, but what his father had said made too much sense to ignore.

'This rider, did you recognise him?'

'Yes, I know him well. It was Will Hodge, Sir Lewis Hearle's groom. He's married to the daughter of Ahab Arthur, one of your fishermen.'

'Then I'll see him and ask the truth of what happened.'

'What difference does it make now? What can you do if I'm proved right?'

Nathan countered with a question of his own. 'How would you set about building a chapel at Pentuan?'

'Why, I'd call for special collections at my open-air services. Not that I could expect to take much money. My open-air services are so popular because those who attend are usually too poor to afford clothes decent enough to wear to church or chapel.'

'We might not need as much as you think. Can any of your Methodists build?'

'Most of them – and there's no shortage of fishermen with time on their hands in winter. Yes, if you're serious about it there are many who'd be only too pleased to help build a new chapel.'

Nathan was satisfied that his father was at last taking a real interest in what was being planned. 'I'll have pen and paper brought to you in your new cell. Draw me a rough sketch of how you want the chapel built. I'll do the rest.'

185

'How will you get word to all my congregation of what is happening?'

'I'll call them to services throughout your circuit – and take the services myself.'

'But you'll need a preaching licence. There isn't a magistrate in St Austell will give one to you.'

'You have a licence. Did it prevent you from being arrested? I'll preach without one. Let them arrest me, if they dare. I'm going now. I have much to do. But I'll be back to see you again soon.'

Nathan called through the grille in the door. A few minutes later he heard the sound of keys jangling as the gaoler hobbled his way along the gloomy corridor.

As Nathan left the cell, his father called quietly to him: 'Nathan? Are you doing all this for the Lord – or for me?'

Nathan knew what his father wanted to hear, but he could not be hypocritical, even when the answer meant so much.

'I'm doing it for you. *You* can further the Lord's cause yourself when you get out of here. I'll do my best to ensure that it's soon.'

Chapter Eighteen

NATHAN headed for Polrudden Manor when he left Bodmin Gaol. Although tired after his long walk and the anguish of finding his father in such a poor condition, he would not rest until he had confronted Sir Lewis Hearle. He wanted to learn the truth of the baronet's part in the arrest and imprisonment of his father.

It was a dismal grey day that had deteriorated into light drizzle by the time he neared the manor-house. When he was almost within sight of Polrudden he saw two riders on Hearle land, riding a parallel course with him. It was a moment or two before he recognised the smaller of the riders as Elinor Hearle.

Nathan's heart began to beat faster at the sight of her, and he had to remind himself of the part Elinor's father had probably played in the events of the past week. Even so, Nathan's mouth became dry with subdued excitement when Elinor turned her head in his direction and he realised she had recognised him, too.

The two horses slowed to a halt, and for some minutes the riders were engaged in earnest discussion. Eventually, and with obvious reluctance, one of the horses moved away. The rider looked back twice before digging heels into the horse's flanks, to be quickly swallowed up in the mist that hid Polrudden Manor from view.

Elinor Hearle waited until the other rider was out of sight before she turned her horse from the bridle path and let it pick a way across the rough grassland to the road where Nathan waited.

Before Nathan had left for Bristol, he had decided that Elinor was deliberately avoiding him, for reasons best known to herself. If this were true, it would seem that something had happened to change her mind. Her smile of welcome began when her horse was still some lengths away. Reaching him, she pulled the animal to a halt, leaped from the saddle, and hurled herself at Nathan, kissing him as though they were in the privacy of her bedroom.

'Nathan, I've missed you. Where have you been? No, there's

no need to explain. I've heard all about your prize-fight in Bristol. Everyone in Cornwall is talking about *our* champion. 'Tis said you are now undisputed champion of *the world*. I am so proud of you.'

Standing close and looking up at him, she put a hand to the extensive bruising about his right cheekbone. 'Your poor face. Does it still hurt?' Without waiting for a reply, she went on: 'Never mind, it's over now. You won. Where have you been today, to see that sister of yours?'

Nathan stiffened. 'No, to Bodmin. My father is in the gaol there.'

'Oh, yes. He was arrested in Pentuan, where all those foolish people threw stones at my father's workmen and then fought the North Cornwall Yeomanry.'

Elinor Hearle spoke so unconcernedly that they might have been discussing happenings in far-off India.

'My mother neither threw stones nor fought the soldiers, yet she died in Pentuan square.'

Elinor Hearle's eyes widened in shocked horror. 'Oh! My poor, poor Nathan. I didn't know. I am sorry . . . so very, very sorry.'

It was very difficult not to believe her. He *did* believe her. After all, she could have had nothing to do with what had occurred. Elinor could not be blamed for Sir Lewis Hearle's complicity.

'My father wasn't involved, either. He was trying to *stop* the stone-throwing. That's why I'm on my way to Polrudden now. I want to speak to Sir Lewis and ask him to use his influence to have my father released.'

It was only a small lie, Nathan told himself. Even so, it was wasted.

'You won't find my father at home. He's in London. He is a very busy man these days.'

Nathan was not sure whether he was disappointed or relieved at the news. He did not know what he would have done had he been able to prove that Sir Lewis Hearle *had* played a part in his father's arrest. He shrugged. 'Then there's no reason for me to go to Polrudden.' He rubbed a hand wearily over his face. 'I might as well go to Venn.'

'Are you *really* going to walk out on me so soon, Nathan?'

188

Elinor began picking imaginary threads from Nathan's shirt front. 'It's been such a long time since you came to visit me.'

Nathan was weary. It had been a long day, and he had much to do – and even more to think about. But this girl plucking at his shirt front was able to stir him in spite of all the physical odds against her.

He grabbed Elinor roughly and kissed her – hard. Immediately, her arms went about his neck and she pressed herself to him. His hands began to move over her body until, gasping, she pulled away from him.

'No, Nathan. Not here. . . .'

Without releasing her, he whispered: 'All right, I'll come to Polrudden tonight. As soon as it's dark.'

'That's impossible.' She slipped away from him. 'We have house guests. It's a damned nuisance, but I have to play at being a hostess for my father in his absence.'

The light drizzle was more persistent now, falling as fine rain. Elinor looked about her. Two fields away the outline of a building stood out from the gathering gloom. It was the shell of what had once been the farmhouse of Polrudden's home farm. Now it was used to store hay.

Nodding towards the building, Elinor said: 'We're getting soaked here. Let's go there and talk.'

Catching the bridle of her horse, Elinor pulled the animal towards her and turned to Nathan. 'Show me how fit your fight has left you. I'll race you to the hay-store.'

After his long walk, the last thing Nathan wanted was a race. But once in the saddle Elinor hung back, taunting him. When they came to a narrow gap in the hedge, between two elm-trees, Nathan squeezed through and began running, leaving Elinor to ride to a gate at the far end of the field. Even so, Elinor won the race and entered the old house ahead of him, laughing and out of breath.

It was dark inside, the grey evening light seeping weakly through a small and dirty window. The whole building carried the scent of hay. It was a good, clean smell. So, too, was the smell of Elinor's hair, damp from the rain, as she took off her hat and shook her hair down about her shoulders.

Without a word, she took his hand and led him to a mound of hay, put out for distribution to the cattle in the morning. When

189

she released his hand she fumbled with the laces at her throat. Moments later she shrugged her shoulders out of the dress. It fell about her feet, and in the dim light Nathan could see the whiteness of her.

'Nathan . . . I'm cold,' she whispered, her mouth close to his. 'Make love to me. Warm me. . . .' Her fingers fumbled at the buttons of his coat. 'It's been so long, Nathan. *Too* long . . .'

They made love in the grey twilight, and again in the full darkness, then Elinor murmured that she must return to Polrudden before they sent out a party to search for her.

Putting on his wet cold clothing in the darkness was a sobering, romance-chilling experience. It did not help when Nathan's many problems returned to his mind to remind him that Elinor's father was undoubtedly responsible for most of them.

The knowledge did not prevent him from taking her arm and pulling her towards him as she was about to pass out of the doorway ahead of him. But when he tried to kiss her once more she moved her face away irritably. 'No, Nathan. I'm wet and I'm cold. I *must* get home.'

He released her reluctantly. 'Will I be seeing you again?'

Untying her horse, she said. 'You want to?'

'Of course.'

'Then you'll think of a way.'

She swung up to the saddle, turned the animal's head and rode away.

Hurt by her manner, Nathan struggled to think of a word to describe his feelings. Her abrupt departure had amounted to a virtual dismissal. The word he finally settled on was . . . 'used'.

Nathan did not go to see Will Hodge, Sir Lewis Hearle's groom, immediately. First he went home, to Pentuan, to clean up and change his clothes. The house was cold and comfortless. Nathan had hoped that Sammy would be at home, but he was probably at Portgiskey Cove. Nathan envied him the warmth and companionship he would undoubtedly be enjoying. There was none of either in the Jago cottage at the moment. Even when he lit a fire it failed to chase away the gloom.

Nathan left the house and was relieved to find it had stopped raining. As he passed the heap of rubble that had once been

Pentuan's chapel, the moon slid briefly from behind the clouds. It gave him a ghostly reminder of the events that had so changed the lives of the people of Pentuan.

When Nathan stepped over the threshold of Will Hodge's cottage, he found all the warmth that had been lacking in his own home. Seated beside a blazing fire, he was treated as a hero. Ann Hodge insisted upon cooking a large meal for him, and young Sarah was brought from her bedroom to say a sleepy 'hello' to the man who had saved her from the stable fire.

Sarah stayed up until a steaming meal was placed in front of Nathan. Not until then did he realise how hungry he was. Over the meal he asked the question he had carried with him from Bodmin Gaol. Where had Will Hodge gone on the afternoon of the 'riot' at Pentuan?

'Why, to Nansladron Farm.' Nansladron was about a mile along the valley from Pentuan. 'That's where the magistrate was waiting with the yeomanry. I'd say they'd probably been in camp there, although the horses were all saddled up and ready when I arrived.'

'Did you carry a message from Sir Lewis?'

'Not a message. It was a sealed letter. Not that it would have made any difference, sealed or not. I don't read. Mind you, now I come to think about it, Sir Lewis did tell me to impress the need for great haste upon the magistrate. I didn't know what he was talking about at the time. I reckon I do now.'

'You believe he knew there would be trouble in Pentuan?'

'He *must* have known. What I don't understand is why he didn't have the yeomanry in Pentuan before the work started, so as to *prevent* trouble.'

'I can answer that,' said Ann Hodge. She had put Sarah to bed and entered the room in time to hear her husband's last statement. 'You haven't lived in Pentuan all your life. You don't know Sir Lewis Hearle as I do. He hates Methodists – Methodist preachers in particular. He didn't want the soldiers in Pentuan until there *was* trouble, with Preacher Jago caught in the middle of it. You said yourself you'd seen the preacher leave Polrudden not half an hour before he was arrested. Sir Lewis knew exactly where he'd be.'

Tears welled up in Ann Hodge's eyes. 'I cried myself to sleep that night, just thinking about your father, poor man. Him in

191

prison, your mother dead, and you away. It was enough to turn his brain. I was so sorry to hear about your mother, Nathan. She was a good woman. I knew her well and never heard her say an unkind word about anyone.'

'Thank you.'

There was no need to say more. Nathan had learned what he wanted to know. Sir Lewis Hearle *had* brought in the magistrate and the yeomanry *before* trouble had started – but not until he knew Josiah Jago was there. Nathan did not believe the stone-throwing had been started by Pentuan men, either. There were probably men in the crowd who had been hired to ensure there *would* be trouble when the military arrived. Nathan knew he would never learn the whole truth of the matter. Sir Lewis Hearle was far too clever to have hired the men himself, but Nathan had no doubt that his suspicion was well founded.

Although reluctant to return to an empty house, Nathan did not remain late at the Hodge cottage. Tomorrow was going to be another busy day.

Will Hodge insisted on accompanying Nathan to Pentuan, saying he would show him a short cut through the gardens of Polrudden Manor.

As they approached the manor-house they could see a great many lights burning in the downstairs rooms, and a number of well-dressed people milling about inside. On the driveway leading to the house, half a dozen carriages were lined up, the horses munching contentedly on the contents of straw nosebags.

Nathan commented that it looked as though there was a party going on inside the house. Will Hodge snorted derisively.

'You'd think Sir Lewis had been crowned King of England, the way things have changed here. I hope he's being paid well in his new government post. He'll need to be. He might have sold some of his farms, but he's spending twice as much as he's getting in. He and Miss Elinor have had to take on more servants to cope with all the folks who want to see them now. They have house guests most of the time – especially the Rodds. They're here at the moment.'

'Rodds? I don't think I've heard of them. Are they a local family?'

Will Hodge chuckled. 'I'm glad old Lady Rodd wasn't around to hear you say you haven't heard of her family. They're very important. They have an estate at Trebartha, on the edge of Bodmin Moor. I think one of the family sits in the House of Commons with Sir Lewis, but they never took much notice of him until he was made an under-secretary. Now they seem to spend more time here than at Trebartha.'

Will Hodge gossiped on happily, pleased to air his knowledge of the family for whom he worked, and of those who came to stay at Polrudden Manor. 'If you ask me, there's a wedding in the offing between young Francis Rodd and Miss Elinor. He dotes on her. Mind you, he'd be a handsome catch. He's heir to all the Trebartha lands, with enough money to solve all Sir Lewis's problems.'

Nathan listened to Will Hodge's prattling with dismay. The talkative groom was mistaken, of course. He had to be. Had he known what had occurred at the old home farm that very afternoon, he would have realised that Elinor could not possibly be contemplating marriage with anyone.

But fate decreed that it was to be *Nathan* who would suffer disillusionment.

Will Hodge suddenly gripped his arm. 'There's someone coming. Quick, hide here. In the bushes.'

He drew Nathan to the deep shadows of a nearby shrubbery and here they waited as footsteps crunched along the driveway, heading in their direction.

There was a faint breeze blowing, and suddenly Nathan caught the fragrance of a perfume he knew well. It conjured up memories of a darkened bedroom, and naked bodies tangled beneath silken sheets. But there were two sets of footsteps – and it was a man's voice he heard first, raised in mild complaint.

'. . . been trying to speak to you for days now. I came riding with you today thinking you'd give me an opportunity to speak my mind. Dammit, Elinor! You *must* know how I feel about you. But what do you do? You take off on that stallion of yours and it's as much as I can do to keep you in view! Then when you did finally slow down, and I was trying to gather enough breath and courage to talk seriously, you packed me off like some disobedient child.'

'Did I, Francis? I'm sorry. But I saw someone with whom I

needed to speak. What was it you wanted to say to me?'

There was a coyness in Elinor's voice that Nathan had never heard before.

'You know full well. You *must* know. I love you, Elinor. I want you to marry me.'

'Francis! This is neither the time nor the place to be saying such a thing!'

Elinor sounded primly shocked. Nathan struggled to keep his own emotions in check, remembering her as he had seen her only a few hours before. Naked in the home farm hay-store.

'I realise it's something that should be discussed with your father first, but dammit, Elinor, we're not children. We don't have to rely upon others to make up our minds for us. I'll speak to your father, certainly. But first I must know how *you* feel. And I want to know *now*.'

There was a long silence during which Nathan realised his fists were clenched so tightly his fingers were hurting.

'Francis, is this a proposal – or an ultimatum?'

Nathan recognised the teasing tone of Elinor's voice. Francis Rodd did not.

'It is not an ultimatum, Elinor. *Desperation*, yes. I'll tell you once more. *I love you.* I want you to marry me. Please say "yes".'

Beside Nathan, Will Hodge began to fidget uncomfortably. He and Nathan were eavesdropping on a very intimate scene. His movements almost caused Nathan to miss Elinor's reply, so softly was it given.

'Yes. Yes, Francis, I'll marry you – if you are quite certain it's what you want.'

Nathan's involuntary sharp intake of breath almost betrayed the two eavesdroppers. Elinor heard and said sharply: 'What was that sound?'

'I heard nothing,' Francis Rodd was determined to allow nothing to detract from this moment. 'I-I'm quite s-sure you are teasing me again. B-but it doesn't matter any more. You've said y-you'll marry me. I feel like sh-shouting the news to the whole world.' In moments of stress, Francis Rodd suffered from a stutter.

Briefly, the two shadowy figures standing on the driveway merged and became one.

194

'Francis!'

Elinor sounded shocked. Nathan's thoughts were in a turmoil, but he could not help admiring Elinor's prowess as an actress.

'I'm s-sorry. That was presumptuous of me. But you've made me s-so happy. May I tell Mother tonight?'

'No.' Elinor was in full command of the situation. 'Keeping our love a secret from your mother will be your way of proving you really love me. You'll tell no one until you've spoken to my father.'

'Dammit, Elinor. I shouldn't have to prove anything. I've told you I love you. Isn't that enough?' Francis Rodd spoke sulkily, but when Elinor gave him no answer he said: 'Oh, very well. But I'm not waiting until your father returns home. I'm going to London to speak to him there.'

'That would make me very happy.'

Elinor could hardly hide the jubilation in her voice. Francis Rodd was probably the most eligible man in the county, and once he had spoken to her father he would have committed himself to marriage without giving his formidable mother the opportunity to raise any objections. Once married, Elinor knew she could persuade the heir to the Rodd fortunes to do whatever she wanted.

Elinor gave Francis Rodd a brief kiss. 'You must go to London and hurry back to me as quickly as you can.' Grasping his arm, Elinor leaned against her intended husband in a display of affection that caused him to puff up with proprietary pride. 'We must return to the house now. If we've been missed for too long, there will be such a scandal that your mother will refuse to allow you to marry me.'

'Sh-she'll never do that, Elinor. Mother doesn't like upsetting me.'

The unofficially betrothed couple walked away along the driveway, returning to the company of family and friends who lived by the strict rules of social etiquette demanded by their society.

Behind her, unseen, and probably already forgotten, Nathan was left to nurse his own foolish, broken dreams.

Chapter Nineteen

WHEN Tom and Nell Quicke received the deeds of Venn Farm, they immediately ceded a piece of land to the Methodist Society, for a church and a burial-ground. They agreed with Nathan that it would prove to Josiah Jago that his work for the Methodist cause was not at an end.

Preacher Josiah Jago was sorely in need of heartening words and deeds. Nathan and Sammy Mizler had been to St Austell in a futile bid to have the preacher released on bail to attend Annie Jago's funeral. They had offered to provide substantial bail money, but the magistrate declared that the crime for which Josiah Jago had been arraigned was of too serious a nature for bail to be granted. He also pointed out somewhat maliciously that Methodist preachers were classed as 'itinerants', travelling from place to place to carry out their religious vocation. Such a way of life could hardly be regarded as settled enough for bail to be seriously considered.

Angry and frustrated with St Austell's custodians of the law, Nathan returned to Pentuan to find a stranger waiting for him. Very tall and vigorous, with a shock of unruly white hair, the stranger spoke with a pronounced American accent. He gave his name as Uriah Kemp – the *Reverend* Uriah Kemp, of the American branch of the Methodist Church.

Kemp explained that he had been on his way from a camp meeting in the North of England, heading for Falmouth to take a return passage to America, when he had heard of the plight of Josiah Jago.

Observing Nathan's bewilderment, Uriah Kemp asked: 'Have you ever attended a camp meeting?'

When Nathan shook his head, the American preacher said enthusiastically: 'Then you've missed one of life's truly great experiences – one that fires the souls of even the most determined unbelievers. Thousands of people on their knees, each promising himself to the Lord, the "Hallelujahs" reaching to the very sky.'

'But why are you here, in Pentuan?'

'I've been guided here by the Lord. . . . You doubt me?'

Nathan thought it would take a very brave man to confess to Uriah Kemp that anything he said was doubted. He shook his head.

'Let me explain, brother. Many years ago, soon after my ordination into the Anglican Church, I was caught up in my country's war of independence. I fought against the British. But something happened to me during those unhappy years. I was converted to Methodism. I ended the war preaching to British prisoners. It's a habit I have never lost. Whenever my footsteps guide me to a town, I head for the nearest prison. There I find souls ripe for the Lord's harvesting. Usually I am given a free night's lodging at the gaol, too. That's what happened when I entered Bodmin Town. I preached mightily for the good of both gaolers and prisoners. My reward was to share your father's cell for the night. He told me of his troubles and I knew the Good Lord had taken me to him because He had work for me again. So here I am. Tell me, what have you done so far?'

Nathan told Uriah Kemp of his plans for the chapel site and the burial-ground alongside, where his mother would be laid to rest. He also told Kemp of the unsuccessful attempt to have his father released on bail.

The Reverend Uriah Kemp nodded sympathetically. 'Bigotry is an enemy we Methodists know well. The best way to help your father is to prove to the authorities – and to him – that his absence affects his circuit not one whit. Let them see that the Methodist Church hereabouts will not collapse with the loss of one preacher. Do this and the reason for holding him has gone. There's little sense in making an example of a man if it doesn't damage his cause in any way. But we'll take things in order of importance. You say your dear mother is to be laid to rest in your new burial-ground? Who is going to take the funeral service?'

'I was hoping one of my father's lay preachers would conduct it, but those I've approached so far are reluctant to commit themselves. One is a good evangelist, but he doesn't read a word and so feels incapable of conducting a burial service. Another is employed renovating the parish church in St Austell, and he fears for his livelihood if he takes the service. The third man I approached simply refused. He says it's a sin to bury my mother with Christian ceremony in unconsecrated ground.'

'Then *I'll* conduct the service. I'll send your mother to the Lord with a reference that will be the envy of every Christian who hears it. As for unconsecrated ground, I'll consecrate it for you. Personally, I don't think it matters a green fig whether the ground is consecrated or not. I've seen men buried where they died, on muddy, unholy battlefields. Many were brave and honest men. I've never doubted that they went straight to the waiting arms of the Lord. I've seen others laid to rest in cathedral aisles, wearing fine clothes inside their satin-lined coffins. I don't doubt they're some of the best-dressed men sitting around the fires of hell. If you're good enough, the Lord will make you welcome. If you're not, no amount of consecrating's going to save your damned soul.'

The Reverend Uriah Kemp glared at Nathan, as though daring him to argue. Once again, Nathan said nothing.

'Now, what arrangements have you made to ensure that regular services are held for Methodist ticket-holders on your father's circuit?'

'None yet.' Nathan spoke hesitantly. 'I think I ought to tell you . . . I'm not a preacher. Not even a lay preacher.'

'I don't give a muleskinner's cuss about that, brother. There are a great many folk who say I don't behave like a preacher, either. But I've given some powerful sermons in my time and shown the road to heaven to a great many sinners. Your pa told me with some pride that you were going to put some backbone into his flock – turn doves into hawks, and make eagles of the chicken-hearted.'

Uriah Kemp was pacing the room on long legs. Round-shouldered and possessing a noble nose, he made a fine caricature of a hawk himself.

'You won't rally your father's flock behind you by pointing out the differences between you and them. You need to show them they can do everything you're doing – and much more. "Look at *me*," you must say to them. "I was born right here, the same as you. I fish for a living, the same as you. Yet the Lord has made me the greatest prize-fighter in the whole world. What are you going to let Him do for *you*?" Rouse them. Let them see that every mother's son and daughter can be a world-beater. You want to build a church? Let *them* do it for you. Persuade a thousand people each to put a stone into the building of a church wall and you have a thousand defenders if the enemies of the Lord try to pull it down again.'

The American preacher stopped in front of Nathan and jabbed a talon-like finger at his chest. 'You want your father out of prison? Right, then let the Methodists of Cornwall show the authorities their strength, not their weakness. Move in on the towns – Bodmin, St Austell, Truro, Launceston. Go there in your thousands – to pray. No marching, no banner-waving – and no leaders. Simply pass the word throughout the county that on a certain Sunday prayers will be said in Bodmin. The week after in St Austell. Let everyone gather in the streets and, at an agreed time, fall to their knees and pray. Set an example for the whole country to follow. Show your government the strength of Methodist support. Make them realise that they'll never stamp out Methodism – unless they are prepared to arrest so many people that there won't be prisons enough to hold them all.'

The hawk-like appearance was accentuated when Uriah Kemp tilted his head to one side. 'You doubt whether it will work, brother? I remember seeing the same doubt on the faces of your generals and colonial officials when told there was a danger of us Americans rebelling and taking the country from you.'

Uriah Kemp laid a long-fingered hand upon Nathan's shoulder. 'All it takes is *faith*, brother. *Faith*. The word has the same number of letters as "sword" and "rifle" – yes, and "Devil", too. But when a man has faith he can take a stand and defeat all three.'

The next week was a busy one for Nathan. It began with the funeral of Annie Jago. She was laid to rest on 3 March 1811, in a coarse-grassed burial-ground, fenced off by a rope that separated burial-ground from unworked pasture. A few yards away, also within the rope fence, the turf had been cut to mark out the shape of the new chapel.

More than a thousand mourners came to pay their last respects to the wife of their preacher – and also to see the American preacher, about whom many rumours were already circulating.

Uriah Kemp did not disappoint them. Both mourners and the curious returned home with their faith revitalised, convinced that Methodism was in the vanguard of the fight against evil and that Uriah Kemp could lead them through fire and brimstone to safety on the other side.

This success was followed by outdoor prayer-meetings in several nearby villages, all of which were on Preacher Josiah Jago's circuit. Advance warning went out that the prayer-meetings would be held, with the result that large, if apprehensive, crowds gathered to hear Nathan and Uriah Kemp conduct their joint services.

Despite Nathan's earlier fears that he lacked the faith and dedication of his listeners, he was able to impress them by his very simplicity, and by his determination to keep his father's circuit active until Preacher Josiah Jago was free to resume his calling.

There was nothing simple about Uriah Kemp's message. He bullied and cajoled, berated and praised his congregation until it had been moulded into a receptacle, perfectly shaped to receive the message he brought to the followers of Wesley.

The fears of the local Methodists were soon conquered. Neither magistrate, nor constable, nor militiaman attempted to break up the meetings, or arrest the unlicensed preachers. It seemed the authorities were aware of the storm that would break if they arrested the nationally famed prize-fighter – one, moreover, who was rumoured to be sponsored by a royal duke.

At only one meeting did the two men meet with any hostility. This was the gathering on the quayside in Mevagissey. Hecklers moved to the front of the crowd when Nathan was talking about the new chapel. They began shouting remarks back and forth among themselves, declaring they did not want drift-fishermen in their village telling them what they should do.

Nathan knew from their flushed faces that the fishermen had been drinking. He braced himself for the fight he felt certain would ensue when they had worked up sufficient courage. Then Uriah Kemp silenced the fishermen in a manner that proved he was used to keeping order at much tougher meetings than this.

The tall American strode forward and seized the two nearest

200

hecklers by the hair. Before they guessed his intention, he brought their heads together with a crack that was heard all around the quayside. One of the fishermen dropped to the ground, unconscious; the other staggered dangerously close to the edge of the quay, holding his head between both hands, dazed to the point of idiocy.

But the Reverend Uriah Kemp was not through yet. Marching up to another of the Mevagissey ringleaders, he tangled his long fingers in the fisherman's thick, black, curly beard – and twisted. The fisherman, his head at a painful angle, was unceremoniously dragged before the crowd. Here he was asked by Uriah Kemp whether he had something to say that was of more importance than the message of the Lord.

The unfortunate fisherman tried to shake his head, but Uriah Kemp was already doing it for him and the man cried out in pain.

'That's the first sensible sound I've heard from you since you arrived,' roared Uriah Kemp. Twisting the man's head still more, he brought him to his knees.

'That's better. This is a prayer-meeting. Now you're on your knees you can beg for the Lord's forgiveness – and you, too!'

His bellowed command and pointing finger took in all the uncomfortable fisherman's companions. One by one, they sheepishly obeyed.

The Reverend Uriah Kemp made the kneeling fishermen repeat a humiliating plea for forgiveness. This was followed by a rendering of the Lord's Prayer, during the course of which he continually called upon the men to raise their voices. Finally, the American preacher led them in a spirited rendering of a well-known Wesley hymn.

Then, with a strength that belied his age, Uriah Kemp threw the bearded fisherman from him. As the unfortunate sinner sprawled on the ground ten feet away, the American preacher dusted loosened hairs from his fingers.

Rising to his feet, the fisherman twisted his head first one way and then the other in a bid to loosen his abused neck muscles, all the while glaring wild-eyed at the tall preacher. When much of the pain had gone, the fisherman took a pace towards Kemp. Nathan was ready and blocked his path.

Although incensed by the treatment meted out to him by

Uriah Kemp, the fisherman was not willing to take on Nathan. With an oath that brought shocked gasps from some of the inland women, he turned and strode away. Most of the Mevagissey fishermen followed him, but Nathan was surprised to see that a few remained to join in the service.

The remainder of the prayer-meeting was uninterrupted, and it ended with a thousand Methodists promising to put in as much time as could be spared to help rebuild Pentuan's chapel.

Later the same evening, a number of lay preachers, shamefaced at their earlier lack of courage, promised that when the call came they would ensure a maximum attendance for the street prayer-meetings in Cornwall's towns.

The lay preachers kept their word. On the following Sunday, Bodmin townfolk were startled and alarmed when more than eight thousand Methodists from outlying villages and hamlets converged on the mid-Cornwall town. Twenty-five militiamen on standby duty were called out. They took one look at the mass of men, women and children advancing towards them and promptly retreated to the safety of their assembly-hall.

The residents of the town watched from behind closed doors and windows in growing apprehension as the Methodists gathered in an uncanny silence, quickly filling the streets about the prison. Then a voice that carried a distinctive American accent began to recite a prayer in a sonorous voice, and the vast congregation sank to its knees and joined in.

Two more prayers followed on behalf of the man incarcerated in the town's gaol for his beliefs before the Methodists rose to their feet and sang a dozen hymns, their voices filling the air to the exclusion of all other sounds. One more prayer, then the vast host turned about and departed as silently and orderly as it had come.

Behind them the stunned townsfolk unbolted their doors to discuss with neighbours the significance of such an assembly. Most knew of Josiah Jago's imprisonment in the town's gaol and all agreed it must have been a declaration of support for the imprisoned preacher. All were deeply impressed by the discipline and peaceableness of the demonstrators. The unusual prayer-meeting had achieved what Uriah Kemp had said it would. It had called the attention of the authorities to Methodist numbers, and showed their determination to uphold a right of assembly.

When the others had left the town, Nathan and Uriah Kemp paid a visit to Josiah Jago. They found him greatly heartened by the hymns and prayers that had been clearly audible inside the grim, grey-walled prison.

Josiah Jago's faith was further strengthened when Nathan informed his father that the walls of the new chapel had reached roof height, and the new burial-ground was already enclosed within four stout walls, and planted with trees and bushes.

The Pentuan preacher was much more comfortable in his surroundings now. The transfer of three golden guineas from Nathan to the gaoler had brought the change about. Josiah Jago now shared a large, dry cell with a cheerful young man of about Nathan's age. The young man's 'crime' was no more than an accusation that he had fathered the child of an unmarried village girl and was refusing to contribute to its upkeep. As he had explained to Nathan on an earlier visit, he would have been most willing to pay maintenance for the child had he honestly believed it to be his. However, he could have named half a dozen men with stronger claims to paternity than his own. The baby's mother had chosen Preacher Jago's cell-mate for the very simple reason that he alone of her lovers could afford to support her misbegotten child. She had already spent a year in prison herself for refusing to give the magistrate the name of her child's father and, for his display of stubbornness, the young man had been resident in Bodmin Gaol for almost two. He had been sent there by St Austell's senior magistrate, Sir Lewis Hearle.

So far, the cheery young man had resisted Preacher Jago's pleas for him to make amends for his profligate ways, but his light-hearted presence had lifted the preacher out of his trough of self-recrimination. Preacher Jago was now ready to stand his trial, when the spring Assizes commenced in a few weeks' time.

On the way back to Pentuan, Uriah Kemp expressed satisfaction at the manner in which their campaign was progressing. He also told Nathan something more of his earlier life in America. So interesting did Nathan find it that the miles passed by almost unnoticed.

Orphaned as a young child, Uriah Kemp had been brought up by an aged Quaker couple of pioneer stock. They provided him with a strict upbringing, substituting religion for affection. They, too, died in a smallpox epidemic when he was only thirteen years old. Uriah Kemp quickly broke his ties with the Quaker background, preferring the less exacting demands of the Anglican Church. He spent three winter seasons trapping the rivers of North America, ranging far ahead of the narrow borders of civilisation. When he had earned enough money to continue his learning, he went back to the East and was eventually ordained in the Anglican Church.

However, Uriah Kemp was by nature a missionary. He had explained earlier to Nathan how he had become a Methodist during the War of Independence, while preaching to British prisoners-of-war. When the war ended, Uriah Kemp moved westwards again, preaching to isolated pioneer families, and to the Indians of the Sioux nations who roamed the lands on both sides of the Canadian border. Privation and hardship became a way of life for this remarkable preacher.

It was late afternoon when they returned to Pentuan, and Nathan suffered a sense of guilt when he saw the sea spread out before them, smooth and inviting. There were no fishing-boats out today. Fishermen did not put to sea on a Sunday, but it had been many weeks since Nathan had been to sea with *The Brave Amy H*.

Nathan knew the boat was going out regularly, manned by Ahab Arthur, Calvin Dickin and the others, but he had little idea of how much fish they were catching. Sammy Mizler was rarely at home when Nathan returned to Pentuan, and on the occasions when he came to the house Nathan was usually deep in discussion with Uriah Kemp about the new chapel or other Methodist affairs. Neither had Nathan seen Amy since the fateful return of the fishing-boat from Bristol. He determined he would find time in the next few days to pay a visit to Portgiskey. He might even spend a day fishing with the crew of *The Brave Amy H*.

With these thoughts uppermost in his mind, it came as a pleasant surprise when he reached the Jago cottage to find both Amy and Sammy Mizler waiting there.

Kissing Amy affectionately, Nathan beamed his pleasure. 'I was just thinking it was time I faced up to my responsibilities and took *The Brave Amy H* to sea again, but I've been kept so busy. No, that excuse is not good enough. I *will* take the boat out – tomorrow! Why don't you come out with me, Amy? Then you can tell me all that's been happening at Portgiskey. . . .'

Nathan's delight at seeing Amy again had made him unusually talkative and it was some minutes before he realised he was receiving no replies. Both Amy and Sammy Mizler were looking at him with embarrassed expressions upon their faces.

'Is everything all right? Has something happened to *The Brave Amy H*?'

Sammy Mizler smiled suddenly. 'Yes . . . but I'm not talking about the boat, but the *real* Amy H.' Reaching out, he took Amy's hand. 'Congratulations are in order, Nathan. Amy has agreed to marry me.'

Chapter Twenty

WHEN he thought about the progress of their relationship, Sammy Mizler told himself he had been in love with Amy since the night she had surprised himself and Nathan in her boat. Even with a loaded blunderbuss in her hands, Sammy had forgotten his fear for long enough to admit that he had never seen a more beautiful girl. With her short black hair and sunburned skin, she might have been a young sabra girl from ancient Israel.

For many months Sammy Mizler kept his infatuation from Amy. More difficult to hide was his deeply felt jealousy when he saw the way she occasionally looked at Nathan. But Sammy was a philosophical man and for a long while he resigned himself to enjoying Amy's friendship, and an occasional shared confidence.

Amy and Nathan struck sparks from each other when they were together. Sammy Mizler, accepting the role of interested spectator, waited for the sparks to ignite an emotional fire between the two partners. It never came. Why, Sammy did not know. He thought perhaps Elinor Hearle was the biggest stumbling-block between the two – and Sammy was constantly reminding Amy of the association between Nathan and the mistress of Polrudden.

Sammy Mizler believed he had lost Amy when he saw how she had shared Nathan's grief at the death of Annie Jago, but her unhappiness passed unnoticed by Nathan himself.

Then, the evening following their return from Bristol, Amy had left Portgiskey to meet Nathan, due back from a visit to his father in Bodmin Gaol. Later that same night, Sammy Mizler had gone to Portgiskey after dark and found Amy crouched in the stern of *The Brave Amy H*, crying as though her heart was breaking.

She never explained what had happened to upset her so, but from that night she began to lean more heavily on Sammy and the name of Nathan was dropped from their conversations.

One fine day, Amy persuaded Sammy Mizler to go fishing with her in her own small boat. He agreed with great reluctance but, much to his surprise, he was not sea-sick. In fact he almost *enjoyed* the experience. So, too, did Amy, and Sammy saw her laugh for the first time in many days.

A week later, Sammy proposed to Amy. It was not easy. Sammy was a careful man, and he had a little money put by in addition to his investment in the Portgiskey fishing venture, but he had little else to recommend him to Amy. He was used to a rootless mode of life – and he was a Jew.

Sammy Mizler had never practised the religious ritual of his ancestors, but the fact remained that he belonged to a race that was persecuted in every country of the world, and treated with contempt and prejudice everywhere. It was not a tempting future to put to a prospective wife, but it was all Sammy had, as he told Amy.

Amy put an end to Sammy Mizler's dogged self-deprecation with a single word. The word was 'Yes'.

Sammy had stared at her in disbelief. 'What . . .? What did you say?'

'I said "Yes". There, now I've said it again.'

'You mean . . .?'

'I mean, yes, I'll marry you. That is, if it's what you really want. Although no one hearing you now could be sure.'

'Even after all I've just told you? Are you quite certain?'

'Sammy Mizler, do you *want* me to marry you, or not?' Amy said in amused exasperation.

'I want it. . . . It's just. . . .'

'Just nothing. You've been very kind to me, Sammy. I'm a lucky girl.'

'When, Amy? When will you marry me?'

Amy frowned. 'Not too soon, Sammy. I'd like a while to get used to the idea of becoming a wife.'

Sammy wondered whether this was the reply she might have made to Nathan, had he asked Amy to marry him. But he said: 'Of course. Of course, my dear.' Not certain what was expected of him now, he wrung his hands in acute nervousness.

'Where will you want us to live when we're married, Sammy?'

'Live? Oh . . . I'm not sure,' Sammy Mizler was unable to think straight. 'Here, I suppose.'

Amy smiled at his confusion. 'Will you really be able to settle at Portgiskey for ever, Sammy? You're a Londoner through and through. You've told me so yourself, many times. Perhaps we could visit London before we marry. I might want to live *there*.'

Sammy Mizler was unable to hide his delight. 'Let's do that, Amy. I will enjoy showing you London.'

'Then that's what we'll do.'

Amy suddenly became matter-of-fact. She kissed her future husband in the same manner, but Sammy Mizler hardly noticed. He had achieved the impossible. Amy had agreed to marry *him*. Sammy Mizler's cup of happiness was filled to the brim. He would not look upon the dregs for a long time to come.

Nathan's enthusiasm for the proposed wedding did not match that of his friends. He offered Sammy and Amy his congratulations, but they went no farther than a handshake for Sammy and a kiss on the cheek for Amy.

His lack of enthusiasm might have put a blight on the apparent happiness of his partners had Uriah Kemp not been at hand to extol light-heartedly the virtues of married life to the pledged couple.

Nathan listend politely for a few minutes, then abruptly announced that he was going to visit the boat at Portgiskey. Aware of Amy's hurt expression and the questioning frown on the face of Sammy Mizler, Nathan made a hasty exit. He had been travelling the lanes of Cornwall, talking to so many Methodists, that he was beginning to feel more like a preacher than a fisherman. But Uriah Kemp was a real preacher and, as a couple about to embark upon matrimony, Amy and Sammy would doubtless want to speak to him without Nathan's presence.

Before Nathan left the kitchen of the Jago cottage he caught Uriah Kemp's glance, filled with concern. But Nathan ignored a gesture that was meant to detain him. He did not want to explain his unforgivable and hasty retreat to anyone. Not even to himself.

His departure left an embarrassed silence behind him in the small Jago cottage, but Uriah Kemp was adept at handling such situations. He told them that Nathan had been very busy working to keep his father's preaching circuit together and was distressed because of his visit that day to Bodmin Gaol.

Nathan walked from the house to the Pentuan foreshore, trying to subdue an unreasonable resentment that was smouldering inside him. He had an absurd feeling that he had been betrayed – and was irritated that he should be entertaining such thoughts. When he arrived at the low barrier of scattered rocks that partitioned Portgiskey Cove from Pentuan Beach, he sat on a rock and tried to analyse his feelings.

Moodily tossing pebbles towards the sea, he felt he needed time to think. He would not be happy until he was able to take up the reins of his life and guide his own destiny once more. As things were at the moment, he felt he was being pushed along an unfamiliar path by the events about him: his mother's tragic death; Josiah Jago's imprisonment; the arrival of the mercurial Reverend Uriah Kemp; Elinor's forthcoming marriage. . . . And now Sammy and Amy's marriage, too.

For some reason, this last announcement had disturbed him far more than it should. He thought that his mood was due to the fact that the future had suddenly become as uncertain as the present, with the fishing partnership under threat.

Nathan looked at the sea. There was only a slight swell with a light breeze blowing from the land. Of a sudden he felt the need to be out there, away from the cares that were on the land. Rising from his rock-seat, Nathan clambered over the rocks to Portgiskey.

From the window of the cottage, Peggy Hoblyn saw him and scuttled to meet him, complaining that she had been left alone all day with neither food nor heat in the cottage. She whined that her daughter did not care for her any more. Nobody cared.

Nathan offered to come to the cottage to light a fire and find some food for her, but Peggy Hoblyn immediately went on the defensive. She declared that no stranger was coming inside her house to report to the villagers of Pentuan how shabbily she was being treated by Amy.

Backing away from Nathan as though he had threatened her life, Peggy Hoblyn turned and ran to the cottage with short, quick steps. She turned for a moment at the doorway, and Nathan called to tell her he was borrowing Amy's small boat. Before the words were out she had slammed the door shut.

209

Moments later he saw the white blur of her face at the window.

Poor Peggy Hoblyn's condition was much worse than when Nathan had last seen her. Her eccentricity now verged on madness. Nathan felt suddenly sorry for Amy and Sammy Mizler. It would be their joint responsibility to care for Peggy Hoblyn in her old age.

Nathan pulled the boat down to the sea until he was standing calf-deep in water and the boat was afloat. Pushing the boat farther out into deeper water, Nathan lay bellydown on the gunwale before swinging himself on board. Rowing clear of the headland, he hoisted the sail and headed out to sea. He had gone about a mile when he passed an empty keg bobbing in the water. Something about its movement made him put the boat about and investigate.

Dropping the sail, he reached over the side and brought the keg inboard. There were two ropes attached to it. One seemed to have an anchor on the other end. The other felt heavy, too, but it moved through the water as Nathan tugged upon it. A fathom's length away from the first keg Nathan found another, but this one was full. The rope led on again, and Nathan brought three kegs to the surface before he gave up. There were probably a dozen kegs attached to the rope. Throwing them all back into the sea, he raised his sail and left the area.

Smiling, Nathan thought it was good to know there were some things that never changed. Smugglers were still active along this part of the coast, even though Amy was no longer among their number. As he remembered Amy, Nathan's smile left him. He wondered how many times he thought of her in a normal day.

He sailed on for another half-hour, towing a fishing-line baited with feathers behind the boat, before he lowered the sail once more and pulled in his catch. He had caught enough fish to bait a long-line. Dropping it in the water, he lit his pipe and sat back to savour the sense of being alone that comes only in a small boat, far from shore.

Inevitably, his thoughts turned once more to Sammy and Amy and it brought an empty feeling to the pit of his stomach. He told himself yet again that it was fear of the marriage bringing the fishing partnership to an end. Perhaps he should have seen it coming, but he was honest enough to admit that

210

since his return to Pentuan his thoughts had been elsewhere for much of the time.

Dusk was approaching when Nathan began bringing in his line. He had caught more than three dozen fine mackerel.

In the distance he had seen a boat leaving Mevagissey harbour a short time before. As it drew closer he saw it was the Revenue cutter. Nathan looked about him uneasily, hoping he had not drifted too close to the anchored line of brandy-kegs. He was relieved that they were nowhere in sight.

The cutter came steadily towards him, and when it was almost alongside the crewmen rested on their oars and a man rose to his feet in the stern. It was Ezra Partridge.

'Well, well, Jago. All on our own out here, are we, sir? What are you carrying?'

Ezra Partridge's manner was more polite than it had been at their earlier meeting, and Nathan looked at the Chief Revenue Officer suspiciously.

'Three dozen mackerel. I wouldn't swear to it, but I doubt if they're from France.' Nathan began carefully coiling his hooked line.

'What are you doing out here?'

Nathan bridled. 'Fishing. That's how I earn my living. I also came out here to get away from people for an hour or two.'

Much to Nathan's surprise, Ezra Partridge nodded, apparently accepting the irritable reply.

'Ay, I've no doubt you'll have plenty to think about. You've not had it easy since you returned from your prize-fight in Bristol.'

Nathan said nothing, but it seemed Ezra Partridge was not expecting a reply. The two boats touched and Ezra Partridge braced his legs to steady himself against the movement of the Revenue cutter. Leaning over the side towards Nathan, he said conspiratorially: 'We're men of the world, you and I, Mr Jago.' He cast a contemptuous look at the crew of the Revenue cutter as they leaned on their oars, chatting among themselves. Reaching out, he grasped the gunwale of Amy Hoblyn's little boat and leaned still closer. In a low voice he said: 'You can do yourself a favour, Mr Jago. With your father a Wesleyan preacher you'll no doubt be against smuggling.'

Nathan stifled a grin. This was a very different man to the

one who had led the raid on the Hoblyn fish-cellar a few months earlier. He wondered what the Chief Revenue Officer would have done had he known that Nathan had once worked for Ned Hoblyn, when that prince of smugglers had been at the height of his nefarious career.

'Help me put a stop to smuggling and you could make yourself a lot of money. I'm authorised to pay a reward of twice the market value for any contraband recovered as a result of information given to me.'

'Thank you. I'll remember,' said Nathan, doing his best to appear suitably impressed.

'Do that,' said Ezra Partridge. 'It's been a pleasure meeting you again, Mr Jago.'

Ezra Partridge pushed off the smaller boat, then called upon his crew to pull away across the bay.

It was quite cold now, and Nathan decided it was time to return to Portgiskey. The wind had strengthened off the shore with approaching darkness, and Nathan was obliged to make a long tack to reach the small harbour against the wind.

He was at the far end of one of his tacks, not far from the entrance to Pentuan harbour, when he thought he heard a sound from nearby. It was dark now and, turning the boat into the wind until it was hardly moving, he listened carefully. For a while there was no sound but the wind and the sea, then he heard the splash of a carelessly handled oar in a leather-muffled rowlock.

'Ahoy there! Can you hear me?'

Three times Nathan called, softly at first. After the third and loudest call, the sounds of rowing ceased and a hoarse whisper came back to him across the water.

'Who's there?'

'Nathan Jago. Is that you, Dan?'

Nathan had recognised the voice of Dan Clymo, his childhood friend.

'Yes. What are you doing out here?'

'That doesn't matter.' Nathan had no need to ask Dan Clymo the same question. Seine-fishermen did not pursue fish at night. Dan Clymo was on his way to pick up the anchored brandy-kegs. 'Turn about and go back to Pentuan. Ezra Partridge and his Revenue men are at sea.'

The anxious muttering of the men in the other boat carried clearly across the water to Nathan.

'How do you know?'

'He stopped me less than an hour ago. Thought I might be interested in helping him capture undutied goods.'

More muttering followed, louder this time. Twice Nathan heard the words 'go back'.

The two boats were drifting apart now as a slight shifting of the wind caught the sail of Amy Hoblyn's boat.

'Head back to Pentuan.' Dan Clymo's voice was barely audible above the slap of the water against the bow of Amy's boat. 'We owe you, Nathan. I'll remember.'

Nathan was battling with the wind now. The tide was on its way in, and the small boat had drifted closer to the shore than he would have liked. However, he cleared the rocks at the entrance to Portgiskey with ample room to spare. Moments later the boat ran ashore on the sand beside the small quay. Someone moved from the shadows and held the bow as Nathan leaped ashore. It was Amy.

'Ma said someone had taken the boat. Her mind is so bad she couldn't tell me who, but I guessed it would be you.'

'I'm sorry if I've kept you up. I just felt like going out for an hour's fishing.' His words sounded stilted, as though he were talking to a stranger. Nathan heard it himself and tried to correct it.

'Where's Sammy?'

'I left him entertaining Uriah Kemp in Pentuan.'

After a moment's hesitation, Amy asked softly: 'What's the matter, Nathan? Don't you want me to marry Sammy?'

'It's none of my business. You won't find a better man.'

'I know. But that wasn't what I asked you. Never mind. As you say, it's my business, no one else's. How about you, Nathan? Have you decided to make your future with Elinor Hearle? Tell me "yes" and I'll believe you. I think you're a man who gets whatever he goes after. Is she what you want?'

Nathan was on the point of telling Amy about Elinor's new love. Instead he said gruffly: 'I'll take care of my own future.'

'Yes. . . . I'm sorry.'

'Amy . . .?' Nathan caught her arm as she went to move away. 'I didn't mean it to sound that way. It's just that I have a

lot to think about just now. You and Sammy getting married **gives** me even more. . . .'

'Oh! I thought you might. . . . Never mind what I thought.' **She** shook her arm free. 'I realise it's going to be *inconvenient* for **you**, but your gallivanting about the countryside hasn't exactly made things any easier for the rest of us. If you'd been here, there would probably have been no talk of marriage between Sammy and me. . . .'

Something in Amy's voice sounded to Nathan like a desperate cry for help. He called to her, but she had gone and the door of the cottage slammed shut behind her. Nathan cursed himself for being an unthinking fool. Scooping up the mackerel he had caught, he set off for home more unsettled than ever.

From inside the cottage, Amy heard his footsteps crunching away as she leaned with her back against the door. She was having difficulty holding back tears. Why did she and Nathan quarrel so much – and why did it matter to her? Sammy Mizler was her man now. Her thoughts should be of him – and they ought to be happy thoughts. She was to be married.

'Amy? Is that you, girl?' Her mother's complaining voice called from a darkened bedroom. 'Are you leaving me to starve to death? I haven't had a bite to eat. . . .'

'All right, Ma. I'll get you something. But there's nothing to stop you doing your own cooking, you know.'

Amy sighed. Physically, her mother was as fit as any other woman of her age, but her mind was making an invalid of her. Peggy Hoblyn's welfare would have to be taken into consideration when she and Sammy discussed their marriage in more detail.

214

Chapter Twenty-One

IN ORDER TO satisfy the many lay preachers who were unhappy at having an unlicensed preacher responsible for the circuit, Uriah Kemp took out a preacher's licence. As an ordained minister of the Anglican Church, he had no difficulty in obtaining such a licence, but the magistrate who issued it warned the American preacher of the consequences of open-air preaching. It was a warning Uriah Kemp had no intention of heeding.

The unorthodox American Methodist was at his evangelical best when preaching in the open air, with no pulpit to enclose him, and no walls to limit the enthusiasm of his congregation. His open-air services became famous throughout the length and breadth of the county. Men and women flocked from miles around to listen to him preach.

The Methodist chapel at Pentuan had been completed within a month of the foundations being dug, but Uriah Kemp declared that Preacher Josiah Jago must be the first man to preach inside its cob walls. Those who came to attend the Sunday services stood in the green burial-ground, beside the chapel, where Annie Jago had now been joined by the late Hannah Hunkin, who died a week after Annie Jago's funeral. Aged ninety-eight years at the time of her death, Hannah Hunkin had been able to remember John Wesley's first and last visits to Cornwall, as well as most of those in between. She had been one of the most respected Methodists in Cornwall. Only days before her death she had declared that she would die happy in the knowledge that she would lie in a Methodist grave in her native Pentuan, and not in St Austell among strangers.

Now that the lay preachers had resumed their duties with renewed enthusiasm, Nathan was content to leave the affairs of the local Methodist church in their hands, with Uriah Kemp supervising their duties. He resumed full-time fishing, but it was not a good time to return. The fish were in short supply.

Nathan took the boat farther west, fishing the dangerous waters around the Scilly Isles, where 'wrecking' was as much a part of everyday life to the islanders as smuggling was to the

Cornish. Sometimes the boat would be away for three or four nights, but by taking his catch direct to Falmouth a good price was obtained from the merchants who supplied the packet vessels plying from the busy port.

Whilst in Falmouth, Nathan received another substantial order for salted fish for the West Indies. For a whole week he ferried hogsheads from Portgiskey, emptying the cellar of their entire stock of preserved fish. Meanwhile, Sammy Mizler was travelling the south-west, securing markets for the coming season's catch, each order marginally more profitable than the last. Amy was usually in evidence at Portgiskey, but no date had yet been set for her wedding to Sammy Mizler.

In early May, Nathan took *The Brave Amy H* just two miles out from Pentuan and located one of the largest shoals of mackerel that he, or any of his fishermen, had ever found. They were present in millions. Almost as fast as the nets were shot, they could be hauled in again, heavy with fish. *The Brave Amy H* returned to Portgiskey carrying more fish than ever before. When they had been hurriedly unloaded, Nathan took the boat out again. Finding the shoal once more, he reaped another incredible harvest.

For three days and nights Nathan and his crew worked the same shoal without making any noticeable difference to its numbers. Then, as suddenly as the fish had appeared, the shoal vanished. Ahab Arthur suggested that the mackerel had been moving with a warm current that had brought them close to the surface. Once the current cooled, they dived well below the depth of a drift-net. Whatever the explanation, the mackerel had certainly gone, but enough had already been caught to keep the Portgiskey cellar busy for many weeks.

Mackerel had always been caught along the Cornish coast, but rarely in such quantities that curing them became accepted custom. However, with so many mackerel at Portgiskey, the only way to avoid wasting them was to cure them in some way. The fish were laid in man-high walls in the cellar, each layer separated by a generous layer of salt. Nathan also had a smoke-house hastily constructed. Here he produced 'fumados', the smoked fish so beloved by Spanish seamen.

Both these processes provided welcome work for the wives of the Pentuan fishermen. The women worked swiftly, though

216

noisily, their shouted conversations and screeches of ribald laughter carrying far across the still waters of the bay.

Outside the fish-cellar, their husbands came to inspect the size of the catches and stayed to view the industry in silent envy, squatting on the quay in small groups, mouthing their comments past the short, stained stumps of their four-a-penny clay pipes. They were happy to have their women working, even though it was for a drift-fisherman. The work brought much-needed money to households that would have little until the pilchard shoals put in their uncertain annual appearance in the bay.

Sammy found markets for the cured mackerel in Plymouth. Some would be sold to the crews of men-of-war, anchored in the Sound. The remainder were to go up-river, destined for French captives, imprisoned behind the high, grim walls of the prison they had built for themselves on Dartmoor.

Nathan brought his almost exhausted crew back to Portgiskey after the disappearance of the mackerel, to find Amy waiting for him in a state of great excitement. She had received a message from Tom Quicke. Nell's time had come. The baby would be born before the day was out.

Leaving the others to secure the boat before they went home for a well-deserved rest, Nathan set off for Venn Farm. Amy went with him, hoping she could be of some assistance to her friend.

It was the first time Amy and Nathan had held any conversation since that night on the quay at Portgiskey, and Nathan opened the conversation with an observation on Sammy Mizler.

'We're having a good year, Amy. It's thanks in no small measure to Sammy's good work in finding profitable markets for us.'

Amy nodded. 'He works hard. He's a good man.'

Nathan looked sideways at her. 'Have you fixed a date for the wedding yet?'

Amy shook her head. 'We're in no hurry.'

'Are you still quite certain it's what you want?'

Amy rounded on him angrily. 'I'm *quite* certain, thank you.'

They walked on in silence for some minutes before Nathan said apologetically: 'I didn't mean to upset you, Amy.' He shrugged helplessly. 'Somehow, I don't seem to be able to avoid it.'

Amy noticed how tired he looked and she felt sudden remorse for having rounded on him so swiftly. With a warm gesture, she reached for his hand. 'I should be apologising, Nathan, not you. But we're still friends?'

He squeezed her hand gratefully. 'Yes, still . . . friends.'

They continued to Venn, walking hand in hand, and in spite of his tiredness Nathan felt more content than he had for a very long time.

A round, motherly woman from a nearby farm was already at Venn Farm with her daughter, and it was clear that further help was not really needed. But Amy was given a number of tasks in the kitchen and was soon as busy as the other two women.

Nathan found Tom Quicke in the outbuildings that opened on to the farmyard. He had cleared out all the animals' sheds and pens, and was now working vigorously moving straw from one place to another. When Nathan taxed him with making unnecessary work for himself, while his wife was in the house giving birth, Tom Quicke readily admitted the charge.

'If I don't keep myself busy out here, I'll be up those stairs to see Nell every few minutes – and the house is no place for a man today.'

Nathan grinned. Taking a pitchfork from a rack on the wall, he set to and helped Tom Quicke to throw straw from the ground floor to a loft.

They were still working here when Sir Lewis Hearle rode into the farmyard. His arrival came as a surprise to both men, neither of whom had known of Sir Lewis's return to Polrudden.

One look at the baronet was enough to see that he was in a foul mood. Tugging on a rein, he caused his horse to turn a complete, head-jerking circle.

'Quicke, what's the meaning of allowing a Methodist church to be built on Venn land?'

Tom Quicke, overawed by the presence of the angry landowner, looked to Nathan for support.

'*I* built the chapel, Sir Lewis. It's to replace the one you had pulled down.'

Sir Lewis Hearle turned a malevolent glance upon Nathan. 'I don't recall addressing you, Jago. Quicke should know better than to associate himself with the son of a discredited preacher. I'll see you lose your tenancy for this, Quicke. I don't know what arrangement you've come to with the Duke of Clarence, but he won't tolerate a dissenting church on his land.'

'I doubt whether the Duke of Clarence cares a fig what happens on Venn Farm,' said Nathan as evenly as he could. He knew that the facts would have far more impact upon Sir Lewis Hearle than anger. It was not easy. This man was responsible for the imprisonment of his father. 'The farm belongs to Tom Quicke and his wife, who also happens to be my sister.'

For a few moments Sir Lewis Hearle was speechless as he stared from Nathan to Tom Quicke in disbelief. 'I don't believe you. When Quicke took on a tenancy from me he could hardly raise the rent money. Where has he found the money to buy Venn?'

'That's his business, and his alone. But the chapel is on Methodist land, properly signed over to them by Tom Quicke. . . .'

Suddenly from the house there came a sound that momentarily halted all conversation. It was the first, long-drawn-out protest of a newborn baby, and Amy's voice was calling: 'Tom, come quickly. It's a boy. A wonderful son.'

In the magic of the moment, Tom Quicke forgot his fear of the baronet Member of Parliament and turned to Nathan with an expression of sheer joy upon his face.

'Go to Nell, Tom,' Nathan said gently. 'She'll be wanting you now.'

Tom Quicke threw down his pitchfork and ran to the farm without another look at Sir Lewis Hearle.

When he had gone, Nathan spoke to the baronet as softly as he had spoken to Tom Quicke. 'You're on another man's land here, Sir Lewis, and that man's wife has just given birth to their first son. It's a happy time – and you have no place in their happiness.'

Sir Lewis Hearle bristled with suppressed rage, and Nathan braced himself for a blow from the riding-crop Sir Lewis was holding.

Instead, Sir Lewis Hearle said: 'I don't know how you managed to get Venn Farm for Tom Quicke, but I'm quite certain it's your doing. You'll regret it one day, very soon. I'll put my mind to the matter once I've seen your father put away.'

Sir Lewis Hearle jerked his horse's head around cruelly and took the animal out of the farmyard at a canter.

Nathan watched thoughtfully until Sir Lewis Hearle passed from view at the end of the farm track. Then he went inside the farmhouse to share Tom and Nell's joy in their son.

Sir Lewis Hearle's return to Cornwall had a twofold purpose. The first concerned his daughter's marriage, and the restoration of Polrudden's fortunes. Francis Rodd had visited Sir Lewis in London, and Elinor's father had bestowed his parental blessing on the union of the two ancient Cornish families.

Since that day, Sir Lewis Hearle had heard nothing from his daughter. He had despaired of marrying her off many years before, and did not intend losing this unexpected opportunity to have the heir to Trebartha's considerable estates as his son-in-law.

Sir Lewis was once again hard pressed for money. The cost of maintaining the standard of hospitality expected of even such a junior government official was much higher than he had anticipated. Furthermore, there had so far been few requests made to him for highly paid favours. He was relying heavily upon the forthcoming marriage of Elinor to save him from further financial embarrassment – but the marriage needed to be soon.

Sir Lewis Hearle also intended combining his paternal duties with a determination to be present at the trial of Preacher Josiah Jago. The Judge of Assize at the spring sitting in Bodmin was to be Mr Justice Vincent, one of the country's most senior judges.

In the past, Judge Vincent had shown himself less than ready to bow to government pressure when giving a judgement on matters of national importance. Sir Lewis Hearle's presence was intended to impress upon the learned judge the need to award Josiah Jago a salutary sentence. The power of dissident preachers and their 'churches' needed to be broken before the seeds of sedition took firm root and a bloody harvest of rebellion was forced upon the country. The memory of events in France and the wholesale slaughter of aristocrats and public officials that followed the act of revolution was still fresh in the minds of King George's ministers.

220

Where the marriage was concerned, Sir Lewis found his daughter equally frustrated in her own efforts to bring Francis Rodd to the altar quickly. The husband-to-be insisted he was as eager as Elinor herself for the marriage. Unfortunately, neither of the young people had been able to induce a similar enthusiasm in the daunting bulk of Admonition, Lady Rodd, the widow of Sir Philip Rodd, KCB.

Named by her naval admiral father after the flagship in which he was serving at the time of her birth, Admonition Rodd was a forceful, domineering woman. She had given her blessing to a marriage between her only son and Elinor Hearle, but she saw no reason why they should rush into the married state.

Indeed, Lady Rodd would have preferred to defer the wedding for a year or two. She wished to be quite certain that Sir Lewis Hearle would prove more durable than many other under-secretaries, and would one day achieve even higher office in Spencer Perceval's Tory government. Her son was too great an asset to waste on the daughter of a junior Minister.

There was another reason for her reluctance to hasten the wedding. Sir Philip Rodd had died when his son, Francis, was a small child. Aware that death was imminent, the Lord of Trebartha had drawn up a tightly detailed will, with the aid of the family solicitors.

Rather than allow the young child to inherit all, and risk manipulation and exploitation by the many influential members of the Rodd family, Sir Philip had left everything to his wife, Admonition. It would remain hers until the day Francis Rodd married. When such an event occurred, Trebartha, its lands and its fortunes would become his. It was not surprising, therefore, that Lady Rodd was in no hurry for her son to take himself a wife.

Elinor, unaware of the terms of Sir Philip's will, tried very hard to apply pressure to Francis Rodd. Unfortunately, the heir to Trebartha was not a strong character. When he was with Elinor he made solemn promises and left her side filled with a determination to be master of his own destiny. But after only a few minutes with his mother all his bold resolution ebbed away.

Plagued with his own monetary problems, Sir Lewis Hearle berated Elinor unfairly, accusing her of doing little to restore the fortunes of Polrudden. He little knew that Elinor, too, had pressing reasons for wanting to become Francis Rodd's wife as quickly as possible.

No more than a week after his confrontation with Sir Lewis Hearle, Nathan was walking to Venn Farm in the late evening. The next day would see Josiah Jago brought to trial at Bodmin Assizes. Nathan wanted a final chat with Nell, to assure her he would be in the court-room throughout the proceedings.

He had reached a quiet spot on the footpath that skirted Pentuan village, when he saw someone seated on the grass verge farther along the path. As he drew closer he was surprised to see it was Elinor Hearle. Grazing some yards away was her stallion, Napoleon.

It all looked very casual, but Elinor had been watching from the top of the hill when *The Brave Amy H* returned to Portgiskey. She waited impatiently for the fishermen to unload the vessel. Then, when Nathan left the boat and made for Venn Farm, she rode to head him off.

Seeing her sprawled carelessly on the grass bank, Nathan felt the familiar excitement for her surging through his veins. A great deal had happened to sour their relationship, but she was still the loveliest girl he had ever known.

Looking up suddenly, Elinor smiled. 'Hello, Nathan. You haven't been to see me for such a long time I thought I must come and find you. It wasn't easy. You're a very elusive man.'

'I'm a *working* man,' said Nathan ungraciously, doing his utmost to dismiss the pleasure her words gave him. 'Besides, I doubted whether you'd want to see me again.'

Elinor smiled mockingly. 'After our last meeting at Home Farm?'

'That was before Francis Rodd asked you to marry him – and you accepted him.'

Nathan had not intended saying anything about the scene he and Will Hodge had witnessed, but he could not hold back the words.

Elinor paled. 'That is a secret between the Rodd and Hearle families. Nothing was to be announced until a wedding date is decided. Who told you? I *demand* to know.'

'It doesn't matter.'

'Damn you, Nathan. It *does* matter. I'll not have my servants carrying gossip to the village.' Elinor stood with clenched fists on her hips, her nostrils flared with anger.

'You didn't come to find me just to get angry about gossip?'

Nathan would have liked to take Elinor and crush the anger and arrogance out of her but, much to his amazement, his words had the same effect. Her arrogance vanished. Suddenly she looked very tired and vulnerable.

'No, I did not come seeking a quarrel with you – and, unless I can find someone to help me very soon, the villagers will have something more than *idle* gossip to talk about. I'm carrying your child, Nathan.'

'*My* child? You're certain?'

'Am I certain it's yours?' Elinor's ready temper flared again and fury accentuated the pallor of her skin. 'Do you think I am one of your village trollops? I should whip you for such a remark, Nathan Jago.'

'That isn't what was meant.' Nathan felt the stirrings of a ridiculous thrill deep inside him. 'There can be no doubt . . . you *are* with child?'

'No doubt at all! That's why I am here to see you. You put it there. Now you can tell me how to get rid of it – and quickly.'

'How long have you known?'

'What does it matter? I suspected I was pregnant about two months ago. I've been quite certain these last few weeks.'

'Why haven't you tried to see me before? Surely you wouldn't have married Francis Rodd knowing you were carrying my child inside you?'

Elinor's chin came up in a defiant manner that Nathan remembered well. 'Would it have been *so* terrible? To give your child an inheritance that included Trebartha and Polrudden?'

Understanding had been slow in coming to Nathan, but it was with him now. 'You haven't been able to arrange the marriage in time, have you? Now you need to rid yourself of the baby before it becomes an embarrassment.'

'I *must*. Another month or so and there can be no question of marriage with Francis Rodd. What can I do, Nathan? Is there a herb or potion I can take? What do the village girls do?'

'Perhaps you should ask the man who shares a cell with my father. Sir Lewis sent him to prison two years ago because of a disputed bastardy order. The unfortunate mother had been in gaol for a year before that, for refusing to name the father of her child. Don't you think she would have got rid of the baby had it been possible?'

Elinor looked at Nathan suspiciously, but suspicion gave way to dismay when she saw no guile in his expression. 'What are you telling me – that nothing can be done?'

'Very little – although I do have one possible solution.'

'Thank God! What is it?'

'Marry *me*, Elinor.'

Elinor's relief turned to anger; then, when she saw Nathan was quite serious, to incredulity. 'Marry you? Marry . . .!'

For some moments Elinor spluttered incoherently. When she regained control of herself, she said in an icy voice: 'What would you have me do, as your wife? Stand in a stinking fish-cellar working my hands raw until the day I give birth to *your* baby? Would you have me become a "good" wife, too? Spending half of each day elbow-deep in salt and fish, the other half caring for a brood of brats that would increase with every year that passed? Is this how you see *me*, Nathan Jago?'

'No,' replied Nathan patiently. 'I won't always be a working fisherman. I own a good boat now and have earned enough money to buy a second. Next year I'll probably buy two more. Before long I'll own the largest fleet of boats on the Cornish coast. You won't have to do anything but remain at home, caring for the child you have inside you now, and thinking of ways to spend the money I'm going to make. You'll be better off than you are now, Elinor.'

Elinor's scornful look cut into him with the keenness of a boning-knife. 'Better off as a fisherman's wife than as Mistress of Polrudden? You're a fool, Nathan Jago. I am the daughter of a baronet – one who might one day become Prime Minister of Great Britain. I am going to marry Francis Rodd. You and I have had . . . fun, together. Because of this I am carrying your child. I thought you might help me. I never realised you entertained such foolish dreams. Never mind. I'll get rid of your bastard in my own way.'

Elinor ran for her horse. Snatching up the reins of the startled animal, she sprang to the saddle. Wheeling the horse to face Nathan, she cried: 'This is one form of abortion your fisher-girls can't try; but it will work, I promise you.'

Elinor brought her riding-crop down hard upon Napoleon's flank and the horse leaped forward, almost bowling Nathan over. Clearing a ditch beside the path in a mighty bound, it then jumped the low hedge beyond. Twenty paces more and the horse was stretching out in a long-striding, reckless gallop down the slope of a field.

Nathan opened his mouth to call to Elinor not to be so foolish, but the sound died in his throat. She was riding like a maniac. Any distraction could be calamitous. Elinor was a superb horsewoman; Nathan hoped she would be able to keep full control of the powerful horse and come to her senses before she had an accident.

But Elinor was courting disaster, and it came to her very quickly. At the bottom of the small field was an untrimmed hedge of briar and bramble. Elinor put the horse to it at full gallop. At the last moment the horse baulked, but it was going much too fast to stop and so made a belated attempt to clear the high hedge. The horse's front legs tangled in the briars, and sheer momentum caused the animal to somersault.

Elinor's scream came back to Nathan, before being cut off as horse and rider crashed to the ground, out of sight beyond the hedge.

Nathan ran to a nearby gate and vaulted over. Running down the slope of the field, he followed the path taken by Elinor. Forcing a way through the tall hedge, he ignored the briars that tore at his clothes and hands.

The stallion was lying dead, its neck broken by the terrible fall. Elinor lay clear of the animal, her right foot still caught in the stirrup. She was dazed, but conscious, and there was no blood to be seen on her.

She appeared to have had an amazing escape, but as Nathan stooped and attempted to free her foot from the stirrup Elinor began screaming.

At first Nathan was unable to get any sense from her. Then she sobbed that the pain was in her back, and when Nathan freed her foot he discovered she could not move her legs.

Nathan was thoroughly alarmed. He had experienced a similar injury on board a man-of-war, when a sailor had fallen from the rigging. His back broken, the sailor had died a pain-filled death two days later.

'I'll need to get help, Elinor.' Taking off his jacket and placing it over her, he repeated his message. It was doubtful whether she heard him, so great was the pain of her injury.

Running to Venn Farm, Nathan found the house filled with neighbouring farmers. With their wives, they had come to see the Quickes' new son. One of the farmers had ridden to Venn, and Nathan despatched him to Mevagissey to find the physician. Then, with Tom Quicke and the other men, he returned to the scene of Elinor's accident, carrying a sheep-hurdle.

As a group of the farmers marvelled at the height of the hedge Elinor and her horse had almost cleared, Nathan, Tom Quicke and two of his neighbours lifted Elinor between them and carefully laid her upon the hurdle. Fortunately, perhaps, she fainted as the men set out with her, bound for Polrudden.

Sir Lewis Hearle was at home and he showed great concern for his unconscious daughter. As the men carrying her began to ascend the wide staircase, the physician arrived.

Dr Ellerman Scott was red-faced and puffing heavily. He had been attending a patient in a cottage on Portgiskey Hill, high above the cove, when the farmer found him. A newcomer to Mevagissey, it was the first time he had been called to the house of one of the area's leading citizens. He set out to create an impression of efficiency and thoroughness.

Supervising the placing of Elinor upon her own bed, he allowed only Elinor's maid to stay in the room. The remainder of the men, including her father, were sent out of the room.

Downstairs, Sir Lewis Hearle served brandy to the farmers, who stood around red-faced and embarrassed as the baronet thanked them for their assistance. Nathan was served with a drink, too, but the baronet avoided looking at his face and said nothing to him.

After a single, large drink, the farmers began to mumble about having work to do and edged self-consciously from the room, Nathan with them.

In the hall outside, Nathan saw the grave-faced physician coming down the stairs. He hung back, in the hope of overhearing what was said.

Meeting Sir Lewis Hearle in the hall, the physician said: 'I have grave news, Sir Lewis. Your daughter's back is broken. I think she will live . . . but she will never walk again.'

Sir Lewis Hearle took the news in stunned horror. 'You are certain? There can't possibly be some mistake . . .?'

The physician shook his head sorrowfully. 'No doubt you will want to call in a surgeon . . . perhaps one of your London acquaintances. But I am afraid he will only confirm my diagnosis. I spent many years treating miners in the St Agnes district, Sir Lewis. I have see many men – *too* many men – with such injuries. By the way, is your daughter's husband in the house?'

'Her husband . . .?' Sir Lewis Hearle looked puzzled.

'Yes.' The doctor had totally misinterpreted Sir Lewis Hearle's response. 'Fortunately – or unfortunately, as it may well turn out – your daughter has not lost the baby she has been carrying for the last three months.'

Flabbergasted, Sir Lewis Hearle opened his mouth to tell the doctor he had made a mistake. Then he saw Nathan standing a few paces away. Suddenly Sir Lewis recalled the look Elinor had given Nathan when he came to Polrudden to negotiate the tithe payments for his drift-fishing venture. He had memories of his own misgivings at the time.

The physician had made no mistake – and Sir Lewis Hearle knew he needed to look no farther than the hall of Polrudden Manor for the father of Elinor's unborn child. He could also hazard a guess why the 'accident' had occurred – and why Nathan Jago had been on the spot.

With a great effort, Sir Lewis Hearle kept his feelings under control. If he allowed them to show now, the news of his shame would be carried to every household in the county within days. The farmers were too far away to have heard the doctor's words, but they had not yet left the house.

Sir Lewis cursed the fates that had allowed the accident to happen without bringing about the miscarriage he believed Elinor had wanted so desperately. He also prayed that Elinor had allowed Francis Rodd to enjoy the liberties she had allowed this . . . this . . . *fisherman*! If she had, it should still be possible to arrange a marriage, quickly and discreetly. If she had not . . . Sir Lewis did not dare contemplate the possible consequences. The county would be scandalised. When the news reached London it could also cost him his future in government.

'Jago. Stay here. I want to see you after the physician has gone.'

Nathan felt a thrill of apprehension run through him. He had been watching Sir Lewis Hearle after the physician had made his unwitting remarks. He knew why the baronet wanted to talk to him.

The physician left after receiving a sherry and the thanks of the Squire of Polrudden. When he had closed the door behind him, Sir Lewis Hearle walked back to the hall, with its magnificent, curving staircase, panelled walls, portraits and faded tapestries. Stopping before Nathan, the landowner made no attempt to disguise the hatred that trembled in his voice as he spoke.

'Jago, you heard what the physician said. I'm not going to give you an opportunity to lie and tell me you're not responsible for the child Elinor is carrying. Everything fits together far too neatly. Elinor has paid the price for her stupidity. God, but she's been punished! Yet, if things do not work out, it might have been better had she been left to die! You may think you've got away scot free, Jago. You haven't. If it weren't for the scandal it would cause, I would horsewhip you here and now. I *will* if I ever see you near this house again. Do you understand?'

'I'm not an innocent preacher who'll turn the other cheek when violence is offered, Sir Lewis. I hit back. What's more, I love Elinor. Yes, it *is* my child she's carrying, and I'll be back to see how she is . . . when my father's trial is over.'

228

Chapter Twenty-Two

THE trial of Preacher Josiah Jago at Bodmin Assizes lasted little longer than the pomp and ceremony that accompanied the opening of the half-yearly court of law.

Mr Justice Vincent arrived at the Assize Court in an impressive carriage, escorted by a troop of Essex Yeomanry, currently performing garrison duties in Cornwall. Behind him came the coaches bearing the Sheriff and lesser dignitaries. All were met at the entrance to the court by the mayors of Cornwall's towns, together with the senior magistrates and court officials.

There were a number of judges on the western circuit. Most enjoyed the ritual pageantry that accompanied the opening of the Assizes, and the subsequent functions and social gatherings that helped to make this one of the highlights of the county year. Some would sometimes spend as long as half an hour at the court entrance, greeting friends and acquaintances, meeting new dignitaries and accepting – or declining – invitations calculated to while away the long rural evenings.

Mr Justice Vincent was not one of these.

Devoid of humour and unsmiling, Judge Vincent regarded himself not as a leading figure in West Country society, but as a servant of England's legal system, chosen to be a judge because of his great knowledge of the law. Scrupulously impartial, Mr Justice Vincent was a forerunner of the incorruptible judges who would one day make Great Britain's judiciary a pattern for the courts of the world.

Nodding his head to acknowledge the obeisance of the gathered officials, the Judge of Assize swept past them all and made his way to the judges' rooms. Ten minutes later, as the occupants of the sombre court-room rose to their feet, the stentorian tones of a court usher announced the approach of the man who would grant life or death, freedom or hell, to the thirty-seven men and women shivering with apprehension in the damp cells beneath the Assize building.

Judge Vincent cut short the many messages of welcome directed at him by court officials. Curtly, he demanded that a roll be called of all those mayors and chief magistrates who were required to attend a Court of Assize. Many were missing, although a few had sent men to make apologies on their behalf. Mr Justice Vincent brushed aside all such apologies, fining the absent mayors forty shillings on the spot. Those mayors and magistrates who had not bothered to send anyone to explain their absence were to receive an even greater shock. The unsmiling judge directed the court to have them arrested and brought before him. His ruling produced a gasp of shock from those dignitaries who were present, but there were carefully concealed smiles of delight from the less respectful junior court officials.

Preacher Jago's case was fourth on the court list. When his name was called, the preacher climbed to the dock looking frail and apprehensive. His arrival prompted a brief burst of hand-clapping from a number of Methodists who had journeyed from the Pentuan area to witness the trial of their minister. Mr Justice Vincent brought the applause to an abrupt end by threatening to clear the court and arrest the offenders.

The prosecution outlined its case and called four witnesses. Two were men who had been demolishing the Pentuan chapel, and another a soldier of the North Cornish Yeomanry.

All three gave evidence that Preacher Jago was present when the Pentuan crowd got out of hand and began stoning the workmen. All agreed that Josiah Jago had been addressing the crowd, but increasingly impatient questioning by Judge Vincent established that not one of the three had heard the preacher's words.

The fourth and last prosecution witness was the landlord of Pentuan's Jolly Sailor tavern. Red-faced and ill-at-ease, Silas Caldicutt spoke of the alarm he had felt when the 'Methodees' gathered outside his premises.

'They was fair angry with they St Austell men,' he added. 'I wasn't at all surprised when they turned nasty on 'en.'

'You saw Josiah Jago addressing the crowd at the time they turned nasty?' The question came from the prosecuting counsel.

'That I did. Standing on the mounting-block outside my tavern, he was. Right outside my window and shouting at they Methodees fit to bust a gut.'

230

'And they responded by hurling stones at Sir Lewis Hearle's workmen, and generally behaving in a riotous manner?'

'They did. They was riotous, right enough. Throwing everything they could lay their hands on. Tore up part of the square. I had to pay my own hard-earned money to make it fit to walk on again.'

'Would you say it was Josiah Jago's presence that incited the men and women in the square to violence?'

'No doubt about it. It were his words that set 'em off, and no mistake.'

Smirking, the prosecuting counsel sat down, satisfied he had at last produced a witness to clinch the case against Josiah Jago.

He had not reckoned with Mr Justice Vincent's obsession with justice. Leaning on his bench and fixing his stern gaze upon the tavernkeeper, the judge said: 'You have said that Mr Jago's words were responsible for the riots. Will you tell this court exactly what those words were?'

'Ah . . .! Ah, well, me Lord. I'm not saying I can remember his *exact* words. I do know they made everyone some angry.'

Judge Vincent looked at the tavernkeeper fiercely: 'The people gathered in the square were men and women of deep religious conviction. Their church was being demolished. I assume they were "some angry" long before Josiah Jago addressed them. You were closer to him than any other witness. You *must* have heard his words. What were they? And I would like to remind you at this stage of the solemn oath you have taken to tell this court the truth.'

The tavernkeeper opened and closed his mouth twice without a sound emerging. He looked at the prosecuting counsel for help, but the barrister was staring at the floor at his feet. He knew better than to break in upon Mr Justice Vincent's questioning. Next, the unhappy tavernkeeper cast a significant glance at Sir Lewis Hearle, seated with his fellow senior magistrates. The Lord of Polrudden Manor was also studiously avoiding the tavernkeeper's glance, leaving him to his own inadequate resources.

'Mr Caldicutt, I am waiting.'

'Preacher Jago told them Methodees he'd been to see Squire Hearle, to ask him not to pull down their chapel. He said Sir Lewis told him it had to come down. Then the crowd started throwing stones.'

Mr Justice Vincent waited for Silas Caldicutt to continue. When nothing was forthcoming, he leaned far over the bench. 'Is this all you can tell me? What did Josiah Jago say when the people began throwing stones – and I'll have the truth, if you please, Mr Caldicutt.'

Running a finger around the neckband of his shirt, suddenly uncomfortably tight, the landlord of the Jolly Sailor tavern croaked: 'He . . . he called on them to stop throwing stones, me Lord.'

'Louder, if you please. I want the jury to hear your every word.'

'He told the crowd to stop throwing stones. Said it would do no good and only lead to trouble.'

Mr Justice Vincent leaned back in his hard, high-backed chair and drummed his fingers angrily on the polished bench in front of him.

'So at last we have the truth of this sordid matter. Far from inciting a riot, it would appear that Josiah Jago was attempting to *end* one. Is there something you haven't told us, Mr Caldicutt? Did the prisoner perhaps behave violently himself?'

'Only when his wife was killed. He pushed one of the soldiers. I . . . I think he wanted to reach his wife.'

The judge sat bolt upright. 'His wife was killed? Was she one of the rioters?'

Silas Caldicutt was about to lie, when he remembered the judge's stern warning. 'No. . . . Annie Jago were no rioter. She were looking from her window and had seen Preacher Jago arrested, I reckon. She were on the way from the house to him.'

Mr Justice Vincent was angry. Very angry. Turning to Richard Oxnam, Sheriff of Cornwall, seated beside him, he said: 'Mr Oxnam, certain matters have been disclosed about this case that I find particularly disturbing. The true nature of this witness's evidence should have been ascertained at the magistrates' hearing. Had that been done, this matter would never have come to court, and the defendant would not have spent months wrongfully imprisoned. I am going to direct the jury to dismiss this case and I want you to instigate an enquiry into the manner in which the hearing at the magistrates' court was conducted.'

232

The judge looked along the line of senior magistrates, and his glance fell upon Sir Lewis Hearle. 'Such an enquiry would normally be the duty of the senior magistrate for the area. However, it would appear that Sir Lewis Hearle has a strong personal interest in this matter. For him to conduct such an enquiry would be quite improper.'

Amidst scenes of uproar in the public gallery, the prosecuting barrister rose to his feet to remind the judge that Josiah Jago still faced charges of 'preaching in the open air'.

Before proceeding farther, Judge Vincent dealt with the uproar in his court-room. When the last of the spectators had been cleared, the judge suggested pointedly that in view of the length of time Josiah Jago had already been held in prison, and the personal grief he had suffered, the prosecution might be well advised to drop all further charges against the Methodist preacher.

Such a 'suggestion' coming from Mr Justice Vincent was tantamount to a directive. The prosecuting counsel promptly announced that no evidence would be offered on the remaining charges.

The decision greatly angered Sir Lewis Hearle. Later, in the judge's private rooms, he had a heated argument with the Assize Court Judge. He pointed out the dangers of allowing ministers of dissident churches to preach against the Establishment and added that the Prime Minister himself had approved a campaign to limit the powers of such men. The Home Office Under-Secretary also hinted that the acquittal of Preacher Josiah Jago would be viewed with great displeasure by the country's first minister.

Mr Justice Vincent gave Sir Lewis Hearle a cold, hard look, his eyes as expressionless as those of a fish. 'I am sixty-seven years of age, Sir Lewis, and have a delightful estate in Hampshire awaiting my retirement. I have no ambition to become Lord Chief Justice, or even a Judge of the Court of Appeal. However, should Perceval wish to dismiss me as an expression of his displeasure, he will need to take his case to both Houses of Parliament. I doubt whether even a man possessed of Spencer Perceval's lack of discretion will embark upon such a course of action merely because an innocent man has been acquitted. Furthermore, I have no intention of distorting the image of justice in order to appease a man who has a personal – and, if I may say so, totally unreasonable – hatred of a noncomformist religious movement. I will, of course, repeat this conversation to the Lord Chief Justice. You may leave now, Sir Lewis – and you have my permission to excuse yourself from attending the remainder of the spring Assize.'

Having dismissed Sir Lewis Hearle, baronet, Under-Secretary at the Home Office, Member of Parliament, Justice of the Peace, and landowner, as though he were a recalcitrant schoolboy, Mr Justice Vincent returned to the court-room to dispense honest justice to the people of Cornwall.

When Preacher Josiah Jago walked from the Bodmin Assize a free man, he looked up to the blue sky, opened his arms wide and allowed the warmth of the late spring sunshine to flow over him. This was something he had missed dreadfully. The opportunity to stand in the open, with the sky above him, and the ability to roam freely and admire God's handiwork about him.

Josiah Jago embraced Nathan and then the American preacher who had served the Methodist cause so well, before setting off on a homeward journey that soon became a triumphant procession. Josiah Jago had become a living martyr to the cause he had always served so loyally.

By the time he arrived in Pentuan, the village street was packed with jubilant well-wishers, and tears of humility glistened on Preacher Jago's face as he looked at his friends and parishioners.

But before he returned to the quiet of his own house Josiah Jago climbed the hill to visit the grave of his wife. When the widowed preacher kneeled by the graveside to offer up a private prayer, everyone who had turned out to celebrate his homecoming kneeled, too. In the surrounding lanes, in the burial-ground itself, and in the green fields of the steep hillside, a prayer went up for the soul of Annie Jago. Nathan thought that he had never before experienced such a moving moment.

Afterwards, Josiah Jago inspected his new church in silence. Nathan, who had been responsible for the construction of the building, waited with some apprehension for his father to approve the work.

It was not forthcoming until Josiah Jago had inspected every aspect of the workmanship and had stood for some silent minutes in the lovingly carved pulpit, gazing out over an imaginary congregation.

Then, looking at Nathan, he nodded his head three or four times, and said softly: 'Your mother would have been proud of you for this, Nathan. It's a pride I happily share. Thank you, son.'

Nathan was reminded of the infrequent occasions when, as a boy, his father would give him a passing pat on the head. It had given a warm glow to the coldest morning. In those days, Nathan would have built ten chapels to receive praise such as his father had just bestowed upon him.

That evening a constant flow of visitors passed through the Jagos' Pentuan cottage, and Nathan was forced to call a halt to them shortly before midnight. It had been a gruelling day, both physically and mentally, for Josiah Jago. He was unused to such activity. He had exercised neither body nor mind during his long imprisonment.

When the exhausted preacher had been persuaded to retire to his bedroom, Nathan and Uriah Kemp sat for a while before the kitchen fire, discussing the events of the day.

'Your father will go to sleep a happy man,' declared Uriah Kemp. 'He's proved that justice can be obtained by a Methodist in your English courts.'

'He was lucky. There aren't too many judges like Judge Vincent.'

'Perhaps not, yet many opressed preachers will take heart from this verdict.' Uriah Kemp looked at Nathan shrewdly. 'But there is still something troubling you, Nathan. Can I help?'

'No, it's something I must work out for myself.' Nathan stood up and reached for his coat. 'I'm going for a walk before I turn in. Don't wait up for me.'

It was a fine night, with a three-quarter moon and a sky full of stars. Nathan went first to the sands that extended from the tiny Pentuan harbour to Portgiskey Cove and he paced the sands for a full hour. At the end of this time he was close to Portgiskey and he sat down, hunched on the rocks at the entrance to the cove.

Deep inside the shadows of the cove was the cottage where Amy slept. Nathan felt he had somehow let Amy down. She had expected more from him than he had been prepared to give to her. Perhaps it would have been different had he never met Elinor Hearle. But the love he felt for Elinor Hearle was stronger than anything he had ever known.

Nathan wished he could convince himself that marriage with Sammy Mizler would bring Amy the happiness she deserved. Sammy was a good man. Nathan believed he was also a kind man, but he really only came fully to life in London. Amy's heart and soul were here, on the Cornish coast. If Sammy Mizler took her to London after they were married, she would wilt and die, as so many country girls had before her. But nothing Nathan could say would change their minds – and he had his own problems to resolve.

Before returning home, Nathan climbed the hill behind Pentuan and stood looking at Polrudden Manor, proud and solid in the moonlight, its crumbling stonework hidden in shadow. There was one tiny light showing from a window. Beyond that window lay Elinor – and his unborn child.

Standing in the shadow of the trees, Nathan remembered how much he had admired this house as a boy. It had always drawn him, although he had never dared to approach as close as this in those days. As he looked, he felt that his destiny lay here; but it was not a comforting feeling. Of a sudden, he shivered violently and shrugged the collar of his coat higher.

Dawn was only an hour or so away. He would go home and sleep for a while. Then he would return here, to Polrudden, and face Sir Lewis Hearle once more.

Nathan's meeting with Sir Lewis Hearle was postponed in a violent and dramatic manner.

The residents of Mevagissey and Pentuan were awakened soon after dawn by the sound of heavy cannon-fire from close at hand. Men, women and children spilled from the houses, latecomers pulling jerseys over their heads as they ran to vantage-points. A sea-battle was taking place offshore between two British sixth-rate frigates, carrying only sixty cannons between them, and four French seventy-four gun ships-of-the-line.

Heading up-Channel, the heavier French vessels had surprised the British ships at dawn and engaged them immediately. The first broadside from the leading French vessel had brought down the mainmast of one of the frigates, preventing the British vessel from making use of her superior speed.

The second frigate might have escaped at this time; instead, her captain chose to engage the French men-of-war in a bid to enable the damaged British ship to escape inshore. It was a brave but futile attempt, and the one-sided engagement could have only one ending.

At one stage both frigates tried to escape by making for Mevagissey's small harbour. Guessing their intentions, the Frenchmen manoeuvred between the shore and the frigates. Refusing to strike their ensigns, the battle became a 'shoot-and-dodge' engagement for the frigates, while the French battle-ships lumbered in like a pack of great mastiffs worrying two crippled terriers.

As the fishermen on shore watched, the foremast of the already crippled frigate crashed to the deck, a mass of splintered wood, torn sail and tangled rigging. A few minutes later, a heated cannon-ball from a French man-of-war found the frigate's powder-store.

The explosion tore the yellow and black hull apart, sending men and timbers hurtling through the air into the sea.

As the spectators on shore gasped in horror, Nathan called: 'Those are British sailors out there – Cornishmen among them, I don't doubt. They need rescuing. Who's with me?'

There was no shortage of volunteers, and Nathan sprinted to Portgiskey, a long line of fishermen of all ages strung out along the sand behind him. He took the first half-dozen to arrive. The remainder, helped by his boat's namesake, heaved *The Brave Amy H* into deep water.

With her sister ship a shattered wreck, the second British frigate crowded on full sail in an attempt to outstrip the enemy. But by now the French men-of-war were ranged on either side of the frigate and were able to concentrate all their considerable fire-power upon her. Soon, two masts crashed to the deck of the frigate and, hanging over the side, they dragged the single-decker around in a tight circle to face yet another broadside.

It was nothing short of slaughter. With the second frigate wallowing helplessly in the water, in imminent danger of sinking, the French admiral called off his vessels. Putting out into the Channel, the four French vessels headed for deeper waters in which to celebrate their victory.

Other fishing-boats had put off from Mevagissey, and all were needed. Dozens of men from the first frigate were in the water, all with wounds and many of them serious. *The Brave Amy H* picked up eight survivors before going alongside the second frigate, which was now on fire, flames licking at the rigging on the remaining mast.

Nathan did not leave the frigate until he had taken twenty-two survivors on board *The Brave Amy H* and could carry no more in safety.

Leaving others to save the remaining seamen, Nathan set a course for Plymouth. There would be Fleet surgeons there, and a hospital where they had experience in treating seamen with battle wounds. Neither Mevagissey nor Pentuan would be able to cope with a hundred and fifty wounded men, many of whom would need to have limbs amputated.

Under normal conditions, the sailing-time to Plymouth from the scene of the battle might have been no more than four hours. Today it was to be much longer. Emboldened by his success, the French admiral unexpectedly returned two of his men-of-war to the English coastline.

They chanced upon a luckless, unarmed merchantman, loaded with tin ore, and a French prize-crew was sent on board. Then the French warships met up with the flotilla of fishing-boats, heading for Plymouth with the survivors from the frigates. In the ensuing chase, two of the Mevagissey fishing-boats were sunk and three taken.

The largest of the fishing-boats was *The Brave Amy H* and one of the French captains tried very hard to capture her. However, emulating Amy on the occasion she had saved the boat from corsairs, Nathan took his vessel close inshore, braving the many rocks that frothed in the sea only feet away.

The Frenchman's answer to this strategy was to cannonade *The Brave Amy H* in a bid to force Nathan out to sea. But Nathan remained close inshore and eventually found the shelter of the tiny fishing village of Polperro. Here he remained until

238

the French men-of-war set off in pursuit of a promising new conquest, hull down on the horizon.

Plymouth was reached at noon. After putting the wounded sailors ashore, close to the naval hospital, Nathan was asked to go to the Admiral's office, on a hill above the naval dockyard. Here he gave the Admiral a first-hand report on the battle between English and French ships, and the subsequent activities of the French men-of-war.

It transpired that there were only two British warships of comparable size at the Admiral's disposal. The remainder had been sent to join two fleets that were at sea hoping to engage much larger French formations.

The survivors of the attack on the rescue fleet were still limping into Plymouth Sound and the Admiral suggested that all the fishing boats should remain at Plymouth, under his protection, until he had assembled sufficient vessels to escort them safely home to their villages.

Three days later a large British fleet of men-of-war, under the flag of Rear-Admiral Keats, entered Plymouth Sound. They had been in action off Cadiz and, on their way homeward, had fallen in with the French admiral and his marauding squadron. One had been sunk, another captured and the remainder put to flight. On board the captured French ship, the British sailors had released many prisoners, among them a number of Mevagissey fishermen. It was now safe for Nathan to return home with *The Brave Amy H*.

Nathan and his crew arrived at Portgiskey Cove to learn that rumours had been rife during their absence. One of the fishing-boats carrying wounded British sailors had turned back to Mevagissey when the French men-of-war attacked. The crew of this boat had seen a French warship in close pursuit of *The Brave Amy H* and had assumed that the Portgiskey drifter had been either sunk or captured. As the days went by without any news, it seemed their assumption was correct. There was even talk of a memorial service being held for the missing men in the new Pentuan chapel!

The Brave Amy H and her crew returned cheerfully unaware of the rumours, and Nathan was startled when Amy hurtled from the cottage and threw herself at him. The other crew members had little time to enjoy Nathan's embarrassment.

Cornish wives and daughters, traditionally undemonstrative, deserted their salting duties and ran from the fish-cellars of Pentuan and Portgiskey to greet their men.

During the days and nights in Plymouth, with little to do, Nathan had found plenty of time to think upon his future, and he had settled on a course of action; but, looking down at Amy as she clung to him, he felt his resolve weaken alarmingly. He put up a hand to stroke Amy's hair and assure her that he was well – and then he saw Sammy Mizler watching them from the doorway of the Hoblyn cottage.

Gently, Nathan put Amy from him and smiled at her before waving cheerfully to Sammy.

'I hardly expected such a warm welcome, after idling in Plymouth for three days and nights,' he said, taking Amy's hand and leading her to where Sammy Mizler waited. 'But the holiday's over now. As soon as the women have satisfied themselves that their men are alive and well, I want the boat made ready for fishing. There's a fine shoal of mackerel not two miles off Gribbin Head. Ahab can take *The Brave Amy H* out. It's at times like this I wish we had another boat. But no doubt one will bring in enough fish to keep the cellar busy for another week or two.'

'And you? What will you be doing while the men are out fishing?'

The relief at seeing Nathan alive and well had threatened to overwhelm Amy a short while earlier, but as she stood at Sammy Mizler's side it was difficult to read her expression.

'I'm going to Polrudden. To keep a promise I made to Sir Lewis Hearle – and Elinor.'

Chapter Twenty-Three

AT POLRUDDEN MANOR, Nathan knocked heavily on the stout wooden door and stood waiting for it to be opened. He displayed far more confidence than he felt. At last the heavy door creaked open and a maid stood in the doorway. Nathan had not seen her before.

'I've come to visit Miss Elinor,' Nathan announced briefly.

'Yes, sir. Will you come inside, please?'

Nathan stepped into the great hall. After taking his name, the maid hurried away in the direction of Sir Lewis Hearle's study.

She returned quickly. 'Will you come this way, Mr Jago? Sir Lewis would like to see you in his study before you visit Miss Elinor.'

If the baronet's reaction to Nathan's arrival had been violent, there was no hint of it in the maid's manner. She chattered on, telling Nathan how pleased the servants were to see Miss Elinor growing stronger with each passing day. Nathan was deeply puzzled.

At the study door the maid knocked, opened the door and announced Nathan. She flashed him a quick smile as he stepped inside the study, and the door closed quietly behind him.

Sir Lewis Hearle was seated close to the window on a captain's swivelling chair. He had his back to Nathan and was looking out of the window, a glass of brandy at his elbow. He must have seen Nathan approaching the house from the lane. In view of the threat he had made when the two men last met, it was more than surprising that Nathan had been allowed to enter the house.

'I'm here to see Elinor.'

'There was talk in the village that the French had either taken or killed you, Jago. You've disappointed me.' Sir Lewis Hearle spoke without turning around.

'As you can see, I'm alive. And I intend to see Elinor.'

'All in good time.' Sir Lewis Hearle swivelled the seat about to face Nathan. He looked at him as though seeing him for the first time, and Nathan could see neither cordiality nor yet dislike in his expression. 'What do you hope to gain from seeing my daughter?'

'I intend repeating an offer I made to her just before she had the accident.'

'You are talking of your offer of marriage, of course.'

Nathan was taken aback. He had not expected Elinor to repeat any part of that conversation to her father. But Sir Lewis Hearle had more to say. 'I must add, of course, that she told me the story to amuse me. What could you possibly offer Elinor – although a girl who will never walk again can have few expectations from life?'

'I would look after her. Give her *loving* care – more than she will ever have at Polrudden. Besides, I feel that I'm responsible for what happened. If she hadn't been expecting my child, there would have been no accident.'

'Is that so?' The look Sir Lewis Hearle gave Nathan was coldly calculating. 'This "loving care" of yours. . . . Does it go beyond having Methodist prayers said for her by your father, and receiving second-rate attention when the brat is due?'

'My father says prayers for every sick person in the area; that's his way. But there would be no interference with me, or Elinor. As for the baby, Elinor would have the best attention that money could buy.'

Sir Lewis Hearle rose to his feet abruptly and turned his back on Nathan, looking out through the window once more. Nathan was puzzled. He was also very excited. Sir Lewis Hearle had not erupted with either anger or mirth – and he had not ordered Nathan from Polrudden. Could it possibly be that he was seriously considering a marriage between Nathan and Elinor?

This was exactly what Sir Lewis Hearle was considering, but his motives had nothing to do with the well-being of his daughter.

Within hours of the accident, Sir Lewis had sent a rider galloping to inform Francis Rodd, at Trebartha. When Sir Lewis returned from the humiliating Assizes, after Josiah Jago's acquittal, he found Francis Rodd waiting at Polrudden. With him was the formidable Lady Admonition Rodd – and a surgeon from London. When news of the accident reached Trebartha, the surgeon had been at the house, brought from the capital to treat her ladyship's troublesome varicose veins.

242

The surgeon had examined Elinor before Sir Lewis's arrival, and his prognosis was gloomier than that of the Mevagissey physician. Elinor's spine was fractured low down on her back. It would cause her periods of acute pain throughout her life – and he confirmed that she would never walk again. Needless to say, the surgeon had also discovered that Elinor was pregnant, although he was of the opinion that the child would be stillborn, as a result of the accident.

He suggested the Mevagissey physician should keep Elinor well supplied with an opium-based painkiller, and trusted that the Lord would grant her a quick release from her sufferings.

Sending the surgeon from the room, Lady Rodd was characteristically blunt with Sir Lewis Hearle. Elinor, she said, should have known better than to put a spirited horse at a high fence at full gallop. Then she added pointedly: 'Although it might have been better had she jumped the horse over a cliff. She's wild, Sir Lewis. Wilder than any girl should be. Why my son ever considered marrying her I'll never know.'

'Are you forgetting the child . . .?'

'I'm forgetting nothing.' Lady Rodd's mouth snapped shut in the manner of a steel gin-trap. 'Least of all *that*! You'd have had Francis marry a girl who carried another man's bastard in her belly.'

She glared at Sir Lewis contemptuously. 'No doubt you were hoping to pass it off as a premature child of the marriage, had I given my permission for an early wedding?'

'I knew nothing of Elinor's regrettable condition before the accident. It *must* be your son's.'

'*It most certainly is not!* I have already asked him. Francis does not lie to me.'

'Others might not agree with you.'

Lady Rodd thrust her aristocratically beaked nose close to Sir Lewis Hearle's face and gave him a look such as a perching buzzard bestows upon a young rabbit.

'I don't give *that* for the opinion of others.' She snapped her fingers loudly – a trick she had learned years before from her sailor father.

Straightening up, she looked disdainfully at Sir Lewis. 'Fortunately for you, Sir Lewis, I am prepared to accept your word that you knew nothing of Elinor's condition before the accident. Any scandal there may be will not originate with me. If Trebartha is to remain in Rodd hands, Francis will need to select a bride elsewhere – and there will be those ready to think the worst of him. I suggest you find some fool to marry your daughter quickly. Now, have my carriage brought round to the door and I will bid you "Goodbye", Sir Lewis. I doubt if you and I shall meet again.'

Sir Lewis Hearle burned with humiliation when he remembered the conversation with Lady Rodd, but he had thought much about it since.

'If Elinor married me, she would want for nothing. . . .' Sir Lewis Hearle had been silent for too long. Nathan was eager to impress him that such a marriage *could* work. 'I have ambitions. . . .'

'Your ambition led you to my daughter's bedroom. Shut up and listen to me.'

Sir Lewis Hearle turned to face Nathan once again. 'All right. You and Elinor may marry – but I'm having no elaborate service. The marriage will take place in Elinor's room, and there will be no guests. If witnesses are needed, I'll find a couple of servants with enough schooling to write their names. After the wedding you will live here, at Polrudden. But I don't want to see you in the main part of the house when I am home. You can have the east wing. It will require a great deal of work carried out before it's habitable. That will be your responsibility.'

Sir Lewis Hearle felt the bile rising in his throat as Nathan's incredulity gave way to delight. He silently cursed Elinor for allowing this oaf to make love to her, thus forcing him to take such a humiliating course of action. He despised himself, too, for not carrying out his original threat to horsewhip Nathan from the house.

But there was far too much at stake.

Quite apart from the scandal of Elinor's pregnancy, there was Sir Lewis's quarrel with Mr Justice Vincent. The judge's report on Josiah Jago's acquittal would doubtless accuse the Home Office Under-Secretary of being dangerously biased against Methodists. Mr Justice Vincent was a highly respected judge, and as the report was being submitted through official channels the Prime Minister would be forced to act upon it – unless Sir

Lewis could prove beyond all doubt that such an accusation was groundless. What better proof could he give than to show that his only daughter was married to the son of a Methodist preacher – the very preacher he was accused of wrongfully trying to convict?

But Sir Lewis Hearle was equally determined that Preacher Josiah Jago's son would not profit from the union at his expense.

'I have other conditions to impose on you. The first is that, while I continue to enjoy all income from Polrudden lands, you will be responsible for the upkeep of the *whole* of this house.'

This was a harsh imposition. The manor-house needed some urgent repairs. Then there were servants' wages to be paid, food bills. . . . It was a high price to pay for a bride. All the same, when Nathan bought his second boat. . . . He nodded his agreement to Sir Lewis Hearle's terms.

'There is more. Whatever happens to Elinor, *you* will not inherit Polrudden. If her child is delivered safely, and is a boy, my title, together with Polrudden and its lands, will pass to him in the event of my death. You will have nothing.'

Sir Lewis Hearle paused and glared at Nathan. 'Finally, your father is never to set foot in Polrudden, not even for the wedding. I'll not have a Methodist preacher in this house. Do you understand?'

It was a humiliating condition – to decree that a man's father could not visit him or the grandchild he would one day have. Nathan hesitated . . . then he nodded once more.

'In that case the marriage will take place just as soon as it can be arranged. *Now* you may visit Elinor.'

Leaving Sir Lewis Hearle's study, Nathan was in a daze. At the top of the magnificent staircase, he paused to look down upon the glistening chandelier, the dark wood panelling and the portraits of former squires of Polrudden. If he had a son, all this would be his inheritance.

Nathan was under no illusions about his own life, here in Sir Lewis Hearle's house. The baronet had imposed many harsh conditions, and he would continue to make things as difficult as he could. But Sir Lewis Hearle would not be able to still the tongues of Cornish villagers.

From the day of his marriage, Nathan would no longer be

Nathan Jago, fisherman of Pentuan. Not even Nathan Jago, champion prize-fighter of the world.

To Cornishmen, Nathan would be something that meant far more to them in this corner of the country. He would be Nathan Jago *of Polrudden*. And he would have Elinor.

BOOK TWO

BOOK TWO

Chapter One

THE marriage of Nathan Jago and Elinor Hearle took place in Elinor's bedroom at Polrudden, on Friday, the last day of May, in the year 1811. The ceremony was conducted by the tight-lipped Reverend Nicholas Kent, rector of Fowey. It was not the happiest of occasions.

Prior to her 'accident', Elinor had been expecting to become the Mistress of Trebartha. Instead, she was marrying a fisherman whose boat had been bought with money earned in a prize-ring. She felt the humiliation keenly.

When Sir Lewis had first told his daughter about the proposed marriage, Elinor had not believed him. Then, when she realised he was telling the truth, she had declared she would not go through with the ceremony. Sir Lewis told his daughter bluntly that she had lost the freedom to choose her own destiny by allowing Nathan to share her bed and becoming pregnant by him. Now he, her father, was making the decisions. Elinor would either marry her fisherman or she would be sent away to spend the remainder of her life in a hospital run by nuns for incurables, not far from London Town. If she chose the latter course, her baby would be taken away from her at birth and placed immediately in an orphanage, with only a faint chance of survival.

Elinor wept and pleaded, but Sir Lewis Hearle remained unmoved. The scandal of an illegitimate child would bring his already uncertain career to an abrupt end.

Given the dark hours of a single night to make her choice, Elinor had accepted the inevitable.

It was not an auspicious beginning to a wedded life already beset by more than its fair share of difficulties. But this was no ordinary marriage.

Sammy Mizler, chosen by Nathan to be the best man, was convinced that Nathan was mad to marry Elinor Hearle, however pressing his reasons. He even tried to talk Nathan out of the marriage, but Nathan was as obdurate as Sir Lewis Hearle. The wedding would take place.

Nathan's family and friends were upset at the haste and

secrecy of the marriage – and none more so than Amy. It did not help to tell herself that she did not *want* to witness Nathan tying himself to Sir Lewis Hearle's crippled daughter.

Sir Lewis Hearle had been drinking heavily before the ceremony and commented rudely upon the incongruity of a Jew being the 'best man' at a Christian ceremony. Only Nathan's restraining hand on his arm stopped Sammy Mizler from giving the baronet a suitable reply.

The bizarre ceremony was witnessed by Elinor's personal maid and a new footman, and was followed by no traditional celebrations. Later, Nathan spent his wedding night futilely trying to convince his bride that there *could* be a happy future ahead of them.

Nathan was determined to make a success of his marriage. Helped by many of the craftsmen who had built the new Methodist church for Josiah Jago, he quickly had the east wing of Polrudden Manor habitable and moved in with his crippled bride.

The move was an uncomfortable one for Elinor. She screamed her agony as she was carried to her new quarters on a litter. Her physician had assured Nathan that she would one day be able to move about the house in a wheelchair, but that day seemed far away.

Nathan had hoped that Elinor would show some improvement once they were established in their own wing of the house, but she refused to listen to his words of encouragement. Indeed, his very presence seemed to upset her for much of the time. It became clear that Elinor blamed Nathan for everything that had happened to her.

Then Sir Lewis was summoned to London to answer the charges brought against him by Mr Justice Vincent. The Tory Prime Minister had attempted to keep the report quiet, but it was receiving much publicity in the capital and looked set to become an embarrassment to Spencer Perceval.

With the departure of Sir Lewis, a new atmosphere began to show itself at Polrudden. Elinor was occasionally seen to smile, and the physician, a frequent visitor, reported that the child inside her was growing normally, despite Elinor's accident.

Elinor had declared frequently that she cared nothing for the unborn baby, but she often found herself thinking about the child and the servants reported to Nathan that she was asking them many questions about feeding and caring for new-born babies.

Then, in mid-July, Nathan went to Portgiskey Cove to take *The Brave Amy H* out for a night's fishing and found Amy and Sammy waiting for him. Inside the small Portgiskey cottage, they broke their news to him. Amy and Sammy had decided to marry at the end of July – little more than two weeks away. But this was not all. After the wedding, Sammy and his bride intended leaving Portgiskey and moving to London.

The wedding was not entirely unexpected, but the decision to move to London came as a surprise to Nathan. He believed Amy would bitterly regret leaving her native Cornwall.

'Who will you put in to run the fish-cellar for you?' he asked Amy.

The answer came from Sammy Mizler. 'That will be for you to decide, Nathan. You and your new partners. Amy and I have decided to put our share of the business up for sale. It makes sense. If we keep it, we'll need to employ people to take our places here. That will cut profits for everyone.'

Sammy spread his arms expressively. 'Today we can afford to do this, but one month of bad weather would result in the business making a loss.'

Amy looked at Nathan apologetically. 'Sammy's right, Nathan. You know that. We realise that new partners might have ideas you can't agree with; that's why we're telling you before we try to sell. We want to give *you* the chance to buy our half of the business.'

'With what?' Nathan stood up and strode to the window. From here he could see the activity in the fish-cellar. Bitterly, he added: 'I haven't got enough to buy out either of you.'

After a few moments of embarrassed silence, Sammy Mizler said: 'All right, so you can't raise all the money by yourself, Nathan. But Sir Lewis Hearle is your father-in-law now. . . .'

Nathan's laugh was short and devoid of humour. 'Sir Lewis Hearle is so pleased to have me as his son-in-law that he's given me responsibility for running Polrudden. I also have to meet all the bills.'

'Oh! We didn't know,' said Amy unhappily.

'It isn't our intention to *ruin* you.' Sammy Mizler was at his businesslike best. 'But we're starting married life, too. We'll need some capital if we're to find ourselves a place in London. However. . . .'

As he was talking, Sammy Mizler's sharp business brain was making rapid mental calculations. 'Can you afford to pay Amy and me a quarter of the value of our share of the business?'

After only a moment's hesitation, Nathan nodded. 'I think so.'

'Then, if Amy agrees, we'll take that. You can repay the remainder over a two-year period. You should be able to manage that.'

Sammy Mizler glanced at Amy, and she nodded her assent. 'Done!'

Nathan clasped an arm about each of his friends. He felt weak-kneed with relief. For a while he had stood eye to eye with total ruin. Now he held a majority holding in the Portgiskey fishing venture. With a great deal of hard work, and a lot of luck, he should be able to make a success of the business.

'Now I suppose I must congratulate you both on your forthcoming marriage. Although why you should want to leave Cornwall I just don't know. . . .'

Amy said nothing. She could not tell Nathan that Cornwall had not been the same for her since the day he had gone to live at Polrudden with his new wife.

Sammy Mizler knew. He had always known of Amy's feelings towards Nathan. He was more aware of them than Amy herself, but he had become adept at hiding his own emotions. To Nathan he replied: 'As you've often said yourself, I'm a Londoner. Nowhere else has the same appeal for me. Cornwall is nice, yes. Beautiful, even. But it's not for me. Besides, there are a few promising prize-fighters about now. I've had some good offers to go to London and train them.'

'But what about Amy?' Nathan looked down at the girl crooked in his left arm. 'How do you feel about leaving Portgiskey?'

Amy shrugged, not meeting his eyes. 'I've spent a lifetime in Cornwall. It's time I saw more of the world. I'll go wherever Sammy goes.'

. . . .

252

The wedding of Sammy Mizler and Amy Hoblyn took place in Josiah Jago's Methodist chapel. It had everything that Nathan and Elinor's wedding had lacked. There was warmth and happiness, and the whole of the tiny Pentuan community was involved.

Sammy Mizler was a stranger in the village – a 'foreigner' from across Cornwall's natural border, the River Tamar. He would never be anything else if he remained at Portgiskey and lived to be a hundred. But his cheery ways and business acumen had gained a firm place for him in the hearts of the Cornish villagers. Amy, too, had moved to Portgiskey from another area of Cornwall, but many village women worked in the Portgiskey fish-cellar and all were fond of her. They gave her a wedding that any Cornish girl would remember all the days of her life.

After the ceremony, a party went on at Portgiskey until early in the evening. Only one person there did not enjoy herself. In truth, Peggy Hoblyn appeared confused by all that was going on. She did not know whether to smile or to cringe from the people who spoke to her.

Concern for her mother was all that marred an otherwise happy day for Amy. Peggy Hoblyn's mental state had deteriorated rapidly in recent months. Amy knew she could not be taken away from familiar surroundings. If she were moved, Peggy Hoblyn's sanity would disappear altogether. She was to remain at Portgiskey, the only other shareholder in Nathan's fishing business. The anticipated income should ensure that she wanted for nothing. A distant cousin, Lizzie Barron, at present living in Mevagissey, had moved into the cottage at Portgiskey to take care of her, and Nathan would ensure that Peggy Hoblyn was looked after.

The party broke up when a hay-wagon arrived to take the bride and bridegroom to St Austell, accompanied by all those wedding guests able to find a few square inches of space on the overcrowded wagon.

In St Austell a patient coachman was holding the London-bound coach for the newly-weds. As their travelling-chests were being lashed down on the coach roof, Nathan said a sad goodbye to his late partners. He and Sammy Mizler had been together for a great many years. Had it not been for Sammy's skills and managerial ability, Nathan would not have gained the success in the prize-fighting ring that had made his present mode of life possible.

The farewell between the two friends was almost wordless, so deep was their emotion. Yet the sense of loss felt greater when Nathan embraced Amy.

Amy clung to him unexpectedly fiercely, and Nathan whispered: 'Goodbye, Amy. I shall miss you. Be happy.'

Pulling away from him reluctantly, Amy did her best to blink back foolish tears. 'If I don't find happiness with Sammy, it will be my fault, not his.'

Looking up at him, Amy added: 'I wish I felt the future had as much to offer you, Nathan.'

Warmed by her concern, he said: 'Don't worry about me. I'll be all right.'

Observing the determined lines of his face, Amy replied quietly: 'Yes, Nathan. I expect you will.'

To the accompaniment of rowdy cheers, Amy was handed inside the mail coach and Sammy Mizler climbed in beside her. Moments later, the mail coach rattled out of the cobbled innyard, its departure signalled by the strident notes of the coachman's long, highly polished post-horn.

The guests who were still in a mood for celebrating hurried inside the inn. They would be thoroughly drunk before they set off for Pentuan in the hay-wagon.

Nathan did not go with them, nor did anyone try to persuade him to remain. He would walk home on his own. Born in Pentuan, Nathan could never be totally excluded from the tight little community, but by marrying into the Hearle family and moving to Polrudden he had set himself apart from them as surely as though he, too, had moved to London.

Chapter Two

PUTTING a deposit on Sammy and Amy's shares of the business had left Nathan desperately short of money. In order to earn more he needed to keep *The Brave Amy H* at sea for every hour of the day and night. He took on an extra crew, putting Calvin Dickin in charge of the day crew and going out with the night men himself.

Nathan was a hard taskmaster, but he had no shortage of crewmen. The pilchards were late coming inshore this year, and fishermen were eager to make what money they could.

Owners of the idle seine-boats blamed Nathan for the absence of the pilchards. They repeated the arguments of generations of seine-fishermen, that the long drift-nets stretched across the mouth of the bay broke up the massive shoals on their way inshore. It was doubtful whether there was any substance in their accusations. In later years, even though existing laws were amended to drive the drifters farther and farther from the coast, and to limit their hours of fishing, the seine-fishermen still enjoyed good years and bad years, as they always had. Some seasons, the pilchards came close inshore in their tens of millions. Other years, they did not arrive at all.

There was no shortage of fish in the deeper waters off the Cornish coast. Night and day *The Brave Amy H* returned to Portgiskey laden with as many pilchards as she could safely carry. Nathan took on additional cellar-women, but they still worked so hard they swore their arms were salt-preserved for ever.

Less than a month after Sammy and Amy had left for London, Nathan decided to take a bold gamble. He used all the money he had made to purchase a second drifter. By naming her *Annie Jago*, Nathan helped to heal the breach with his father, brought about by Nathan's unusual wedding at Polrudden.

Annie Jago was not a new boat. She had been put up for sale by a fishing syndicate in nearby Fowey, whose luck did not match Nathan's own.

For a couple of weeks it seemed that Nathan's gamble was

going to pay him handsomely. Both vessels worked together, and the catch doubled. Then a south-easterly storm blew up and raged the length of the English Channel for a whole week. During this time not a boat put to sea from the south Cornish ports.

At Polrudden, Nathan paced the floor of his bedroom night after night, as the storm raged outside. He listened in vain for some change in the tone of the wind howling off the sea, and there was no slackening in the rhythm of the rain beating against the diamond-paned windows of the old manor.

Occasionally Elinor would call querulously from the adjacent bedroom, wanting something that lay just out of reach, or simply demanding that he keep her company and read to her. She could be safely propped up in her bed now, but she preferred to lie down, complaining that unless she did so the child kicking inside her made life unbearable.

It was not a happy time for Nathan. Worried about his fishing business, he found neither sympathy nor affection at home.

Then, one stormy night when the wind was rattling the windows in their frames and swooping down wide-built chimneys to scatter the ashes of dead fires around cooling fireplaces, Nathan was awakened by strangled screaming. The sound came from Elinor's room.

Fearing that the baby was coming early, or that Elinor might have somehow fallen out of bed, he threw back the bedclothes and hurried to her.

Elinor lay with her eyes closed, twitching as though she were having a fit, the skin of her face glistening with perspiration.

Alarmed, Nathan leaned over her. 'Elinor . . . what's the matter? Wake up. . . .'

Elinor continued twitching and a low, long-drawn-out animal noise rattled in her throat.

'Elinor. Wake up.' Nathan shook her by the shoulder.

Suddenly, Elinor's eyes opened, filled with fear. A moment later they filled with tears and she reached up for him. Incredibly relieved, Nathan held her to him as she began to sob as though her heart were breaking.

'Hush! It's all right, Elinor. Everything is all right.'

Gradually the sobs subsided, but still she clung to him.

Looking down at her pale, dark-eyed face, Nathan brushed back a long strand of dark hair. 'You must have been having a bad dream.'

She nodded. 'It . . . it was horrible.' Her fingers dug into him as details of the dream returned. 'Nathan, put out the candle and lie with me for a while.' She whispered the words.

Reaching across her to the bedside table, Nathan snuffed out the ragged yellow flame and slipped into bed beside her. It was the first time he had shared her bed since their marriage and he put his arms about her, careful not to twist her body.

'Nathan?' Elinor's hoarse whisper cut across his thoughts. 'I haven't been very kind to you, have I?'

'You've been in a lot of pain. With that and the baby, I haven't exactly been the best thing to come into your life.'

'I've thought about that, too – a lot. After the accident my father told me I had chosen my own destiny when I let you make love to me. It's quite true, Nathan. You neither ravished nor seduced me. *I* wanted *you*.'

In making her admission to Nathan, Elinor said more to him than at any time since their improbable marriage, and Nathan had never known her in such a self-critical mood as this.

'I wanted you, too. I loved you very much, Elinor.'

'Do you still love me, Nathan?'

'Yes. Nothing has happened to change that.'

'Thank you.' Elinor pulled Nathan to her fiercely, kissing him with all the exciting ardour he remembered from nights when he had entered this same house secretly. Resting her cheek against his, she said: 'I dreamed you had stopped loving me and told me you were going away. I . . . I didn't like it very much. It mattered to me.'

'People who put great store by such things say you should always reverse your dreams. So you see, your dream was really telling you that I'll never leave you.'

Elinor would not tell him about the remainder of her dream, of watching him walk into terrible danger, a small child clutching his hand. The child looked like Nathan, and she knew it was *their* child. She called, but neither of them heard. She tried to run to them, to warn of the danger, but she was crippled. She could not move. Then they turned, and she held out her arms, begging them to come back to her. They did not see. Turning away, they walked on. There was nothing more she could do to save them. That was when she began to scream, and scream. . . .

In the darkness of her room that night, as Nathan held his wife close, he felt their child stir inside her crippled body. Elinor smiled at the wonder in his voice. Nathan had discovered the miracle of life, but she, too, had made a wonderful discovery. On this wild and stormy night, as the result of a terrifying nightmare, Elinor had discovered that she loved her husband.

When Nathan awoke the next morning, he was immediately aware of something different. For a few minutes he lay still, telling himself it was no more than the unfamiliar shape of his wife's room. Then he realised there was no wind rattling the windows. No rain beating against the panes.

Easing himself gently from the bed, so as not to wake Elinor, Nathan went to the window and looked outside. The sky was a miscellany of rain-washed pastel shades. Blues and pinks and yellows, and a delicate mauve, with not a hint of grey. The storm had finally blown itself out.

Back in his own room, Nathan dressed hurriedly in his fisherman's clothes, anxious to take advantage of the change in the weather.

'Nathan? Where are you?'

'In here. The storm is over. I'll be able to take the boats out again.'

Nathan entered her bedroom in time to catch the pout she tried to hide. 'Must you go? I don't *want* to be left.'

'I must. We've already lost a week. We need the money.'

Elinor said no more until he came into the room again to kiss her farewell. Hugging him to her, she whispered: 'Hurry back. I shall miss you . . . husband.'

That morning Nathan arrived at Portgiskey as happy as any fisherman has a right to be. Unfortunately, the feeling did not survive the day. *The Brave Amy H* and *Annie Jago* put to sea together, both crews eager to bring in good catches after a week of enforced idleness, but the fish were not to be found. Hand-lining, in an attempt to locate them, the boats beat up and down the Channel across the wide mouth of St Austell Bay before being forced to accept the truth. The fish had gone.

Bringing both boats to Portgiskey that evening, Nathan was filled with gloom. The women in the fish-cellar were still noisily salting fish caught before the storm, but unless more were brought in before the end of the week the number of women would have to be reduced. The uncertainty of the remainder would cast a pall over Portgiskey.

Day and night the two Portgiskey drifters took it in turn to go to sea. Each time they returned with no more than a basket of fish to show for their efforts. Convinced the fish *must* be out there somewhere, Nathan took his boats farther and farther from Portgiskey. Still they returned empty. It was as though the fish had deserted the coasts of Cornwall for ever.

The situation rapidly became serious. Nathan had bought *Annie Jago* in anticipation of at least a normal fishing season. Now he had no fish, and an extra crew to pay.

Nathan brought *The Brave Amy H* home to Portgiskey after yet another fruitless search, to find the one-armed Calvin Dickin waiting for him on the quay. Skipper of *Annie Jago*, Dickin was a good fisherman but he was having no more success than Nathan.

'No luck?' The question was unnecessary. Calvin Dickin could see for himself the empty baskets piled high in the boat.

'If I didn't know better, I'd swear the storm scared every last fish from around the coast.'

Nathan looked tired, and Calvin Dickin knew that worry was beginning to take its toll on him.

'Things are going hard just now.'

'If they don't soon improve, I'm going to have to put one of the boats up for sale and take a loss on it.'

'So it's as bad as that?' Calvin Dickin began skilfully packing a pipe with his one hand and as dexterously brought it to life with the aid of a tinder-box. Tucking the box away inside a pouch suspended from a cord about his neck, Calvin Dickin removed the pipe from his mouth. Breathing smoke, he said quietly: 'I can offer you a way out of your troubles – if you're the man I believe you to be.'

Nathan looked at Calvin Dickin sharply. The one-armed man had worked for Ned Hoblyn as a full-time smuggler. 'You're suggesting I become a "night trader"?'

259

'There's harder ways of earning a living. Less certain ones, too.'

'The days of making easy money from smuggling are long gone, Calvin. There are too many men like Chief Revenue Officer Ezra Partridge around today.'

Calvin Dickin spat expertly over the edge of the quay into the water below. 'Ezra Partridge is blinded by your prize-fighting title. He'll not bother *you*. You've got the perfect smuggling arrangement here. Ned Hoblyn earned a good living for many years. . . .'

Calvin Dickin looked about him quickly, to ensure he was not being overheard. 'I've been approached by a customer who wants brandy in larger quantities than most boats can carry. I also know a French captain who is sitting out there in the Channel at this very moment, hoping someone is coming to relieve him of a prime cargo. All I need is a boat, and space to store it for a night or two.'

'So you thought of me . . . and Portgiskey?'

'Would you rather I approached someone else? This is a chance for you to make money, Nathan. Perhaps your only chance. Not only that, if the Revenue men ever look like getting close to Portgiskey you've got room at Polrudden to hide cargoes from a whole fleet of night traders.'

Nathan wondered how Sir Lewis Hearle would feel if he knew Polrudden was being considered as a hiding-place for undutied goods. But Nathan took Calvin Dickin's proposal seriously. He did not *want* to use his two boats for smuggling, but if he did not earn some money very soon he would have no boats.

'Where is this French ship?'

'She'll come in to anchor off Deadman Point tonight, and the next two nights.'

'All right, I'll do it. Get *The Brave Amy H* ready. She'll outsail anything we're likely to meet, if the need arises.'

Nathan glanced to where his crew were spreading the nets from *The Brave Amy H* on the quayside. Some were men he did not know well.

'I'll leave you to choose a crew – and choose carefully. Take no one you can't trust. I'm going to Polrudden now. I'll see you here at sunset.'

Nathan arrived at Polrudden to find that Elinor had prepared a surprise for him. A table was laid in her room and, carefully dressed to hide her pitifully wasted legs, Elinor sat in a chair, cushions piled about her to prevent her from falling. Her face was freshly powdered and her long black hair had been washed and brushed until it shone.

Nathan's astonishment at finding her out of bed delighted Elinor, but she was to surprise him even more. Holding out her hands for him to take, she squeezed his fingers and declared: 'Nathan, I am going to walk again.'

He looked at her in alarm, afraid that the strain of leaving her bed had been too much. As gently as he could, he said: 'We'll talk about that when you're stronger. Both the physician and the surgeon said—'

'Damn the physician! And damn the surgeon, too!'

Elinor used the mode of speech that had disappeared with her accident. Nathan kissed her and hugged her to him happily. 'When you use that "Hearle" tone of voice to tell me you're going to walk I *have* to believe you. Why, the Lord himself would give way to such arrogance!'

The determined line of Elinor's chin softened and she smiled. 'Perhaps He already has.' Her excitement bubbled over again. 'I'm getting feeling back in my feet. I am quite certain of it. Watch my big toe. I'll make it move for you. No, the *right* foot. Hurry now, before I exhaust myself *talking* about it.'

Nathan removed her slipper carefully and looked at the thin, white foot. After a couple of minutes' silence during which Elinor watched his face eagerly, she exclaimed: 'There! Did you see it move then?'

'You could be right. . . .' Nathan did his best to sound convincing.

'You *didn't* see anything.'

Nathan feared Elinor would burst into tears.

'I'm not saying it *didn't* move,' he lied. 'I think it *did*. But I don't want you building your hopes too high, that's all.'

To Nathan's great relief, her chin rose in an expression of renewed determination. 'It doesn't matter. I *know* my toe moved – and it's only a beginning.'

She smiled at him, and he saw that her disappointment had not entirely disappeared. 'One day I'm going to ride to

Portgiskey to meet your boat when it comes in. I'll put on my best clothes and have every fisherman's wife in Pentuan hate me for my airs and graces.'

Nathan grinned. 'They can hate you as much as they like. The day you are well enough to sit a horse I won't care if you ride stark naked through Pentuan and Mevagissey. I'll cheer you every inch of the way.'

Elinor smiled with him. 'Such a ride has already been made, my love, by a certain Lady Godiva. But I promise I won't even think of such a thing until I've got rid of this.'

She patted her swollen belly, and the baby obligingly writhed beneath her hand.

'He has too much room to move about in there. A belly full of food will put a stop to his nonsense. We'll eat, then you can carry me to the window so I can watch the sunset while you read to me. After that you can take me to bed and hold me all night to keep my bad dreams away.'

Nathan remembered the plans he had agreed with Calvin Dickin for the night. 'I'm sorry, Elinor. I have to take the boat out again at sunset.'

Elinor's dismay almost persuaded Nathan to change his mind, but he desperately needed money. He could not pass up such an opportunity.

He kept silent when Elinor argued that, with no fish being caught, there was no need to put to sea. 'Even if they were, you employ enough men to take out the boats without you,' she added.

Nathan still said nothing, and Elinor studied his face as he began the meal brought in by a maid.

'This is not a fishing trip, is it? You are going smuggling.'

'We need money, Elinor. I must make it any way I can.'

Elinor was aware of Nathan's problems. She also knew that Polrudden was an additional burden he had taken on for her sake. Reaching across the table for his hand, she said: 'Please be careful, Nathan. It has taken me so long to realise that I need you.'

Later that evening, when Nathan had left the house, Elinor lay in her darkened room with the curtains drawn, gazing out at a full moon – a smuggler's moon. She was reluctant to sleep. Sleep brought too many nightmares. They were haunting her all too frequently lately, and every one had the same theme. The loss of Nathan.

There had been a time, even after her accident, when Elinor would have scorned a suggestion that she would one day become dependent upon a man – any man. That had now changed dramatically. For the first time in her life Elinor was in love, deeply in love. The knowledge that Nathan loved her, too, gave her great happiness. There was also a thrill in the thought that his baby lived inside her body. All she needed now was to regain the use of her limbs – and she *would* walk again. Determinedly, Elinor gritted her teeth and *willed* life into her foot. The toe *had* moved. She was quite certain of it. . . .

Nathan was watching the same moon with something less than enthusiasm. Ezra Partridge and his Revenue men could sit on the cliffs at Chapel Point, south of Mevagissey, and see everything that went on for miles around. With the aid of a good telescope they might read the name of every vessel in St Austell Bay.

Not until *The Brave Amy H* was more than a mile offshore, hidden from Chapel Point by the tall and dangerous rock island known as The Gwineas, did Nathan relax a little.

He kept *The Brave Amy H* close to The Gwineas until past midnight, and the crew talked in whispers as they strained their eyes across the calm, moonlit waters. Suddenly, Calvin Dickin gripped Nathan's arm excitedly. 'Look! There on the starboard bow. It's a ship.'

'About time, too. I'll signal to him. The sooner we load up and get on our way the better I'll like it.'

The speaker, one of the seamen, was about to strike life from a tinder-box when Nathan knocked it from his hands.

'That's no French ship. It's far too small. Quick, start shooting the nets.'

Startled into action, the fishermen began throwing nets over the bow while Nathan raised the drift-sail. As the nets splashed into the water, a line of cork floats began to drift away from *The Brave Amy H*.

The other vessel turned towards them, and the fishermen could now see it was a large cutter, propelled through the water by an impressive number of oars.

As it drew closer, pitch torches spluttered into life and Nathan called: 'Stay clear, whoever you are. We've a line of nets upwind.'

The cutter changed direction and came alongside *The Brave Amy H*.

'Is that you, Mr Jago?' It was Chief Revenue Officer Ezra Partridge. He sounded both disappointed and suspicious. 'I haven't seen you fishing over this way before.'

'With the luck I've been having lately I need to fish new waters.'

'Ay, I've heard things aren't going too well for you.'

The Revenue cutter was close enough now for Ezra Partridge to peer inside *The Brave Amy H* as the flickering pitch torches held aloft by his men threw dancing shadows into the recesses of the fishing-boat.

When he had satisfied himself that *The Brave Amy H* carried no contraband, Ezra Partridge ordered his men to extinguish their torches – a feat that was accomplished by plunging them in the sea.

'I wish you luck, Mr Jago.'

'May none come your way – or the way of any King's man,' muttered Calvin Dickin under his breath.

When the Revenue cutter was well out of hearing, Calvin Dickin asked Nathan: 'What do we do now? We'd be foolish to wait for the Frenchie with Ezra Partridge out of harbour.'

'We'll put in an honest night's fishing,' declared Nathan. 'If we haul in the nets and go home now, Ezra Partridge will know exactly what we are doing out here. If we continue to fish, he'll never be certain.'

It was a profitable decision. When the nets were hauled inboard at dawn, they held a good catch. Nathan went home to Elinor a happier man.

Chapter Three

THE weather was more to Nathan's liking when he made his next attempt to rendezvous with the French smuggler, on the following night. The sky had been overcast since early afternoon. By the time night fell the moon was sandwiched between thick banks of dull, grey cloud, emerging for only brief periods.

Nathan took both boats out with him on this occasion, but left *Annie Jago* fishing off the Gwineas, where the previous night's catch had been made. He then took *The Brave Amy H* out into the deeper waters of the English Channel, hoping to meet the French ship on her way in.

Everything worked out exactly to plan. Three miles from The Gwineas, Nathan saw the brief winking of a candle-lantern and a reply flickered out from the fishing-boat. Fifteen minutes later *The Brave Amy H* bumped gently against the side of a dark-sailed French schooner of rakish lines, with three open gunports on either side.

Nathan went on board the French vessel with Calvin Dickin and was introduced to the French captain. The introductions over, Calvin Dickin pointed to the captain's leg which ended at the knee and was supplanted by a wooden stump. 'Between us, Cap'n Pierre and I just about make one good man.'

To the Frenchman, Calvin Dickin said: 'This is my captain – Captain Nathan. He was at Trafalgar, too.'

'Ah! So we are both sailors of war, eh? Which ship, monsieur – at Trafalgar?'

'*Victory*.'

'Indeed! Admiral Nelson's own ship. I am honoured. I was the First Lieutenant in *Bucentaure*.'

'Then you, too, served with a great gentleman,' acknowledged Nathan.

Bucentaure had been the flagship of the gallant French Admiral, Pierre Charles Jean de Villeneuve. During the battle of Trafalgar, *Bucentaure* lost all her masts, and the Admiral had been forced to strike his colours. The following year, after Villeneuve had been repatriated to France, he was threatened with a court martial for his conduct in the fierce battle. Broken-hearted at the unjust criticism levelled at him by his countrymen, Villeneuve committed suicide by thrusting a long pin through his heart.

Memories of their respective admirals kept the hands of the two men clasped in a mutual regard that only men who had fought each other well and honourably would understand. It mattered not that it was *Victory*'s guns that had shot off Captain Pierre's leg and killed a hundred of his shipmates.

For twenty minutes Nathan remained with the French captain, drinking his best brandy and exchanging reminiscences of the great sea-battle. During this time the crew of the French smuggler were passing cask after cask of brandy down to *The Brave Amy H*.

Their business completed, the two vessels parted company. Agreement had been reached for a fortnightly rendezvous, and the crew of *The Brave Amy H* were happy at the success of their midnight business. The mood held until the moon appeared momentarily, and Calvin Dickin called that he could see a vessel making for them in the darkness.

The moon disappeared before Nathan could glimpse the other boat, but Calvin Dickin was certain it had been the Mevagissey Revenue cutter.

'What will we do?' One of the men asked the question apprehensively. It was his first smuggling trip.

'Crowd on every inch of sail,' was Nathan's crisp reply. 'With this breeze behind us there's nothing afloat in these waters can catch us. It could have been especially ordered for *The Brave Amy H*.'

'If Ezra Partridge saw us, he'll head straight for Portgiskey and be there before we've unloaded half our cargo.' The comment came from Calvin Dickin.

'Possibly,' agreed Nathan. 'But we won't be unloading at Portgiskey. Do you know the old quarry dug into the cliff below Polrudden?'

Calvin Dickin did. Stone from the quarry had been used to build many churches and fine mansions in the area. Idle for many years, the quarry was now overgrown by bushes and coarse grass. A boat could drive to within feet of the workings at high tide. It would make an ideal hiding-place for contraband.

By the time the moon appeared once more there was no sign of the Revenue cutter, but, as Calvin had predicted, Ezra Partridge *had* thought he recognised *The Brave Amy H* and he was on his way to Portgiskey.

The Chief Revenue Officer and his crew waited impatiently at Portgiskey before accepting that their quarry was not on the way home to the little cove. Putting to sea again, they searched until the grey light of dawn showed *The Brave Amy H* hauling nets off The Gwineas, not half a mile from *Annie Jago*.

Unwilling to accept that he might have been mistaken, Ezra Partridge went alongside Nathan's boat and carried out a thorough search. All he found on board was a good haul of pilchards that increased with every net that came inboard. To all intents, it seemed the two Portgiskey vessels had been fishing all night.

For Nathan, it was a highly successful night's work. The fish had returned, and he had a substantial amount of contraband stored in the disused quarry.

Nathan's career as a smuggler suffered a setback the following evening. When he set off from Polrudden, Calvin Dickin was waiting for him outside the manor entrance. One look at Dickin's face was enough to tell Nathan that the one-armed fisherman was the bearer of bad news.

'It's our buyer . . . for the brandy,' said Dickin in answer to Nathan's question. 'He's gone. Fled the country one step ahead of the Revenue men. If the reports are to be believed, he's taken a ship for America.'

'Can you find another buyer?'

Calvin Dickin shrugged miserably. 'Probably, but it will take time – and Cap'n Pierre will be back again in two weeks. We've got too much money tied up in that brandy to allow it to lie in the quarry doing nothing. What's to be done, Nathan?'

The two men walked on in silence for some time. Then Nathan stopped and snapped his fingers in sudden jubilation. 'What price were we expecting for our brandy?'

'At least twenty-four shillings a gallon.'

'What if I told you I could get *forty-eight*?'

'That's madness! Good brandy is hard enough to come by these days, but no one is fool enough to pay that much for it.'

'You're wrong, Calvin – and our fool is none other than Ezra Partridge himself.'

Quickly, Nathan told the fisherman of the offer the Chief Revenue Officer had made to him some months before, to pay double the market price for any contraband he found and handed in.

'How many kegs do we have?'

'Fifty.'

Calvin Dickin tried to work out their worth at the Chief Revenue Officer's unrealistic price. He gave up, leaving Nathan to arrive at a figure.

'I make that close to nine hundred pounds. It will leave us with a handsome profit.'

Calvin Dickin nodded his head in stunned agreement. They stood to make a colossal sum.

That night the crew of *The Brave Amy H* reloaded the kegs from the Polrudden quarry and sank them close to Deadman's Point, with a small marker buoy to mark their position.

The next morning Nathan went to Mevagissey and sought out Ezra Partridge. The Revenue man was delighted with Nathan's information about a cache of spirits discovered off the Deadman's Point. He confirmed that the reward would be twice the value of the contraband goods and insisted that Nathan immediately show him where the cache was located.

Declaring that he could not risk being seen putting to sea with a Revenue man, Nathan met the Chief Revenue Officer outside the fishing village and together they walked the four miles to Deadman's Point.

After showing the marker buoy to the eager Revenue officer, Nathan walked him the four miles back again. By the time he reached Mevagissey, Ezra Partridge was perspiring like a blown horse and staggering from sheer exhaustion. But he would not rest. Before Nathan was halfway home to Polrudden, Ezra Partridge had set off for Deadman's Point in his Revenue cutter.

A fortnight later, Nathan made another 'find', this time of sixty kegs. He had decided upon the greater number because Ezra Partridge had paid out on only forty-five kegs on the previous occasion, assuring Nathan with a great show of sincerity that only forty-five had been found.

268

When the second consignment of brandy was taken to the Revenue Collector's warehouse in Fowey, the Area Revenue Officer complained that if many more such rewards were paid out the Revenue Service would have to accept a cut in salary to afford them.

By now word of what was happening had leaked out, in spite of all Nathan's precautions. The fishing community of Mevagissey cast glances of contemptuous amusement at Ezra Partridge whenever he passed by.

Nathan realised that such a lucrative source of income would not continue for much longer, and when he next made a rendezvous with the French smuggler he took a hundred kegs of brandy from the French captain, and a large quantity of tobacco, sealed inside a barrel.

On this occasion Nathan carried the whole cargo direct to Mevagissey and handed it over to the Chief Revenue Officer in the presence of his officers. Ezra Partridge had been greedier than before with the last haul, rewarding Nathan for only fifty kegs instead of sixty.

As Nathan had expected, Ezra Partridge's gratitude on this occasion was tempered with more than a little suspicion. It was heightened by the presence of a number of grinning fishermen, standing on the quayside nearby.

Nathan was grudgingly paid his reward, but Ezra Partridge informed him that if he 'found' any more contraband the circumstances surrounding the discovery would be thoroughly investigated.

The story of how the Chief Revenue Officer had been tricked spread through Mevagissey like a thatch fire. Women grinned saucily as he passed, and cheeky children called after him to ask if he had 'found' any brandy lately. Soon Ezra Partridge had only to see two men in conversation to imagine they were talking about him. He decided to do something quickly to put a stop to the malicious amusement.

By October the pilchard shoals had still not moved inshore, although Nathan was catching them regularly further out to sea. Along the coast more fishermen were following his example. Those who could afford to do so were selling their seines and buying larger boats in order to take up drifting.

269

One evening, Nathan's two boats put to sea as usual, shortly before dusk. Calvin Dickin took *Annie Jago* to the area beyond The Gwineas, while Nathan and *The Brave Amy H* worked the deeper waters out beyond the Fowey Estuary.

At dawn Nathan and his men hauled in their nets and returned to Portgiskey laden with a very satisfactory catch. *Annie Jago* was nowhere in sight, neither was she alongside the quay in Portgiskey, but there was nothing in this to alarm Nathan. *Annie Jago* might have drifted a mile or two out to sea and, consequently, was taking longer to return to the cove.

However, when *Annie Jago* had not returned by the time *The Brave Amy H* was unloaded, Nathan sent a young member of his crew to the top of the cliffs above Portgiskey, to see if he could sight the missing fishing-boat.

When the young fisherman returned to say he could see nothing of *Annie Jago* anywhere, Nathan felt uneasy for the first time. Calvin Dickin would have begun hauling in his nets at dawn. Whether or not he had made a good catch, he should have been back by now.

There was no need for Nathan to communicate his concern to his crew. They, too, knew that Calvin Dickin and *Annie Jago* should have returned before this. They quickly made *The Brave Amy H* ready for sea again. Minutes later the fishing-boat was heading for The Gwineas.

Nathan scoured the sea for miles about The Gwineas without making a sighting of *Annie Jago*. In spite of this, Nathan still expected to see his second fishing-boat unloading at the quay when he returned to Portgiskey. After all, it had been a calm night, and Calvin Dickin and his crew were all experienced fishermen.

Annie Jago was not at Portgiskey, but when *The Brave Amy H* berthed all the women from the fish-cellar crowded round to tell Nathan what they had learned. At first, Nathan received an excited and garbled account of what had happened, but gradually a story began to emerge. Calvin Dickin and his crew had been arrested on a smuggling charge. Ezra Partridge had taken them to Fowey during the night. Once ashore, the fishermen had been taken to the lock-up in St Austell, while *Annie Jago* remained at Fowey, confiscated by the port Revenue authorities.

Nathan was dumbfounded. Captain Pierre and his ship were not due for another week. Calvin Dickin must have been engaged in an illicit deal about which he had told Nathan nothing.

Cursing Calvin Dickin for putting *Annie Jago* at risk without telling him, Nathan hurried home to Polrudden. After telling Elinor what had taken place, Nathan saddled a horse and set off for St Austell. He was not a good rider, disliking riding, but he was tired and there were many miles to be covered before dusk.

Nathan went first to St Austell. There he found his despondent crew crowded inside the tiny lock-up. Allowed to speak to them, Nathan demanded to know what Calvin Dickin had been doing to get himself and his crew arrested.

'That's the damnable part of this whole business, Nathan. We weren't doing anything except fishing.'

'But the gaoler has just told me that four kegs of brandy were found in *Annie Jago* by Ezra Partridge.'

'It's easy enough to find something when you've put it there yourself,' said Calvin Dickin bitterly. About him, the nodding heads of the other fishermen provided confirmation that the one-armed fisherman spoke the truth.

'Ezra Partridge deliberately put kegs of brandy in *Annie Jago* and then arrested you for smuggling them? Did any one of you see him do this?'

This time the heads were equally unanimous that no one had seen anything.

'Ezra Partridge brought the Revenue cutter alongside before dawn,' explained Calvin Dickin. 'He stayed with us until we began hauling in the nets. That's when he found the brandy, sitting among the fish-baskets. They were there, right enough, but they certainly *weren't* on board when we shot the nets last night.'

'But why *Annie Jago*? Had he put the kegs in *The Brave Amy H* when I was on board it would have made some sense. But to do this to you. . . .'

In truth, Nathan was shocked that Ezra Partridge should have fabricated evidence in such a manner. Smuggler and Revenue man bitterly opposed each other's stand on the issue of smuggling. They fought on many occasions, and blood was frequently spilled. But there had always been a grudging

271

mutual respect between the two sides. Lying in order to secure a conviction was a despicable act that would be neither forgiven nor forgotten among the fishing communities of Cornwall. Ezra Partridge had broken the unwritten laws of the game, and all Revenue men would be subjected to some rough handling as a result.

'I fancy Ezra Partridge was disappointed that it wasn't *The Brave Amy H* he'd found,' said Calvin Dickin. 'But no doubt he thought we'd do instead.'

The one-armed fisherman tried to appear nonchalant, but he failed miserably. 'It's me for transportation this time, Nathan. I was convicted of smuggling ten years ago and spent six months on the treadmill for my sins. The judge won't treat me so leniently this time.'

'That was ten years ago. You've lost an arm since then. He'll treat you as a new offender. He's bound to.'

Nathan's optimism was ill-founded. Calvin Dickin's fellow-fishermen were each sentenced to six months on Bodmin Gaol's treadmill, with instructions to use the time so employed to contemplate the error of their ways.

Calvin Dickin was labelled a 'hardened criminal' and sent to the Assizes for sentence. Two weeks later, heavily chained and fettered, the one-armed fisherman left Bodmin Gaol to begin a seven-year sentence in the penal colony of Botany Bay. The judge felt obliged to explain the 'leniency' of his sentence. He had, he said, taken into account Calvin Dickin's disability. Having only one arm, the prisoner would have to work harder than his fellow-convicts at the business of survival. Such moments of 'benevolence' earned for the judges of His insane Majesty King George's courts the right to have the word 'merciful' included in their funeral eulogies.

Nathan had already learned that the law was less benevolent in the matter of his boat, *Annie Jago*. The magistrates ordered its confiscation after Ezra Partridge had insinuated that Nathan was fully aware the boat was being used for the purpose of smuggling. Nathan was at the hearing and leaped to his feet demanding that the Chief Revenue Officer substantiate his accusation, only to be ordered from the court-room until the trial was over.

272

It was a disastrous setback for Nathan. He now had little hope of surviving the stormy days of winter, when fishing would be impossible for weeks at a time. His only hope lay in stepping up his smuggling activities. But he would first need to do something about Ezra Partridge.

Nathan's opportunity came in early November, at a time when his own participation in fishing was restricted to daylight hours. Elinor was suffering great discomfort, and there were signs that the baby might come earlier than expected.

Nevertheless, when the time came round for another rendezvous with Captain Pierre and his smuggling vessel, Nathan knew he must take a chance and sail *The Brave Amy H* to meet him. He would have liked to leave the task to Ahab Arthur, Nathan's new lieutenant; but, although the old fisherman had willingly taken on the night-fishing trips, he had none of Calvin Dickin's knowledge of smuggling.

Elinor worked herself into a state of near-hysteria about Nathan's night trip. She still suffered the recurring dream about reaching out and not being able to touch him, and many nights she sobbed herself back to sleep in his arms.

Had there been any other way, Nathan would have foregone the night rendezvous, but with only one drifter working the bills were piling up.

Nathan set off from Polrudden, leaving Elinor weeping behind him in the care of a maid who would stay with her throughout the night. It was a crisp November evening. A new, early-rising moon hung over the sea, and there was just a hint of early frost in the air.

The crew of *The Brave Amy H* stowed a minimum of fishing-gear on board. They needed to satisfy the passing glance of a Revenue man with a telescope, looking down at them from a cliff-top hideout above Portgiskey Cove.

The Revenue man had been seen on the cliff-top for some nights now. It made the fishermen nervous. The fate of Calvin Dickin and the crew of *Annie Jago* was still fresh in their minds. They left Portgiskey that night wondering whether they would be returning to their families in the morning.

Nathan headed *The Brave Amy H* towards The Gwineas. Hidden from the view of much of the mainland, it had become customary to wait here for full darkness before heading out to meet the Frenchman.

Their course took them past the entrance to Mevagissey harbour and they were not far past it when Ahab Arthur said quietly to Nathan: 'There's a boat coming out of Mevagissey. It looks mighty like Ezra Partridge and his Revenue cutter to me.'

Quiet though Ahab Arthur's words were, they were overheard by two of the fishermen, and they waited anxiously for Nathan to give the order to return to Portgiskey. There were not enough nets on board to remain at sea and make a pretence of fishing. But, instead of giving the order, Nathan nodded his head in acknowledgement of Ahab Arthur's words and said brusquely: 'I saw the boat. It *is* the Revenue cutter.'

'It's turning our way,' exclaimed one of the anxious fishermen. 'We'd best be putting back to Portgiskey. The amount of fishing-gear we've got on board won't fool anybody. Not Ezra Partridge . . . nor a magistrate.'

'Ezra Partridge won't be coming close enough to see what fishing-gear we're carrying,' said Nathan. '*The Brave Amy H* can outsail any cutter built for a Revenue man. But I don't think we'll need to put it to the test just yet. My guess is that someone's been talking. Probably a relative of one of our men in Bodmin Gaol. It means Ezra Partridge will know there's a rendezvous due. But he won't make a move until he's certain we've got dutiable goods on board – not a second time.'

'You'll not go ahead with the rendezvous? Not now you know Ezra Partridge is out?'

'There are Revenue boats out all along the Channel coast tonight. Do you think they'll keep every night trader from putting to sea?' Nathan scoffed at the man's alarm. 'You don't need to worry yourself. I'm no more anxious to see the inside of Bodmin Gaol than you.'

The suggestion that they should return to Portgiskey was not repeated, but the fishermen were unhappy. The men spoke to each other in low tones, and more than one baleful glance was cast in Nathan's direction.

The Brave Amy H remained close to The Gwineas until an hour after dusk. Then Nathan set sail and headed out into the Channel. The moment they got underway the crew of the fishing-boat were hanging over the side, peering anxiously to see whether the Revenue cutter was following.

274

It was. Only minutes after they had left the shelter of the rocky island, one of the fishermen called to Nathan in a hoarse whisper: 'They've spotted us. Ezra Partridge is following!'

'Good.' Nathan's reaction was not what the crew were expecting, but he gave them no opportunity to debate the matter. 'Instead of wasting all your time trying to fall overboard, clear some space for the brandy. I'm taking a double cargo on board tonight. Keep a look out for the Revenue cutter. I want to be sure we don't lose it. Jump to it, now.'

Nathan's tone allowed for no argument. Although deeply concerned about their fate, the fishermen did as they were told. For half an hour Nathan maintained the same course and speed. Suddenly he said: 'Right, now we'll crowd on every bit of sail we have. You've wanted to lose Ezra Partridge; this is your chance.'

The men did not need to be told twice. The farther they were from Partridge, the happier they would all be. Soon *The Brave Amy H* was surging through the water, hitting ever low wave with a thump that jarred the bones of each man on board. Now that Nathan had drawn the Revenue cutter out to sea, the fishermen believed he would put about and return to Portgiskey, outstripping Ezra Partridge.

Much to their surprise, Nathan maintained the same course. Surprise turned to alarm when a light winked at them from the darkness and Nathan told Ahab Arthur to signal a reply.

Even Ahab Arthur could not believe that Nathan was going to keep the rendezvous and take brandy on board with a Revenue cutter in such close attendance.

'How far behind do you think Ezra Partridge will be when we reach the Frenchman?' Nathan asked his lieutenant.

'Not much more than twenty minutes.'

'That's all the time I need. Hurry and reply to that signal. I want Cap'n Pierre to heave-to out there. The farther he is from the coast, the better it will be for the plan I have in mind.'

Fifteen minutes later *The Brave Amy H* bumped alongside the French vessel and Nathan scrambled on board the larger craft. To the men in the fishing-boat he called: 'Get the brandy on board as though the Devil were nipping at your heels – and if you're not quick enough he might be.'

Captain Pierre was on deck and greeted Nathan warmly. 'I

have been worried about you, my friend. I thought something might have happened to you. But where is Calvin? He is not with you tonight?'

'Calvin's been taken by Revenue men and sentenced to transportation. The same Revenue men followed me out here tonight. We have less than twenty minutes. Tell your men to place as much brandy in my boat as she'll carry. In the meantime I want to talk to you – in your cabin. There's something I want you to do for me – and for Calvin.'

The French smugglers and Nathan's crew had *The Brave Amy H* fully laden in fifteen minutes. As Nathan swung over the side of the French vessel, he called back: 'Goodbye, Cap'n Pierre. I won't see you for a month. You'd best avoid this part of the coast until then. Good hunting!'

Once in *The Brave Amy H*, Nathan gave the order to cast off. But then, instead of turning back to Portgiskey, he headed out into the Channel. Behind them the voice of the French captain called soft orders to his crew and Nathan heard the once-familiar rumble of cannon being run out through open ports.

On board the Revenue cutter, Ezra Partridge peered out across the choppy waters, the darkness of the night relieved by the soft light from the stars and a thin crescent moon.

He cursed his tired crew for not keeping up with *The Brave Amy H* when Nathan had crowded on sail. The Revenue cutter was large, and with her twelve oarsmen was capable of a fair speed, but oars were no match for a sailing vessel in a good breeze.

'There's something up ahead.' The coxwain of the boat pointed to where a tell-tale bow wave reflected pale green luminescence against the darker green of the sea.

'It must be Jago on his way back.'

'No, it's too large.' Suddenly the coxwain put the tiller hard over. 'It's a ship – probably the French smuggler!' To the listening oarsmen he called: 'Pull hard. The Frenchman's trying to run us down!'

But Captain Pierre had no wish to sink the Revenue cutter. Nathan's plan was far more subtle than sending a boat and her crew to the bottom of the English Channel. At the last minute the French sailing ship heeled over and turned into the wind.

276

'Ahoy there! Come alongside. I wish you to come on board my ship.'

The English words, spoken with a strong French accent, rang over the water.

'Pull away from here quickly,' Ezra Partridge hissed at his men.

The cutter turned, but she had gained no more than ten lengths when a cannon was fired from one of the open ports along the French ship's side. So close was it that the flash and roar threw the oarsmen into utter confusion as acrid smoke drifted about the cutter.

'The next shot will sink you. You will do well to obey my order.'

Captain Pierre's amused voice called across the water once more. He had seen the effect of his first shot.

When the cutter bumped against the side of the French ship, Captain Pierre ordered her occupants to come on board.

The huge bulk of Ezra Partridge had to be helped up the side of the French smuggling-ship. When he eventually stood on the deck, trembling with a mixture of fear and anger, he blustered: 'You'll regret this. I am a Chief Revenue Officer in His Majesty's service. . . .'

'And your country is at war with mine, monsieur. Very soon you will be a prisoner of France. Until then I am happy to offer you my hospitality.'

The disappearance of Mevagissey's Chief Revenue Officer, together with his cutter and crew, created a furore. Revenue boats from Falmouth and Fowey, and a frigate from the naval dockyard at Plymouth scoured the seas about the coast for three days. On shore the militia was called out to search the rocky coastline for signs of wreckage.

Nothing was discovered, of course; and when word was received six weeks later that the Chief Revenue Officer and his crew were prisoners the mystery deepened. The information said that they and their coastguard cutter, still flying the British flag, had been captured by the French navy in the Gironde, the forty-five-mile-long river estuary that brought the world to Bordeaux, and provided access to the vineyards of Cognac. The Gironde was more than three hundred miles from Mevagissey!

Chapter Four

NATHAN kept *The Brave Amy H* heading away from the shore until he heard the report of the French smuggler's cannon in the distance. Not until then did he turn his boat round and head for the disused quarry below Polrudden Manor.

The nervous fishermen wanted to know what had happened to Ezra Partridge and his crew, believing that the French vessel had sunk the cutter. Nathan would say only that the less the fishermen knew about the incident, the better it would be for everyone. They would learn the truth in due course, but the thought that the Chief Revenue Officer might have been killed would keep them tight-lipped when the Revenue authorities began their enquiries. Telling them now would give them a story that not one of the fishermen was capable of keeping to himself.

When the brandy was safely hidden, Nathan took *The Brave Amy H* back to Portgiskey. It was still a couple of hours short of dawn, but there was no sense in going out again. Ezra Partridge was out of the way and there was no one to question the reason they had returned without fish.

It had been a night to remember. Nathan looked forward to sharing the story of the night's adventure with Elinor. Letting himself quietly into the east wing of Polrudden Manor, he made his way quietly upstairs.

He frowned when he saw no light shining beneath the door of Elinor's room. The maid staying with Elinor must have fallen asleep and allowed the candle to burn out. Opening the bedroom door quietly, Nathan immediately became aware of a low moaning, as though someone was in deep pain.

Thoroughly alarmed, he made his way to the bed. He was still a pace away from it when his foot touched something on the floor. Bending down he ran his hands over the cold form of Elinor, lying on her side.

Elinor's stomach muscles contracted beneath his hand, and she moaned again. Hurriedly, Nathan lifted her bodily from the floor and placed her on the bed. Then he searched at the bedside for a light. He found the burned-out stub of a candle in the holder with another lying on the table beside it. Striking a light, Nathan set the candle in a small spot of hot candle-wax on the cabinet top before turning his full attention to Elinor.

She opened her eyes as he leaned over her, but she was delirious with pain and showed no recognition. She was also in labour – but there was no sign of the maid who should have been in the room.

'Elinor, can you hear me?'

Nathan bent low over his wife, but she gave him no sign that she could hear him.

Distracted with concern for Elinor, Nathan was momentarily at a loss. There were no servants in this wing of the house. Those who did not live out were accommodated in the attic of the main house. Then suddenly Nathan knew where he would find the maid who should have been with Elinor. She and a new stable-boy had been seen walking hand in hand in recent weeks, and the stable-boy lived in a partitioned-off corner of the hay-loft.

Nathan was halfway to the door when Elinor moaned again. Hurrying back to the bed, he was beside her when she opened her eyes; but this time there was recognition in them.

'Nathan. . . .' Her hand reached up to him, and he took it in his. 'Where have you been? The baby is coming. . . .'

A pain racked her body, and she gripped Nathan's hand hard. When the pain eased she gasped: 'I was frightened. It was dark. . . . I remembered my dream.' Her hand gripped his once again, and he knew it was almost time for the baby to come. 'I tried to reach for a new candle. I must have leaned too far. I fell. . . .'

'It's all over now. I'm back. Everything will be all right. Lie still and sstrength.'

Nathan thought of Elinor lying alone in the darkness of the room, aware that the baby was coming and having no one at hand. Beneath his breath he cursed the maid who had left her alone. But he needed help.

'Elinor, I must leave you for a few minutes and send someone for the physician.'

The fear returned to Elinor's eyes, but she was able to control it better with Nathan standing beside her. She nodded. 'Be quick, Nathan. The baby won't be long now.'

The pain returned yet again, and Nathan waited it out before he slipped from the room.

Dawn was showing in the east as Nathan ran to the barn. A lamp was burning low in the stable-boy's makeshift room – and the maid was coming down the ladder from the hay-loft. Hair tangled and dishevelled, it was clear she had dressed in a great hurry.

When she saw Nathan, the maid's eyes opened wide in fear – and with just cause. Nathan had actually drawn back his hand to strike her when reason returned to him.

'Wake someone to help you, then go to Mistress Elinor's room – *now!*'

He shouted the word, and the maid fled from the barn. A tousled head appeared at the hay-loft trap-door, and Nathan called: 'Get down here quickly. Take a horse and ride to Mevagissey to fetch the physician. Tell him it's Mrs Jago. The baby's almost here.'

Nathan returned to Elinor's bedroom. A few minutes later an elderly woman, Sarah Davey, a part-time kitchen help and wife of the Polrudden gardener, hurried to the room. Dropping Nathan the briefest of curtsies, she came to the bedside and looked down at Elinor with motherly concern.

'Hello, me dear. 'Tis your time, then. Never you mind, my love. We'll soon have you to rights.'

'Where's the maid? I told her to come here.' Nathan's anger with the girl flared once more.

'And I told her to go to the kitchen to light fires, boil water and get things cleaned up down there.' Sarah Davey sniffed expressively. 'She's no good for anything else. She's shaking like a leaf – and with good reason, I've no doubt. Now, I'll thank you to find something to do elsewhere for a while, Mr Jago. There's chores to be done here that no husband should see. There's no need for you to fret. She's in good hands. I've had nine children of my own and delivered fifteen grand-children without losing a single one. Off you go, now.'

Nathan looked uncertainly at Elinor, and she attempted a tired smile. 'Don't go too far. I want to see your face when I give you a son.'

Leaving the room, Nathan felt guiltily relieved at handing responsibility for Elinor to someone else.

280

He had washed, shaved and changed by the time the physician arrived, full of brisk *bonhomie*. 'Don't you worry yourself,' he told Nathan, patting his shoulder reassuringly. 'Go away and find a close friend. Share a celebratory bottle of something with him. Childbirth is no time for a man to be alone with his thoughts.'

Dr Ellerman Scott was less cheerful when he came to find Nathan four hours later. 'I've sent your groom to fetch Surgeon Isaacs from Bodmin. He has had much experience in cases of childbirth. The fact is, when a baby is due to be born, the bones of the pelvic region become more pliable, to allow the baby to pass through. This has not happened to your wife. It probably has something to do with her accident. The bones are rigid and we're getting no help from her muscles, I'm afraid.'

'What does it mean? What's going to happen?'

'I don't know.' Dr Ellerman Scott spoke with alarming candour. 'I wish I did. However, Surgeon Isaacs will know what to do. He is excellent in cases like this. I knew his name long before I ever came to Cornwall.'

'This Surgeon Isaacs is not likely to be here for hours. Can I go in to see Elinor?'

'Yes, but don't tire her with too much talking. We need to conserve her strength as much as we can.'

When Nathan entered the bedroom he was shocked by Elinor's appearance. Tired and drawn, she looked at him with eyes that expressed weary resignation. Nathan was alarmed, Elinor was a fighter. She had always been a fighter. That she should give up now was quite unthinkable.

Taking her hand in both his, he forced a smile for her. 'It won't be much longer now. The physician has sent for a childbirth expert, one who's famous all over the country. When he gets here the baby won't dare cause any more trouble.'

Elinor licked dry lips before speaking. 'Your son is making his mark on the world early. You'll be proud of him, Nathan. I know you will.'

A labour pain gripped Elinor, and Nathan saw how very tired she was. The spasm drained all life from her for many minutes.

'We're *both* going to be proud of our son,' declared Nathan in desperation. 'I . . . I think you should rest now. I won't be far away. . . .'

281

'No! Don't leave me.' Elinor's fingers tightened on his.

'All right, I'll stay. But only if you promise to sleep.'

Elinor nodded wearily and closed her eyes.

The next few hours were long ones for Nathan. Twice when he thought Elinor was sleeping he tried to leave the bedroom. Each time she opened her eyes, and he had to remain.

Late in the afternoon, Dr Ellerman Scott came to the room. He had been in and out for most of the day, and Nathan took little notice until the doctor placed a hand on his shoulder. When Nathan looked up, the physician motioned for Nathan to accompany him from the room.

Elinor's eyes were closed, and on this occasion Nathan was able to take his hand from hers without disturbing her. Outside the room, Dr Ellerman Scott's manner was grave as he told Nathan that the messenger had returned from Bodmin – alone.

'Surgeon Isaacs is in London. He will not be returning for two weeks. We can't wait even two days, Mr Jago. I very much doubt whether we can really afford to wait for another two *hours*.'

'I don't understand. Wait for what? If you can hurry the birth along, why haven't you done so before?'

'I can't hurry the birth along any faster than the Lord himself is doing. The baby wants to come. It's trying hard to be born; but you can't push a cow through a sheep's gate, Mr Jago – and that's the fact of it. The baby is large, and the gap in your wife's pelvis is small. What's more, because of her accident she has no pushing power.'

'Then what do you mean by saying you'll have to act before another two hours have passed? What more can you do?'

The physician looked ill-at-ease. 'If we allow things to go on as they are, both mother and child will die. If I operate to remove the baby, there is a chance that I can save the child.'

'And Elinor . . . my wife?'

The doctor's silence provided its own dramatic answer, and Nathan recoiled in horror. 'You're suggesting I allow you to . . . to *kill* Elinor in order to save the baby? Is this what you're saying?'

'I am merely suggesting a way to save one life. The alternative is to lose two. I realise it is not an easy decision to make. . . .'

282

'Decision? Decision, you say? You're asking my permission to murder my wife! *That's* a decision?'

Dr Ellerman Scott's shrug was a combination of embarrassment and resignation. 'I understand how you must feel, Mr Jago. It is a decision I trust I will never be called upon to make for myself; but for some families an heir is all-important. When there is a title in the family – a baronetcy, for instance, or even higher rank now Sir Lewis has government office. . . .'

'Damn Sir Lewis, and his titles.' Nathan paced up and down the corridor outside Elinor's bedroom, his thoughts in a turmoil. 'I'll send a messenger on the next mail coach to this Surgeon Isaacs. I'll ask him to return immediately.'

Dr Ellerman Scott shook his head sadly. 'If I thought it would save your wife's life, I would ride to London myself. Sadly, things have already gone too far. Go in and remain with her, Mr Jago. I'll be there soon. If you change your mind— No, of course you won't.'

Without another word, Nathan went in to Elinor. He thought she was asleep, but as he sat down wearily by her side she opened her eyes.

'I am a worry to you, my husband.'

Her voice was so weak he had to put his head close to hers to catch the words.

'Of course you're a worry to me. Childbirth is a worrying time. Why, I can remember how Tom Quicke was when my sister Nell was having their child. . . .'

Nathan was trying desperately to give Elinor hope and strength, but she shook her head and relieved him of the need to lie.

'This is not the same. I know. It doesn't matter for me . . . not now. But your son. . . . I want him to live, Nathan. For you. For me, too. . . .'

Elinor's eyes closed and her mouth dropped open as another pain came. When it passed away she lay on the bed breathing shallowly. Nathan thought she had sunk into unconsciousness, but then her lips moved again.

'Tell the physician . . . to do what must be done. Save the baby. Please, save the baby.'

'No, Elinor. No!'

Nathan's cry brought Dr Ellerman Scott to the bedside.

'What is it? What happened?'

Nathan shook his head, unable to speak, and the physician took Elinor's wrist.

'She's very, very weak.'

Nathan knew the physician was waiting to hear him say he had changed his mind, but he shook his head. Nathan was aware that nothing short of a miracle could save Elinor now, but he could not bring himself to give the doctor the role of executioner.

Seated by Elinor's bedside, Nathan *willed* her to live. For a few unbelievable hours soon after dusk it appeared that a miracle might occur. At least, Elinor grew 'no weaker. Then, when the moon rose faint beyond the curtains, her strength ebbed away and she slipped into unconsciousness.

Shortly before midnight, Elinor opened her eyes and looked directly at Nathan. Her lips moved, and he put his ear to her mouth. He could never be certain, but afterwards he swore that the two words she spoke were 'Our son'. Immediately afterwards her eyes closed as though she would sleep – but Nathan knew she was dead.

'Doctor. . . . Doctor!'

The shout came from the gardener's wife, who had not left the room all day. It brought Dr Ellerman Scott bounding up the stairs, two at a time. He looked down at Elinor for a few moments, then slid a small hand-mirror from his waistcoat pocket and held it in front of her mouth. Removing it, he turned it towards Nathan. There was not even a hint of the mist of life upon the glass.

Next the physician picked up a small instrument shaped like a funnel from the table beside the bed. Putting the small end to his ear, he drew back the sheets and placed the other end upon Elinor's swollen belly.

His eyes opened wide in disbelief and he beckoned to Nathan. 'Quickly, listen to this.'

Nathan put his ear to the funnel-like instrument, and heard something that sounded like the heartbeat a man hears in his ears when he wakes in fright in the darkness of night.

'It lives! We might save it yet. For God's sake, man. Let me try!'

Fighting back his tears, Nathan nodded his head blindly;

284

then nodded again so there could be no mistake. Rising to his feet, he stumbled from the bedroom. He was unaware that, even as he was leaving the room, Dr Ellerman Scott had made his first incision in Elinor's body.

Such was the speed of the Mevagissey surgeon that Nathan was still at the head of the stairs, composing himself before breaking the news to the servants, when he heard the baby's first cry.

He turned in disbelief – and met Dr Ellerman Scott in the doorway of Elinor's room. Jubilantly, the physician placed a bloody bundle of humanity into Nathan's arms. Half-choked with unaccustomed emotion, he said: 'Here. . . . It's your wife's last gift to you. The son you damned near refused.'

Looking down at the screwed-up face, fighting to close its tiny lips about a bloody fist, Nathan sank to his knees in the doorway and wept. He wept for his dead wife, and for the future of the child in his arms, and his tears washed Elinor's blood from the tiny, naked body of their son.

It was 6 November 1811. A day Nathan would never forget.

Chapter Five

NEWS of the birth and death at Polrudden was carried to the village by the servants within minutes. Half an hour later Josiah Jago was knocking at the door of the manor, hat in hand. Roused from his bed, he had hurried to offer comfort to his son. At his own request, the preacher was taken to see Elinor. Kneeling by the bedside, he said a prayer for her.

Rising to his feet again, he looked down at the bloodless face. 'I find it sad to be gazing in death at the face of a daughter-in-law I never knew in life.'

'I was only just beginning to know her myself,' replied Nathan, his voice unsteady.

'Then your loss will be all the sadder for that,' said Josiah Jago. Taking Nathan's arm, he led him from the room and together they walked to the nursery where Nathan's son lay sleeping, wrapped in a white sheet. A maid, her eyes red from weeping, sat in the room nearby.

Preacher Jago reached out a gentle hand and caressed the baby's cheek with a finger, stopping when the child stirred.

'If only your mother could have seen him,' the preacher said gruffly. 'It's been a sad year for us, Nathan. Will you be burying Elinor in our little burial-ground?'

'No. I'll not let Elinor's death be the cause of a quarrel between Sir Lewis Hearle and myself. She'll be buried with the other Hearles, in St Austell.'

Josiah Jago nodded his understanding. 'She'll have our prayers from Pentuan. No doubt you'll be bringing my grandson to live in the village?'

Nathan shook his head vigorously. 'This is where he was born. This is where he'll stay. Polrudden is his heritage. I'll give Sir Lewis no excuse to keep it from him.'

'But who will feed the poor mite?'

'I've sent for our Nell. Baby Tom gets all the sustenance he needs from that new cow of theirs, and he's already taking solid food. Nell was complaining the other day that her own milk was showing no sign of drying up. The doctor says there's another woman heavy with milk in Mevagissey, but she's just lost her own baby through some mystery illness. I'd rather not put Elinor's – *my* son at risk.'

'Our Nell will welcome the opportunity to pay you back for giving her and Tom their farm. That was a very generous and brotherly thing to do, Nathan. It makes me very proud of you whenever I think about it.'

Looking down at the sleeping child, Preacher Josiah Jago swallowed the lump that rose in his throat. 'You deserve better fortune. Life hasn't always been kind to you.' Shaking his head, Josiah Jago added: 'The Lord works in mysterious ways, Nathan. My Annie, and now your Elinor. . . .'

Abruptly, the preacher turned away and walked from the room. At the doorway, he paused. 'You are right not to allow your wife's death to cause argument. Lay her to rest where her family have always been buried. But there will be a service for her in the church you built for me. I would like to see you there, my son.'

Sir Lewis Hearle reached Polrudden Manor four days after Elinor's death. Nathan met him on the east-wing staircase. The baronet looked very tired after his journey from London and he wasted no time on either pleasantries or commiserations.

'Where is she?'

'In her own room. I'll—'

Sir Lewis Hearle brushed Nathan to one side and hurried up the stairs.

Nathan was in the baby's room when the baronet left the bedside of his dead daughter and came looking for his grandson. Nell was in the room feeding the baby, but when Sir Lewis entered the room she pulled her teat from the baby's mouth and slid her breast inside the bodice of her dress. Robbed of its feast so unexpectedly, the baby continued sucking, not understanding what was happening, or why.

It was impossible to know what Sir Lewis Hearle was thinking as he stared at his hungry grandson. When he did speak it was to jab a forefinger in Nell's direction.

'Who is this?'

'My sister Nell. Tom Quicke's wife.'

'Wife to the man who had a chapel built upon his land? I'll have no *Methodist* wet-nurse in this house.'

Nathan's eyes glittered angrily. The baronet had made no mention of Elinor's death.

'Wrap the baby up well and take him to Venn Farm, Nell. I'll come later.'

Nathan's words took Sir Lewis Hearle by surprise. 'What? Where do you think you're taking him?'

'My son is going where he'll be warm and well fed. Where he'll continue the progress he's made since he was born.'

'It's a pity you didn't show such concern for your offspring before. You came within an ace of having him branded a bastard, and crippled his mother . . . my own daughter. . . .' Sir Lewis Hearle's hate and grief spilled out in the open, but with a visible effort he regained control of himself again. 'Find another woman for him.'

'The only other woman available is in Mevagissey. There's an epidemic of stomach sickness there – her own child died from it. I'll take my son from this house rather than expose him to such a risk.'

Sir Lewis Hearle fought a fierce mental battle between his hatred of anything that smacked of Wesleyism, and common sense.

'All right, the wet-nurse can stay. Just keep her out of my sight.'

Sir Lewis Hearle took another look at the baby. 'Have you given the brat a name?'

'Yes. Beville Hearle Jago. It's the name Elinor and I decided upon many months ago.'

'H'm!' Sir Lewis directed another expressionless look at the baby, then left the room without another word.

'We've a bad-tempered old boar at Venn with better manners.' The vehemence of Nell Quicke's words startled the baby, and he began to cry in a high, thin voice. Nell quickly silenced him by putting him to her breast once more.

'Sir Lewis finds it difficult to show any emotion except anger,' explained Nathan. 'But he'll cause no trouble for you. He couldn't take his eyes from his grandson.'

Nathan rested his hand lightly on his son's head. 'Beville Hearle Jago has just won the first and most important round of the fight for his heritage.'

. . .

Baby Beville might have won over his maternal grandfather, but Nathan was no more acceptable to the baronet than before. Sir Lewis even suggested that Nathan should stay away from Elinor's funeral, hinting that his attendance would be an embarrassment.

Nathan countered by pointing out that *he* could insist on the funeral taking place at Pentuan's chapel, where Sir Lewis would be received with courteous respect, and where there would be no such embarrassment.

Nathan's presence did cause a stir at the funeral service held in St Austell parish church, but the mourners were sharply divided in their attitude towards him. Most ignored Nathan, offering their condolences only to Sir Lewis Hearle. Others went out of their way to express sympathy to Nathan. The latter were, for the most part, people who had known Elinor personally, and had heard the story of her first meeting with Nathan. Marrying the prize-fighting champion of the world was in keeping with Elinor's wild nature and undisciplined upbringing. These mourners believed Sir Lewis Hearle's daughter might just as readily have eloped with a stable-lad or a wandering gipsy.

After the day of the funeral, the two men saw little of each other. Nathan had expected Sir Lewis Hearle to tell him to leave Polrudden Manor. The order did not come, but Nathan knew his presence was tolerated only for the sake of Beville – and because of the bills Nathan paid for the upkeep of the house.

The baronet never came near the baby when Nathan was at home, but Nell and the maids said Sir Lewis spent much time with his grandson. He had even been heard talking to him in a language strangely akin to 'baby talk'.

Any thoughts that Sir Lewis Hearle might be softening his attitude to the world in general were quickly dispelled on his return to London in mid-December.

The baronet arrived to find that anti-Methodist feeling had now reached an unexpectedly high level among those in the capital who were responsible for running the affairs of the country.

In Nottingham and other centres throughout the newly

industrialised Midlands, workers were clamouring for higher wages to meet the soaring cost of buying food to feed their large and undernourished families. They were also calling for the removal of the machines that were taking the places of men in the factories. When their demands were not met, angry voices were raised against the employers and a number of the more impetuous workers called for universal action.

Older men were reluctant to take the law into their own hands against the men who paid their wages, however meagre the sum might be, but hot-headed younger men were not. A number of weaving-frames were deliberately smashed by the discontented labourers, and the Midlands drew in its breath and awaited retribution.

None came. Mill-owners were playing the affair down, hoping the very act of destruction was enough to shock the workforce into the realisation of their responsibilities. Unfortunately, the mill-owners had miscalculated the mood of the workers. The more militant weavers took the lack of action to be a sign of weakness. The discontented workers set out on an orgy of wrecking. In two months more than nine hundred frames were smashed. The militia were mustered and troops despatched hurriedly to the area. Hundreds of workmen were arrested and some were killed or wounded.

The actions of the weavers brought rumblings of sympathetic discontent from the colliers, who had themselves been seeking higher wages for many years. For a while it seemed that the workers of the Midlands would unite in common cause.

Because of this hitherto unknown display of co-ordination between all sections of the working population, the authorities, in desperation, sought a scapegoat for the troubles they were experiencing.

Quick to seize upon such an opportunity, Church leaders pointed to the Methodist Church, whose rate of recruitment appeared to be advancing in proportion to the growth of industrial unrest. Here, they said, was a dissenting church whose name invoked discipline and 'method', who drew its recruits from those very people who were terrorising the countryside, destroying machinery and the means by which law-abiding people earned a living.

These critics ignored the fact that Methodist preachers were standing up and pleading with their congregations *not* to join the lawless bands who roamed the countryside smashing machinery, and that unrepentant agitators suffered dismissal from the Methodist Society.

Spencer Perceval saw no reason to question the accusations made by his leading churchmen. Methodism would serve well as a scapegoat for the shortcomings of his own administration.

When three rioters were arrested after a number of weaving machines were smashed in Manchester, the Home Office reported that the three had demanded the services of a Methodist minister. It was conveniently ignored that their request was refused because all three men had been expelled from the Methodist Society some months before.

In Parliament, Sir Lewis Hearle listened with great satisfaction as the anti-Methodist storm gathered momentum. Talkers began to compare Methodists with the Puritans of the seventeenth century – agitators who had overthrown the King and plunged the country into bloody civil war.

In the House of Lords ecclesiastical dignitaries angrily decried their nonconformist brethren. The Bishop of Gloucester called them 'malignant' and 'subtle adversaries', accusing them of concerting measures to undermine the country's civil and religious constitution.

Once again Methodist preachers were arrested on the most ridiculous charges, and convicted on the flimsiest of evidence. In Cornwall the magistrates were wary of arresting Preacher Josiah Jago yet again. Instead, Sir Lewis Hearle found another way to hit hard at the Cornish Methodists. He had Uriah Kemp taken into custody.

Immensely popular with the Methodist community, the American had fallen in love with Cornwall. He tramped the length and breadth of the county, drawing huge crowds to his meetings. By ordering his arrest, Sir Lewis Hearle made a very shrewd move. Government officials were becoming increasingly aware that war with America was inevitable. In accusing Kemp of stirring up disaffection, Sir Lewis Hearle added further fuel to the rumour of Methodist disloyalty. One great advantage to the Government was that it was not even necessary to bring the American to trial in a court-room, where his oratory might prove an embarrassment. After a two-minute appearance in St Austell's magistrates' court, Uriah Kemp was ordered to be deported from the country. Immediately after the order had been made, the American preacher was bundled into a prison van to begin a long and uncomfortable journey to London.

But, as on so many previous occasions, the well-thought-out ministerial ploy foundered on human frailty. As the journey to London progressed, the distance between stops at the numerous inns along the way grew shorter. One week after setting out, the prison van stood outside a Wiltshire inn for three long hours. When the driver and guard finally lurched back to their vehicle, Uriah Kemp demanded to be taken inside to a privy.

After a drunken discussion about which of the two escorts should take their prisoner inside the inn, both men went inside with him. Whilst there, each in turn returned to the bar for yet another drink to see him along the road.

The inn was crowded, and both escorts had made the acquaintance of a number of fellow-tipplers. When they finally staggered separately from the inn, each thought the other had locked the prisoner inside the van. Not until they arrived at Salisbury Town lock-up, where the prisoner was to spend the night, did they discover their drunken error.

The chief magistrate of the area was informed and immediately ordered out a troop of Dragoon Guards stationed in the town. The soldiers galloped back to the inn, but Uriah Kemp had disappeared.

A futile search was carried out among the lanes and highways for miles around, but no trace was found of the American preacher.

The escape was well publicised in newspapers throughout the country and provoked considerable admiration for Uriah Kemp's resourcefulness. War with America had still not been declared, and it was even hinted that *if* war came it would be the fault of the British navy. Stories were circulating of American ships stopped on the high seas and their crewmen ordered to prove American citizenship. Those who failed, for whatever reason, were accused of desertion from the British navy and impressed into service in His Majesty's men-of-war.

Sea-port towns and coastal villages of Great Britain had long and bitter experience of the activities of the naval press-gangs.

Until war came and British lives were lost, there would be much sympathy for the American cause in Britain. Consequently, there was no pressure on the Methodists to return Uriah Kemp to the authorities and thus demonstrate their loyalty to the Crown.

Chapter Six

IN FEBRUARY 1812, seven months after the wedding of her daughter to Sammy Mizler, Peggy Hoblyn's finely poised mental balance dropped violently on the side of insanity. She murdered Lizzie Barron, her housekeeping cousin.

Had there been anyone at Portgiskey who cared sufficiently for the ageing fisherwoman, the grisly tragedy might have been averted. As it was, much of the story had to be pieced together by a coroner's court.

Lizzie Barron had been steadily increasing the pressure on her simple-minded cousin. She was far more interested in enjoying her own life than in caring for Peggy Hoblyn. When Lizzie Barron went out for an evening with her friends, Peggy Hoblyn was locked in her own bedroom. Nathan remonstrated with the cousin on two occasions, but Lizzie Barron merely bided her time, ensuring that Nathan was out of the way before she went out.

Peggy Hoblyn hated being locked away in such a manner. The women in the nearby fish-cellar would frequently hear her hammering on the door to be let out, when she felt she had been in the room for long enough.

The breaking-point came when Peggy Hoblyn's cousin went to St Austell market early one morning and stayed on to enjoy a drink with some friends. The women in the fish-cellar had heard Peggy Hoblyn banging on the door of the bedroom for most of the day, alternately demanding to be released and pleading for someone to come to her assistance. One of the fisherwomen *did* try to go to her, but the outside doors of the cottage were also locked. No one thought of contacting Nathan, who had been night-fishing and was sleeping at Polrudden.

By the time Nathan reached Portgiskey for his night's fishing, the women from the cellar had gone home and all was quiet inside the Hoblyn cottage. Nathan was a little later than usual and, after checking his boat, he put to sea without going to the cottage.

What happened that night would never be known. Peggy Hoblyn's cousin was known to have been drinking heavily before she left the St Austell inn to return to Portgiskey, and this was the last occasion on which she was seen alive.

The following morning, Nathan brought *The Brave Amy H* back to Portgiskey Cove to find the women from the fish-cellar crowded about the door of the cottage. When Nathan leaped to the quay, the women rushed to tell him what was happening.

'Something terrible's happened inside the cottage,' explained one of them. 'No doubt about it.' After telling Nathan of Peggy Hoblyn's cries the previous day, the woman added: 'I went to the cottage this morning to see if Peggy was all right – and she jumped out on me like some wild beast, screaming fit to frighten the Devil.'

All about Nathan the women were nodding their agreement, and Nathan's informant went on: 'I don't mind telling you, I feared for my life. There's no sign of that cousin of hers; but the door's unlocked, so she must have come home.'

'All right, come away from the door. I'll go inside and find out what's been going on.'

Pushing his way through the women who were reluctant to give up their individual vantage-points, Nathan reached the door. Once inside, he closed the door behind him, much to the chagrin of those waiting outside.

Nathan searched the downstairs rooms and ascertained no one was there before mounting the creaking stairs. He was about a third of the way up when Peggy Hoblyn appeared at the top and began screaming incoherently at him.

'It's all right, Mrs Hoblyn. It's me . . . Nathan Jago. I'm a friend of your Amy, remember?'

At first his words made no difference, but very gradually Peggy Hoblyn becam The physical signs of her madness were clearly in evidence this morning. Wild-eyed and tangled-haired, she crouched with fingers extended like the claws of a defensive wild cat.

Talking all the while, Nathan gradually edged his way upstairs, pausing whenever Peggy Hoblyn appeared to be particularly agitated. When he was almost within touching distance of her, Peggy Hoblyn retreated backwards inside the bedroom. Slowly and cautiously, Nathan followed.

He was inside the room before he saw Lizzie Barron. She lay sprawled untidily on the bedroom floor. It was clear to Nathan before he leaned over her that Lizzie Barron was dead, and her face told its own story. Nathan had seen more than one unfortunate sailor hanged from the yardarm of a ship. The dead woman's face had the same purplish hue, her eyes starting from her head, an expression of terror glazed permanently upon them.

Nathan did not need to see the dark bruises on Lizzie Barron's neck to know she had been strangled.

On a table in the corner of the room was a pile of stale crusts, and an overturned water-jug lay beside a cracked and stained mug. The room stank of continuous occupation, and the stout bolt on the outside of the bedroom door completed the wordless story for Nathan. Peggy Hoblyn had been kept prisoner in this bedroom for long periods. Her gaoler had paid a grim price for the lack of concern for her deranged cousin.

There was no way in which the death could be kept a secret. A runner was sent to inform the St Austell coroner, while a couple of nervous fisherwomen cooked a meal for the insane murderess. Peggy Hoblyn was ravenously hungry, and the fear of the fisherwomen turned to pity as they watched her wolf down plate after plate of cooked fish. It was apparent that Peggy Hoblyn had been kept hungry as well as a prisoner in her room.

The coroner arrived at Portgiskey accompanied by a magistrate and two constables, and Peggy Hoblyn was taken in custody to St Austell. Two days later, after the coroner had recorded a verdict of 'murder' on the dead woman, Peggy Hoblyn was brought before the magistrate. Nathan was present to hear her found not guilty of Lizzie Barron's murder by reason of her insanity and he visited her in the cells beneath the court. Then she was transferred to the old lunatic asylum in the nearby village of Lostwithiel.

Had Amy been at home, Peggy Hoblyn might have been discharged into the custody of her daughter, but Nathan had no London address for her and was unable to prevent Peggy Hoblyn from being sent to the asylum.

Two days later Nathan travelled to Lostwithiel to see how the Portgiskey woman was settling in at her new 'home'. He was deeply shocked by what he saw. The unfortunate Peggy Hoblyn was lodged in a large, stone-walled room that was reminiscent of a medieval dungeon. She shared this accommodation with a number of other inmates, all with a history of violence. Each occupant had a stinking straw pallet for a bed, a canvas bag in which to keep her meagre possessions, and two wooden buckets, one to hold water, the other slops. Each woman wore an iron belt about her waist from which a chain led to a stout ring set in the wall behind her pallet. The chains were positioned to give each woman a degree of free movement, whilst keeping her at least an arm's length from her neighbour.

The smell in this part of the asylum was appalling, and twice one of the chained women rushed at Nathan in a vain attempt to claw his face, screaming abuse when the chain brought her to a halt.

Peggy Hoblyn would not speak to him and started nervously at each sudden movement made by her fellow-inmates. There was just cause for such nervousness. The seven women chained in the room had been responsible for thirteen deaths. One woman had killed her husband, mother and two children.

These details were given to Nathan when he gave the Superintendent of the asylum money with which to buy Peggy Hoblyn a few luxuries. Nathan was aware that most of the money would go straight into the Superintendent's own pocket, but the knowledge that someone cared for Peggy Hoblyn would at least ensure that she received her full dues. Many others in the asylum were less fortunate.

When the heavy, iron-studded doors slammed shut behind him, Nathan breathed unfouled air deep into his lungs and looked back at the dirty, grey stone asylum building. He knew he had to get word of Peggy Hoblyn's plight to Amy.

It was a quiet time of the year at Venn Farm. Nathan had little difficulty in persuading his sister to come to Polrudden to look after Beville while Nathan was in London finding Amy. Beville Jago was now three months old and Nell's own son six months older, and Nell enjoyed caring for both children together.

It was eighteen months since Nathan had last seen London. In that short time the great, greedy city had gobbled up vast tracts of the surrounding countryside. From the coach Nathan was astonished to see that houses now reached almost to Kensington and Paddington villages. But his business did not lie here, among the houses being built by merchants and traders. He was heading for the narrow streets of London's 'East End'. Here were tens of thousands of dingy houses. They owed their origins to medieval peasants who built their hovels against the stout walls of the Tower, in the vain hope that its garrison would afford them protection.

Since those earlier years, this fringe of London had developed a unique character of its own. It was a maze of alleyways and crooked streets, the dark windows of its houses patched with rags and scraps of stained paper. In the shadow of the houses, shoeless, undernourished children played in stinking pools, surrounded by piles of rotting rubbish. The residents here were a breed of Londoner noted for their guile and sharp wit, with a slang language that had no meaning for anyone who lived outside the area. In addition, the 'East End' Londoner possessed a will to survive unmatched by any of his countrymen.

Sammy Mizler had been born here. In common with the vast majority of his fellow 'East Enders', he was truly happy living nowhere else. It was here that Nathan would find Amy.

Nathan entered this cockney kingdom on foot. No hackney-carriage driver would risk his purse, or his horse and vehicle, in the lawless streets and alleyways beyond the ancient east wall of England's capital.

Nathan visited two inns he had once frequented with Sammy Mizler, only to learn that the landlords had changed. His questions brought only hostile glances from both owners and customers alike.

He was more fortunate in the third tavern only because a customer recognised him. But the presence of the prize-fighting champion caused such a commotion that it was some time before he was able to put his question.

'Sammy Mizler?' The landlord worked a finger in his ear as he nodded slowly. 'Yus, I knows him. Leastways, I know *of* 'im. Good little fighter in his day, 'e was. Come up in the world since then, I do 'ear. Some of the boys 'ave see 'im up west, running wiv the Duke of Clarence's crowd and spending 'is young wife's money.'

'Do you know where his wife is?' asked Nathan eagerly.

The landlord shook his head. 'No, but Charlie Harrup

might.' Raising his voice, he called across the crowded tap-room. 'Charlie? You know where Nathan Jago can find Sammy Mizler's missus?'

Charlie Harrup turned a pock-marked face towards the speaker and wiped a watery eye with the back of a dirty hand.

'Dunno for sure.' Charlie Harrup sniffed, wiped his hand with a greasy sleeve, then with a hopeful grin held up an empty pewter pot. 'Perhaps anuvver drop o' 'Ollands might 'elp me mem'ry.'

The landlord looked enquiringly at Nathan. After a moment's hesitation, Nathan nodded. He watched as the mug of gin passed from hand to hand until it reached the widely grinning Charlie Harrup.

Taking a long swig, the cockney pulled a face, then smacked his lips noisily. 'Ah! That's better. Wonderful wot a drink does for a geezer's memory. Sammy Mizler's missus. . . . Nah, is she a dark-'aired little piece? Got bags of go in 'er?'

Nathan smiled at the description. 'That's her. You know where she's living?'

Much to Nathan's annoyance, Charlie Harrup shook his head. 'Nah, dunno that. . . . But I've seen 'er a few times in 'Aggerston market. You go there and ask Tillie Carver. She runs the fish-stall. Tillie's Cornish 'erself. She'll be able to tell yer.'

Leaving the landlord with a shilling to keep Charlie Harrup in cheap gin for the remainder of the afternoon, Nathan set off for Haggerston market.

Half an hour later he was knocking on the door of a pokey little house, built in the space between a tallow works and a brewer's stable.

Nathan waited with a sense of apprehensive excitement for the door to open. The Cornish stallholder, rendered garrulous by the appearance of a fellow-Cornishman, had told the same story as had the tavernkeeper. Sammy Mizler was not likely to be at home, preferring the company of his London friends to that of his bride of only seven months.

Then the door opened – and Amy stood before him. Her face registered a mixture of joy and disbelief. Then she was in his arms, hugging him.

'Nathan! Is it really you? What are you doing here? Why

haven't you written?'

Suddenly, Amy held him off, her face registering alarm. 'Is something wrong? Yes, I can see by your face it is. It's Ma, isn't it? Is she . . . dead?'

As she spoke, Nathan was looking more closely at her. This was not the carefree, healthy girl he had known in Cornwall. Amy was thinner, pinch-faced and pale. Dreadfully pale.

'No, Amy, she's not dead. But . . . can we talk about it inside?' Nathan had fought and trained in this area. Ostlers from the brewery stables had recognised him and were crowding from their building on to the street.

Amy drew him quickly inside the house. When the door closed behind them, Nathan told Amy details of the tragedy that had occurred at Portgiskey.

Amy was shocked, horrified and deeply distressed. 'Poor Ma. . . . Oh, poor Ma! I should never have left her on her own. I should have realised she wouldn't be able to cope without me to look after her. Where is she now, Nathan?'

'The lunatic asylum in Lostwithiel. I went to see her there. It . . . it's not a good place to be, Amy. But they won't allow *me* to take her away.'

'Then *I* must go to her. When is the next mail coach?'

'Tomorrow morning at eight o'clock from the Bell inn at St Paul's.'

'I'll need to leave early. It's two miles to St Paul's. But how long has she been as bad as this? Why didn't you write and tell me?'

'I had no address for you. I've spent most of today making enquiries. It was Tillie Carver who finally told me where you and Sammy lived.'

'But my letters . . . didn't you get them?'

'You disappeared from my life when I waved goodbye to you and Sammy on the London-bound coach from St Austell. There has been no word from you since.'

'I wrote *three* letters. . . .' Amy closed her eyes for some moments, as though she were in pain. 'Sammy. . . . It *has* to be Sammy. I gave the letters to him to send off for me.'

'Where is he? What time will he be home?'

'I don't know. It's been three days since I last saw him. He . . . he doesn't come home very often.' She finished lamely, as though the words constituted an explanation. 'But you must be famished. There's plenty of time before I need to pack for the journey. I'll give you some food.'

Nathan followed Amy to the kitchen, and as she busied herself preparing a meal for him he sat at the table asking endless questions about her life in London. It was a form of self-defence. He had no wish to answer any of Amy's questions about the happenings in Cornwall.

He learned that Sammy had been a warm and attentive husband for only a very short time before he gravitated to the growing circle of followers about the Duke of Clarence. The Duke's brother, George, had recently been appointed Regent, to rule in the place of their insane father, King George III. With the advent of the Regency, the Duke of Clarence had advanced a number of rungs up the ladder of nineteenth-century society. He was now the brother of the man who effectively ruled the country and no longer a rather happy-go-lucky younger royal son.

Nathan also learned that Sammy Mizler had founded a club in Shepherd's Market, under the sponsorship of the Duke of Clarence. The object of the club was to advance the cause of prize-fighting. Here Sammy encouraged promising young pugilists and taught the art of 'fisticuffs' to blue-blooded gentlemen of the 'Fancy'.

While Sammy was enjoying the company of his aristocratic friends, Amy kept herself occupied helping the local Methodist Society to feed near-starving children in the worst slums of nearby Hoxton. Many were the sons and daughters of soldiers serving in the ranks of Wellington's victorious army. In varying stages of malnutrition, they suffered the ills and diseases that attacked many children who lived in the overcrowded slums of the largest city in the world. For some, the only way of life they knew was picking over the accumulated filth in narrow streets as foul-smelling as the sluggish, contaminated waters of the River Thames.

Then Amy put the first of the questions Nathan had been dreading.

'We've done nothing but talk of me since you arrived. What's been happening at Portgiskey? Is Calvin still with you?'

'No. He was transported – for smuggling.' As Amy

temporarily abandoned her cooking, Nathan told her of his second boat and the events surrounding Calvin Dickin's arrest and sentence.

'So Portgiskey is once more a haven for smugglers,' commented Amy quietly. 'It's a foolish way of life, Nathan. My pa got away with it, and so did many other men of his time, but times are changing. There are far more Revenue men now. How long do you think it will be before you are arrested, too?'

When Nathan did not reply, Amy asked: 'Does Elinor . . . your wife, know what you are doing?'

At last the name of Elinor had entered the conversation. It hurt, as Nathan had known it would. He had realised he would have to talk about Elinor, but he found it necessary to compose himself before replying.

'Elinor's dead. She died in childbirth.'

Amy had been watching Nathan closely and had anticipated his reply. Tears filled her eyes, and now it was her turn to struggle for the words she wanted to say.

'Oh, Nathan, I'm *so* sorry. I know how much she meant to you. What . . . what happened to the baby?'

Nathan's taut expression softened immediately. 'Beville? He's a grand boy. Nell is at Polrudden looking after him while I'm away.'

Tears were still lurking in Amy's eyes when she asked: 'Beville? Does the name have anything to do with my brother?'

'Yes.'

'Thank you, Nathan. I'm so glad your son lived. If only. . . .'

The hoarse-voiced Amy never completed the sentence. Clouds of dark smoke rose from the fish cooking in the frying-pan on the fire behind her. Snatching up the pan, Amy hurried it to the back door. As the door opened, Nathan caught a glimpse of a tiny, flagstoned yard behind the house. It was dark and damp, tall buildings on either side blocking out the sun. At Portgiskey, the Hoblyns had enjoyed a large, shrub-filled garden, with the sea and distant cliffs on one side, and a green, steep valley extending behind the house to woodland at the top of a hill.

When Amy returned, Nathan had opened the kitchen window, allowing the smoke to billow out.

'I'm sorry, Nathan,' Amy said despondently. 'I so rarely have an opportunity to cook for anyone. Then, when a chance arises, I make a mess of everything.'

She looked so crestfallen that Nathan said: 'Never mind about cooking a meal. I'll take you out to eat. I remember one or two good taverns from my prize-fighting days.'

Amy's face lit up instantly. 'I would like that. I haven't been out very often since Sammy and I came to London.' Amy gave Nathan a doleful half-smile. 'It's strange, isn't it, to feel lonely surrounded by thousands of people? Yet I'm lonelier here than ever I was at Portgiskey.'

Amy gave a rueful shrug. 'But my troubles are nothing when compared with yours. I'll go and fetch a shawl.'

The tavern Nathan chose was no more than half a mile from Amy's little house and they walked there arm in arm. It was a cold, raw London evening, but the tavern was warm and cheerful. The landlord had once been a prize-fighting champion himself and he greeted Nathan effusively. When Nathan introduced Amy as the wife of Sammy Mizler, only the very best would do for the tavern's two guests.

Shifting the tables about, some already occupied by early diners, the landlord secured Amy and Nathan a place beside the cheerful fire. At the same time, he confided to Amy: 'Your husband was the first man ever to beat me in the prize-ring. Nathan here is a good champion, I'm not denying that. But that fight 'twixt me and Sammy was one of the best ever seen in London. Sixty-four rounds, with not a man willing to risk his money on which of us would win. Then Sammy brings up a punch that felt as though it had travelled all the way from Billingsgate – and gaining speed every inch of the way.'

The cheerful landlord rubbed his jaw in rueful memory. 'They told me I was out cold for an hour and a half. I was in no state to argue for days afterwards.'

Winking at Amy, the landlord added: 'Taught me the most important lesson of my life, did Sammy. Until that fight, I thought I was unbeatable. But while I was nursing my jaw I got to thinking. What Sammy Mizler had done, another fighter might do, too. I started choosing my fights a bit more carefully, and putting away the money I earned. The result was that when I was beaten again – by Nathan this time – I had enough money put by to buy this tavern. Now I can entertain those friends who helped me along the way. Now, what's your pleasure? Tonight, everything is on the house – and I'll take it as an insult if you don't order the very best.'

For almost three hours, Nathan and Amy were able to push to the back of their minds all the problems that awaited them in Cornwall, and to enjoy the conviviality of the tavern, its landlord and customers. It was Amy's first opportunity to observe at first hand the all-embracing warmth of the cockney out to enjoy himself. Tapping her foot in time to the fiddler, or clapping her hands in time to the bawdy singing, Amy became more like the young girl Nathan had known in Cornwall.

Regretfully, when the party was still in full swing, Nathan decided to bring the evening to a close. Amy would have things to do to prepare for her trip to Cornwall in the morning. Nathan himself had to get back to his room at the Bell inn, from whence the mail coach would leave. Before then he wanted to go to the boxing club in Shepherd's Market, to tell Sammy Mizler of his wife's impending departure for Cornwall.

Outside the tavern, Amy's hand found Nathan's for a moment. 'Thank you, Nathan. This was the nicest evening I've spent since leaving Portgiskey.'

'I find that very sad, Amy. I felt sure you and Sammy would have a good life here together.'

'So did I.' She turned her face towards him as they walked along. 'But you mustn't blame everything on Sammy. When we first came here I missed Cornwall so much I cried myself to sleep most nights. I couldn't have been much fun to live with. In fact, had my letters reached you, and you replied, I would probably have packed up and come home. It's not really surprising that Sammy began to find things to do that would take him out of the house.'

'There are many places he could have taken you,' said Nathan. 'The tavern where we've spent this evening, for instance.'

They walked together in silence until they turned a corner and came within sight of the little house that was Amy's London home.

'There's a light showing. Sammy must be home.'

Nathan was unable to tell from the tone of Amy's voice

whether she was pleased or apprehensive. Her steps quickened and she hurried Nathan to the door. Pushing it open, she called: 'Sammy? Sammy, look who's here.'

Sammy Mizler appeared at the door of an upstairs room, the sleeves of an expensive, lace-trimmed shirt flapping loose. When he first saw Nathan, Sammy's face lit up with uninhibited delight, but as he took the first step down the stairs the pleasure was chased away by a frown.

'Where have *you* been,' he growled at Amy. 'I've been home for almost two hours.'

'You've *not* been home for three days,' corrected Amy. She gave Nathan an embarrassed look before returning her attention to her husband. 'Nathan has come from Cornwall to tell me Ma's in serious trouble. I'll need to go home to her for a while.'

Sammy had reached the bottom of the stairs. Adjusting the lace cuffs of the shirt he wore, he looked at Nathan almost casually and, without proffering his hand, passed on to the tiny parlour.

'When did you reach London?'

'This morning. I spent half the day asking for you. It seems most of the landlords we once knew have moved on. Your address was eventually given to me by the Cornish fish-seller in Haggerston market.'

Sammy Mizler eyed Nathan for a few minutes. When he finally accepted that Nathan was telling the truth, Sammy relaxed. His suspicions could hardly have been clearer had he spoken them. Sammy had believed that his old friend had been staying at the house for a day or two.

'There should have been no need for Nathan to seek us over half of London,' said Amy to her husband. 'I've written three letters since we came here. You took them to a post office for me, Sammy. What happened to them?'

Sammy Mizler shrugged. 'Who knows? The mail has never been reliable since all the best men went off to war. Probably some drunken mail-coach guard lost them along the way.'

Amy opened her mouth to pursue the matter, but Sammy had turned back to Nathan. 'I'm going out for a drink and something to eat. You'll come with me?'

'I'll need to get back to the Bell inn, at St Paul's. I'm catching the morning mail coach back to Cornwall.'

'Leaving London so soon? Well, if you must, I suppose there's nothing I can do about it. But you'll stay here tonight. We've a spare room, and you and I have a lot to talk about. I want to tell you about my club. I've got some fine fighters training there. Abraham Dellow is one of them. Remember him – the negro slave you fought in Bristol? He's good, Nathan. You'd be hard put to beat him now. He's the Regent's favourite. I spoke to the Regent only the other day and he said to me—'

'Sammy . . . Sammy!' Amy had been vainly attempting to gain her husband's attention while he was talking. When he turned to look at her, she said: 'Can you talk about nothing but prize-fighting? I'm leaving London in the morning, too. Ma needs me.'

Sammy Mizler's suspicions returned. 'What's wrong with her? Is she dying or something?'

'She's been committed to a lunatic asylum. Chained to a wall there like an animal. She'll not survive long if I don't get her out quickly.'

Amy did not tell Sammy the full story, and Nathan did not feel like amplifying her brief outline of the situation. Instead, he said: 'Why don't you come with us, Sammy? There are many old friends who will be happy to see you again. Not as many as there were, but enough to give you a real Cornish welcome.'

'I've got too much to do. The Duke of Clarence has plans. . . . But come out with me. I'll tell you about them over a drink.'

At the doorway, Nathan cast an apologetic look back at Amy and saw her standing forlornly in the centre of the room. He wished he could have invited her, too, but Sammy Mizler had joined the ranks of those husbands who did not take their wives out with them. Nathan also suspected that the couple found much to quarrel about. He had no wish to add something more.

Sammy Mizler was full of the plans he and the Duke of Clarence had for Sammy's prize-fighting club, and the 'nobs' to whom Sammy was teaching the rudiments of a prize-fighter's art. On the infrequent occasions when Amy's name entered the conversation, Sammy dismissed her with a derisory remark that jarred upon Nathan. Sammy Mizler also drank far more than in the past. It was not the comfortable evening between old friends that it might have been, and Nathan brought it to an end as quickly as he was able.

That night, Nathan lay in bed in the Mizlers' tiny house and could hear the sound of low voices in the adjacent bedroom. Later, in the early hours of the morning, when sleep still eluded him, Nathan was certain he could hear the sound of Amy weeping.

Chapter Seven

SAMMY MIZLER did not accompany his wife to the Bell inn, but put in a brief, bleary-eyed appearance at the top of the stairs as she and Nathan set off to begin the long journey to Cornwall. Sammy reminded Nathan that a payment was almost due in respect of the dissolved Portgiskey fishing partnership.

Shouldering the bundle that held all the possessions Amy was taking with her, Nathan set off from the tiny house in the dingy back street with a feeling of relief. Beside him, Amy walked along in silence. She had lightly powdered her face in an attempt to hide the puffiness about her eyes, but Nathan suspected she had shed a great many tears in the darkness of the bedroom she shared with her husband.

Misreading the cause of her unhappiness, Nathan said gently: 'Perhaps Sammy will change his mind and come to Portgiskey after all.'

'He'll have to if he wants to see me again,' declared Amy fiercely. 'I'll not return to London. I hate everything about it, and what it's done to Sammy – to us.'

Nathan remembered the warning he had given to Sammy Mizler about marrying Amy and taking her from Cornwall. He said nothing. Sammy and Amy had learned the hard lesson for themselves. Amy belonged to London no more than did Sammy Mizler to Portgiskey.

They reached the Bell inn with only minutes to spare. Two other passengers were on board, both elderly gentlemen who spent the first hour of the journey complaining about the hardness of the coach seat. They consoled each other with copious draughts of brandy, contained in the numerous flasks both had concealed about their persons. The brandy proved an acceptable substitute for the upholsterer's failings. By the time the houses gave way to fields and trees, the two men were slumped against each other, snoring noisily.

The first glimpse of the countryside after so long in the crowded alleyways of London's East End put new life into Amy. She smiled for the first time that morning and nodded in the direction of their two fellow-passengers. 'Do you think all the grumbling was part of their regular travelling ritual, or merely an excuse to bring out their brandy-flasks? Look at them; they're sleeping like babies now.'

Nathan smiled. 'I think it must have been a bachelor who first thought of the expression, "sleeping like a baby". It certainly doesn't apply to Beville. He thinks the night hours are for playing.'

'You have him in the room with you?'

'When I'm not fishing. I see too little of him otherwise.'

'You're very proud of your son, Nathan.'

'Yes. He'll be a fine man one day.'

The offside coach wheels dropped into a deep pothole, but a quick glance at their fellow-passengers assured Amy that they were still sleeping. 'What will Beville think when he learns his father is a smuggler?'

'What did you think when you discovered *your* father was a smuggler? Beville will understand that I have no choice. It's the only way I can keep Polrudden.'

'Is Polrudden so important to you.'

'More than ever before. It's my son's heritage. I'll ensure that it isn't lost to him.'

The mail coach was fast. At dusk the following day it pulled on to the yard of the Talbot inn in Lostwithiel, to the accompaniment of long and noisy blasts on the coachman's horn. Here, Nathan and Amy climbed stiffly from the vehicle, grateful that the long journey was over. Their two sleeping companions had left the coach at Salisbury, but others had joined at stops along the route and the passengers squeezed uncomfortably close together inside the coach. A few rowdier travellers clung tenaciously to the outside, hurling abuse and an occasional bottle at the inhabitants of villages along the route.

The lunatic asylum looked even more forbidding in the half-light. Inside its dark and draughty corridors, candles flickered in smoke-darkened recesses. As they walked behind the Superintendent, shadows from the swinging lamp he carried reached into cells where the minds of chained and manacled lunatics gave them grotesque substance in the tragic world of the insane.

Walking beside Nathan, Amy jumped nervously at each new cackle of mad laughter that reached out at her.

'Take no notice,' said the Superintendent reassuringly, as he led the way along the dark, evil-smelling corridors. 'They're always worse at this time of day. If there's going to be trouble, this is when it usually happens. We say it's the Lord of Darkness taking the roll call of his servants – begging your pardon, Miss. Meaning no offence, of course. Here we are. This is the room where you'll find your mother. Stand back a minute now, while I check they're all fit to be seen.'

Taking a heavy ring of keys from his belt, the Superintendent selected one and inserted it in the lock. Turning the key, he swung the door open and held the lamp up to see inside the large room. Immediately, a screaming form hurtled from the darkness and flung itself upon the Superintendent, knocking him to the ground.

For a moment there was pandemonium in the corridor, the mad woman's screams taken up by her companions and the occupants of nearby cells. Then Nathan got a grip on the struggling woman and hauled her off the asylum official. He was amazed by the strength in her puny body, but he held her in the air as she kicked and fought in his arms.

Struggling to his feet, the Superintendent cursed the woman as she hurled vile abuse at him. He drew back his fist to strike her, then remembered that Nathan and Amy were visitors and not asylum staff. Picking up his lantern, he relit the extinguished candle from one burning in the corridor and held it to the woman's face.

'Oh, it's *you*. Bring her over here.' Reaching down a chain and manacles from the wall, the Superintendent fastened the woman's wrists and ankles swiftly, then linked a chain to them and secured it to a ring in the corridor wall.

'She's lost weight and slipped the band about her waist. It sometimes happens, especially with the women.'

'Is it *really* necessary to chain her like this?' Amy asked indignantly as the Superintendent bent the woman double and added another, smaller chain, linking her ankles to her wrists.

'Necessary?' echoed the Superintendent. 'I'll say it's necessary. This woman has already killed four people. She'll kill more given half a chance.'

'And she's been sharing a room with my ma?' Amy was horrified.

'Your mother is in here because she, too, killed someone,' retorted the Superintendent brutally. To Nathan he said: 'Keep the young woman here, sir. I'd like to look inside that cell before I allow you in.'

'But my ma . . .?'

'Do as he says.' Nathan took a firm grip of Amy's arm.

The noise of the struggle had aroused the inmates of cells leading off the corridor in which they waited. The din was terrifying. Screams, shouts, curses and other sounds that Nathan found difficult to believe originated in human throats were hurled at them from all sides.

Then the Superintendent backed out of the cell, but as Amy started forward he slammed the door shut behind him.

His face pale in the lantern light, the Superintendent said to Nathan: 'That mad bitch has raised her score to six! There's two women in there strangled with their own chains. Two others badly hurt. I need to fetch a surgeon. I must ask you both to leave for now.'

'But what about my ma?' cried Amy. 'Is she all right?'

'Mrs Hoblyn is one of those who's been hurt,' replied the Superintendent. 'I can't tell how bad she is at this stage. . . . She's unconscious.'

'Oh, my God! I want to see her. She's my mother. . . .'

'I'm sorry – but the sooner I can bring a surgeon here the better it will be for her.'

'He's right.' Nathan put his arm about Amy, who was still inclined to protest, and led her away. Over his shoulder he called to the Superintendent: 'We'll be staying at the Talbot inn tonight. Should there be any cause for concern about her you'll let us know?'

The Superintendent nodded. Then, roaring at the shrieking inmates of his institution, he hurried past Amy and Nathan and unlocked the door for them.

At the Talbot inn, Nathan was able to book two rooms for himself and Amy. Then he called for a bottle of the landlord's best brandy and forced Amy to drink down a large tumblerful. The brief glimpse of the inside of the lunatic asylum had badly shaken her. Concern for her mother was now coupled with a renewed determination to have her released as soon as was possible.

Nathan talked to Amy for a long time that evening, and he insisted that she try to eat a meal. She was in no mood for eating but obligingly pushed the food about her plate with her knife, occasionally picking at it with a fork.

When the desultory meal was almost at an end, the door opened and a man stepped into the room, blowing warm air into cupped hands. Nathan recognised him as the magistrate who had dismissed the case against Preacher Josiah Jago eighteen months before. He must have been brought from St Austell to deal with the incident at the Lostwithiel lunatic asylum.

Telling Amy he would be back in a few minutes, Nathan went to the table close to the hearth, where the magistrate had settled himself. Amy saw a frown appear on the man's face as Nathan began talking. Then both men looked across the room towards her. The stranger nodded to Nathan and, after a few more words, rose to his feet and accompanied Nathan to where Amy was sitting.

'Amy, this is Mr Carlyon. He's the magistrate who was asked to come here by the Superintendent.'

Amy started up, all her earlier fears returning. 'What's happening? Is Ma going to be all right?'

'Your mother was still alive when I left the lunatic asylum, only a few minutes ago.' The magistrate's expression became grim. 'In that she is fortunate. A third victim died shortly before my arrival. However, I don't want to build your hopes too high. The surgeon who examined your mother could find no indication that her skull was broken, but he feels it is probably cracked. She received a violent blow to the side of the head, most probably with a heavy wooden stool that was normally kept by the door, out of reach of the inmates. I discovered blood and hair adhering to it. . . .' Observing the stricken look on Amy's face, the magistrate coughed noisily to cover his embarrassment. 'The surgeon fears she may be unconscious for many days. It is even possible she may never regain consciousness. I am sorry to be the one to give you this news, but I feel you have a right to the truth.'

Amy gave Nathan a grief-stricken look, and he wished there was something he could do for her. When she spoke, it was to

312

the magistrate. 'Must she stay in that place as she is so ill?'

The magistrate looked thoughtful. 'Your mother was committed to the lunatic asylum because there was no relative willing to accept responsibility for her. I understand you were living in London at the time. Have your circumstances changed?'

Amy hesitated for only a moment. 'Yes, I've returned home now.'

'And are you willing to accept full responsibility for her?'

'Yes. . . . Oh, yes!'

'Very well. Come to my office tomorrow – or whenever the surgeon says she may be moved. I will give you the necessary authority to remove her from the lunatic asylum. But I suggest you consult the surgeon on the best mode of transportation for her. Now, if you will excuse me, I see the landlord's wife with the meal I ordered. Good evening to you both.'

Amy was greatly cheered by the magistrate's decision, and Nathan had to remind her that Peggy Hoblyn was still unconscious and the future uncertain for her.

'I know,' replied Amy. 'But when she's home where she belongs, where she's loved, she'll improve. I'm quite sure of it. Thinking about her being in that *horrible* place all this time, with no one to care for her, makes me want to weep.'

Amy shuddered, then looked at Nathan gratefully. 'Thank you for coming to London to fetch me, and for bringing the magistrate to speak to me just now.'

'I wish I could have done more, and sooner. I've always felt guilty that I didn't know what was going on at Portgiskey, and wasn't there when I was most needed.'

Amy reached across the table and squeezed his hand. 'None of it was your fault. You've had problems enough of your own.'

'Did you mean what you told Mr Carlyon – about returning to Cornwall for good?'

Amy withdrew her hand from his and looked down at her plate. 'Yes.'

'What about Sammy?'

Amy looked at Nathan defiantly. 'I went to London expecting to be an important part of Sammy's life. I knew I wouldn't enjoy living in a city, but I was willing to try for Sammy's sake. He didn't give me a chance. From the moment we arrived he busied himself seeking out old friends from the

313

prize-fighting world. I might not have existed for him.'

'The prize-ring has always been the most important thing in Sammy's life, Amy. I thought you understood that?'

'I do, and I don't mind – but I wanted to be *part* of that life. Instead, Sammy cut me off from it completely. I was "the little woman" or "the old lady", as I heard myself called by one of his London friends. I was expected to wait patiently at home, ready to do the bidding of my lord and master, on the rare occasions when he returned home – usually just to get a change of clothing.'

Amy's chin came up in a way Nathan remembered well. 'I'm not a "little woman". Neither am I an "old lady". I was fishing and smuggling with my own boat for too long to allow all my independence to be suddenly taken away – by anyone. I went to London with Sammy because I knew that was what *he* wanted, and because I felt he needed me. I was right about him wanting London, but wrong about him needing me. He only needed me while he was *here*, because Sammy was a stranger in Cornwall. In London, Sammy has prize-fighting – and he needs nothing more. After he met up with the Duke of Clarence I was lucky if I saw him twice a week. I'm not prepared to live that way. I told Sammy so.'

'What was Sammy's reply to that?' Nathan prompted, when Amy fell silent.

'He said I'd feel different when I had a brood of "kids" to look after. He made having children sound like taking a dose of physic. I told him I didn't want the children of a man who felt like that about them.'

'Was that why you were crying, that last night in London?'

'You heard? I'm sorry. Yes, he tried. . . .' Abruptly, Amy stood up. 'I . . . I'm going to my room now, Nathan. It's been a long day. I'm very tired.'

'Of course. Don't worry about your ma. We'll go and see her first thing in the morning. Then we'll get her home to Portgiskey. Everything will come right for you, you'll see.'

Amy leaned over and kissed Nathan on the cheek. 'Thank you for listening to my problems, Nathan. And thank you especially for caring.'

Peggy Hoblyn went home to Portgiskey two days later. Still

unconscious, she travelled on a bed of hay in Tom Quicke's high-sided wagon. Nathan drove, with Amy in the back of the wagon, at the side of her mother.

Nathan allowed the horses to rest for a while at the watering-place, before going on to tackle the long and steep hill that dropped down past Polrudden to Pentuan. It was here that Nell Quicke found them. A servant from Polrudden accompanied her, and with them Nell's young son, Tom, and baby Beville.

When Amy jumped down from the wagon and took the baby from the servant, Beville, always ready to please an audience, obligingly gurgled and cooed. Clinging to her finger, he gave Amy a lop-sided, gummy smile. Amy was completely captivated. For many minutes she was so engrossed with Nathan's son that she forgot the others who stood and watched her.

When Amy finally raised her head from the baby and saw she had everyone's attention, she was only mildly embarrassed. 'He's *lovely*, Nathan. Such a happy baby. Poor Elinor.'

Amy hugged Beville to her again, then reluctantly handed him back to his nurse.

After seeing Nell Quicke, the servant and two babies on their way to Venn Farm, Nathan guided the horses slowly along the lane, and down the steep hill to Pentuan village.

As was so often the way in Cornwall, news of Peggy Hoblyn's return to Portgiskey travelled ahead of the wagon. It might have been an unguarded remark made by Tom or Nell Quicke, or a piece of gossip passed on by one of the Polrudden servants.

What was more certain was that not all the villagers were well disposed towards Peggy Hoblyn's homecoming. As the wagon creaked through the village women stood around in small, disapproving groups and not a welcoming smile was to be seen. Nathan sensed the hostility, but he knew better than to say anything. If he could get Peggy Hoblyn to her home without incident, the village would soon forget about her – as it always had in the past.

It was not to be. A group of seine-fishermen, some holding pewter tankards half-filled with ale, stood in a loose-knit group outside the Ship inn, which, with the Happy Sailor, catered for the drinking needs of Pentuan's fishermen.

The group of men extended halfway across the narrow village street. As Nathan approached, they gathered together in a tight bunch, blocking the way. Nathan considered whipping up the horses and driving them straight through the fishermen's ranks, but common sense prevailed. Nathan's livelihood and the future of his son depended very largely upon this community. If something needed to be said, it was better to have it out in the open here and now.

Nathan hauled on the reins and the two horses leaned back in their leather harnesses, bringing the wagon to a halt.

A babble of sound immediately rose from the assembled fishermen.

'You shouldn't have brought her home.'

'We don't want Peggy Hoblyn close to our village. There are children here to be considered.'

'Nothing personal to you, Nathan.'

'Just a minute.' Nathan held up his hand for silence. When it came, he said: 'I'm not going to attempt to speak to everyone at once. Is there anyone who would like to speak for the rest?'

A number of the fishermen looked at Dan Clymo, Nathan's boyhood friend.

'You've got something to say to me, Dan?' Nathan sat easily on the wagon seat as the fisherman was pushed somewhat reluctantly to the front of the group.

'Nothing aimed at you personally, Nathan,' said Dan Clymo eventually. 'But we heard you were bringing Peggy Hoblyn back to Portgiskey.'

Nathan jerked his head to indicate the back of the high-sided wagon. 'You heard right. She's in the back, with Amy.'

The crowd about the wagon began to talk and gesticulate excitedly, but it seemed to Nathan that no more than half were perturbed about Peggy Hoblyn's return. The remainder were expressing more interest in the presence of Amy, whom they had last seen setting off as Sammy Mizler's bride.

'It's said Peggy Hoblyn killed someone else in the lunatic asylum in Lostwithiel. We don't want her back here. No mother will feel safe letting her child out to play. . . .'

The hay behind Nathan erupted, and Amy's angry face came into view.

'There's not a child in Pentuan has ever had to fear my ma –

316

and they never will. She's looked after your children often enough, Dan Clymo. Or have you forgotten? When your wife was off helping to bring in the harvest on some farm while you sat in the Jolly Sailor for month after month, waiting for the pilchards to come in and give themselves up, remember? Yes, and she looked after your wife more than once, too, when she returned from the farm so drunk on harvest cider she couldn't carry her own child without falling over.'

As men about him sniggered, Dan Clymo's face became as red as Amy's own. 'That was before your ma went mad,' he retorted. 'She hadn't killed anyone then.'

'My ma killed a grown-up woman who was keeping her a prisoner for no good reason she could see,' said Amy. 'There was no one about her she knew, and her mind snapped. I'm not excusing murder; I'm just explaining what happened. Ma is no child-killer, as well you know.'

'Then what about the business at the lunatic asylum? I've heard—'

'Whatever you've heard is wrong, Dan Clymo. You should take no more notice of such rumours than I or my ma ever did about rumours of your wife's carryings on with other men. I'll *tell* you what happened in Lostwithiel. Someone who'd killed four times before broke free in the asylum. She killed three times again – and badly injured my ma. Here, all of you. Come to the back of the wagon and you'll see the woman you're so frightened of. She's been unconscious for two days and two nights, and she may never regain consciousness again. . . .'

Here, Amy's voice broke with emotion and one or two of the fishermen crowding about the wagon looked embarrassed.

'That's all very well,' Dan Clymo persisted doggedly, 'but suppose she *does* come round. What'll happen to her when you go back to London to your husband?'

'You don't have to lose any sleep over that. I'm not going back.'

Dan Clymo shuffled his feet uncertainly for a minute or two, then he turned away without another word. He had not succeeded in preventing Peggy Hoblyn's return, but seeing her unconscious in the back of the hay-wagon he doubted whether she would ever pose a threat to anyone. Moreover, Amy had provided Pentuan with a piece of gossip that would last longer than the return home of an unconscious lunatic. Amy Mizler had left her husband after only a few months of marriage. What was more, she had returned home in the company of Nathan Jago!

A few of the men in the crowd outside the Ship inn were interested in neither Nathan Jago nor the Hoblyn family. They had been drinking for many hours prior to the gathering of the fishermen in the street outside the tavern. They had anticipated some excitement and were disappointed because nothing had transpired.

Now they stood their ground in front of the wagon, and Nathan was forced to make a quick decision. Amy had succeeded in winning the Pentuan crowd to her side but, if the handful of drunken men caused trouble, opinion was likely to swing against her and Nathan once more.

Nathan climbed down from the wagon seat and walked to the head of one of his horses. Taking hold of the bridle, he clicked his tongue against the roof of his mouth and the horses moved forward. They took a couple of paces before stopping, heads tossing uncertainly. Four drunken men barred the way. Nathan realised that time had run out for diplomacy.

Before any of the drinkers guessed his intention, Nathan released his hold on the horse and stepped forward quickly. Grabbing two of the men by the hair, he crashed their heads together, as he had once seen Uriah Kemp deal with Mevagissey hecklers.

One man collapsed to the ground immediately. His harder-headed companion dropped his tankard and staggered away, too dazed and drink-sodden to realise who was responsible for what had happened. One of the two remaining men opened his mouth to protest, but the words had not left his mouth when his head came into violent collision with that of his remaining companion.

Both men would have dropped to the ground instantly had Nathan not kept his grasp on them and laid them to one side.

So swift had the action been that not more than two or three fishermen standing to one side of the wagon saw what had occurred. Nathan gave them a brief grin, then took the bridle of his horse once more and led animals and wagon past the men on the ground. Serious violence had been averted, and Peggy

318

Hoblyn was almost home.

But the day had not yet given up all its surprises. When Nathan eased the wagon down the steep hillside behind the Hoblyn cottage at Portgiskey Cove, he found his father waiting by the door of the fish-cellar.

Calling a delighted greeting, Nathan said: 'Hello, Pa. It's nice of you to come and meet us. I'm glad you weren't one of the "welcoming" party who tried to turn us back outside the Ship inn.'

'I see they didn't succeed,' commented Josiah Jago. 'But my presence here has nothing to do with Peggy Hoblyn. I've just received news that Uriah Kemp has been recaptured in Plymouth. He was arrested near the naval dockyard in Devonport – and has been charged with spying.'

'That's absurd!' Nathan cried incredulously. 'Uriah is a preacher, not a spy. Who is he supposed to have been spying for?'

'For his own country. America. There's been a sea-battle off the coast of Cornwall. A British man-o'-war tried to board an armed American merchantman, to impress seamen. The American ship opened fire and dismasted the British man-o'-war, which then ran aground and sank. To make matters worse, Napoleon has declared his support for America. It seems that a declaration of war between America and Great Britain is likely any day now.'

Nathan was stunned. Uriah Kemp was in serious trouble, but Nathan would never believe that he was a spy. He was a fine preacher and a good man.

'There's more yet.' Preacher Josiah Jago was grim-faced. 'When your father-in-law announced Uriah's arrest in Parliament, he claimed that the Methodist Society was behind his activities. He's proposing a Bill to have us outlawed.'

Chapter Eight

THE REVEREND URIAH KEMP refused to take seriously the charges brought against him, at first. Having escaped from the prison van and eluded the Dragoons sent out after him, he had been making his way towards Falmouth in an almost leisurely fashion. Once there, he intended taking a ship for America. On the way he decided to call at Plymouth, to visit the spot from which the members of an earlier persecuted sect of dissenters had sailed to colonise America, almost two hundred years before.

It was ill-fortune that one of the St Austell constables should have been in Plymouth that day. Recognising the fugitive preacher, he arrested him and took him before a Plymouth magistrate. News of the action between the British and American ships had been received in Plymouth only an hour before, and the American preacher was closely questioned about his reason for being in Plymouth Town.

Not satisfied with the replies he was given, the magistrate ordered Kemp to be held in custody in Plymouth's Citadel, and sent a report of the matter to London. Here it passed through the hands of a number of Home Office clerks until one noticed that the report was about a Methodist minister. He promptly passed it on to Sir Lewis Hearle.

Sir Lewis seized the opportunity afforded by Uriah Kemp's arrest eagerly and sent for the Plymouth magistrate to come to London immediately.

In London the magistrate had numerous meetings at the Home Office with the Under-Secretary. Later, at Sir Lewis Hearle's club, he was introduced to members of London Society whose views on Methodism coincided with the baronet's own. All were prepared to go to great lengths to suppress the thriving religion.

The Plymouth magistrate returned to his home town armed with Sir Lewis Hearle's assurance that, if he were able to produce sufficient evidence to send Uriah Kemp for trial, the country would be eternally grateful.

Within a week of the magistrate's return, Uriah Kemp was

sent to London to face trial as a spy and on this occasion was given no opportunity to escape. Chained and manacled, he was conveyed in a frigate of the British navy to the Pool of London. Here he was taken through the busy streets of the capital to Newgate Prison.

Even now all might have gone well for Uriah Kemp had not a tall, pale-faced man with the gleam of insanity in his eyes stepped from the shadows in the lobby of the House of Commons with a pistol in his hands to change the course of Great Britain's political history.

Spencer Perceval, the Tory Prime Minister, was shot through the heart at point-blank range by the deranged Liverpool businessman John Bellingham in the early evening of Monday, 11 May. Uriah's Kemp's trial was to be held in the same week.

A few days after the shooting, Uriah Kemp and John Bellingham shared a cell beneath the Old Bailey Hall. Both were waiting to face trial before London's Recorder, in the presence of the Lord Chief Justice of England.

John Bellingham's trial was biased to the point of vindictiveness. His counsel entered a plea of 'Not guilty, by reason of insanity', and produced evidence that Bellingham had a history of insanity. Indeed, his father had died insane before him.

In spite of this, the defence plea was rejected. Then judge and jury listened impatiently for eight hours to the story of Bellingham's life of failure before pronouncing his guilt to a waiting nation. He was sentenced to be hanged at eight o'clock on the morning of Monday, 18 May, barely a week after committing the murder for which he was to die.

With the formality of Bellingham's trial over, rumour spread through the corridors of the Old Bailey Hall that Bellingham had merely been the tool of a sinister society. Its aim was the overthrow of responsible government in Great Britain. A dozen countries and organisations were named as being behind the society. Among these were France, America, the Midland industrial agitators – and the Methodist Church.

Such totally unfounded rumours were denied by all those named. Before he died on the gallows, Bellingham himself declared that the assassination had been the result of a personal grudge he held against the unfortunate Spencer Perceval.

321

The denials came too late to save Uriah Kemp. In an atmosphere of near-hysterical suspicion, it was disclosed to a beetle-browed Recorder and the jury of upright citizens that Kemp had been a chaplain to the American rebels during the War of Independence. Returning British prisoners-of-war had spoken of his frequent visits to their camps.

Since the end of that war, Uriah Kemp had been a regular visitor to Great Britain. His travels in the British Isles were related to the court, together with details of the 'happenings' that followed his progress.

Uriah Kemp had preached many times in the Midlands, where public unrest had become the cause of great concern. From here he had made his way to Cornwall, whereupon that most loyal of counties had experienced its first serious riot for many years. The American Methodist minister had in fact been arrested in Cornwall, but had proved his remarkable resourcefulness by escaping in a 'daring' fashion when being conveyed to London. After his escape, Kemp had made his way to Plymouth, evading all efforts to recapture him. He was arrested in the vicinity of the naval dockyard only hours after a ship from the port had been sunk by an American vessel off the Cornish coast. Finally, whilst awaiting his trial in the cells beneath this very court-room, Kemp was seen to be uncommonly friendly with the man who had been convicted of murdering the Prime Minister of Great Britain.

There was much more so-called 'evidence' against Uriah Kemp. All of it was circumstantial, much was hearsay, some mere speculation. Unfortunately for Uriah Kemp, the trial of John Bellingham had been so brief it had not satisfied the populace of the capital. Vengeance, wearing the guise of 'justice', demanded more.

A judiciary reeling under the assassination of the country's leader dared not oppose such strong popular feeling – certainly not for the sake of an eccentric American Methodist preacher.

Uriah Kemp had ministered to a wide spectrum of humanity for many years. He recognised the feeling that gripped the people of London as being akin to mass hysteria. He also understood the workings of government, and the principles they would sacrifice in order to remain in office.

Uriah Kemp realised he was to be the Tory government's sacrifice. The Lord he served had been offered to the multitude for similar reasons, eighteen hundred years before.

Standing in the dock of the Old Bailey Hall, Uriah Kemp expressed his feelings succinctly and forcefully, but wholly unsuccessfully. Looking at the set faces of the Recorder and the jurors, he knew his words fell on deaf ears. He had been pre-judged, not on the facts of his own case, but as a result of the trial that had gone before.

His speech serving no useful purpose, Uriah Kemp brought it to a dignified close. Standing tall and proud before his accusers, he concluded: 'Gentlemen, I stand innocent of all the charges levelled against me in this court-room. Whilst in your country I have served no master but the Lord. I wish I might have served Him better. However, if I am to be convicted, however unjustly, of serving any country, I could not wish to suffer on behalf of a finer or more honourable land than my own.' With a stiff bow to the jury, Uriah Kemp added: 'May the Lord guide your deliberations.'

'So be it,' snapped the Recorder brusquely. 'But first the jury will need to listen to what *I* have to say.'

With that the Recorder began a summing-up that in less emotionally charged surroundings would have been scurrilous. His words left no room for an acquittal and so it came as no surprise when, after only the briefest of discussions among themselves, the jury returned a verdict of 'guilty' against the Reverend Uriah Kemp.

'Uriah Kemp' – the Recorder deliberately spurned the use of the epithet 'Reverend' – 'Uriah Kemp, you have been justly convicted of a dastardly crime against a country whose hospitality you have grossly abused. I am in no doubt that your conduct has deliberately provoked much of the industrial troubles we have experienced in recent years. It matters not which country you serve, be it France or America. Both were spawned in violence and insurrection, subjects in which you are apparently well versed. It is my solemn duty to pass upon you a sentence to deter others, and to remind them that Great Britain will not tolerate treasonable acts committed in this realm. You will be taken from here to a place of execution. There you will be hanged by the neck, taken down while you yet live, and suffer execution on the block. May the Lord have mercy on your soul.'

The sentence, traditional for acts of treason, brought a gasp from many of those in the hushed court-room. Decapitation was no longer a fashionable mode of execution. The excesses of those who had employed 'Madame Guillotine' during the recent revolution in France had caused Englishmen to lose all taste for the executioner's axe.

Uriah Kemp paled and momentarily swayed in the dock, but he angrily shook off the steadying hand of the gaoler.

'I fancy *you* will have more need of the Lord's mercy than I, when the time comes for you to meet Him. I trust you will not then be judged in the manner you judge others.'

With these words Uriah Kemp turned and left the dock, his heavy ankle-chains rattling noisily as he shuffled awkwardly down the stairs to the cells beneath the Old Bailey Hall.

Preacher Josiah Jago stepped off the coach in the Bell innyard the day after Uriah Kemp's trial and stared upwards in wonder at the great dome of St Paul's Cathedral. It was the Methodist preacher's first visit to London and he was already overawed by its size and bustling activity.

Josiah Jago had travelled alone to the capital to see his friend, Uriah Kemp. Nathan had originally intended travelling with his father, but two days before the proposed journey *The Brave Amy H* had been rammed and holed by a Mevagissey seiner as the night crew brought her in after a successful fishing trip. It was not certain whether the incident had been an attempt to put Nathan out of business, or merely a careless accident, but Nathan could take no chances with his only boat. He remained at Portgiskey to see the repairs carried out, and to ensure there was no repetition of the incident.

Neither Nathan nor his father had fully realised the seriousness of the charges against Uriah Kemp. Consequently, it came as a great shock to Josiah Jago when he overheard excited servants at the Bell inn talking of the American preacher's conviction and sentence.

Filled with horror at the thought of Uriah Kemp's plight, Josiah Jago did not delay even to change his clothes. Dressed in his dusty, ill-cut serge suit, the Cornish preacher hurried to the

324

house in City Road where John Wesley had once lived. It was currently the headquarters of the Methodist Society.

Josiah Jago hoped to learn what was being done by Britain's Methodists to overturn the verdict on Uriah Kemp. Instead, after he had given his name to a rather bored clerk, he found himself warmly received by the senior officials of his church, fêted as a hero. It was many minutes before Josiah Jago was able to explain his reason for coming to London.

Immediately, the joyous reception he was being given lapsed into embarrassed silence.

'Ah, yes. . . . The American evangelist. Most distressing. *Most* distressing.' The awkward silence was broken by a Methodist preacher who had achieved senior status for no other reason than that he had accompanied John Wesley on one of his innumerable provincial tours. He had never been invited on another, but to those who came after Wesley's death it was enough merely to have spoken to the founder of the Methodist Church.

Josiah Jago waited for the doyen of the Methodist Church to add something to his murmur of polite sympathy. He waited until it became clear that the other man had no more to say.

Preacher Jago stared about him in disbelief. 'Is *nothing* being done to save Uriah Kemp? In God's name. . . . His only offence is to preach the word of Our Lord in the manner taught to us by John Wesley himself. Should he be condemned to die for this? If so, not one of us here is safe.'

None of the men about him would meet his eyes, and Josiah Jago asked: 'Well, how is Uriah bearing up? You *have* sent someone to console him in prison?'

'You don't understand, Josiah. These are difficult times for us. Uriah Kemp's name has been linked with that of John Bellingham, the assassin who murdered Spencer Perceval. There are many men in government and the Church of England who would dearly love to involve the Methodists in such matters.'

'I don't doubt you. But Uriah is one of *us*. He and my son kept the Methodist Church alive in Cornwall when I was in prison. It's for this he's been convicted, not for anything else. He's as innocent of all other charges as you and I.'

'Josiah, these are difficult times for our church.' Laying a hand upon Josiah Jago's shoulder, the senior preacher spoke to him as he might a young child having difficulty learning the lesson set by a Sunday-school teacher. 'We are being accused of all manner of crimes against government and public order. Sir Lewis Hearle has asked Parliament to ban the Methodist Society and he has powerful support in the House of Lords. We must be careful to give him no more fuel for his sacrificial fire.'

'Even if it means Uriah Kemp must die abandoned by those to whom he has given his faith and friendship?'

'Even so. If he is as true a Christian as you believe him to be, he will understand and find comfort in the Lord.'

Josiah Jago looked about him at the nodding heads of his fellow-preachers. Suddenly he realised he was a stranger among them. Here at the heart of Methodism, in the home of its founder, he felt the cause to which he had dedicated his whole life crumbling about him.

'Uriah Kemp has always found comfort with the Lord. The years he spent in the American wilderness brought him closer to Him than we, who find ourselves distracted by the material things of the world about us.'

Overcome by tired emotion, Josiah Jago's Cornish accent was so heavy that some of the London preachers had difficulty understanding his words. But there could be no mistaking the depth of his feelings.

'Uriah Kemp has always preached that faith will reap its own reward. *I* believe the Methodist Church will survive all the trials it's suffering today. The Lord will see to this. But Uriah Kemp has always maintained faith not only in the Lord, but also in his fellow-men. I intend showing him that this faith is not unfounded. I am going to visit Uriah Kemp in prison, gentlemen. I would welcome your company, for Uriah's sake. I also intend asking permission to accompany him to the scaffold. I crave your indulgence if I appear to be going against the wishes of the Society. My conscience will not allow me to do otherwise. It's the same conscience that prompted me to do the things for which you called me a hero when I walked into this house – the house that was once John Wesley's. I bid you good day. I doubt if we shall meet again.'

Preacher Josiah Jago was not a big man but, as he walked

away from the policy-makers of his church, dignity gave him a stature that dwarfed every man there.

Getting permission to see Uriah Kemp proved to be very difficult. For two days Josiah Jago was told that the American preacher could have no visitors. Apparently it was a government directive. Not until Uriah Kemp's execution was only eighteen hours away did the Governor of Newgate Prison take it upon himself to allow Josiah Jago to enter and see his friend.

Uriah Kemp had accepted his fate with a calmness typical of the man, but he was touchingly grateful to the Cornish preacher for travelling so far to see him. He enquired after the journey and hoped that Josiah was not tired. Had it not been for the grim surroundings, it might have been the meeting of two old friends at a wayside inn.

Not until Josiah Jago repeated his conversation with the Methodist preachers at City Road did the American show any emotion.

'If they believe the way for our church to survive is by not offending those who seek to destroy us, they are sadly mistaken. We must assert the right to worship in our own way. If the arrest and, yes, *execution* of one man will stop Methodists from standing up and *shouting* our beliefs for the whole world to hear, then we have no right to claim recognition as an independent church. As a person I am of no more importance than that fly climbing up the wall. Neither are you, Josiah, my good friend. Yet you and I, and all those who believe as we do, represent a revived faith. The Methodist Church has been responsible for showing thousands – no, *tens of thousands* – of sinners the way to God. It is *this* which is important. Our work must pause for *no* man, whether he be a friend or against us.'

Uriah Kemp's oratory was interrupted by the arrival of the Governor, accompanied by two turnkeys. In his hand, the Governor carried a document written in careful script. At the foot of the paper was a large and impressive seal.

Addressing Uriah Kemp, the Governor said: 'Reverend Kemp, as you know a plea was sent to the Regent on your behalf, begging him to exercise mercy towards you. I regret that he feels unable to overturn the findings of the court. However, I am pleased to inform you that instead of being hanged and then beheaded, you are now to suffer hanging only.'

Josiah Jago's hopes, which had soared when the Governor entered the cell, now plummeted. He had imagined the Governor had come bearing a pardon for his friend.

If Uriah Kemp had held out the same hope, he concealed it well, even managing a quip for the Governor. 'Does this mean I'll be any *less* dead when the hangman's through with me?'

Unsmiling, the Governor said: 'There are many ways for a man to die, Reverend Kemp. Death by the axe is not one of the more pleasant forms of execution, either for the victim or for those of us forced to watch. I have never met a sober executioner. While I appreciate his need for alcohol, it adds nothing to such meagre skill as he might possess. However, such talk is out of place here and now. Your friend may remain with you until dusk, but I regret he will not be allowed to accompany you to the scaffold in the morning. I can flout orders within the walls of Newgate Prison, but I must needs be more circumspect with half of London's populace gathered to bear witness of my deeds.'

Josiah Jago stayed with the American preacher until two gaolers entered the cell, bearing lamps to keep at bay darkness and the thoughts it afforded a condemned man. The gaolers would remain with Uriah Kemp until the macabre procession comprising Governor, doctor, padre and hangman arrived to escort the condemned man to the plank-wood platform where the grim reaper had his throne.

After sharing a prayer, kneeling on the cold flagstones of the American preacher's cell, the two friends embraced. Then, blinded with tears, Josiah Jago was escorted away through the dark prison corridors.

When the heavy gates slammed shut behind him, Josiah Jago found himself standing on the pavement outside the high-walled prison. Not far away was the scaffold where the insane John Bellingham had died at the end of the hangman's rope and where Uriah Kemp would hang in a few hours' time.

In the dim light from nearby windows, and lanterns hung high on the prison walls, Josiah Jago could see that the street was littered with all manner of debris. Left behind by the great crowd that had assembled to witness Bellingham's execution, the rubbish was being methodically turned over and examined by two old crones who placed useful and edible items in the folds of tattered and grubby skirts.

In the shadow of the scaffold, Josiah Jago sank to his knees. With his chin sunk upon his chest he began a night of prayer for the soul of Uriah Kemp. As the night wore on he was joined by others. Most were there to ensure they had a good view of the morning's execution, but a few joined Josiah in prayer.

By the time dawn arrived, a thousand or more people were already gathered about the scaffold. Soon afterwards there was a sudden movement in the noisy throng and two of the Methodist ministers to whom Josiah Jago had spoken at City Road sank to their knees beside him.

Too weary to express surprise, Josiah Jago turned a haggard, unshaven face towards them.

'You have been here all night, Josiah?'

He nodded without speaking, and one of the Ministers laid a hand on his arm. 'We should have been here to share your vigil, but we were busy. Our efforts have not been in vain. When Uriah Kemp walks out to the scaffold, almost every Methodist in London will be here to send his soul soaring straight to heaven.'

Josiah Jago was so tired that his face registered blankness rather than surprise. The hand on his arm tightened sympathetically. 'You shamed us with your words, Josiah, and you were right. John Wesley would be ashamed of us were he alive today. He was a man like yourself – one who went out and followed the dictates of his heart. He would not have cowered in a corner, keeping quiet and hoping to escape the notice of those who sought to kick him. But enough of words. Will you lead us in a prayer, Josiah?'

By the time the prison bell began to toll, announcing to the waiting crowd that the condemned man and his escort had begun the walk to the scaffold, there was no room for a child as far as the eye could see. Josiah Jago could not believe that the vast majority of such a huge crowd were Methodists, until Uriah Kemp, his hands pinioned behind his back, appeared on the platform above them.

Instead of a roar from a spectacle-seeking crowd, there was a sudden silence. It was broken by a single tremulous voice singing the first line of Charles Wesley's hymn, 'Jesu, lover of my soul'. As the singer progressed to the second line, 'Let me to thy bosom fly', thousands of voices joined in.

The sound swelled impressively, and Josiah Jago raised his eyes to the scaffold. Uriah Kemp smiled down at him as he, too, joined in the hymn, joyously aware of the composition of the great crowd. Those on the scaffold about the condemned man were aware of it, too, and the hangman was ordered to carry out his task as quickly as he could.

Uriah Kemp tried to shake off the hood as the hangman put it over his head, but even as his lips framed the 'No!' the black mask was pulled down, hiding his face.

As the voices of the crowd faltered and came to a ragged halt, the hangman took a step backwards. Grasping the lever that released the trapdoor beneath Uriah Kemp's feet, he gave it a sharp tug. The condemned man dropped almost from view. Only the shrouded head remained above the level of the scaffold floor, jerking grotesquely.

In most executions, this was the signal for the crowd to roar its approval. Today, it brought only an involuntary gasp. Then, as the prison bell ceased to toll, an uncanny silence fell upon the vast crowd. It was more impressive than any uproar.

Moments later the vast concourse dropped to its knees and the leaders of the Methodist Church led their followers in a prayer for the soul of the Reverend Uriah Kemp.

It was a convincing demonstration that the death of Uriah Kemp had not succeeded in crushing Methodism. The message was not lost upon the Earl of Liverpool, the new Tory Prime Minister. He had watched the proceedings from the upper window of a building opposite the prison, the guest of Sir Lewis Hearle.

Chapter Nine

PEGGY HOBLYN lay unconscious at Portgiskey for a full week, and Amy despaired that she would ever recover. Then one morning Amy looked in the small bedroom at Portgiskey cottage and saw her mother lying still in her bed, her eyes fixed upon the curtains flapping at the open window. Overjoyed, Amy hugged her mother, certain that everything was going to be all right again. Holding the frail, thin body in her arms, Amy promised she would never go away again; that mother and daughter would live happily at Portgiskey once more.

Peggy Hoblyn said nothing at all. Neither words, nor tears, nor affection produced any response from her. The long period of unconsciousness had wiped Peggy Hoblyn's memory as clean as a rain-washed slate. She remembered nothing, and no one. Even speech came to her with great difficulty.

When Peggy Hoblyn was strong enough to walk, she wandered about the cottage, running exploratory fingers over once-familiar furniture, and gaping open-mouthed through the windows at the work being carried on in the fish-cellar and on the quay at the water's edge.

When she could venture outside, the fisherwomen in the fish-cellar were at first apprehensive. After all, they had seen the strangled body of Lizzie Barron, the woman Peggy Hoblyn had murdered. But, as it became increasingly evident that she was no longer to be feared, the fisherwomen began to poke cruel fun at her. So innocent and childlike was she now, that Peggy Hoblyn would do everything she was told. She ate the raw fish given to her by the fisherwomen, and retreated in distressed bewilderment at their laughter. She raised her skirts to the fishermen when so ordered by the other women, and obediently repeated dictated obscenities when told to do so.

Amy remonstrated angrily with the fisherwomen when she caught them playing tricks on her mother, and Nathan dismissed one of them as a warning, but the unkind tormenting continued.

Then, only a week after Preacher Josiah Jago returned from London, cholera reached Mevagissey. For many months the disease had been sweeping through the towns and cities of Europe, claiming tens of thousands of victims. Around the coast of Great Britain, the authorities in every sea-port had taken stringent precautions to prevent the killer disease from spreading to these islands. Any ship with sickness on board was held in an anchorage well clear of the port until doctors were satisfied that the malady was not cholera.

The precautions worked well until a Sicilian vessel, bound for Sweden, made an unscheduled stop at Mevagissey. It had been a bad voyage for the crew of the Mediterranean ship from the moment she sailed from Gibraltar into the deeper waters of the Atlantic. One after another the members of the crew fell ill. Two died and were buried at sea. Then, becalmed off the Scilly Isles, the ship's captain collapsed and was carried to his cabin, protesting vainly that he was not seriously ill. The wind picked up from the south-west, and the vessel was off Mevagissey before the captain died. With the mate too ill to assume command, the crew voted unanimously to make for the nearest landfall.

The Sicilian ship rode the tide into Mevagissey's small fishing-harbour just as dawn broke. When the village awoke, half the crew were ashore, collecting fresh water, searching for fresh provisions, and seeking the services of a doctor.

Dr Ellerman Scott was called to the ship just as he was about to sit down to his breakfast. Listening to the symptoms, explained partly in halting English and completed in mime, he hurried from the house, leaving his untouched meal on the table.

His diagnosis was immediate and unequivocal. There was cholera on board.

Those members of the crew still ashore were quickly rounded up and returned on board. The contaminated vessel was then towed clear of the harbour by Mevagissey's new Revenue cutter, and the unfortunate Sicilians abandoned to their fate on the high seas.

It was too late. During the short time they had spent ashore, the effusive Sicilians had shaken hands with half the men in Mevagissey, and patted the heads of countless black-haired children. In addition, two of the crew, with an instinct inherent in professional seamen of the time, had found their way to a decrepit cottage, standing no more than a hurried prayer from the vicarage. Here a sleepy but accommodating troll tested their Sicilian gold coins between bad teeth and, in an equally businesslike manner, relieved them of the pent-up passions accumulated in the course of their long sea-voyage.

One week later, four fishermen, two wives and three children were dead. A hundred more lay sick in their beds.

In a village where each household could claim a blood relationship with at least ten others, doors were locked against neighbours for the first time in living memory, and friends crossed to the other side of narrow streets to avoid each other.

In this atmosphere of fear and death, Dr Ellerman Scott toiled day and night in a vain bid to contain the epidemic. His only helper was the troll of Vicarage Hill. For the first time in her lurid life, the doors of respectable homes were opened to her. Her tireless and selfless efforts encompassed men, women and children; churchman and sinner alike. The Sicilian gold she had earned was spent on herbs to ease the pain of her patients, and much more of her money went the same way.

Pentuan closed its doors to fisherfolk from Mevagissey, but a young Pentuan fisherman was courting a Mevagissey girl and the two met unobserved in the woods on the hill between the two villages. Three days after the girl's brother died in Mevagissey, the illness struck down its first Pentuan victim.

Cholera swept through Pentuan with alarming rapidity, and when the disease was confirmed in three Polrudden servants Nathan sent Beville to Venn Farm. He believed the isolated farmhouse to be probably the safest place in the whole of the area. Tom and Nell Quicke had no need to leave the farm for anything. Their cow gave them milk from which they made butter and cheese, and they had all the produce and meat they required.

There was no doctor in Pentuan and, because villagers were frightened to enter a house where sickness was present, much of the work of caring for cholera victims fell to Josiah Jago, as the village preacher.

When two of the women working at Portgiskey contracted the sickness, Nathan closed down the fish-cellar and helped his overworked father to tend to his patients.

For weeks there was no fishing anywhere along the length of

the Cornish coast. Cholera had now spread to most of the fishing communities, and a rumour began that the disease was in fact contracted by eating fish. There was no truth in such an absurd assertion, of course, but the ignorant and frightened populace was ready to listen to any advice in a bid to end the present epidemic. The housewives of Cornwall stopped buying fish.

The day after Nathan closed down the fish-cellar, Peggy Hoblyn was struck down with cholera. The illness was the final blow to a constitution weakened by weeks in prison cell and asylum. Forty-eight hours after the first symptoms showed themselves, Peggy Hoblyn was dead.

Nathan and Josiah Jago were with Peggy Hoblyn when the end came. Both sought to comfort Amy, but she remained remarkably calm. Amy declared it was enough for her that Peggy Hoblyn had died in her own home and not in a lunatic asylum, surrounded by uncaring strangers.

However, when a summer storm threatened later that night and Nathan returned to Portgiskey to check that *The Brave Amy H* was properly secured, he found Amy huddled beside a huge pile of fish-baskets on the small quay, crying as though her heart would break.

When he lifted her to her feet she clung to him desperately and he held her until her sobbing subsided. When she eventually spoke, her words were punctuated by long-drawn-out sobs that shook her body.

'Wh-what do I do, Nathan? I've lost Sammy . . . and now Ma. What will I do?'

Drying her eyes gently, Nathan said: 'This doesn't sound like the girl who put to sea with me in a storm and saved a fishing-boat from being wrecked. The first thing you'll do is to stop trying to work out your future all alone in the dark with your ma lying dead in the house. There will be time enough for that in the morning, when you're rested and with friends.'

'I think you . . . must be the only friend I have left.'

Nathan smiled, but was glad that the darkness hid it from her. Amy was not yet nineteen years of age, but in that moment she sounded far younger and terribly vulnerable.

Acting upon affectionate impulse, Nathan cupped her face in his hands and kissed her. He knew immediately that it had been a mistake. After the first moment of surprise she stiffened. When he dropped his hands from her, she took a backward pace away.

He tried to think of the right words for an apology, but Amy spoke first.

'You shouldn't have done that, Nathan. You shouldn't have kissed me.'

'I know. I'm sorry.' He felt embarrassed and awkward. 'You're a married woman now, not a young girl. . . .'

'That isn't what I meant.' She spoke fiercely. Then suddenly she was kissing him with an ardour that took him by surprise. His arms went about her and he pulled her to him. With body pressed hard against his, Amy felt his need for her – but then she twisted away.

'Nathan, why couldn't you have wanted me like this before?'

After flinging the unexpected question at him, Amy turned and fled to the cottage and Nathan heard the thud of the heavy wooden bolt slamming into position.

Peggy Hoblyn was buried the next day in Josiah Jago's Methodist burial-ground, her body carried to the village on board *The Brave Amy H* and from there in a Polrudden wagon. It was a brief, simple ceremony. In these times people did not gather together for funerals, especially when the burial was for a cholera victim. Only the gravedigger remained as a disinterested bystander. Too old to fear death, he was too drunk to care.

As Josiah Jago closed his book Amy turned to him, dry-eyed. 'How many villagers are ill with cholera now?'

'Twenty-four . . . although I've just been told that young Dolly Kittow and her brother are sick, too.'

'Can you do with some help?'

'Can I . . .? My prayers are a constant cry for help. But are you ready to take on such a burden, so soon after the funeral?'

'It can't be soon enough. I'm in sore need of something to occupy my mind until I've decided where my future lies.'

As she spoke, Amy glanced swiftly at Nathan, who was listening nearby. Josiah Jago missed neither the glance nor the significance of her words.

'Your future lies with your husband, my dear,' he said quickly. 'But you can't risk carrying cholera to London Town.

It would spread through those crowded streets like the wrath of God. In the meantime I'll find plenty to keep you busy.'

When Nathan returned to Polrudden to change his clothes after the funeral, he found Sir Lewis Hearle in the house, newly arrived from London. The baronet was in his study, tugging futilely at a bell-pull. He was in a furious mood.

'What the devil is going on here, Jago? Where are the servants? Where's my grandson? Dammit, I leave the place for a month or two and everything stops. Well, don't stand there like some stupid village oaf. Tell me. Are things so bad that you can't afford to keep the servants on?'

'Not yet. But if this cholera epidemic doesn't soon end they will be.'

'Cholera epidemic? Here?' Sir Lewis Hearle looked startled.

'Surely the news has reached London? Cornwall is very badly hit.'

'I had heard it was at Falmouth, and an unconfirmed report of a case at Plymouth. I never dreamed it would be here, in Pentuan. Is it bad?'

'I've just come from the funeral of Peggy Hoblyn. She's the fourth to die in Pentuan. Things are much worse in Mevagissey. Three of our servants here at Polrudden have the sickness. I've told the remainder to stay away, as a precaution. For the same reason I've sent Beville to stay with my sister and her husband at Venn Farm. He should be safe there.'

Sir Lewis Hearle raised a half-filled brandy-glass to his lips with a shaking hand. He had turned suddenly pale. 'This is dreadful. I must return to London at once.'

'Is death by cholera so much worse than death at the end of a rope, Sir Lewis? Or do you consider your life of more value than an American preacher whose only crime was to love God and his fellow-men?'

Colour returned to Sir Lewis Hearle's face in a sudden rush of blood. 'Uriah Kemp was convicted in an English court of law. The man was an agitator and a convicted spy.'

'He was a Methodist,' retorted Nathan. 'Nothing more. But no doubt it was sufficient cause for you and your friends to have him put to death.'

'If I consider Methodism to be contrary to the interests of my country, I will not shirk my duty,' declared Sir Lewis Hearle pompously. 'As for Uriah Kemp, before you say something you will regret, I think I should tell you his country has just declared war on Great Britain. No doubt Kemp's information was intended to give America the numbers of the warships still in harbour and not fully engaged against Napoleon's navy. If so, it was a fruitless exercise. This country has enough men-of-war available to tackle any American threat to our shipping.'

Sir Lewis Hearle poured himself another brandy and looked across the room waspishly at Nathan. 'Pass my information on to your father. It should interest him to know the company he and his Methodist friends have been keeping. Oh, and you can give your fishermen friends some news, too. These are hard times. I'll be increasing tithes for the coming pilchard season. Tell them not to spend their money unwisely until I have discussed a new rate with my solicitors.'

Nathan looked at Sir Lewis Hearle in disbelief. Then he startled the baronet by laughing. The moment of apparent merriment was brief. When his eyes met Sir Lewis Hearle's a moment later there was no mirth in them.

'I have news for *you*, Sir Lewis. Go to Pentuan and check on the boats and the fish-cellars. You'll find neither working. Half the boats, including mine, are rotting away for lack of work. Nobody has brought in fish for weeks, because no one is buying. Raise the tithes as much as you like. A sixth of nothing is no more than a twentieth – and that's exactly what you'll be getting. Nothing!'

Chapter Ten

THE American declaration of war gave renewed strength to Sir Lewis Hearle's anti-Methodist campaign. He had taken a gamble in having the American Methodist preacher indicted for spying. Now he had been vindicated by the actions of that country. It also threw further suspicion on the loyalty of the whole Methodist movement. It was well known that Uriah Kemp had been preaching to open-air Methodist meetings throughout the land. Sir Lewis ensured that the arrest of Methodist preachers for breaches of laws and by-laws received maximum publicity. When three Midlands 'Methodists' were convicted on charges of inciting riots and smashing valuable weaving machinery, anti-Methodist feeling was already running high.

In the House of Lords, bishop after bishop rose to his feet to launch scathing attacks on the Methodist Church, calling upon Great Britain's new Prime Minister to declare the Methodist movement unlawful.

Paradoxically, Methodists were also coming under attack in the Midlands from those newspapers who supported the activities of the discontented workers. They denounced Methodists as 'enemies of the people', because of their alleged support *for* the Government!

The stage was set for a final assault on Methodism. The Home Secretary introduced a Bill that would effectively curb all those in the Methodist Society who declared themselves to be 'preachers'. The Home Secretary claimed derisively that among their ranks were cobblers, tailors, pig-drovers and chimney sweeps. He proposed that every so-called 'preacher' should have to prove his qualifications to a local magistrate before being issued with a licence allowing him to preach. It was also proposed that the two-hundred-year-old Toleration Act should in future be rigidly enforced. This Act stipulated that even a licensed preacher must preach only in the town or village where he resided.

By these two moves the Home Secretary would give local magistrates absolute jurisdiction over the granting of licences to dissenting preachers. He would also wipe out the very cornerstone upon which Methodism had been founded: the circuit preacher.

Throughout the country, Methodists realised their church was facing extinction. But now, when it was most needed, they received unexpected support. Other dissenters realised that the Methodist fight was theirs, too. Any new laws or restrictions would affect them just as much as their Methodist brethren. Their leaders met with Methodist preachers, and all across the land lamps burned in chapel meeting-houses until their meagre glow was lost in the greater light of dawn. Meanwhile, Methodist worshippers approached every reasonable man of influence with whom they could claim acquaintance, begging for help to keep Wesley's church alive. It became apparent to all at Westminster that this was to be a hard-fought battle.

Only in Cornwall did this bitter war for religious survival pass almost without notice. Preachers like Josiah Jago were busy fighting a battle of a different kind, this one for the lives of their congregations, struck down by cholera. They had little time to spare for involvement in something that was little understood and quite remote from life here, in the extended toe of England.

Gradually, the two villages of Mevagissey and Pentuan began to win their fight against the cholera epidemic.

In Mevagissey, the troll of Vicarage Hill had nursed the sick of the fishing village through three dread months of epidemic. By this time there were thirty-seven bodies in the roped-off corner of the churchyard, and the gaunt and exhausted village physician declared that the cholera had finally run its course.

The troll returned to her decrepit cottage, and not for ten days did anyone give her a thought. When the physician entered her house, he found that she had probably been dead for at least half that time. Alone and untended, she was the last victim of the disease she had worked so hard to contain.

Only now was it realised that no one knew the troll's full name. To the doctor she had been 'Nan', but she was also known by at least five other forenames. Her surname had never been mentioned in the village. She was buried in an unmarked corner of the mass cholera grave, among those she had tended so diligently. In a few weeks it was as though she had never been.

In Pentuan, as walls and houses were whitewashed and cleaned, the village slowly came to life again. Neighbours no longer avoided one another. Instead, somewhat shamefaced, they stopped and enquired after families and friends, exchanging harrowing details of the ordeals each had survived.

During these difficult weeks, Nathan saw little of either his father or Amy. With no servants at Polrudden, he did all the work of feeding animals and tending crops.

Both Amy and Preacher Jago also worked hard, tending the sick day and night. For a while they were helped by a mission doctor, newly returned from India. It was hoped that his experience of cholera would prove invaluable. Unfortunately, all his experience had not given the doctor immunity from the sickness. After only a week he contracted cholera himself and died three days later.

Then, late one evening, Nathan went to the village and discovered Amy and his father sitting in the kitchen of the Jago cottage, enjoying a cup of tea together. Both looked weary. Amy, in particular, looked as though she should sleep for a week. But Josiah Jago looked up at his son and smiled happily.

'We've finally won through, Nathan. There has been no fresh case of cholera for three days, and I believe all those patients we already have will recover.'

Nathan pulled a chair out from the table and sat down. 'Good. It means I'll be able to bring Beville home. I miss him.'

Josiah Jago shook his head. 'I'd leave the little chap with our Nell for another day or two yet – perhaps another week. By then we'll know for certain that the epidemic's over.'

'We've come out of it better than some villages,' said Nathan grimly. 'In Mevagissey they've lost whole families. But the sooner things are back to normal, the better it will be for everyone. I need to find a market for the fish I have in the cellar at Portgiskey soon. I've no ready money left.'

'It will feel strange to be sleeping at Portgiskey again,' commented Amy. 'What little sleep I've had since Ma died has been here, in this house.'

'I gave Amy the use of your room,' explained Josiah Jago to Nathan. 'She would never sleep until she reached the verge of collapse and wouldn't have made it to Portgiskey.'

'I won't make it tonight unless I leave now,' said Amy, rising to her feet. 'I've been putting off returning to Portgiskey, but I'll have to go back some time.'

'Leave it until tomorrow,' urged Josiah Jago. 'Stay here for tonight.'

'It's time I went home. There are lots of things to be done there.'

'I'll walk to Portgiskey with you.' Nathan pushed back his chair and stood up.

'No!'

Amy knew immediately that she had answered too quickly, in too positive a manner. Josiah Jago had been startled. Now he looked from Amy to Nathan suspiciously.

'I don't mind walking there on my own,' explained Amy, doing her best to make the words casual. 'It will be nice to breathe in good, sweet air and think about something more than the next case of cholera.'

'You'll have all the time you need to be alone and think. I doubt if the Portgiskey fish-cellar will be working for another week or two. Besides, I'm not offering to walk with you just to be chivalrous. I go to Portgiskey every night to check my boat.'

Watching Nathan and Amy leaving the house together, Preacher Jago thought they would have made a splendid couple. He had always thought so; but now Amy was another man's wife, and her husband was many miles away. He should have said something to keep Nathan at the house while Amy went home alone. But he was too tired for guile. Shaking his head, Josiah Jago closed the door of his cottage and made his way wearily up the stairs to his bedroom.

He had always known that Nathan and Amy had made a great mistake in not marrying each other. He sincerely hoped they would never reach the same conclusion.

Crossing the narrow Pentuan bridge, Amy turned towards the beach, but Nathan stopped her with a touch on her arm. 'The tide's in too far. We'll need to follow the road and double back through the valley.'

They were the first words either of them had spoken since leaving the Jago house and they effectively broke the silence that had sat awkwardly on both of them. Each was thinking of the last occasion on which they had been alone.

341

'You've worked hard these past few weeks. My father couldn't have carried on without you.'

'*He's* the one who's been working too hard. But for him, Pentuan and most of the people in it would have died.'

A silence descended upon them again for some minutes before Nathan asked: 'What are you going to do, Amy? Will you go back to London? To Sammy?'

'Your pa thinks I should. He says that's where my duty lies.'

'He would. He's always taken "duty" seriously. If he hadn't, I would never have run away from home – and perhaps my mother would have been alive today. Think very carefully before you make up your mind, Amy. You have a right to be happy – and you're not happy with Sammy. I know it, and so do you.'

'At the moment I'm not sure about anything.' Amy stopped and turned towards him. 'But thank you for caring, Nathan.' She was silent for a few moments, before adding quietly: 'I would like you to leave now.'

The feeling that had come to both of them on the night he had kissed her had inexplicably returned. Nathan wondered what would happen if he kissed her again now.

'Good night, Nathan.' Amy turned and hurried away into the darkness – and Nathan hurried away after her.

It was some moments before Amy realised he was behind her. When she did, she whirled to face him. 'Nathan, I don't *want* you to come to Portgiskey with me . . . please!'

'All right, walk ahead of me, if you wish, but I have business to attend to at the cove.'

'Checking your boat? I'll do that for you.'

'I *do* check my boat regularly, but I have other things planned for tonight. I have a rendezvous to keep.'

'Oh, of course. You need to bring in smuggled goods if you're to keep Polrudden.'

'That's right. I've lost weeks of fishing. I must make money somehow.'

Amy suddenly became thoughtful. 'How will you manage *The Brave Amy H* without a crew?'

'I can't. I shall do what I did for the last rendezvous – take your small boat and bring back what I can.'

There was a strong breeze blowing at their backs as they

made their way along the descending valley towards Portgis-key. The cliffs and surrounding hills meant that Portgiskey Cove was well protected, but beyond the bay it would be rough.

'This is no night to take a small boat out as far as you'll need to go. Do you have such need of money that you must risk your life to get it?'

'Yes. One day I intend buying another boat. With only one I can barely pay my debts, even in a good year. When Sir Lewis raises his tithes, I'll be hard pressed to do even that.'

'You can forget everything you owe to me, Nathan. Ma left more money than I knew she had. It must have come from Pa. I don't need more from you.'

'That's very generous of you Amy, but I can't accept such an offer. You'll be paid, you and Sammy, but more of the money will come from smuggling than from fishing.'

'Then you'd better make as much as you can – before the Revenue men put an end to smuggling, once and for all. You can only do that with the drifter. Take her; I'll crew for you.'

'You? You'd fall asleep if I left you alone for a moment. No, I'll take the small boat. Besides, there's a new Chief Revenue Officer in Mevagissey. He'll no doubt be eager to make a name for himself. I won't risk having you caught.'

'There's not a Revenue boat built that can catch *The Brave Amy H*; you've said so yourself, many times. Remember how we gave the slip to those Moorish pirates when we brought her from the boatbuilder's yard?' Amy's eyes sparkled with an infectious enthusiasm.

Nathan grinned at the thought of that exciting chase. It seemed to have happened a lifetime ago, yet it was hardly two years.

'Do you *really* feel up to making a trip?'

Nathan knew he should not be asking her, but Amy was right. *The Brave Amy H* could bring back ten times the amount of contraband that her own little boat could carry – and Nathan was desperately in need of money.

'Of course I do. I can't think of anything I'd rather be doing. It will be marvellous to breathe fresh sea-air and get the smell of sickness and unwashed bodies out of my nostrils. Come on, hurry yourself. The thought of going to sea again has given me new energy. It's been months and months. . . .'

343

Half an hour later, with the moonlight giving the water the appearance of beaten pewter, *The Brave Amy H* slipped her moorings at Portgiskey. Catching the wind almost immediately, she heeled over and headed out towards the deep water of the English Channel.

The wind was almost dead astern, and *The Brave Amy H* was soon away from the shelter of the coastal headlands.

It must have been close to midnight when Amy called: 'There's a sail coming up from the south, no more than a mile away. It looks like Captain Pierre's ship.'

'That's the one I'm looking for. Haul in the sea-anchor. I'll show him a light before he goes away again.'

There was a brief flicker of answering light from the dark-sailed ship approaching from the Channel and the two vessels closed each other rapidly. Minutes later, Nathan brought *The Brave Amy H* alongside the smuggler as French seamen lowered plaited rope fenders over the side. There was a heavy swell, and damage might easily have been caused to the smaller fishing-boat.

From the deck of the French vessel, Captain Pierre looked down into Nathan's boat. 'Welcome, Captain Nathan – but please do not come aboard. The cholera, you understand?'

'Of course.' Nathan understood the sailor's fear of cholera. Once on board a ship it would almost certainly affect every member of the crew. 'But with any luck the epidemic is over in this part of the country – as my crew can tell you. She's nursed the victims in Pentuan back to health.'

The captain stared down at Amy, standing in the bow of *The Brave Amy H*, shadowed by the bulk of the French vessel. 'Who is that? Can it be my beautiful Amy? It is? Ah, *ma chérie!*' He gave a loud groan of Gallic despair. 'To meet you again after so long and not be able to kiss you. This is torture, indeed!'

To Nathan he said: 'Captain Nathan, you will kiss her for me. A Frenchman's kiss, if you please. Not like one of your English chickens. You understand me?'

'I do – but you'll need to persuade Amy.'

The banter continued, with Amy occasionally contributing a remark of her own, while the French crew lowered small kegs of brandy and waterproof packs of tobacco to the deck of *The Brave Amy H*.

Nathan had told the French captain he would take every keg of brandy and packet of tobacco that could comfortably be carried. But the fishing-boat was no more than half-loaded when there was a cry from the look-out that caused alarm among the Frenchmen.

Captain Pierre had disappeared from the side of the ship at the first shout. Now he reappeared.

'It is a ship, Captain Nathan. Coming from the direction of your English coast. I think it may be a warship. Cut your ropes quickly.'

Already the French vessel was under way, crowding on sail and dragging *The Brave Amy H* through the water with her.

Nathan was attacking one of the mooring-ropes with his knife, when something struck the side of the ship not four feet away from his head and splinters of wood flew about him. He felt a searing pain in his arm, and as he tumbled to the bottom of *The Brave Amy H* he heard the familiar rumble of a cannonade.

'That was British shooting. . . .'

As the thought was passing through Nathan's mind he heard Amy's cry. Suddenly he realised that the peculiar angle at which he was lying had nothing to do with his fall. The rope he had been cutting was still holding. *The Brave Amy H* was being towed through the water by the rear mooring-rope and bouncing awkwardly over the waves. Amy was sawing away at the rope, but it was eventually severed by an axe-wielding French seaman on board the boat towering above them.

Scrambling to his feet in the wildly rocking boat, Nathan helped Amy to hoist the sails. As he did so, he saw that the man-of-war with the outline of a British frigate had altered course to pursue the French vessel. The new course did not prevent a gunner from firing off a smaller cannon at *The Brave Amy H*. Fortunately, the shot fell well short, and Nathan was able to alter course and pass well astern of the pursuing naval vessel.

As he brought *The Brave Amy H* round in a wide circle to take the craft shorewards, Nathan felt another sharp pain in his arm. Reaching up to explore his upper arm, he discovered a deep groove carved in the flesh, and his finger came away sticky with blood.

'Are you all right?' The moonlight was bright enough for

Amy to be able to see Nathan exploring his arm with his fingertips.

'It's nothing. A splinter of wood must have caught me when the man-o'-war opened fire.'

'Let me have a look.' Amy clambered aft to stand beside him. His shirt sleeve was already torn, and now she ripped it still more in order to examine the wound better.

'It's not pretty, but fortunately it's not *too* serious. I'll bind it up for you.'

Amy had a kerchief about her neck. Taking it off, she folded it into a long, narrow strip and bound it about the wounded arm. 'That will do until we get ashore and I can bind it properly.'

The bandaging over, Amy remained beside Nathan, looking out across the water to where both the French vessel and the British frigate had vanished into the gloom of the distance.

'Do you think Captain Pierre will be all right?' Amy asked anxiously.

'Sure to be,' replied Nathan confidently. 'He has a good ship. It will outrun a man-o'-war.'

'Where did the frigate come from? Was it on patrol, do you think?'

'I doubt it. I'd say it was outward bound from Fowey. It was probably sheer bad luck for us that the captain was keeping such a good look-out. He wasted no time running out his guns, either. Nelson would have been proud of him.'

Nathan shook his head ruefully at Amy. 'Things have a nasty habit of happening to us when you and I are at sea together.'

'Yes.'

Amy did not pursue the conversation. When she had seen Nathan take a bloody hand away from his arm she had felt a moment of panic. Not until she had learned for herself that it was not too serious had the panic subsided. She had been so relieved she could have hugged him. The urge to do so was still there.

Leaving Nathan's side, Amy stepped into the well-deck, just aft of the wheel. She took only one step before turning hurriedly back to Nathan.

'There's water in the boat! It must be a foot deep.'

'Damn! I thought she wasn't handling as she should. Take

the wheel for me while I have a look.'

Handing the wheel over to Amy, Nathan dropped into the well-deck and took up the bottom boards. Amy was right. There was at least a foot of water in the bottom of the boat. If any more came in, the drifter's handling would be seriously affected. Nathan worked his way forward, trying to locate the damage, but he was unable to find the spot where the water was entering the boat.

'Some of the planks must have sprung when we were being battered against Cap'n Pierre's ship,' he called to Amy. 'Head straight for Portgiskey. We'll have to risk the man-o'-war coming back to find us. I'll crowd on all the sail we've got and then start pumping. We should make it all right.'

They almost did. With sails close-hauled, Amy kept the boat's bow pointed towards Portgiskey, while Nathan worked the bilge pump as hard as he could.

It soon became apparent that the water was gaining, but Nathan continued to pump until his muscles were numb and the blood from his wound ran down his arm, making the pump-handle slippery. Then, with the cliffs about Portgiskey no more than a mile away, the bilge pump become blocked. Water had seeped inside some of the packets of tobacco and split them open. Their contents completely clogged the pump.

Nathan worked furiously to clear the tobacco, but soon realised it was an impossible task. The water was rising too fast. *The Brave Amy H* was now so low in the water that small waves were breaking over the side.

Making his way to Amy, Nathan said: 'The pump's blocked. The boat will go under at any moment. We'll need to swim home. I'll take the wheel and keep her on course for as long as I can. You strip off. You can't swim in those clothes.'

As he was talking, Nathan grasped the wheel. Holding it firmly with one hand, he bent down and unlaced his heavy boots, kicking them off into the bottom of the boat.

Looking up again, he saw that Amy, too, had removed her shoes, but she was standing with her hand poised uncertainly on the unlaced cord at the neck of her grey linen dress.

'For God's sake, Amy! This is no time for modesty. You'll need to swim close on a mile . . .!'

Amy tugged the cord free and dropped the dress from her

shoulders, then down over her breasts. As it fell to the wet deck at her feet, she wriggled out of her cotton petticoat. At that moment, *The Brave Amy H* shipped a wave that surged over the bow and swept the length of the boat. Nathan had to hold the wheel with all his strength to prevent the boat being swept broadside on to the sea and swamped.

The Brave Amy H was still making headway, but she handled heavily and sluggishly. Nevertheless, Nathan was determined to bring his boat as close inshore as was possible before abandoning her.

Another wave rose over the bow into the half-filled boat, but still the sturdy drifter ploughed on towards the cleft in the cliffs that was Portgiskey Cove. They were less than half a mile from shore now and the wind coming off the high land was beginning to play tricks on them, yet still *The Brave Amy H* ploughed shoreward.

Amy was kneeling in the bow of the boat now. Looking at her, bare-breasted in the moonlight, Nathan was reminded of a beautifully carved figurehead he had once admired on the prow of a French merchantman, captured in the Mediterranean.

Amy looked back at him and called excitedly: 'We're going to make it, Nathan. *The Brave Amy H* will get us home.'

The words had hardly been spoken when the wind dropped away suddenly, leaving the boat wallowing heavily in the lee of the cliff. Seconds later a low wave, hardly more than two feet high, broke against the side of *The Brave Amy H* and hundreds of gallons of sea-water poured inside the foundering fishing-boat. It was the end. Slowly, the boat tilted and began to slide beneath the water.

'Jump!'

Nathan matched word with deed and leaped over the side himself. As he struck out for the shore, he called to Amy. To his relief, she answered him from near at hand as they both swam into the long shadows cast by the cliffs.

'Keep going. I'm right behind you,' he called. He knew that Amy was a strong swimmer and he began heading towards Portgiskey Cove, grateful for the fact that the tide was in their favour.

The salt water was stinging his wounded arm, and Nathan

348

stopped swimming for a few minutes to remove the neckerchief that was beginning to chafe the wound.

Looking back, Nathan saw that *The Brave Amy H* had somehow righted herself. Although filled almost to the gunwales with water, she still refused to sink.

The Brave Amy H represented Nathan's sole means of earning an independent livelihood. Treading water and looking at the vessel, Nathan knew he could not allow her to sink without some attempt to salvage the vessel.

Making a sudden decision, Nathan struck out for the boat. Minutes later he dragged himself back on board. He swiftly located a length of rope long enough for his purpose. Knowing just how deep the water was along this part of the coast, he paid out enough to mark the drifter's position when she finally went under. On most trips he and his crew were in the habit of putting out a few lobster-pots, with wooden keg marker-buoys. Pulling one of the small buoys from a water-filled locker, Nathan secured it to one end of the rope. The other end was secured to a brass ring screwed into the gunwhale.

The work was completed just in time. As he slipped back into the sea and struck out for the shore once more, *The Brave Amy H* dipped her bow into a wave and failed to rise again. Slowly, the two masts slid beneath the water until only the keg buoy and a few loose packs of contraband tobacco were floating on the surface of the water to mark her position.

With a heavy heart, Nathan turned his back on the spot and struck out strongly for Portgiskey Cove.

When he reached the shallows, Nathan found Amy in a desperate panic. As he pulled himself to his feet and staggered ashore, he saw Amy frantically dragging her own small boat to the water's edge.

'What are you doing?'

At the sound of his voice, Amy spun round to face him.

'Nathan. . . . Oh! Thank God!' She rushed at him with such eagerness that she almost knocked him back into the water. As he held her, he felt her naked body tremble uncontrollably in his arms.

'What happened! I thought you were right behind me, but when I came ashore you were nowhere to be seen. I called and called. When you didn't answer I thought something must have happened to you. Your arm. . . . I didn't know what to think.'

'I didn't hear you. There's so much noise out there – the wind, and the sea crashing against the rocks. I saw *The Brave Amy H* was still afloat. I went back to fix a marker to her.'

'You fool! You frightened the life out of me.' Amy clung to him as though he might rush back into the sea again. 'When I thought you were lost I didn't know what to do. I . . . I've never been so panic-stricken in all my life.'

Nathan tried to push her gently away, in order to look down at her face, but she clung to him tenaciously.

'No. Just hold me. Please, just hold me.'

It was not a difficult duty to perform. Her wet body was smooth beneath his hands as he stroked it in what began as a bid to calm her nerves. Nathan never knew at what moment his compassion became desire – but Amy knew. She knew, too, that she should have slipped from his arms and hurried inside the Portgiskey cottage. She did neither. The events of this night had badly shaken her resolution. She raised her head as his lips came down upon her mouth and the next moment she was meeting his ardour with a passion that took his breath away. His hands grew bolder, and for long, gasping moments Amy writhed to their touch. Not until now did she break away from him.

As Nathan tried to take hold of her again, she took his hand and held it up to her cheek. 'Not here, Nathan. Let's go inside.' Her voice was husky with the same desire that held Nathan in its grip, and hand in hand they went to the cottage together.

Nathan was awakened in the morning by the raucous crying of gulls outside the window. It was a moment or two before he realised where he was. Then he sank back on the feather-filled pillow and thought of what had happened only a few hours before.

'You'll never raise *The Brave Amy H* by lying abed all day.' Amy came into the room. Much to Nathan's disappointment, she was fully dressed.

'The sun is hardly up yet. Come back to bed.'

'No, Nathan.' She leaned over the bed and kissed him lightly on the forehead, eluding his hands.

He smiled up at her, but saw no answering smile on her face. Raising himself on one elbow, he said: 'What do we do now, Amy?'

Amy went to the window. Drawing back the curtain, she looked out across St Austell Bay before answering.

'Unless we want to change everything – to lose everything that we both enjoy here – we do nothing. We must go on as though last night never happened.'

'We can't do that! Not after . . . everything. Amy, you know I love you?'

'Things would have been very different had you discovered that before I went away, Nathan.' She spoke with her hands clenched tightly at her side. 'I'd have done anything – gone *anywhere* – with you.'

'What are you saying, Amy?'

She turned to face him. 'I'm saying that I'm no longer Amy Hoblyn, a little girl in love with a man who's blinded by the daughter of the manor. I'm Amy *Mizler* now – the wife of another man.'

'But you don't love him.'

'No, and I don't think I ever have. Poor Sammy was a means of escape. I used him. I couldn't stay here to be constantly reminded that *you* belonged to someone else. I was ashamed of my reason for marrying Sammy at first. Then I learned that he hadn't really married *me* for love, either.'

'I'm sorry, Amy. I don't understand.'

'No, I don't suppose you do. It's probably never occurred to you that Sammy was jealous of you from the first moment you met. You were on the way up then, a future prize-fighting champion. Sammy was on the way down. He'd never *quite* managed to be the best, and now he never would, because you would always be ahead of him. You became "friends"; but at any gathering, at any prize-fight, it was always *you* people wanted to see, to talk to. He was just Sammy Mizler, the man who arranged *your* fights. The little man who looked after *you*.'

Nathan listened to Amy in astonishment. 'I don't believe it. I don't believe Sammy ever felt that way.'

'It's true enough, Nathan. When I was in London it came out every time Sammy had too much to drink – which was most nights he was home.'

'But what has this to do with him marrying you?'

'Ah! That's where Sammy thought he was being clever. He convinced himself a long time ago that it was *me* you really loved, not Elinor. Even after you'd married her he believed that one day you'd realise your mistake and want me. But it would have been too late then. I would be his. Whatever happened, he would have had me first. He had beaten you for the very first time.'

Nathan was deeply shaken. 'I'm sorry, Amy. I never realised Sammy hated me so much. I always thought we were good friends.'

'He doesn't hate you. He *envies* you. He envies you so much it's become an obsession with him. He *has* to prove he can beat you.'

'But, if this is true, why do we have to forget last night? I can make you happy, Amy. I know I can.'

'Yes, Nathan. You could make me happy. But. . . . Oh, I'm so confused at the moment. I only know that I'm still married to Sammy. Try as I might, I can't just put it behind me as though it never happened. I told you once that Pa brought me up as a Methodist. Perhaps that's got something to do with it.'

'You managed to forget it last night,' Nathan reminded her.

'Yes . . . and I'm not going to say I'm sorry about it. But it mustn't happen again, Nathan. I want you to promise me it won't happen again.'

Nathan shook his head.

'Please, Nathan. Unless you promise, I must leave here – probably go back to London. Yes, I know it's foolish, but I *can't* let you make love to me while I'm another man's wife. Try to understand.'

Nathan knew he would never understand, but Amy had worked herself up to such a highly emotional state he believed she really would go away if he did not give her the promise she demanded.

'All right, Amy. I promise to try.' It was a promise that would be almost impossible to keep, but it had to be given.

Amy sagged with relief. 'Thank you. If you hadn't agreed, I would have gone away. Then I would have had nothing left at all. Now I have Portgiskey – and I have you, too, don't I,

Nathan? I've taken over Ma's share of the business, so we're partners again.'

Nathan wondered which of them would weaken first but, throwing back the bedclothes, he swung his feet to the floor.

'Yes, Amy. We're partners.'

Chapter Eleven

NATHAN and Amy were working on the beach at Portgiskey Cove when Sammy Mizler arrived.

Riding a horse he had hired in St Austell, his approach along the sands from Pentuan had gone unnoticed by the busy couple.

The Brave Amy H had drifted inshore, as Nathan had anticipated, and was lying on her side in no more than a fathom of water. Amy had rowed Nathan out to the boat, where he dived to attach a very long rope to the sunken drifter. He had already salvaged everything movable – together with a dozen kegs of good French brandy that were now safely stowed beneath the fish-cellar.

Amy saw her husband first. She and Nathan were kneeling together in the sand, their heads close as they spliced a rope to extend the length attached to *The Brave Amy H*.

Nathan heard Amy's gasp of disbelief and looked up to see the blood rush from her face. She swayed as though she might faint. He reached a hand out hastily to steady her, but she scrambled to her feet after giving him a dismayed glance. Then Nathan, too, saw his one-time partner and prize-fighting companion.

'Well, now, here's a fine scene of domestic industry,' said Sammy Mizler mockingly. 'But you've made a mistake, Amy. *I'm* your husband, remember?'

'I remember it every waking hour,' replied Amy, gathering her wits together.

'What do you want, Sammy?' Nathan put down the half-joined ropes and stood up to face the other man.

'Is that the way to greet an old friend? "What do you want, Sammy?" How about, "Hello, Sammy. It's nice to see you, Sammy," or "Hello, Sammy, I'm pleased to see you because I owe you some money for the partnership I bought out"?'

Nathan pointed to where the long rope disappeared beneath the sea. 'There's your money, Sammy. Sunk in a fathom of water, but with the help of your horse we may be able to haul *The Brave Amy H* clear.'

Sammy Mizler shook his head. 'No, my friend. You are

354

wrong. That's *your* money beneath the water. I'll thank you to pay mine in golden guineas. As for this horse. . . .' Sammy Mizler cuffed an ear of the sway-backed animal upon which he sat. 'I've paid good money for its hire – as a *riding*-horse. You'll need to find yourself a cart-horse if you want your boat pulled from the water. You don't seem to have had much luck with your boats, Nathan. First *Annie Jago*, and now this one.'

Sammy Mizler leaned forward in the saddle. 'Could it be that your thoughts are too occupied with other things?'

Angrily, Nathan took a pace towards Sammy Mizler; then he remembered what had happened between himself and Amy the previous night, and he stopped. Anger left him and a sense of shame took its place. Sammy Mizler had been his friend for many years. Together they had climbed the ladder of success in the prize-fighting world and reached the top.

'You didn't come all this way just to be insulting, or to collect a few guineas. Why are you here, Sammy?'

'A few guineas, Nathan? I'm due a hundred now, I believe. Then there's what you owe my wife. . . .'

'*I'll* manage my own business affairs, thank you, Sammy. And I'm just as curious as Nathan to know why you're here.'

'I don't doubt it, my dear wife. Would you believe me if I were to say I've come all this way to enjoy your charms once more? No, I can see you wouldn't. But suppose you and I go inside the house while Nathan plays with his boat. You can talk to me while I change my travelling-clothes, then I'll let you cook me a meal. Is your mother in the house? Or did you decide it would be more "convenient" to leave her in the lunatic asylum?'

Mention of her mother struck Amy like a blow. During the weeks of epidemic she had worked hard, pushing thoughts of her mother to the back of her mind. Now Sammy had brought her cruelly and abruptly face to face with the reality of her death. Amy was not yet prepared for it. Turning away, she ran to the house, leaving Sammy staring open-mouthed after her.

'Peggy Hoblyn's dead. She died of cholera, here at Portgiskey.'

'Cholera?' Sammy Mizler's sallow London complexion paled even more. It was a typical reaction when the disease was mentioned. 'You've had cholera here?'

'We still have. My father said last night there were more than twenty villagers ill in Pentuan, and the burial-ground has been the busiest place in the village these last few weeks. I believe Mevagissey is faring even worse.'

Watching Sammy Mizler's expression come close to sheer terror, Nathan was reminded of the obsession Sammy had always had with his health. Nathan had known him leave a room or a tavern bar because someone had sneezed.

'Ask Amy for the details when you go inside. She's been nursing the worst cholera cases throughout the whole epidemic.'

'Amy has . . .!' Sammy Mizler sounded as though he was being strangled.

'Yes. She's been staying in the village with them. Last night was the first she'd spent at Portgiskey for five weeks.'

Sammy Mizler might have an obsession with his health, but he was no fool. He knew that Nathan was quite capable of using this knowledge to drive him away from Cornwall – and from Amy.

'I don't believe you.'

Nathan shrugged. 'Please yourself, Sammy. Go to Pentuan and ask my father. If he's not there, go up to the burial-ground and count the number of graves. Better still, go to Mevagissey and check there. I hear they've fenced off a whole area of the churchyard for those who die of cholera. You won't be able to ask the preacher; he was one of the first to die. Now, I'm sure you'll forgive me, but I've got a boat to salvage. If you want your money, come to my father's house tonight. I'm owed money in the village. I'll collect from those well enough to pay and give you whatever I raise.'

Nathan turned away, but Sammy Mizler called after him. 'I'll have no money that's passed through the hands of anyone with cholera. You can bring it to London when you come.'

Sammy Mizler's words brought Nathan to a halt.

'That's right. You've business in London. Pressing business. I'm here to tell you that the Duke of Clarence thinks it's time you honoured the agreement you made with him. He's arranged a prize-fight for you. On 6 November, at Bushy Park, close to his estate. He expects to attract the largest crowd ever seen at a prize-fight. It's mooted that the Prince Regent himself will be there.'

Nathan had almost forgotten that he had agreed to a second fight for the purse the Duke of Clarence had put up early the previous year. Now he was being called upon to fulfil that promise, and on his son's first birthday.

Sammy Mizler was watching Nathan closely. 'Can I tell the Duke you'll be there? Or shall I tell him you honour *your* word in the same manner as some women honour their marriage vows?'

Nathan flushed, but controlled his anger. Sammy Mizler had every right to make such a jibe.

'I seem to recall that the marriage service also demands that a man should "love and cherish" his wife, Sammy. You can tell the Duke of Clarence that I'll be there. Who will I be fighting?'

Sammy Mizler smiled triumphantly. With more than a touch of malice in his expression, he replied: 'Abraham Dellow. Remember him? The negro slave you fought in Bristol. He's much improved now, Nathan. Greatly improved. I've trained him for many months and he's the best prize-fighter I've ever seen in action. Even better than you were in your prime. I've told the Duke it will be a one-sided fight – that he ought to match my man against a good, strong, young fighter, not a has-been – but the Duke wants you. He wants Abraham to become the undisputed champion of the world.'

Still smiling, Sammy Mizler flicked the reins of his horse and brought the animal round in a half-circle. 'Tell Amy I'll not bother to claim my rights as a husband on this visit, but she'll do well not to forget she's married to *me*. I'll be back for her some day. Goodbye, Nathan. I'll see you in London in November. You'll need to provide your own men in your corner; I'll be with Abraham Dellow. But for old time's sake I'll use my skills to bring you round when the fight's over.'

With this parting jibe, Sammy dug his heels into the flanks of his ribby nag. The animal set off along the seashore with a resigned gait, heading for the St Austell road.

From the window of the cottage, Amy saw her husband leaving and hurried out to Nathan's side.

'What's happening? Where's Sammy going?'

'Home. Back to London.'

Amy looked at Nathan in disbelief. 'But why? I thought. . . .' Sudden relief overcame her and she took Nathan's arm. 'When he spoke of coming back to me I . . . felt sick. I couldn't live with Sammy again.'

Gripping Nathan's arm with both her hands, she said fiercely: 'I'd kill myself before I let him touch me again. I *swear* I would. . . .'

'Hush!' Nathan watched Sammy Mizler until he rode from view beyond the rocks separating Portgiskey Cove from the Pentuan sands. 'We won't have to think about that for a very long time. I told Sammy there was cholera in Pentuan, that you'd been nursing the victims. You know what he's like about coming into contact with illness. The thought of cholera terrified him. Had he been riding any other horse, he'd have galloped all the way back to St Austell.'

'But why did he come all this way, Nathan? It wasn't just to collect the money you owe him, surely? Sammy can live very comfortably on what the gentlemen of the "Fancy" pay him to teach them prize-fighting.'

Nathan became suddenly thoughtful, and Amy said: 'There is something else. . . . Tell me, Nathan.'

'The Duke of Clarence wants me to defend my title against Abraham Dellow again. This time near London.'

'The slave you fought in Bristol? Nathan, you *can't*. You've been away from the prize-ring for too long. You told Sammy so, of course?'

'When the Duke of Clarence gave me a purse large enough to buy Venn Farm, he made it clear it was for *two* fights. I must honour the promise I made then.'

'But . . . does it have to be Abraham Dellow? Sammy has been training him hard. He's been prize-fighting ever since he went to London from Bristol.'

Nathan nodded ruefully. 'Sammy says he's the best – and no one is a better judge. The most damnable part is that I doubt if I'll make a penny from the fight.'

Nathan shrugged. 'But I've got two months to worry about the fight, and only about four hours in which to haul *The Brave Amy H* to safety before the tide comes in. When I've finished that splice, I'd like you to bring the rope up the beach as far as you can and secure it to a rock or a stake – anything. I'm going

358

to Venn. Tom hired a team of oxen to plough his steepest fields. If he's still got them, I'll bring them down here.'

'And if he hasn't? There's a storm blowing up—' Amy stopped. There was no need to say more.

'If he hasn't, I lose my boat.'

Fortunately, Tom Quicke still had the oxen and he brought them to Portgiskey as fast as the steady, slow-plodding animals would travel. All Nathan's crew turned out to add their strength to the combined weight of the oxen. Slowly but surely, *The Brave Amy H* was tugged from the water. A great cheer went up from the men and a few watchers as the drifter cleared the water and slid on her side across the sand to a patch of sloping shingle beside the Portgiskey quay. Here *The Brave Amy H* would remain until she was made seaworthy once more.

Nathan's speed in salvaging his boat saved her from becoming a total wreck. That night a fierce storm broke along the length of the south Cornish coast. Boats were torn from their moorings, waterside houses flooded and deep-sea vessels scurried to mid-Channel, there to ride out the storm, well clear of dangerous Cornish rocks. The storm raged for two days and two nights before moving on, leaving the sea exhausted and the land washed clean.

Things quickly returned to normal at Polrudden. There had been no more cases of cholera in Pentuan village, and the servants had returned to their duties. But now they were working they would expect to be paid – and Nathan's boat lay on her side at Portgiskey.

On his way to Portgiskey on the first morning after the storm, Nathan called at Venn Farm and he arrived at the cove shouldering the ten-month-old Beville.

Ahab Arthur and two of Nathan's fishermen were already at Portgiskey, shaking their heads pessimistically as they examined *The Brave Amy H*. Amy had seen Nathan approaching and she ran from the cottage to take Beville from his father. The expression on her face as she took the baby from him caused the fishermen to nudge each other knowingly.

'Have you got the timber we're going to need?' Nathan asked Ahab Arthur sharply. He had seen the men's knowing glances, and they annoyed him.

359

'I've got it, but there's no certainty we'll be able to make *The Brave Amy H* seaworthy again. As well as the sprung planks there's a broken stem and a couple of broken ribs. I don't know what you hit, Nathan, but whatever it was you hit it damned hard.'

He looked at Nathan slyly. 'By the way, there was a man-o'-war left Fowey the night you had your accident. She returned only yesterday evening. It seems the crew had a rough time in the storm. 'Tis said they surprised a French smuggler not a mile or two off Fowey and chased her halfway to the French coast. The Frenchie got clean away. I thought you'd likely want to know.'

Nathan had not told his crew how *The Brave Amy H* had been damaged – and he would not. Such a yarn would be repeated, and the fewer men who knew of his smuggling activities the safer he would be. But he could not prevent men from arriving at their own conclusions.

It took the men five days of frustrating work before *The Brave Amy H* was righted and floated on the waters of Portgiskey Cove to check on her seaworthiness. Much to everyone's delight, the boat rode the water perfectly, none entering between the newly caulked planking. Two hours later *The Brave Amy H* was heading out to sea, with Nathan at the helm, to lay her nets.

The fish ran well for Nathan. He found an abundance of pilchards well off shore, and the Pentuan women were able to return to full-time working in the fish-cellar at Portgiskey once more. The market had revived, too. The foolish rumours that fish had been responsible for spreading cholera had been discounted by learned medical men in London. In fact, the physicians declared that fish was actually *beneficial* in warding off the much feared sickness.

This conclusion was, in all probability, no more sound than the rumour it was intended to discredit, but it had the effect of creating a sudden demand for fish that Cornish fishermen were unable to meet. There was still cholera in one or two fishing villages, and no more than half the county's boats were at sea.

The clamour for fish coincided with a disastrous harvest throughout the land. Only a fraction of the corn needed to meet the needs of Britain's growing population had been harvested.

360

With grain from the Continent denied them by Napoleon, a crisis was at hand. Already prices had soared beyond the reach of ordinary working people, and discontent was spreading rapidly. All over the country militiamen were being urgently called up for service and sent to towns far from their own homes. By detailing the militia for garrison duties in other counties, it was hoped their sympathies would not be so easily aroused as they might in their own towns and villages.

When bad weather finally brought fishing to a temporary halt, Nathan spent some hours in the Portgiskey cottage, working on his accounts. Beville was playing on the floor with Amy, and every so often Nathan would pause in his work and watch them for a while.

Glancing up from the simple game she was playing with the child, Amy caught Nathan in one of these moments. 'Are we disturbing you, Nathan? Would you rather I took Beville to the kitchen to play?'

Nathan smiled. 'No, I enjoy listening to Beville chuckling – and to you too, Amy. There's been little to make you smile for a very long time.'

'I'm happier now than I can ever remember. I know there's so much more that I want – that we both want – but it's wonderful to have Beville here.'

Beville crawled to Amy and tried to pull himself to a standing position, using her dress. Losing his grip, he fell backwards, landing heavily on his bottom. Before he had made up his mind whether to laugh or cry, Amy picked him up and whirled him high in the air.

As Beville chuckled, Amy hugged him to her. 'Ooh! You young rapscallion. I wish you were all mine. . . .'

Her words caused Nathan to recall Elinor and the night almost a year ago when she had died without ever seeing the child she had carried inside her body for so long.

Amy saw Nathan's change of expression and guessed at the cause. She could have bitten off her tongue. To give him something else to think about, she asked: 'How have you done during the past few weeks? Has *The Brave Amy H* made a huge profit?'

'H'm? Oh, yes, she's made money. But not as much as I need. The tithes are due this month. Then there's Sammy's money, your money – and Polrudden. *The Brave Amy H* just can't catch enough fish to pay all the bills.'

'Then let's buy another boat.'

'It's just not possible,' replied Nathan patiently. 'Every penny I earn is taken up in one way or another. I simply can't afford to buy another boat.'

Amy stooped down to move a tempting, charred piece of wood out of Beville's reach before answering.

'I have.'

'You buy me a boat? No, it's out of the question.'

'It's nothing of the sort,' Amy retorted. 'And I wouldn't be buying it for you. Not entirely, that is. I've inherited my ma's share in the business, right?'

Nathan nodded.

'That gives me a quarter interest, so it means I have *some* say in what goes on at Portgiskey. Ma also left me some money – rather a lot of money. If I use some of it to buy another boat, and we agree to forget the money you owe me, would you accept me as a full partner?'

'Would I . . .?' Amy's generous offer made sound business sense and it had been put in a way that Amy hoped would be acceptable to Nathan.

Nathan could hardly hide his elation. Another boat would pull him clear of the near-poverty in which he now found himself. But he had to be certain Amy was not doing this merely because of her feelings for him.

'You'll be risking a lot of money, Amy.'

Amy snorted loudly. 'I'll be risking nothing. You're the best drift-fisherman on this coast. You've made money when others were being forced to sell off their nets and boats. Most of the money I have now was earned by my pa. You knew him. What would he have wanted me to do with it? I'll tell you: he would have wanted me to have a good boat and a share in Portgiskey. If it also happened to help a little boy, named "Beville", after his own son, that would clinch it.'

Hugging Beville to her, she smiled at Nathan. 'Besides, we'll still be carrying on pa's own trade. He'd have to approve of that.'

Chapter Twelve

NATHAN bought his new boat in a Falmouth auction. A fine French-built lugger, she had been taken as a prize by an English man-of-war in a daring raid on a French harbour. Nathan was well pleased with his purchase and proudly showed off her paces to Amy when he brought the boat back to Portgiskey.

As they scudded across St Austell Bay, running before a stiff breeze, Amy agreed it was a fine craft.

'But she'll never mean quite as much to us as *The Brave Amy H*,' she added nostalgically. 'You and I were the first to sail in her, and she was our very first boat. There will never be another like her. What will you call this one?'

'Well, we've had an *Annie Jago*. How about *Peggy Hoblyn*?'

'Yes, I'd like that very much.'

Amy's hand found Nathan's, on the wheel. If any of the crew noticed, not one of them made any comment.

Nathan still did his share of fishing during the day, but he would not be taking a boat out at night until after the fight. Instead, he spent his evenings training. Common sense told him that he had little chance of retaining his title, but he was determined that the giant ex-slave would leave the prize-ring well aware he had been in a fight.

There were more drifters working the coast now. Many of the older seine-fishermen still harboured a deep-rooted resentment against the drifter, but more and more fishermen were coming to realise that drifting offered them an opportunity for a year-round living. Because of this, Nathan had no difficulty finding crews to keep his two boats at sea day and night, and the Portgiskey fish-cellar was busier than ever before.

With the arrival of the second lugger, Nathan hoped his money troubles were over for a while. He thought he might even be able to purchase a third boat once Sammy Mizler had been paid off. But this would mean buying another fish-cellar. . . .

Meanwhile, events were taking place in London that would ultimately concern Nathan deeply.

.   .   .

Sir Lewis Hearle's well-planned final assault on the Methodist Church had foundered.

The combined might of the Established Church and many of the country's great landowners had failed to push Sir Lewis's Bill through Parliament. Indeed, the dissenting churches were united as never before, and as they never would be again. In unity, they learned they were not without influence themselves. The Earl of Stanhope, acting as their champion, utterly demolished the arguments of Sir Lewis Hearle and his friends.

Visiting Lord Liverpool, the country's new Prime Minister, at his Downing Street home, the Earl of Stanhope pointed out that the Methodist religion was now beginning to attract solid citizens to its ranks – men with votes. He provided the Prime Minister with a wealth of impressive statistics, clinching the argument with the result of a recent survey. This showed that in the area covered by the survey the Established Church possessed 2533 places of worship, most of them no more than a third full for each Sunday service. By contrast, the dissident churches had 3454 churches and chapels, all of them packed to capacity for every service, be it Sunday or weekday.

Lord Liverpool and his government, later to be known as the best-hated cabinet England had ever known, had no wish to earn the enmity of such a vast percentage of the populace at this early stage of Lord Liverpool's reign as First Minister. There was serious trouble in the Midlands with disgruntled weavers, and farmworkers and miners were on the verge of riot because of low wages and the high price of corn. Meanwhile, the Irish, taking full advantage of the absence of the army who were fighting Napoleon in the Peninsula, seemed poised for open rebellion. Lord Liverpool could not risk trouble from yet another section of the populace, especially one with such deeply held beliefs.

Summoning Sir Lewis Hearle to his office, Great Britain's Prime Minister berated the Home Office Under-Secretary for bungling the brief given to him by Spencer Perceval. If the Government followed Sir Lewis Hearle's advice, it would bring the Tory administration down and provoke rioting on a scale that would overwhelm the overburdened forces of law and order. The stage would then be set for a popular uprising such as that which had choked the gutters of Paris with the blood of

France's aristocracy.

In a remarkable political *volte-face*, the Tory Prime Minister made an astounding announcement.

'After giving this matter a great deal of thought, Sir Lewis, I have reached a conclusion. I prefer to have the bulk of the Methodist Church on my side and not against me. I therefore propose to give them full religious freedom: the right to practise their religion as they see fit, without let or hindrance.'

Standing before the leader of the party he had supported for all his political life, his face pale and strained, Sir Lewis Hearle fought to maintain control of himself.

'Will you allow me to resign my office? Or do you intend dismissing me?'

'Dismiss you? My dear sir, of course not. Submit your resignation couched in the usual terms. Pressure of private business commitments . . . something like that. I will accept it with regret, and publicly thank you for your hard work whilst in office. You already have a baronetcy or my gratitude would take a more tangible form. Perhaps I could persuade his Royal Highness, the Prince Regent, to make some additional gesture. . . .'

'That will not be necessary, my Lord. I have no son to inherit my titles. I have *no* children . . . now.'

'Very sad, Sir Lewis. Now, if you will excuse me? I have much work to do. My secretary will show you out. Thank you for coming to see me.'

Outside, in the streets of London, it was drizzling. Apart from shrugging his cloak higher about his shoulders, Sir Lewis Hearle hardly seemed to notice. He walked slowly in the direction of his club, thinking of the bleak future that lay before him. The post of Under-Secretary was to have been merely a beginning – the first step on the ladder that might have taken him to the highest office in the land. Sir Lewis Hearle snorted angrily, frightening a passing governess carrying a small child. What was left to him now?

The tide of the Napoleonic war was beginning to turn in Great Britain's favour in Europe. It was being said that the mercurial little French General had over-extended his army in Russia and would soon begin a disastrous retreat from that vast, unconquerable country. If peace came, Lord Liverpool would

365

no doubt call an election. After gaining and losing a ministerial post during his present term of office, it was doubtful whether Sir Lewis would be chosen by Fowey's fickle voters to represent them again, so strongly were they influenced by the county's gentry.

Sir Lewis knew he would have little difficulty obtaining a nomination to another seat, but it would need to be closer to London. Such a move would break all his ties with Cornwall. His wife was dead. Elinor was dead. He had only Polrudden there – and Beville.

The baby was Elinor's son, of course. His only grandson. But he had been cut from Elinor's dead body. The brat bore as much responsibility for her death as did its father. The child was not even a Hearle, but a Jago. Sired by a prize-fighter – a fisherman – and the son of a Methodist minister. Sir Lewis could not prevent his grandson from inheriting his title, but should he have Polrudden, too?

Sir Lewis Hearle stopped in his tracks. Behind him, a fat washerwoman bearing a heavy basket on her shoulder was forced to step from the footway into the filth of the gutter, grumbling at the inconsiderate ways of the class of person for whom she was forced to work.

'Dammit! I've had this millstone about my neck for years – and for what? So it can be enjoyed by a *fisherman*? Or in order that a brat steeped in Methodism may claim it for his inheritance? No, by God! I'll sell it first! That's what I'll do. I'll sell Polrudden.'

Sir Lewis Hearle banged fist into palm, and passers-by ushered their children from the footpath, giving a wide berth to this wet, wild-eyed man who stood muttering angrily to himself.

The decision made, Sir Lewis Hearle felt marginally better. He was a ruined man, of course. He had overcommitted himself in a gamble on his political future. But selling Polrudden would keep him going until he had established himself in a new constituency. He contemplated changing his allegiance and joining the Whigs, but dismissed the idea immediately. His well-known anti-Methodist views were not popular with them. He could expect little advancement in their ranks, should they come to power in the foreseeable future – and that in itself was highly unlikely.

Sir Lewis had been walking as he was thinking and now found himself in St James's Street, where his club was situated. A respectable club was essential to any man with political aspirations – but they had more to offer than respectability. The son of more than one great house had gambled away his inheritance here, on a session of hazard that might have lasted for two days and nights.

There was excitement in the air when Sir Lewis Hearle entered the club. He thought it probable there was a 'hot' game underway, but when he sat down and called for a drink he quickly learned the truth. One of his fellow-MPs came across the room and spoke to him – a certain indication that news of his removal from office had not yet reached the House. Once it was common knowledge, Sir Lewis Hearle knew he would be avoided as though he had the plague.

'I would have expected you to be in the thick of the argument about the outcome of the prize-fight, Sir Lewis. After all, the champion *is* a fellow-Cornishman, though I fear he'll not be champion for very much longer.'

'Nathan Jago is fighting?'

'Yes, it surprises me, too. He's been a good champion and I would have thought he'd have the sense to rest on past glories. But it seems he's indebted to the Duke of Clarence and has to fight Clarence's man. Poor fellow, I wouldn't take his place if they offered me the Regency. I've been over to Mizler's club and watched Clarence's man sparring. Huge black chap named Dellow. Freed from slavery by Jago himself, they say. If it's true, there's damned little gratitude in him. He's boasting that Jago will fail to make the mark before the fifth round. I, for one, don't doubt it. Dellow's a *giant* of a man. I saw him knock out three sparring partners in one evening, one after the other. Clarence says he's the best prize-fighter he's ever sponsored. The clubs certainly believe him. They're offering five to one against Jago everywhere in St James's.'

Looking about him quickly, the informative MP bent low over Sir Lewis Hearle. 'Mind you, I know an old Jew who's willing to offer evens on Dellow. That's a sight better than you'll get here. You'll be lucky if you can persuade anyone to take your money.'

Sir Lewis Hearle was not a gambling man. On any other occasion he would have dismissed his fellow-MP's offer without another thought. But money matters were foremost in his mind today. He thought he saw a desperate way out of his immediate problems. Yet, even now, he was reluctant to commit himself.

'You say you've actually seen this ex-slave prize-fighting?'

'He gives an exhibition in Mizler's club every evening. I'm on my way there now. Come with me.'

The uninformed Member of Parliament was delighted at an opportunity to advance his acquaintanceship with an under-secretary.

Sir Lewis arrived at a sudden decision. 'Dammit, I *will* come! What's more, if he's as good as you say, then I'll place a handsome wager on him, too.'

Abraham Dellow did not disappoint his spectators, each of whom had paid five guineas for admission to the prize-fighting club. To a chorus of admiring gasps and appreciative applause, the big ex-slave quickly disposed of a burly stevedore, and two bulging-muscled coal-heavers with dust-stained bodies. His fist was a devastating weapon, and the three unfortunate sparring partners were helped from the ring glassy-eyed. If anyone noticed that the three men reeked of cheap gin, nobody blamed them. Few men would be fool enough to provide a target for Dellow's iron-hard fists when sober.

Watching the superb fighter in action, Sir Lewis Hearle remembered Nathan as he had seen him some mornings. Grey-faced and round-shouldered with exhaustion, Nathan looked anything but a champion prize-fighter. In Cornwall, the problems of earning a living from the sea constantly with him, Nathan would have little chance to train himself for a championship fight. Dellow, on the other hand, had every opportunity. Furthermore, with royal patronage and the hero-worship of the public to spur him on, he had all the incentive any man could ask for to become the next world champion.

'Well?' Sir Lewis Hearle's companion posed the half-question as they left Sammy Mizler's club.

'I think you'd better take me to your Jewish friend before he shortens the odds on Dellow.'

Sir Lewis Hearle had no money, but such was the standing of

a parliamentary baronet that he could lay a bet and pick up his winnings without having to find a single guinea. A signature from a gentleman on a simple IOU was sufficient, even for the five thousand guineas Sir Lewis Hearle wagered on the outcome of the prize-fight.

Sir Lewis Hearle returned to Polrudden in mid-October. There were many reasons for his departure from London. The first was to escape the snubs of his colleagues and the speculation that followed upon his removal from office. His letter of resignation had been made public, as was the Prime Minister's politely worded letter accepting the 'resignation' of the Under-Secretary, but few people had been fooled. Lord Liverpool had not yet announced his intention to free the Methodist Church from petty restrictions, so rumour was rife about the real reason for Sir Lewis's sudden downfall.

Sir Lewis Hearle also wanted to see how fit Nathan was. There was no possibility he could reach Abraham Dellow's high standard, but the baronet had a great deal of money riding on the outcome of the fight. He felt the need to reassure himself. No doubt the news he bore would help his cause, by giving Nathan Jago something else to worry about.

Nathan learned of Sir Lewis's return when he came home from a day's fishing, running up the steep hill from Pentuan as part of his preparation for the fight. As he approached the door of the east wing, the window of Sir Lewis Hearle's study opened and the baronet's head appeared there.

'Jago, come up here. I want to speak to you.'

Nathan stopped beneath the window and looked up. 'If it's about the tithes, I'll bring the money to you tomorrow.'

'Bring them tonight. I have something to tell you, but I have no intention of shouting for the whole of Cornwall to hear.'

Half an hour later Nathan entered Sir Lewis Hearle's study and placed a heavy leather pouch on the desk in front of the baronet. 'There's your tithe money. I'll have a receipt before I go.'

'You'll have a receipt when I've counted the money.'

Sir Lewis Hearle scrutinised Nathan anxiously. Nathan was fit, very fit. But in attaining such fitness Nathan had sacrificed more weight than a champion prize-fighter would care to lose.

He was a big man, yet he must have weighed at least three stones less than Abraham Dellow, and he lacked Dellow's recent experience in the prize-ring. Sir Lewis Hearle relaxed in his chair, satisfied that his stake in the fight was secure.

'I hear you're defending your prize-fighting championship soon? I watched your opponent the other night. He's good, Jago. *Very* good indeed. So good that a gambling man can get odds of five to one against you winning.'

'He was good when I beat him in Bristol,' said Nathan, with more confidence than he felt about the outcome of the fight, but he was gratified at the effect his remark had upon Sir Lewis.

'You've fought him before . . . and beaten him?'

'That's right. He was wielding a whip on an American slave-ship in those days.'

Sir Lewis Hearle felt suddenly uneasy. No one had told him the two men had already met in the prize-ring. But the negro must have improved a great deal since then. No one in London had any doubts about the outcome this time.

'He's been well trained since then by an old friend of yours. Mizler . . .? Is that his name? You won't beat Dellow this time, Jago. I've bet money on the outcome, and I don't back losers.'

'I've heard those same words spoken by many a gambler who has followed the fortunes of the prize-ring. Most ended their days in Newgate's debtor's gaol, wondering what went wrong. Is that your reason for calling me up here? If so, I hope you've enjoyed our little chat. I'll have my receipt and bid you good evening. I have other things to do.'

'Don't be in such a hurry, Jago. When you've gone from Polrudden you'll probably wish you'd made more use of your time here.'

'When I've gone from Polrudden? Are you telling me I have to leave?'

'I'm telling you that I'm selling the manor. Lock, stock and barrel.'

'You can't! It's Beville's inheritance. That's why I've kept things running here. . . .'

'You're the one who has had the pleasure of living here. As for your son, you'll need to make your own arrangements for him. I'm selling up and concentrating my interests in London.'

Sir Lewis Hearle smiled maliciously at Nathan's dismay. 'Of

course, if you can raise six thousand guineas, you're quite welcome to remain at Polrudden Manor – as the new owner.'

'You know very well I can't raise a tenth of that – hardly a hundredth, thanks to your tithes and the money I've already spent keeping Polrudden running.'

Nathan spoke with great bitterness. 'It's as well Elinor isn't here to see how little you think of your grandchild. Her son.'

Sir Lewis Hearle's good humour vanished abruptly. 'If it had not been for your brat, and your attentions, Elinor would still be a lively, healthy girl with a wonderful future ahead of her. Now leave me, Jago. Get out. I want you and your brat clear of Polrudden by the end of this month. Prospective buyers will be coming around after that. I don't want them wondering what a fisherman is doing behaving as though he belongs here.'

Nathan spoke to his father the next morning, asking whether he and Beville could come and share the little Pentuan cottage with him. The Methodist preacher agreed immediately, but he listened to details of Sir Lewis Hearle's intended sale of Polrudden Manor with scarcely concealed impatience. He had news of his own. News of *truly* great importance. Rumours had reached the Methodist Executive Committee in London of Lord Liverpool's intentions. As with most rumours, this one had lost nothing in the retelling.

Excitedly, Josiah Jago told his son that the Methodist Church was to be given full parity with the Church of England. Its ministers would be recognised – even by the gatekeepers on the country's turnpikes, who had instructions to allow ministers of the church free passage on the toll roads, but who delighted in taking money from the 'Methodees'. Methodist ministers were also to be authorised to administer the sacraments and to perform weddings. In short, the Methodist Church was to be allowed to go forward proudly, and not forced to fight for its very existence.

With such a heady prospect in view, it was hardly surprising that his son's more material problems hardly registered with Josiah Jago. He was eager to fetch out his old donkey and spread the glorious news among his far-flung flock.

Amy was much more sympathetic, and genuinely distressed at Sir Lewis Hearle's actions. She said: 'But Polrudden is your home – yours and Beville's. He can't just sell it and throw you both out. He has a duty towards Beville, at least.'

Nathan shook his head: 'He can do just as he likes – and he's selling Polrudden.'

Amy knew how hard Nathan had worked to keep Polrudden, and she was distressed to see him so unhappy. For the first time since she had known him, Nathan Jago looked a defeated man.

'What will you do with Beville?'

'He'll live with me in Pentuan eventually. But while I'm in London for the prize-fight he'll go to Nell at Venn Farm.'

'No, he won't,' said Amy firmly. 'Beville will stay with me. He's happy here, and he knows you always come back to Portgiskey. He can wave to the fishermen, and I'll let the fisherwomen spoil him, just as they always do. It will be much better for him, especially as Nell's expecting another.'

Nathan knew Amy's idea was sensible. Nell was six months pregnant again; she would not want another child thrust upon her. He nodded. 'All right. If you're quite certain you want him.'

'*I want him. God, but I want your child, Nathan Jago! If only he were mine, too. . . .*'

The words were not spoken aloud, and Amy closed her eyes for a long moment before she trusted herself to speak.

'You mustn't worry, Nathan. It won't matter to Beville whether he's brought up in a cottage or in a manor. He'll be happy, you'll see.'

Nathan looked at Amy, but the faraway expression on his face told her that he was not thinking of her. 'Polrudden is Beville's birthright, Amy. Sir Lewis is doing this quite deliberately. He knows he can't prevent Beville from inheriting his baronetcy, but he's determined his grandson will have nothing else belonging to the Hearles.'

'Beville will inherit the baronetcy? You mean he'll become *Sir* Beville when Sir Lewis Hearle dies?'

'That's right.' Nathan's face relaxed for a moment as he witnessed her astonishment. '*Sir Beville*. But who has ever heard of a baronet living in a cottage belonging to a penniless Methodist preacher?'

'Is *this* the reason Polrudden means so much to you?'

'Of course. What other reason would I have?'

Amy did not reply. She was not certain what she had thought, but she had believed that Nathan's reason for wanting Polrudden so much had something to do with his memories of Elinor.

'Nathan, you told me that Sir Lewis Hearle mentioned your prize-fight – that he had wagered money on the outcome?'

'Yes, he's wagered that I will lose the fight. It seems most of London is behind Dellow. They are offering odds of five to one against me.'

'You don't think this talk of selling Polrudden is a ploy to worry you – to affect your preparation for the fight?'

'I don't doubt that Sir Lewis hopes it *will* upset my training, but I believe he's telling the truth about putting Polrudden on the market.'

'Are you going to allow him to succeed in everything, Nathan – to sell Polrudden *and* make certain you lose the fight?'

'There's nothing I can do about Polrudden . . . unless I can find six thousand guineas quickly. As for the prize-fight, they say Dellow is one of the best fighters ever seen in this country.'

'You beat him in Bristol. You can do it again. I *know* you can.'

'Amy, I love you.'

They were standing on the quay, looking out across the cove. When Nathan put an arm about Amy's shoulders and gave her a kiss, there were catcalls from the women working in the fish-cellar, who had been watching Amy and Nathan's earnest conversation with a great deal of speculative interest.

Nathan ignored them. 'Amy, you've solved my problem of what to do with Beville while I'm in London, and done your best to assure me that I'm not an absolute failure. Perhaps you'd like to try to persuade Sir Lewis Hearle that he doesn't need to sell Polrudden? Although I doubt if even the Devil's own persuasion could change his mind about that.'

Chapter Thirteen

NATHAN left for London at the end of October. He intended having a week in London before the date of the fight. He was as fit as he had ever been, even at the peak of his prize-fighting career, but he needed to spend the final week sparring with some of the prize-fighting friends he had made in the past. By the time a week was over he would have a better idea of his chances against Dellow.

At the last moment, Amy tried to persuade Nathan to let Beville go to Venn Farm after all, and to take her with him to London. Nathan refused, even when Amy became surprisingly persistent. He needed to concentrate on his preparations for the fight. He did not want the additional worry of having Amy in London, within reach of Sammy Mizler.

On the journey to London, Nathan startled the other passengers by leaping from the coach at the first steep hill and running to the top beside the labouring horses. However, when the reason for this unusual behaviour was explained to the passengers and coach driver they became excited about having the prize-fighting champion of the world on their coach. Whenever Nathan alighted from the coach at the bottom of a hill the driver obligingly adjusted the pace of his horses to suit Nathan, while the passengers shouted encouragement to him from the windows.

When the coach stopped at an inn for the passengers to dine, a word from the driver was enough to ensure that sufficient food was set before Nathan to satisfy a whole farmer's family.

In London, Nathan put up at the Plough inn, in Carey Street. The landlord was John Gully, himself a former great prize-fighting champion. Not only did Gully promise to supply Nathan with all the tough sparring partners he required, but he also declared his willingness to become one of their number.

That very first evening, after a full hour's training in the innyard, the heavily perspiring Gully declared it was time for a respite. Clapping a 'muffler'-encased hand upon Nathan's shoulder, he boomed: 'You're good, boy – damned good – but you'll need to be even better if you're to keep your title against

Abraham Dellow.'

Inside the inn, Gully called for the tapster to bring two tankards of best ale.

'You'll have one?' he asked Nathan.

'No. I'll take porter with my meals, but nothing in between.'

John Gully nodded his approval. 'There have been more prize-fights lost in a tavern than in a ring. This fight of yours could prove to be one of them. Dellow's taken a great liking to strong drink, so I've heard. He even calls for it between rounds. He hasn't enough years of drinking behind him to have developed the belly to hold it. He would have tasted little beer on a slaver.'

The wily former prize-fighter winked at Nathan. 'Watch him carefully, boy. If you see him drinking between rounds, you'll know you have the beating of him in a long fight – say, over twenty or thirty rounds. After that you'll only need to sink a good solid right hand in his belly and you'll tap him like a good barrel of the Plough inn's best. Remember that, Nathan; it's good advice. Now, if you're not drinking you'll want to be fighting, and I can see just the man for you coming through the door at this very minute. Ned . . . Ned Panter! Over here. You've told me often enough you're going to be a champion one day. Here's your chance to show us just how good you are.'

After Nathan had gone, Amy remained at Portgiskey with Beville for twenty-four hours before taking the small boy to Venn Farm.

Young Tom was out in the cart with his father, and Nell Quicke was alone in the house. Heavily pregnant, Nell looked a picture of health. Amy thought, with a tinge of envy, that Nell and Tom Quicke would probably have a happy, healthy family of ten or twelve children, bringing the old farmhouse well and truly to life.

'Hello, Amy . . . and young Beville, too! Well, what a lovely surprise.' Nell Quicke held out her arms, and Beville went to her eagerly for a warm hug.

Smiling at Amy, Nell Quicke said: 'Nathan told me you'd be looking after Beville. I'm pleased. He's a little boy who brings his own love with him. You'll both be good for each other.' She drew Beville to her. 'Dear little mite, I love him as though he were my own.'

'I know. That's why I'm here to ask if you'll look after him for a few days.'

Nell Quicke said nothing, but her eyebrows posed a question.

'I want to go to London. I think Nathan may need me – and there's a chance I may be able to save Polrudden for him. Nathan said something before he left that gave me an idea.'

Amy was talking in riddles, and Nell Quicke understood none of it, except that Amy intended going to London to see Nathan.

'But your Sammy? He's in London.'

Amy smiled. Nell Quicke had travelled no farther from her home than to St Austell. She had no conception of London's size.

'London's a big place, Nell. I'll be able to keep out of Sammy's way. But it might be better if you said nothing of my whereabouts to your father. He wouldn't approve.'

Nell's snort made Beville jump. 'Right now you could tell Pa the world had come to an end and he wouldn't hear a word. News has come from the Methodist Conference that Lord Liverpool has announced the changes in the law that Pa's been expecting. There are to be no more arrests of Methodist preachers. They can go their way without hindrance, and we are free to worship in the way John Wesley taught us. Methodists are now respectable people, Amy. Pa is riding his circuit on that old donkey of his, passing on the glad news to anyone who isn't sick to death of hearing about it. He says these are the greatest days of his life. Poor Pa, but he *has* suffered more than most for his beliefs.'

Nell Quicke was a simple, emotional girl. Moved by her own thoughts, she smiled tearfully at Amy. 'If only you hadn't married Sammy Mizler. You and Nathan always did make a lovely couple.'

'But I *did* marry Sammy – and Nathan married Elinor Hearle.'

Amy spoke more sharply than she intended. She had too much on her mind to indulge in thoughts of what might have been.

'Will you look after Beville for a few days?'

'Of course I will, won't I, me darling?' Nell kissed Beville, then over his head said: 'I don't know what you have in mind, but I'll help you do anything for our Nathan. He gave Venn Farm to Tom and me, and we'll neither of us ever be able to repay him for that. He deserves more happiness than he's found in life so far. You give him that, Amy, and you'll always be in *my* prayers, whatever Pa or anyone else says about it.'

Amy caught the mail coach from St Austell the next morning. She endured a cold and bumpy ride to London in the company of a clergyman, his wife and four daughters. They complained bitterly about everything, from the lack of comfort in the coach to the poor standard of food and accommodation along the way. The reverend gentleman was constantly putting his head out of the coach window, demanding that the coachman drive more carefully. Instead, the horses were urged to even greater speeds and, as the coach bounced over the potholes, the passengers were tumbled in a shrieking heap upon the coach floor.

Once in London, Amy quickly found a room in a quiet and respectable inn, only a short distance from the coaching tavern. Then she set about locating the Duke of Clarence. It was not easy. First, Amy tried the clubs in the vicinity of St James's. As they were all male haunts, and there was a very real likelihood of Sammy being in one of them, she hired a hackney carriage. While she waited in the carriage, the somewhat reluctant driver was sent to make enquiries for her.

By the end of the day it became apparent that the Duke of Clarence was not in London, but was at his Bushy Park home, some miles outside the city. Amy decided she would go there the next morning.

It was a pleasant ride. Crossing the bridge at Westminster, the carriage followed the river for a couple of miles before turning south, through the pretty villages that would one day be swallowed up by the ever-expanding capital.

After skirting the royal park of Richmond, the hackney carriage turned through a pair of impressive but unpainted gates and followed a driveway that led eventually to a mansion set among trees, lawns and tangled gardens.

Here Amy's self-confidence temporarily deserted her. She had come to London with a simple plan in mind, a plan that she

377

hoped would enable Nathan to keep Polrudden. Now, seeing this great house, realisation came to her that she, Amy Mizler, of Portgiskey Cove in Cornwall, daughter of a Cornish smuggler, was calling upon the Duke of Clarence, son of King George III, to ask a favour.

In a moment of panic Amy leaned out of the carriage window to tell the driver to turn the carriage about and return to London. The coach had cleared the trees, but as she put her head out of the window a young girl darted from some bushes, into the path of the horse.

The driver hauled back on the reins, at the same time stamping on the brake, causing horse and carriage to skid to an untidy halt on the gravel of the driveway.

The child escaped without injury, but Amy's cheek came into sharp contact with the window-frame. The blow stunned her for a few minutes. When she raised a hand to her face, it came away stained with blood.

It was no more than a scratch, but it looked far worse. When a matronly, blowzy woman appeared on the scene, surrounded by children of various sizes, her hand flew to her mouth in a dramatic gesture.

'Oh, my dear child! Your poor, poor face. It was that naughty Sophie. You must come inside and allow me to clean that wound for you. Driver, don't sit up there on your seat gawping. Help the young lady out. Quickly now!'

The driver leaped from his seat and, despite her protests, Amy was handed from the carriage and hurried inside the house by the woman who had come to her aid.

Amy was taken to a small, untidy sitting-room. Procuring a bowl of water, Amy's rescuer began bathing her face. As she worked, she chattered incessantly, and in a relieved tone declared that the wound was not as serious as she had at first feared, although Amy was told she would have a bruised cheek for a week or two.

From outside the sounds of children engaged in rough play drifted in through a window. Believing the woman to be a housekeeper, or perhaps a children's maid, Amy said: 'I didn't expect to find so many young people here.'

'Nobody ever does, my dear. Most of them are the Duke's, although I believe they have some friends in today. Sophie – the girl who ran in front of your carriage – is one of the Duke's favourites. She is also the wildest. . . . Ah! Here she is now. Sophie, come here at once and apologise to this lady. You caused her to injure her poor face. Come now, apologise immediately.'

For a moment it seemed as though the young, tomboyish girl might refuse. Then, with a reluctant 'Yes, Mamma,' she dropped a curtsy to Amy. After murmuring a brief apology she fled from the room.

Amy was hardly aware of the brevity of the expiation. She was looking at the matronly woman with something akin to awe. 'She called you "Mamma". Then you must be . . . the Duchess of Clarence?'

The woman gave an amused snort. 'Duchess, indeed. No, my dear. Royal dukes do not marry actresses – and that is what I was when Willie, the Duke, first saw me. Now after bearing ten of his children I am still Mrs Dorothea Jordan, the Duke's "companion".'

Dropping the cloth into the water, she said: 'There, that's stopped the bleeding. Some salve will ensure that it heals satisfactorily.'

Looking up from the bowl, Mrs Jordan caught Amy's expression and she laughed: 'Why! I do believe I've shocked you, child. Who are you that you don't already know of me? Where do you come from, pray?'

'I'm Amy Mizler. Mrs Mizler, ma'am. From Portgiskey, in Cornwall.'

'Are you, indeed? You seem hardly old enough to be married. But what is a little country girl doing coming to Bushy Park in a hackney carriage?'

'I've come to see the Duke of Clarence, ma'am. To beg a favour.'

'Indeed?' Mrs Jordan's expression hardened, and she stood up abruptly. 'And why do you think the Duke of Clarence might feel inclined to oblige you with a "favour"?'

'He helped a friend of mine, Nathan Jago, some time ago. He needs help again. It . . . it's very important.'

'Nathan Jago?' Mrs Jordan repeated the name. 'I've heard Willie and his friends talking of him. Isn't he the prize-fighter?'

'Yes, but at home he's a fisherman, with two boats of his

own. Him and me are partners.'

Amy felt unusually inexperienced and awkward in the presence of this woman. Still blowzily attractive, Mrs Jordan was astonishingly down-to-earth. Yet this woman had given ten children to one of King George's sons. She must be intimately acquainted with the Prince Regent and everyone at the King's Court. Amy looked at her in awe.

But Mrs Jordan was smiling again now. 'Indeed, my dear. I like to tell the Duke that he and I are partners in the business of producing children. It's something we do rather well, I think. Now, do I sense an intrigue between you and this partner of yours?'

'An intrigue? Is this something I should know about?'

The Duke of Clarence had entered the room silently through a door behind the two women and he stood in the doorway beaming benevolently.

Amy attempted to get to her feet to curtsy to the Duke, but with a hand on Amy's shoulder Mrs Jordan pushed her firmly down in the chair again.

'Willie, dear. This child has travelled all the way from Cornwall to beg a favour – only to have Sophie frighten her horse and cause her to injure her poor face.'

Mrs Jordan twisted Amy's head so that the Duke of Clarence might see the graze.

The Duke dutifully looked at Amy's slightly grazed face, but it was not the injury that made him frown.

'You and I have met before, young lady. What's your name, eh?'

'Amy. Amy Mizler. We met when Nathan Jago fought in Bristol.'

'That's it. You watched the fight with me. But your name wasn't Mizler then. Are you related to Sammy Mizler, who runs the boxing club?'

Amy nodded. 'I'm his wife . . . but I've come to see you about Nathan Jago.'

'Have you, now?' William, Duke of Clarence looked at his mistress with a faint smile. 'Damned if you're not right, Dorothea. There *is* an intrigue here. Have someone bring a drink, then lock the door to keep the brats outside. I want to hear all about this.'

A servant was summoned, drinks were served, and the Duke of Clarence and his mistress sat back to listen to Amy's story.

Hesitantly at first, but gaining in confidence as she went along, Amy told the story of Nathan's life at Portgiskey during the previous two years. She spoke of Preacher Josiah Jago's arrests, the death of Annie Jago, and why Nathan had wanted the Duke of Clarence to buy Venn Farm from the earnings of the Bristol fight. Amy described Nathan's struggle to earn a living from his fishing-boats, and choked on her emotion when she related the tragedy of his marriage to Elinor and his life at Polrudden. During the course of her story, Amy also touched briefly on her own disastrous marriage to Sammy Mizler.

When Amy had no more to tell, Dorothea Jordan dabbed at her eyes with a ridiculously flimsy lace handkerchief and looked questioningly at the Duke of Clarence.

'H'm! I had no idea Jago had been a naval man. Fought with Nelson, you say?' The Duke seized on an aspect of Amy's story of particular interest to him.

'He was Nelson's coxwain. My brother was in *Victory*, too. He died at Trafalgar, at the same time as Nathan was wounded.'

'Well, I'm damned . . .! Well, I'm damned!' For a full minute, the Duke of Clarence was lost in his own reminiscences. He, too, had spent a number of years in the Royal Navy, and one day, as William IV, he would be known as 'The Sailor King'. By mentioning Nathan's service in the King's navy, Amy had guaranteed him the Duke's fullest sympathy.

Bringing himself back to the present, the Duke said: 'You didn't come all this way to tell me a story, no matter how interesting it might be. What is it you want?'

Amy seized her opportunity eagerly. 'Before Nathan came to London he told me it was possible to get odds of five to one against him retaining the championship. Is this still so?'

Puzzled, the Duke of Clarence nodded. 'There was a time when they were quoting *six* to one at the club. But, yes, five to one sounds reasonable. Why?'

'I'd like you to bet some money on Nathan for me.'

Neither the Duke of Clarence nor Dorothea Jordan dared to look at each other. For years they had lived in a state of regal poverty, much of it brought about by the Duke's extravagence and his love of gambling. There had been many occasions when

Dorothea Jordan had threatened to leave him unless he spent less of both time and borrowed money in the gaming clubs of St James's. Yet here was this unsophisticated young girl from a remote Cornish fishing hamlet asking the Duke of Clarence to place a bet for her!

Clearing his throat noisily, the Duke asked: 'How much money do you wish to bet on Nathan Jago?'

'Fifteen hundred pounds,' said Amy proudly. Oblivious of the incredulous looks that passed between the Duke of Clarence and his mistress, she opened the leather pouch she carried and took out a piece of paper, which she passed to the Duke. It was a note, drawn on the bank of Philip Ball & Son, of Mevagissey. It promised the sum of fifteen hundred pounds to whoever should present the note.

'My dear girl! This is a *vast* sum of money for you to risk on the outcome of a prize-fight! Are you quite certain you know what you're doing? I mean, if Jago *loses*, you've thrown away a considerable fortune. . . .'

'He won't lose,' said Amy confidently. Then, doing her best to appear nonchalant, she added: 'Besides, the money really doesn't matter to me. It was left by my pa. I've already spent some to buy another boat for the partnership – Nathan's and mine. But Nathan wants Polrudden far more than anything I'll ever want to spend the money on.'

The Duke of Clarence looked in astonishment at Amy. 'You are a remarkable young lady. Don't you agree, Dorothea?'

'I think this Nathan Jago is a very fortunate young man,' replied Mrs Jordan, reaching out and squeezing Amy's hand affectionately. 'I would very much like to meet him. But tell me, dear. What does he want with a manor-house? You've told us that when the prize-fight is over he'll go back to fishing once more.'

There had been gaps in Amy's narrative. Dorothea Jordan was attempting to fill some of them.

'He wants it for his son, for Beville. It's his heritage. But now Sir Lewis Hearle has put it up for sale, even though he knows Beville will become the fourth baronet one day.'

Amy spoke proudly of Nathan's son. 'Beville can hardly have the title and no manor-house, can he?'

She smiled at the Duke of Clarence, who was having great

difficulty in absorbing this latest astounding piece of information. 'That brings me to my second favour. You arranged for Venn Farm to be bought for Tom and Nell Quicke. Would you do the same with Polrudden? Buy it with my winnings, for Nathan. It might be better if you did it through a friend, though,' she added as an afterthought. 'Sir Lewis Hearle was very upset when he learned it was really Nathan who'd bought Venn Farm.'

The Duke of Clarence began spluttering uncontrollably. Amy was uncertain whether the cause was mirth or anger. His words did nothing to help her.

'Dammit! I asked Jago once before whether he regarded me as some sort of estate agent. Now I know! I'll soon have the whole of Prinny's blasted Duchy after me to buy and sell land for them!'

The Duke of Clarence was referring to the huge land holdings that came to every Prince of Wales, together with his hereditary title of 'Duke of Cornwall'.

Rising from his seat, the Duke of Clarence took a handkerchief from his sleeve. Putting it to his mouth, he hurried from the room, making sounds as though he were choking.

'Have I angered him?' Amy asked anxiously, as the door banged shut behind the departing Duke.

'My child, you are absolutely *priceless*,' declared Mrs Jordan, hugging Amy to her suddenly. She was having great difficulty controlling her own amusement. 'Willie will place your bet for you. Yes, and he'll purchase Polrudden for your gladiator. *I'll* see to that. But I doubt if I'll be able to bear the suspense on the day of the prize-fight. Willie will have to take both of us to watch from his carriage. Now, you must stay here at Bushy Park with me until the day of the fight. No, I'll take no argument from you. I am absolutely *starved* of company, so far away from town. Mind you, it's going to be a unique experience, having a guest give me *honest* replies to all my questions.'

Chapter Fourteen

THE day of the fight dawned crisp and clear. Nathan drove from London to Bushy Park accompanied by John Gully and Ned Panter. Panter had insisted on acting as Nathan's second cornerman, even though he sported a swollen and colourful right eye as evidence of Nathan's powerful punching.

Nathan knew that, win or lose, he would be fighting in front of a huge crowd on such a day. This was confirmed by the time they came to within two miles of Bushy Park. People were streaming towards the scene of the prize-fight from all directions. Prize-fighting was unlawful, but here, where the Duke of Clarence sponsored prize-fights between the best boxers in the land, no magistrate would risk his standing in county society by invoking the law.

The crowds and the gentlemen in carriages were reluctant to give way to anyone, but the booming voice of the coachman calling 'Make way for the champion of the world' was enough to clear a path and bring resounding cheers from the crowds. The odds might be heavily against Nathan Jago, but he was an *English* champion. The people of England were strongly behind him.

Bushy Park itself was heaving with spectators. Some were forced to stand so far from the prize-fighting ring that they could not possibly have a clear view, even though the ring had been raised on a huge wooden platform. Around the ringside, in the area reserved for members of the 'Fancy', friends of the Duke of Clarence would watch from the comfort of their own carriages, obstructing the view of the spectators even more.

When Nathan and his seconds drove up, Abraham Dellow was already in the ring. Striking exaggerated poses to demonstrate his impressive muscles, he was drawing roars of approval from the throats of thousands of waiting spectators.

'We'll stay in the coach a while longer,' said the wily John Gully cheerfully. 'There's a cold wind out there, and it's well known that Dellow doesn't like the cold. It will stiffen his muscles and have him calling for strong drink to warm him before the fight's even started. Ned, do you have a pack of cards in your pocket?'

Ned Panter had no cards, so John Gully began pointing out well-known members of the 'Fancy' to Nathan. John Gully knew them all, their family backgrounds, mistresses and children. He also entertained Nathan and Ned Panter with a wealth of anecdotes of these men who promoted and encouraged the art of prize-fighting. John Gully was displaying the knowledge that was soon to earn him a fortune gambling on horse racing and prize-fighting, and take him to the House of Commons as a Member of Parliament.

When half an hour had passed, Abraham Dellow gave up exhibiting his body. He stood in his corner, wrapped in a large, warm overcoat and sipping from a silver brandy-flask. Beside him, peering peevishly along the road from which he expected Nathan to arrive, was Sammy Mizler.

The crowd was growing restless. Looking from the window of the carriage, John Gully said: 'Nathan, boy. There are two classes of people entitled to keep others waiting – brides and champions. They've had their waiting, out there. Now it's time for them to feast their eyes on you. Out we go.'

The three men climbed from the carriage, but for a few moments no one in the huge crowd recognised them. Then a mighty roar went up. Some of the spectators were angry that Nathan had deliberately kept them waiting. The remainder, realising why Nathan had remained in the carriage, roared noisy approval.

Climbing the short ladder to the wooden platform, John Gully was the first of the trio to duck beneath the single rope of the ring and he held it high for Nathan.

Once in his corner, Nathan acknowledged the shouts and cheers of the crowd. Stripped to the waist, he pranced about in his corner for a few minutes, slinging punches at imaginary opponents. It served to loosen a boxer's muscles and, over the years, the spectators had come to expect the brief exhibition.

In the far corner, Abraham Dellow was doing the same. Now both men were stripped, the discrepancy in their weights was evident. Dellow's black shoulders bulged heavily with muscle. Nathan's were hard and sinewy, and far less showy.

Sammy Mizler had not acknowledged Nathan and had given

him only one brief glance. But that look was sufficient to tell him that Nathan was as fit as he had ever seen him. Abraham Dellow would win – but it would not be the walkover that many were expecting. Dellow *had* to win. Boasting incessantly that Nathan stood no chance, Sammy had taken money – a *lot* of money – from gamblers loyal to the champion, offering them odds that varied from four to one to six to one. One such gambler was the Prince Regent himself.

The referee called both men to the mark in the centre of the ring and satisfied himself they were ready. Then, signalling to the timekeepers, he hurried from the ring and called on the boxers to begin fighting.

Abraham Dellow came straight into the attack. Driving Nathan across the ring before him, he scorned the left jabs with which Nathan tried to keep him at a distance. Ducking and moving all the time, Nathan escaped most of the other man's blows for more than three minutes, until Dellow backed him against the rope. Crowding in on him, Dellow caught Nathan in a wrestling hold and threw him to the ground.

Immediately, a break was called. Nathan returned to his corner to perch on the knee provided by Ned Panter, while John Gully rubbed his body briskly with a rough towel to prevent him becoming chilled.

'You're doing fine, boy,' said Gully. 'Make him come to you. Hit him when you have the chance. But *keep out of trouble*. The longer you make him work, the better it will be for you. Dellow has never fought a long fight and he may not have the stamina.'

Abraham Dellow was not relying upon a second to keep out the cold. He had a flask to his lips and was pouring best smuggled brandy down his throat, while Sammy Mizler remonstrated with him.

Time was called for the second round and both prize-fighters met again in the centre of the ring. The pattern of the first round was repeated until Nathan caught Abraham Dellow with a blow to the face that stung the bigger man. Dellow came back with a speed and ferocity that took the champion by surprise. Nathan took a crashing blow to the left eye, and another to the side of the jaw that dropped him to his knees.

Back in his corner, Nathan's seconds worked hard to clear his mind before he needed to toe the mark for the next round. As

Ned Panter sponged icy cold water on the back of the champion's neck, John Gully burned a fistful of feathers beneath his nose.

Nathan made the mark, but spent the whole of a long round retreating before Abraham Dellow, who was convinced he already had Nathan beaten. Dellow won this round also, but then lost the next two. However, by this time, Nathan's left eye had almost closed and his vision was severely restricted.

Taking advantage of Nathan's handicap, Abraham Dellow kept his attack coming from Nathan's blind side. On three occasions he succeeded in tripping him to the ground. The prize-fight had now settled into a punishing pattern. Nathan landed one or two good punches in every round, but in terms of knockdowns Dellow was winning three rounds out of every four.

Nathan had already absorbed more punishment than in any prize-fight he had taken part in before. His body was badly bruised, great red blotches standing out from the pale skin. But it was Nathan's face that caused John Gully to look anxiously at his fellow-second, over the top of Nathan's bowed head, during the interval after the twenty-sixth round.

Nathan rose from Ned Panter's knee for the twenty-seventh round – and thirty seconds later was back in his corner. Gasping with pain, he had been felled by a low blow that the referee had missed – or chosen to ignore. A minute and a half later, Nathan was back again, knocked to the boards of the ring in similar circumstances.

This time John Gully protested vehemently to the referee that the blow had been low, but the referee shook his head.

'I reckon he's got failing eyesight,' grumbled Ned Panter, as the disgruntled John Gully returned to the corner.

'More likely a small fortune riding on Abraham Dellow,' scowled John Gully. 'I've met him before. He refereed the last fight I lost. I swear to this day I was never given a full half-minute to come to the mark.'

Nathan said nothing. He ached in every limb. From his one sound eye he hazily saw Abraham Dellow grin at Sammy Mizler before taking another swig – from a bottle this time, the flask being long emptied.

Nathan closed his eyes and leaned his head back. He should

never have agreed to this fight. He had been out of the prize-ring for too long. Then he was being pushed to his feet and led across the ring to the mark, to come face to face with Abraham Dellow once more.

The twenty-ninth, thirtieth and thirty-first rounds passed in a haze of pain. It seemed to the crowd that the big negro was playing with Nathan now, using him to demonstrate his own boxing skill as he cut Nathan's face to ribbons with angled, slicing punches.

During the brief intervals, John Gully and Ned Panter tried to persuade Nathan not to come up to the mark for another round, but stubbornly Nathan lurched to his feet and plodded to the centre of the ring.

As Nathan slumped to Ned Panter's knee at the end of the thirty-first round, blood gushing from his nose, there was a sudden commotion outside the ring, only yards from the corner where he sat. Nathan was too weary to do more than register the disturbance until the shrill voice of a woman cried: 'Let me go. Let me get to Nathan.'

It was Amy!

Suddenly she was at the ringside, and he could see her expression of despair as she looked at his battered face.

'Nathan, give up. Please. . . . Don't go on.'

At that moment the referee called for the two men to meet at the mark in the centre of the ring for the thirty-second round. Only John Gully escorted Nathan to the mark. When he glanced over his shoulder, Nathan saw Ned Panter forcibly preventing Amy from getting inside the ring.

His astonishment gave Nathan a new and unexpected strength. Abraham Dellow moved in, instructed by a grim-faced Sammy Mizler to end the fight quickly, only to be met by a barrage of blows that dropped him to one knee in the space of five seconds.

Almost before the referee had declared it to be a knockdown, Nathan was back in his corner.

'What are you doing here? Where's Beville?'

It was the first time Nathan had used his voice during the fight and his jaws moved stiffly, the muscles of his face battered and bruised.

'Beville's with Nell. I came to see you fight. But you've had enough, Nathan. End it now. Come back to Portgiskey . . . and Beville. Please. Please!'

As Amy talked of Portgiskey and Beville, it was as though she was pumping new strength into Nathan. He thought of the sea, of Portgiskey, and the small, unchanging village of Pentuan; of his life there as a fisherman. And he thought of his son. Today was Beville's first birthday. This was not the day to make him the son of a *defeated* prize-fighter, an *ex*-champion.

There was something else, too. Across the ring, Sammy Mizler had stared open-mouthed at his wife when she first fought her way to Nathan's corner. Now, ashen-faced, he glared across the ring, his lips drawn together in a tight, thin line. Amy was Sammy's wife. In the eyes of the law she was no more than a chattel – and the law was inclined to ignore what a man did with his own. If Nathan was beaten into the ground, here in this prize-ring, Sammy would reclaim his 'property'. No doubt he would then teach her a harsh lesson for shaming him in front of so many of his friends.

'Did you come all this way just to see me beaten?' Nathan mumbled painfully.

'That doesn't matter now. Just finish the fight, here and now. Let Dellow take the championship. What good is a prize-fighting title to a fisherman? You've got so many other things. . . .'

Once again the shout of the referee brought the two prize-fighters to their feet. Nathan wasted no time getting to the mark, but he was no quicker than Abraham Dellow. The negro fighter had been ordered to end the fight in this the thirty-third round.

For a full two minutes the two prize-fighters stood toe to toe, each throwing punches that would have felled most men. The action set the crowd roaring its approval. Then Nathan ducked low beneath Dellow's muscular arms and sunk a mighty punch into his opponent's stomach, putting all his weight behind the blow.

A look of agony contorted Abraham Dellow's face. Clutching both hands to his stomach, he doubled up and sank to the boards, groaning.

The crowd went wild as Dellow's seconds hurried to treat him where he sat in the ring. Straightening him out, Sammy

Mizler desperately rubbed and kneaded his fighter's tender stomach muscles while the other second tried to pour brandy down the suddenly reluctant throat of the challenger.

When the referee called for the men to step up to the mark, Dellow was still on the ground; but Sammy Mizler was equal to the occasion. Leaving his fighter, he turned to the referee. Protesting loudly, he called on him to declare that his man had been put down as the result of a low blow.

Before Nathan could say anything, John Gully had crossed the ring to denounce Sammy Mizler as a liar. As the two men argued heatedly, the crowd of spectators erupted in a roar of disapproval, calling for the fight to be continued.

It was a full minute before order was restored and both seconds ordered back to their respective corners. But Sammy Mizler's interruption had served its purpose. Abraham Dellow was on his feet. Although still hunched over with pain, he was able to toe the line.

It was a brief respite. As Sammy Mizler screamed instructions to the still dazed challenger, Nathan repeated the last punch of the previous round; but this time he did not stand back to watch the result of his blow. As Dellow folded forwards, Nathan straightened him with two hard uppercuts. His final punch was a superb right cross that exploded on Dellow's chin and dropped him to the ground at Nathan's feet.

The challenger lay on the ground without so much as a muscle twitching, and Nathan knew he was still the champion.

The crowd knew it, too. They were going wild long before the referee performed the formality of calling the fighters to come to the mark. With Abraham Dellow still lying on his back, arms outstretched, the referee declared Nathan to be the winner.

Grinning as widely as his battered face would allow, Nathan returned to his corner to be hugged by John Gully, Ned Panter . . . and Amy. But there were many disgruntled losers in the crowd, and when they began to get out of hand John Gully suggested that they should leave the ring as quickly as possible.

Nathan agreed but, gripping Amy's arm, he said: 'On the way you can tell me exactly what you are doing here.'

Amy looked up at him, her concern for his injuries hidden

beneath a happiness that, for the moment, supplanted all other feelings. Beyond her, across the ring, Nathan saw Sammy Mizler standing alone, his expression that of a man who was living out a nightmare.

'I think you'd better come with me, Nathan.' Amy was talking. 'There's someone here who can tell you better than I can.'

Amy guided the three men to where a liveried coachman stood beside a plum-coloured carriage. On the side was the motif of a ducal crown. Nathan knew to whom the carriage belonged before an aristocratic man with high forehead and a genial expression opened the carriage door and said: 'Come inside, Nathan. You'll be ready for a seat that's a sight steadier than Ned Panter's bony leg.'

It was William, Duke of Clarence.

The hours that followed the fight were cloaked in an air of unreality for Nathan. Even with Amy clinging to his arm he was so dazed and battered that he was still not certain she was really beside him. Nathan was introduced to Dorothea Jordan and was forced to endure her tearful administrations as she smoothed balm on his badly battered face.

They drove to the home of the Duke. By the time they arrived, Nathan was so stiff and sore he had to be helped from the carriage by two of the Duke's footmen.

Once inside the house, Nathan had his battered face dressed yet again by Dorothea Jordan, while a whole series of awe-filled young faces swam in a vague sea of unreality about him, and a succession of huge brandies were forced upon him.

Then, ignoring Nathan's demands to be told what was happening, Dorothea Jordan ushered him off to bed, telling him firmly there would be ample time for explanation when he was thoroughly rested.

Nathan was convinced he would lie awake for hours, going over the exciting events of the day, but within minutes of stretching his aching body on the soft bed he was fast asleep.

When he awoke, the room was in darkness, only a faint light coming from the square of dark grey sky filling the window. For a moment Nathan could not remember where he was. When everything came back to him, he sat up suddenly. All the aches

391

and pains returned to his battered body and he sank backwards once more with a groan.

A tinder-box scraped in the room and moments later it was illuminated by the soft, yellow glow of a lamp. Then Amy was kneeling beside the bed.

'At last! I thought you were *never* going to wake.' She took his hand and hugged it to her, tangling his fingers in hers. 'I've got so much to tell you.'

Her happy excitement was contagious. Nathan grinned – and immediately regretted the facial movement. It would be many days before he would be able to change his expression without the muscles of his face reminding him of the battering they had taken at the hands of Abraham Dellow.

'I've got a few questions to ask you, too. What you're doing here, for instance.'

'I came to London to place a bet on you winning the prize-fight.'

'You did what . . . ?' Nathan repeated his earlier mistake and tried to sit up. This time he succeeded, but at great cost. When he turned his head he discovered he had vision in only one eye. The other was tight-closed. He put a hand up and carefully traced the extent of the swelling with his fingertips.

'God, but I took a battering.'

'Yes, but you won the fight, Nathan. You're still the champion – and I won my bet.'

'How much did you win?'

Nathan was puzzled that Amy should make so much of a wager. Until he learned of the sum involved.

'I won seven thousand five hundred pounds.'

In an instant all aches and pains were forgotten. Nathan's mouth dropped open in utter astonishment. When he spoke again his voice came out as a hoarse whisper of disbelief.

'Amy. . . . How much did you wager on the fight?'

'Fifteen hundred pounds.'

'But that was all the money you had. The money your father left you.'

Nathan felt sick when he thought how close he had come to losing the fight. Then he rememberd how Amy had urged him to give the fight to Abraham Dellow because he was being badly battered. As the thoughts went through his mind, he squeezed

Amy's fingers so tight she winced painfully.

Nathan was immediately filled with concern. 'I'm sorry, Amy. It's just . . . I don't know what to say. What are you going to do with your fortune?'

This was the question for which Amy had been waiting. She could not conceal her delight, as she said: 'It's already spent. Well, much of it. I've bought Polrudden – for Beville.' Amy added the rider hastily, as she saw Nathan's expression changing.

'You've . . . bought Polrudden?'

'Yes. Sir Lewis Hearle also bet on the fight. Only he thought Abraham Dellow was going to win. He owed five thousand guineas to a moneylender who would have sent him to Newgate Gaol had he not been able to pay him immediately. He was desperate for money. When a friend of the Duke of Clarence offered him five thousand guineas for Polrudden, he accepted immediately. Gratefully, too, I understand.'

Nathan sank back on his pillows again and tried to make sense of all that Amy had just told him. It was impossible. It all mattered far too much. If what Amy said was true. . . .

'Amy, why should the Duke of Clarence be so kindly disposed towards me? He's Abraham Dellow's sponsor. He must have lost a lot of money on the fight.'

'He *would* have done had I not come to London. When I convinced him that *you* would win he managed to switch his money to you – or something like that. Whatever he did, he won a lot of money. Far more than I did.'

Nathan was silent for a while. Then he said: 'I can't take Polrudden from you, Amy. You can see that, surely?'

Amy shook her head vigorously. 'No, I *can't*. Anyway, I've told you. It's for Beville. You can't take it away from *him*.'

She gripped his hand tightly in hers and spoke in near-desperation. 'Nathan, listen to me. I haven't lost by this. Even after giving you Polrudden I'm going home much richer than when I arrived in London. Please don't refuse my gift, *please*. It means more to me than anything I've ever done before.'

Nathan withdrew his hand and, ignoring his complaining muscles, he put his arms out and pulled her to him. 'Amy, I know why you've done this, and I love you for it. You've saved

Polrudden for Beville – and for me. All right, I'll live there – but as your tenant until I can raise the money to buy Polrudden from you.'

Amy was about to argue that she had bought the house for Nathan and his son, and would attach no conditions to the gift, but she bit back her reply. Nathan had said he would remain at Polrudden. It was enough for the moment.

Chapter Fifteen

NATHAN and Amy spent that day and a further night at Bushy Park as guests of the Duke of Clarence and Mrs Dorothea Jordan. It was a warm and friendly stay, if somewhat hectic. Most of the children of the union seemed to be of an indeterminate age, caught between childhood and adulthood, and each had a crowd of friends who spent much time at the house. They passed through the room where Nathan rested continuously, pausing to chat with the easy-going Duke of Clarence, or just standing gazing admiringly at Nathan's battered face.

It soon became evident that the crowd of young people would not have been nearly so large had Nathan not been staying at the house. Dorothea Jordan was convinced her own children were charging their friends for admittance to see him.

When it was time to leave there was genuine warmth in the farewells said between Dorothea Jordan and Amy. The one-time actress had taken a great liking to Amy that was in sharp contrast to her manner towards most young women of the Duke's acquaintance. As she led Amy to the Duke's carriage, which was taking Amy and Nathan to London, Mrs Jordan gave her a few words of advice.

'You've got a fine young man there,' she told Amy, patting the arm that was linked through her own. 'Don't lose him because a few narrow-minded busybodies say it isn't right for you to love him.'

She looked back to ensure that the Duke of Clarence was not within hearing. 'Had I listened to the advice of others, I would never have spent so many happy years with Willie. They are coming to an end now, but I'll always have the children, and Willie is a kind man. He'll never take them from me.'

Amy looked at her new-found friend in some bewilderment. 'Take them away – but why should he? You are all so happy here together.'

Dorothea looked at Amy's face quickly but saw no guile there. She gave a wan smile. 'Forgive me, my dear. I keep forgetting you're an uncomplicated little girl from Cornwall, far away from the dreary intrigues of the Prince Regent's Court. Willie is the third of King George's fifteen children. Alfred never survived infancy, and poor Amelia died two years ago, but the remainder are tenacious survivors. The male members of the family are also prolific procreators of children – out of wedlock. As such, they are a serious drain on the funds of the poor old King, their father. Consequently, they are all under constant pressure to marry into money, especially poor Willie. Then, of course, there is the question of the accession to the throne. The Prince of Wales and Caroline have only their daughter, Princess Charlotte. They are unlikely to produce any more – at least, not by each other. If anything should happen to Charlotte, the succession to the British throne would be thrown wide open once again and there would be an unseemly scramble to make "suitable" marriages, and beget legal offspring.'

Dorothea Jordan laughed gaily, but Amy detected a deep bitterness in the sound. She was also aware that the Duke's mistress cared more for her royal lover than was good for any woman in such an uncertain situation.

At the coach Mrs Jordan kissed Amy and embraced her warmly. 'Goodbye, child. Promise you'll write and let me know how you and your champion are getting along.'

To Nathan she said: 'Take care of this young lady. She is rather special.' Then she kissed Nathan, too, adding: 'If I am ever in the West Country I will visit Polrudden – and I expect to see you *both* there.'

The Duke of Clarence was less emotional, but considerably more practical. At the last moment he pressed a weighty bag upon Nathan. 'Here's five hundred guineas. It's the money that would have gone to Abraham Dellow, had he won. It's yours, Nathan. You've earned it and proved yourself a great champion. Dammit! Can't I persuade you to defend the championship just once more? I'll give you the largest purse ever. *Two* thousand guineas . . . two thousand *five hundred*.'

The Duke had to shout his last offer. Mrs Jordan had given a signal to the coachman, and he had driven away before Nathan could give the Duke of Clarence an answer.

Nathan and Amy went to the Plough inn before returning home to Cornwall. Here, in the company of John Gully, Ned Panter and their friends, they enjoyed a riotous party. Nathan had trained at the inn and was well liked and respected there. In addition, many of the staff and customers had backed him to retain the championship. Now they had an opportunity to express their gratitude, and spend some of their considerable winnings.

The singing and dancing went on throughout the night, although Nathan and Amy left the party early. They were catching the morning coach. The hard springing of a mail coach and the potholed roads upon which it travelled made no concessions to a head heavy from an excess of brandy and porter.

Nathan and Amy were pleased they had not stayed to greet the dawn when they saw the state of John Gully, Ned Panter and the other revellers who came to see them on their way the next morning. Still far from sober, their bleary eyes and general air of fragility set them a world apart from those about them who shouted farewells to Nathan and Amy's fellow-travellers.

At Andover the coach stopped at an inn to allow the passengers to enjoy a meal before facing the wide open spaces of Salisbury Plain. It was here that the Duke of Clarence's emissary caught up with the coach. He bore a letter addressed to Amy and written in the Duke's own bold hand.

Puzzled, Amy broke the seals on the letter and opened out the large sheet of paper. As she read a variety of expressions crossed her face. They ranged from shock and anguish to a sudden realisation of new hope.

'What does it say?' Nathan asked when he could contain his curiosity no longer.

Instead of replying, Amy handed the letter across the table to Nathan. Setting down her knife and fork, she left the dining-room hurriedly.

Nathan squinted through his one good eye to read the letter. His expressions followed the same course as had Amy's. When he had read the letter through twice, Nathan sat back in the chair and closed his one good eye, as a host of jumbled thoughts chased each other through his mind. The letter he held in his hand informed Amy of a tragedy that had taken place in London – one that would change the whole course of Nathan and Amy's lives. Aware of the importance of his news, the

Duke of Clarence had penned the letter hurriedly and sent a horseman to overtake the coach.

It informed Amy that Sammy Mizler was dead – killed by his own hand.

Carried away by his own boasting, Sammy Mizler had convinced himself that Abraham Dellow was unbeatable and could not possibly lose to Nathan. Sammy's prize-fighting club was frequented by many of London's richest men, a few of whom favoured Nathan. Sammy Mizler had stupidly accepted wagers from these wealthy clients – almost twenty thousand pounds, at odds of up to six to one. In the belief that he was making himself a rich man, Sammy had then taken the money to the gambling clubs of St James's and used it to back his own man to win the world championship.

When Abraham Dellow failed to reach the mark for the thirty-fifth round of the championship prize-fight, he left Sammy Mizler owing the gentlemen of London more money than he could ever hope to raise – six thousand guineas of it to the Prince Regent himself.

The situation was an impossible one for Sammy Mizler. Faced with social annihilation, and a lifetime in Newgate's debtor's gaol, Sammy Mizler returned to London's East End. Here, in the tiny Haggerston house tucked between the tallow works and the brewer's stable, he consumed a quart of brandy before cutting his throat inexpertly with a kitchen knife. He then bled to death on the cheap carpet.

Nathan thought it was a tragic end to the man who had been his friend and companion for many years, even though the friendship had turned sour for both of them.

But Sammy's death had set Amy free. She was no longer another man's wife. . . .

Nathan found Amy outside the inn, where the newly harnessed coach-horses blew clouds of vapour high in the cold air, while driver and guard exchanged crude jokes with the inn's hostler and a tapman who had brought out brimming tankards of porter for the two coachmen.

Amy looked pale and taut, but there were no tears for her late husband. Nathan took her hand and they walked across the road from the inn to stand looking over a low wall at a fast-running stream.

398

Amy spoke first. 'It's awful to think of Sammy dying like that. No one should die so . . . so *alone*. I know I should feel sorrow for him, weep for him . . . but I *can't*. I'm sorry for the way he died, but all I can feel is a great relief. A tremendous weight has been taken from me. Nathan, help me. I'm so confused. . . .'

Suddenly, in complete contradiction of all she had said, Amy burst into tears and turned to Nathan. He held her until she stopped crying, then dried her eyes, aware that the coachmen were watching them curiously from the innyard.

'Feel better now?'

Amy nodded. 'Yes. I'm glad I was able to cry for Sammy. Just once. I gave him little else.'

'You're wrong, Amy. Sammy gained the greatest victory of his life when you married him. But now he's given us back a future again. Let's think of him kindly.'

Amy nodded, saying nothing as from the innyard a coachman blew a long brass horn to summon passengers to the coach.

Nathan and Amy made their way across the road and climbed inside the coach. A few minutes later the creaking vehicle lurched from the innyard and gathered speed on the smooth stretch of road that linked town cobbles to country lane.

Amy's fingers slipped into Nathan's hand. Leaning against him, she whispered: 'Nathan? Will you accept Polrudden as my dowry . . .?'